THE
FIFTH
SEED

To my wife Shelly, who always believed.
And to my daughters:
Genevieve, a young author in the making;
and Olivia, my little dreamer.
You inspire me every day.

"That I may understand whatever binds the world's innermost core together, see all its workings, and its seeds."—Faust

PRELUDE

THE ESCAPE

S eeing the foursome, one never would have suspected they were running for their lives. Three men and a woman—young and full of energy—and they darted in and out of shops at the Mall of America, wrapped in the excitement of their newfound freedom. On September 2nd they had escaped from a private treatment center for troubled youth, secreted away in the extreme northern reaches of Minnesota, just northeast of Bemidji on the outskirts of the Chippewa National Forest. What follows are excerpts from a journal kept by one of these extraordinary individuals, describing their first few days of freedom—and their last days together.

Excerpt from Joe Meyer's Journal

September 2nd: Pre-Dawn

Well, we have finally done it and life on the outside seems strangely abnormal. Our escape from Northwoods Mental Health Treatment Center has left the four of us exhausted and at odds about the future. But at least we are free and together . . . if only for now.

I can't say as I write by the light of a full moon, resting for a few brief moments before we push on, that it was easy. But so far it seems everything has gone to plan. It certainly helped to have aid from the inside. Our thanks to an old friend at Northwoods who I shall never name here on these pages—for should this journal ever be ripped from my possession, this blessed friend, our saving grace, would be in grave danger. Still, this individual's contribution should be noted.

I won't go into the exact details of the escape. That is best left for another day, another time, when we do not live with the constant fear of being hunted and forced to return. With my freedom only hours old, I already can't imagine life any other way. I won't accept life any other way.

To the group's knowledge we have not been followed. Yet we are quite certain the search has begun for us in earnest, as dawn begins to stoke up the horizon into a smoldering red sky to the east. To this point we have been on foot, yet as we pause now to break into pairs and find the separate roads we seek heading west, we pray for good weather, good fortune and helpful strangers to aid us in our journey.

I can't imagine having to say goodbye to Curt and Anna, not so soon after we have sipped from the same cup of freedom. But after much heated discussion, and Trent's unwavering insistence that we stick to our plan, we finally agreed it was for the best. Pairs will still give us strength, a friendly shoulder to lean on and will make hitchhiking a more realistic possibility. Yet if the unimaginable happens, and Northwoods swoops down upon us one night, like a hawk snaring its unsuspecting prey, we hope separating might ensure at least two may slip through their grasp, to someday tell our story.

God willing, we will rejoin somewhere northwest of here, in a town called Grafton, a town I scarcely knew existed only a month ago . . . and today still only know by name. There, another friend of our cause awaits, another link in the underground chain, to propel anyone who might survive this ordeal onto the next leg of our freedom's journey. But for now, my weary legs must move again . . . we are heading out.

September 2nd: 8:00 p.m.

Trent and I are in a run-down motel in a $15 room paid for out of the cash our few friends at Northwoods had smuggled to us over time. Yet even in this broken down rattrap I feel more alive than I can ever recall. The past

12 hours have been a living hell. Heavy rains hampered our travel, and of the few drivers who passed us, even fewer were kind enough to stop.

You cannot imagine the turmoil we faced each time we spotted a set of disembodied headlights racing toward us down a water-slicked road. Trent and I each wishing out loud for them to slow and then stop—yet in the same breath praying that those huddled figures inside the cars, obscured by torrents of rain, washing way any figments of human shape, had not been sent for us.

The one ride we did get came from a kindly old farmer, attending the funeral of one of his cousins, right here in this tiny town of three hundred souls. To our luck and his sorrow, the trip was long and we parted with our 'thank yous' and sincere sympathies as he drove out of our lives in a wash of rain.

As rain still plinks in a steady crescendo off the rooftops, we have not seen Anna or Curt since our parting, and we wonder how they might be faring. The route they chose runs due west to Grand Forks then north into Grafton, while ours runs a more direct northwesterly route to the same destination. By distance alone they should arrive after us, but who knows when you are traveling by thumb. I pray they are okay, and wonder if perhaps in tonight's dreams we might find them well.

Tonight I go to bed, for the first time in as long as I can remember, tired but free.

September 3rd: Noon

We woke today to an unpleasant discovery. According to a map from a local gas station, the town we are in is farther west and nearer to Grand Forks than we planned to be. So far off our intended route are we that Trent and I wondered whether Anna and Curt might be sleeping in the room next to us. As it was, we haven't seen them, and our dreams held no clues. Who knows exactly why or when these beautiful and horrid minds, we have for some reason been blessed with, will let us see what we see. Again I write, praying they are well. Yet I can't help wondering about the broken relationship Curt and Anna once shared, and the hurt feelings that lingered. I hope they are getting along.

At least luck for Trent and me seems to have rediscovered us like the day's welcome rays of sun. For as I pen these words in the back seat of an old Ford Crown Victoria, we have made it back to the road we detoured from last night, and are again heading northwest. The young man who picked us up is in auto parts sales and told us his next stop was a Minnesota town near the North Dakota border. He'll take us that far, which by the map I have sprawled out beside me appears to be less than a half hour's drive from our ultimate destination.

Still, I can't seem to relax. Every now and then I look back through the rear window to see the same damned car hanging back about a quarter mile. I try to look away and dismiss it as nothing, but my mind won't let me stray long, and I forever feel I must take another look. When I do, the car is still there.

Logic tells me I'm being foolish, for where else is there to go on this lonely stretch of flat, treeless road cut from the farm fields but straight ahead. Twice I've thought about broaching the subject with Trent, but could not bring myself to do so—not in mixed company at least. I hope I am not overreacting. I hope my next entry in this journal finds me a fool.

September 4th: Morning

I have reason to believe the car behind us was a false alarm, but more on that later. Curt and Anna are here! All of us are now in Grafton, safe and sound in the home of a friend. We all arrived within hours of each other last night, and this morning we celebrate with a breakfast buffet out. Though we are all overjoyed, Anna is the happiest: she received her first word of Mary Jane in almost a year. Our gracious host even offered insight as to where she might be living and informed us she was well. Mary Jane's dismissal from Northwoods a year ago had changed Anna terribly; leaving her depressed and dejected much of the time. Today Anna could hardly contain her excitement: in a few days she plans to reunite with the woman she adores like a mother.

For now, we will stay here to rest and recover. We have no set timetable, but tentative plans to travel with Anna by bus to the Twin Cities where perhaps we might all spread out and explore the world for a while on our own. As it is, this is as far as our post-escape planning had taken us and we hope the rest of our lives are open for us to write. Perhaps we are too giddy with our recent successes, but we can't imagine Northwoods having the resources to discover us here, or stake out the bus stations of every rural town in the region.

Still, I have a concern. Curt and Anna are at each other again. Their trip together seems to have ripped open old wounds that never healed, rather than bringing them closer together. Even now, Anna's happiness seems to be wearing on Curt. And I am starting to have suspicions about Curt's health. He says he had his addictions under control, but I can see the bags under his eyes and the muscle twitches that tweak his body relentlessly. I suspect he wasn't clean, as he had reassured us only days before our escape.

There's more to tell, but I have gone on too long. Everyone is getting ready to go.

September 5th: 1:15 a.m.

Oh my God, I am drunk . . . we celebrated together all day and partied all night in a great little bar called the Extra End. Curt and Anna are arguing again. I wish they would stop. I need sleep. Until tomorrow.

September 5th: 3:45 a.m.

I had a dream. No, a nightmare. I can't even fathom its meaning. I pray it is wrong but I'm not sure. How can I be sure? In a month, I fear only one of us will remain.

September 5th: 12:30 a.m.

We celebrated again tonight, but I did not feel like drinking. I still have concerns about my dream, but if any of the others shared it, they are not saying. Anna seems too happy for such thoughts and Curt is too strung out. He got blitzed tonight and almost got us thrown out of the bar. I'm not sure about Trent . . . though he seemed enough like himself today.

So now, I hold this secret . . . and wonder if I should tell them . . . but I can't bring myself to. How can I when we all have felt so alive these past few days? I can't dash their hopes on something I am so unsure of. What should I do?

Sleep can't be far off . . .

September 6th: 3 p.m.

We departed Grafton today for the Twin Cities. Just before we left our host sprung a surprise on us, handing over $15,000 to each of us. She explained it was from Mary Jane, and was to go toward starting our new lives. We are all extremely grateful. The money seems to have sealed it . . . we have decided to separate, at least for now. The thought scares me, as I have no place to go. Anna is going to try to track down Mary Jane and Trent seems to want to travel—to where he has not said. Curt talks of family in San Francisco, but I can't imagine where he will start to look. Like many of us, he was turned over to Northwoods at about age eleven or twelve—most likely with his parents' approval and probably an exchange of cash. Still, I hope for his sake he finds them.

For now, we share some of our last moments together, perhaps our final moments if my dream comes to fruition. The bus we ride on is a tour bus headed to the Mall of America in Bloomington. We will disperse from there, with plans to meet again about a month from now. It was Curt's idea to come back together, and that it should be our secret . . . shared with no one else or risk endangering the group. I can't imagine whom we might tell, but we have all agreed. I just hope there is more than one of us at the reunion.

Their time together now almost at an end—Anna, Trent, Joe and Curt slowly made one last trip around the massive indoor mall. Their feet finally paused at the center of the large indoor amusement park. There they hugged, kissed and laughed away tears as young children screamed nearby, oblivious on their rides. In a month, God willing, the four would all meet again. But for now, each spread out in different directions. These widely divergent paths had been planned to avoid long goodbyes and re-intersecting paths. But as Anna got lost in a moving sea of unruly families and overburdened shoppers, one silent observer watched fitfully.

CHAPTER 1

A Father's Plea

The man who called himself Bruce Jenkins gazed blankly out the newly installed bay window of a quaint Craftsman bungalow. The St. Paul home, tucked back along the scenic river bluffs of Merriam Park, was being gradually restored by its owner.

Bruce's watery eyes fell momentarily on a small squirrel nestled in at the foot of a giant oak. He watched absent-mindedly as it dug in a nut for winter storage. As he stood there, contemplating his story, stray words popped into his mind: *purposeful, deliberate, intuitive . . . yet pitifully stupid.*

"You were saying," a voice nudged carefully from behind him.

Bruce, a large burly man with close cropped salt and pepper hair, stood almost six-foot four inches tall. He turned abruptly to face the voice.

The man who'd spoken was ex-FBI agent Grady Hamilton. It was his home office in which Bruce now stood. The office appeared to be immaculately kept, with Grady's antique mahogany desk taking up the vast majority of the room's smallish footprint. The young private investigator sat with his back to a floor-to-ceiling bookcase crafted of dark stained oak. The shelves were crammed with leather-bounds—but the office and the books were all show. Grady rarely used the library behind him, doing all his research online these days.

At the moment, Grady's eyes were focused intently on Bruce's massive frame, blocking his view of the bay window he'd installed himself and of the backyard beyond. It was there Bruce began grasping for his next words . . . the right words. What he was about to explain required the utmost care and tact.

After a moment's pause Bruce appeared to compose himself. "As I said, I want you to locate my daughter."

"And her full name?" Grady inquired, asking what he already knew.

"Anna Rae Jenkins." Bruce replied swallowing hard, perturbed by Grady's oddly repetitive line of questioning. "As I said, I haven't seen her in over a year."

"Yes, yes . . . I recall you saying something like that on the phone. But you said you couldn't or perhaps wouldn't elaborate then."

"No, I needed to meet you before we went into details."

"And?" Grady prodded again.

"You'll do." Bruce said with a bluntness he regretted immediately.

"I can't thank you enough for your overwhelming show of confidence," Grady jabbed back sarcastically.

Go to hell were the first words that came to the tip of Bruce's tongue, but he held back. He wasn't about to blow it . . . not now. Instead, Bruce tempered his response. "I'm sorry, I'm a little emotional right now."

"How so?" Grady inquired with rapid-fire skepticism. "From our brief phone conversation you and your wife sent your daughter off at the age of twelve to a special center for problem children—someplace up in northern Minnesota.

"It's called Northwoods, and yes, it's near Bemidji," Bruce answered, "but . . ."

"In any event," Grady said cutting Bruce off, "from my standpoint you abandoned your responsibilities as parents, paid what I assume was top dollar to institutionalize your own flesh and blood in a private home, and then washed your hands of her for the last six years, visiting her on what I will respectfully describe as an irregular basis. Excuse me for being harsh, but that certainly doesn't fit the loving, caring father role all too well."

"You must understand. There have been complications." Bruce paused, flushing with a show of apparent grief.

Impatient, Grady nudged him forward. "Go on."

"My wife, you see. She's sick. Has been for the last two years. The last year it's been complicated . . . anyway the doctors don't think she'll make it." Another choke of emotion cut him off.

For the first time in the interview, Grady backed off and sighed. "I'm sorry Mr. Jenkins. I didn't know."

Still apparently grief-stricken, Bruce tried awkwardly to wave Grady off and turned back toward the same squirrel digging at the base of the old oak.

Grady watched as Bruce's body heaved a couple of times with silent sobs, and for a brief moment he felt a sliver of guilt for the hard tack he had taken with Mr. Jenkins. But this was Grady's style. In his three plus years of working as an investigator for hire he had seen more than his fair share of clients walk through his door. Most of them had a story. And most of them lied, especially to him. In this business he had developed a detached, less-than-empathetic attitude toward those who retained his services. It was this hard line of questioning that usually helped him figure out who was telling the truth and who was giving him a dump truck full of bull.

A minute passed before Mr. Jenkins spoke again, still facing the window. "You see Mr. Hamilton."

"Call me Grady . . . everyone does," he offered, a little more politely.

"Okay, Grady. As I told you on the phone, my daughter is missing. Actually I guess you'd call it an escape. Anyway, she walked out of Northwoods along with three other patients about a week ago. You must understand, all her young life she has been treated for clinical depression, mild schizophrenia, and drug abuse."

"I see, which for you, justified the home."

"Yes," Bruce spoke turning back to Grady, letting the man's jab slide this time. "At age twelve . . . my God she was only twelve." Another sob. "She got in with the wrong crowd. She was always smart—perhaps too smart. Martha, my wife, and I saw it coming. She started getting bored

3

in school . . . lost interest in her studies. Her A average quickly slipped to a B and then a C, and still lower. We tried everything, from tutors to psychologists. Everyone said the same thing. Anna was amazingly intelligent, but her mind wandered terribly. She started having horrible nightmares, fell into fits of depression and was caught skipping school on more occasions than I could count. It was then that we discovered her stash."

"Do you know what kind of drugs she was into, Mr. Jenkins?" Grady asked evenhandedly.

"We only found a baggie of pot, but after she had spent some time at Northwoods they told us she admitted to drinking and experimenting with meth."

Grady watched Bruce closely as he spoke. The man seemed amazingly composed after his short breakdown only a few seconds ago. Something was odd about him. He seemed to slide in an out of his emotions quickly, and his words were now more deliberate . . . or rehearsed. Grady was sure Jenkins was hiding something, and he thought he knew what it was.

"I'm sorry, Mr. Jenkins, but I have to ask. Your daughter . . ."

"Yes." Bruce asked cautiously, as if sensing what was coming next.

"Was she abused?" Grady asked, his unblinking eyes never leaving Mr. Jenkins' own.

Bruce eyed Grady with contempt. "Christ! I don't need this shit. There are twenty other investigators I can get to take this damn job," he yelled, snatching his coat off the back of a chair as he stormed for the door.

Grady was intrigued by Mr. Jenkins' quick response. Grady had never directly suggested Mr. Jenkins was the abuser, but the man seemed to have taken it that way. Still, Grady let him go, watching as Bruce blew past his desk, out of the office, on his way to the front door. No longer able to see Mr. Jenkins, Grady played his last card. "Why didn't you call them first then . . . the other investigators?" he shouted after Mr. Jenkins.

At first there was no answer, but Grady never heard the front door open. So he waited, hands clasped in his lap and head down, waiting patiently for Bruce to reply or leave. To Grady, it really didn't matter either way. But then Grady heard the soft shuffle of footsteps across his hardwood floors, signaling Bruce's slow return. Out of the corner of his eye, Grady saw the man reappear, pausing just inside his office doorway.

"You're so smart?" Bruce said after a long, deliberate pause. "You tell me."

Lifting his head, Grady turned, swiveling slowly to face Bruce. "Because I'll find your daughter."

CHAPTER 2

FALLING

Two Weeks Later

Peering through the thick, dense fog, like a lone, ominous eye it came toward him: a round object, at first only a glimmer of yellowish-white light, glowing dimly, and then ever so slowly brightening.

Curt stood the only ground he had, fiercely clinging to a broad metal column rising up beside him, his knuckles whitening against the cold, brisk breeze that buffeted the Golden Gate Bridge. Below him, his sneakered feet rocked precariously on the outermost rust-orange rail, the final impediment separating pedestrians and cars from the churning waters of the bay below.

In his mind's eye he could sense the throng of observers who had stepped from their cars and now clustered on the walkway behind him. Their shouts to come down only vaguely registered in his troubled mind. Instead his thoughts centered upon the irony of his situation. For years his life had not been his own. For years he had longed to be free, to live as he chose, as he wished, and not by another's code. Yet here he was tonight, finally free, as he had been for the last few weeks. Yet now his life seemed somehow even more unlivable.

Curt knew all too well the darkness would eventually find him. He knew deep down, like few people could truly understand, that his captors were closing in, and that what lay before him was his only way out. He so desperately wanted to be away from them . . . those horrible people and the sheer terror of what they could do to him . . . and the things they could make him do.

Teary eyed, he lifted his gaze skyward once more at the eye hovering out in the mist, parting the thick night sky. The light's brilliance now accompanied by the deep thumping chop of helicopter blades as they beat the crisp autumn air with a vengeance. The hanging bird closed in, the spotlight finding Curt's trembling body, bathing it in an almost spectral white glow, as the wind wash from the churning blades tore unrelentingly at his clothes.

Curt gazed, nearly blinded by the light, trying to see past its beam, where he could vaguely make out the sleek, streamlined shape of the helicopter behind. His eyes fell once more to the blackness below. He couldn't see the water—certainly there beyond the mist and darkness—but he could just barely hear its waves lapping at the bridge's massive support columns, waiting for him.

Yet what he heard next wasn't the waves, and it sent a violent shiver through him, as though someone had just poured ice water down the length of his spine. It was a mere whisper, set upon the wind and delivered only to his ears. An eerie voice, that rose above all the others, was spoken with such softness it might have come from his very own mind. He knew its origin, though. He knew it was not his. It was them . . . it was *him* . . . The Fifth Seed. They had found him, just as he had anticipated, just as he had known all along they would. It was why he was here in the first place tonight, wasn't it?

Instinctively he glanced over his shoulder to see who could have gotten so close to speak this single word. So close he could almost feel the puff of breath tickling the short hairs on his neck. But he knew even before he saw—no one had come within twenty feet of his precarious perch.

Now Curt knew he had no choice. If there was a part of him that would prevent him from tossing himself to the waves, it was now gone. His self-preservation instincts had suddenly been shoved aside by the wicked and foreboding voice that goaded him in a one-word whisper. "Jump."

Gathering himself, he breathed his last words, "Goodbye, Anna. I love you. I'm so sorry." With that Curt heaved himself out into the air, his body seemingly hanging there momentarily before plummeting in a terrifying descent to the murky black of the turbulent water below.

As the crowd looked on aghast—screaming out in combined shock and horror—a lone dark figure observed from a safe distance, finding immense pleasure at the sight. And riding on the connection that was just made, he offered his own parting words to the wind. "I'm coming for you, Anna," he whispered, before fading away once more into the thick, hanging mist.

CHAPTER 3

THE CONNECTION

Half a continent away, in a townhouse set in a sprawling Minneapolis suburb, the connection was completed, and Anna Jenkins woke with a terrible shiver. The white cotton tank top she wore to bed was soaked with sweat and her hands trembled uncontrollably. Glancing at the clock on the nightstand she saw the neon display flash over to 12:01 a.m. Dashing across the floor she flicked on the wall switch, hoping the bright light would wash away the sick and frightened feeling she had. She crawled back into bed and curled up in the fetal position, hugging a thick floral comforter to her like a massive security blanket. There she began to weep softly.

In her mind, she had experienced the same events, like a horrible nightmare, yet she knew it was not a dream at all. After all, she was the connection. Horrified, she could feel Curt falling through the black void, the terror he felt and the presence that had pushed him literally over the edge. She knew this, to her utter horror and revulsion, like a twin might sense something terrible had happened to a sibling—only ten times more vivid. She knew what her mind told her to be true: Curt was lost, and The Fifth Seed was coming for her. Now there were only three.

CHAPTER 4

STAKEOUT

G rady Hamilton watched patiently from the soft leather bucket seat of his 1999 metallic-blue Ford Explorer. As he did, a light winked on in the front room of the townhouse, number 3345—the home he had been watching for the last five hours. On a yellow pad on the empty seat beside him, Grady scribbled the following: "12:03 a.m . . . . light on . . . front upstairs window." The entry followed a whole host of observations he had strung together, but as of yet, they offered no solid clues.

From under the pad, Grady pulled a large legal-size leather folio in which he had been keeping information he had gathered on the case. With one eye on the townhouse Grady dug into the file's contents. It had been nearly two weeks now since Bruce, Anna's father, had stormed to Grady's front door, threatening to leave. Yet the overwrought father had eventually settled down and handed Grady the case.

At the time, Mr. Jenkins had unequivocally stated that he had never abused his daughter. Still, Grady wasn't so sure—there was obviously something traumatic in this young girl's life. But the issue had been dropped for the time being. Right now Grady had other things to worry about, like what was going on behind the windows of 3345. Was Anna inside? He wasn't sure, but so far it was the best lead he had.

From the file Grady pulled out a photo of Anna. He had looked at it many times before, so he set it aside. He couldn't look at her anymore, finding it hard to imagine this young lady had so many problems. In Grady's mind's eye she seemed too well put together . . . too self-assured. Yet the information he had received from Northwoods, through Mr. Jenkins, was unmistakable. She had a history of drugs, had been released to halfway houses four times—each and every time returning to drug abuse within a month of supervised release. The file also indicated Anna had attempted suicide twice, and nearly overdosed another four times. Still, the question Grady had was why?

Momentarily pushing those disturbing thoughts from his mind, he returned to his file, retrieving a stack of papers nearly a half-inch thick. This was the fully typed transcript of Grady and Mr. Jenkins' conversation, along with observations he had inserted after the fact. Grady always recorded his sessions with clients, but rarely offered that tidbit of information to his customers. It was probably a legal issue, but if they never found out, what was the harm? Ultimately he was amazed at how much he could discover by referring back to the conversations once he was further along in his investigations—especially inconsistencies that arose in people's stories over time. But he had read the transcript dozens of times, so it too was quickly set aside.

Next, Grady removed brief bios and photos of the other three escapees, tossing them into a stack with the other items, before finally retrieving four photocopied newspaper articles fastened together with a paper clip. Absent-mindedly, Grady thumbed through the news clippings, catching their headlines and little else. He had read and reread each many times over. The first was the most recent, a story from the *Minneapolis Star-Tribune's* regional section. It was short, and the headline simply read: "Four escape from Northwoods."

The second article was longer, but covered the same topic—though this one had been retrieved from Grady's local library and had run in Bemidji's own weekly rag. Both articles detailed a lapse in security at Northwoods caused by a series of suspect errors that ultimately led to the escape of four of its troubled patients.

The escape had taken place several weeks ago now. Speculation was that an orderly failed to lock in one of the patients, and that patient,

Curt Browning, had released the other three, including Anna. From there, a malfunctioning door alarm on a delivery entrance, and a security camera system that mysteriously was down during the escape cleared a path for the patients to slip unnoticed off the grounds. Grady suspected an inside job, but neither article posed that possibility. The stories went on to give brief descriptions of the escapees and the unsuccessful attempts to track them down. None were described as dangerous, except possibly to themselves.

The third article was from about two years back, again retrieved from the library archives. The feature article from the *Rochester Post Bulletin* was titled, "Medical Mind Games." Grady was quite sure it held no significance to his case, but a search using the keyword "Northwoods" had pulled it up from the library's files. The article went into some depth about recent medical studies authored by a doctor at the Mayo Clinic dealing with increased brain function through different physical and mental activities, including games. Northwoods appeared only at the end in a brief reference to the doctor's bio. Apparently the man had served as a consultant to the facility in some capacity.

The last article held what Grady was looking for. It was an article from a medical journal about another doctor by the name of Mary Jane Henderson and the color photo offered a crisp, clear picture of her round smiling face. Mary Jane was a psychologist, specializing in childhood disorders, particularly as they related to savants—and she had served as a caregiver at Northwoods for nearly five years. He wondered why a woman with her background, with an expertise in matters of savants, would spend part of her promising career dealing with the bratty children of rich families and their various vices—particularly at a private treatment center in the middle of nowhere Minnesota. Something didn't quite fit. Unable to resolve it at the moment, he tucked this anomaly in the back of his mind.

Perhaps the answers would come soon, as it was Mary Jane's home that Grady now watched. Grady had been given her name by Mr. Jenkins, along with some other pieces of information that weren't published in any articles or journals. Apparently, while at Northwoods,

Mary Jane had been assigned to Anna's case and had developed an unnatural motherly attachment to Anna. Then, a little over a year ago, Mary Jane had been released from her duties at Northwoods. The parting was officially termed a resignation, though Bruce seemed to indicate it was actually more of a firing.

Mr. Jenkins seemed to think—with his daughter becoming so attached to her—Anna might try to seek out Dr. Henderson after her escape. For Grady, it seemed like a long shot, but it was the only lead he had to go on. While Bruce had been able to get Northwoods to release some of Anna's files, Grady had no luck trying to get the private facility to share any details around the escape or the other escapees. In fact, he'd been told unceremoniously that the police were looking into the matter . . . period. With that door shut, and little else to go on, Grady had gone about the task of trying to locate Dr. Henderson.

Doing so ended up being much more difficult than he ever anticipated. For shortly after Mary Jane left Northwoods, she seemingly disappeared. Grady even tried calling in a few favors owed to him from his Bureau days, but a discreet search, provided by an old friend and colleague, failed to turn up anything concrete on Mary Jane's whereabouts. It was actually the article he held in his hand that began to slowly expose the trail of a woman who didn't seem to want to be found.

From the article, Grady discovered Mary Jane's last place of employment. Prior to joining Northwoods she had been with the University of Minnesota's medical research department, dealing specifically with young savants. Grady called an old girlfriend, Marie, who worked in the university's personnel department. They were still on friendly terms, and so, against university policy, she dug into her computerized files to see what she might be able to unearth. It was a long shot that initially didn't pay off. The search yielded nothing. Mary Jane had not had any contact with the university in the last year and their most recent address for her was five years outdated.

Discouraged, Grady had been just about to hang up when Marie threw him a bone in the form of a phone number. After running a cross-search of personnel from Mary Jane's department, Marie had come across the name of another woman who appeared to have partnered with Mary Jane on several research projects. The woman had since left the university, but was still in town. She had left her forwarding address and phone number. After Grady promised not divulge where he got the name, Marie recited the information to him over the phone.

Thankfully, Abby Turnbill was a gossip—Grady could tell that ten seconds into their call. Representing himself as a reporter, wanting to do a follow-up story on her old colleague Mary Jane, Abby had immediately opened up, offering any assistance she might be able to provide. Without any prompting she began to relate what she described as a stormy partnership between the two research professionals, with Abby emerging in the limelight. Grady did all he could to feign interest before he had to cut her off and get to the meat of what he wanted.

"You want to know where she is?" Abby had said incredulously, as if she were the only person Grady would need to talk to. "I haven't spoken to her in over nine months."

But it was the glimmer of hope Grady was looking for. Nine months meant Abby must have seen Mary Jane after she had vanished.

With a bit of prompting, Grady soon discovered Abby had run into Mary Jane at one of their favorite restaurants, the Uptown Café. According to Abby, Mary Jane seemed flustered, and in a hurry to leave, so much so, that she left before the waitress could return her credit card. "I was so surprised," Abby had said to Grady, "when the waitress ran out with her card calling after her . . . Miss Flannigan! So, I asked her if she got married and she just looked at me all embarrassed before finally saying yes. Then she grabbed the card from the waitress and ran off."

Thanking Abby, Grady instantly began his search anew, looking for a Mary Jane Flannigan. Still, he couldn't find a Mary Jane Flannigan or M.J. Flannigan listed anywhere in the Twin Cities metro area. And the two M. Flannigans listed turned out to be male. It took a week's worth of cold calls to hospital, clinic, and medical research facility receptionists to finally find a Mary Jane Flannigan employed at MediView, a small research clinic.

Upon arriving at the clinic itself, Grady discovered it to be a newer building, located on the site of the old Meyer Brother's dairy in the wealthy suburb of Wayzata, an area he knew well. For the two days following, Grady staked out the company's parking lot armed with the photo from the article. He must have missed Mary Jane the first night, or perhaps she hadn't come to work that day, but he struck gold the next, seeing her leave the facility and get into her 2001 Mitsubishi Gallant. Based on the old photo from the article, she had changed her hair color, but it was definitely the same round friendly face from her earlier days.

After that, the rest was easy. Grady simply followed Mary Jane home, bringing him to where he was now, staring at a light in a window, hoping Anna was somewhere behind the veil of white curtains. A few minutes later, at 12:46 a.m., the light in the front window flashed off again. Grady recorded the time in his ledger. It would be his last observation of the night. For the rest of the evening the townhouse remained in darkness.

CHAPTER 5

FITFUL SLEEP

Mary Jane wandered down the dimly lit hallway from her master bedroom in the rear of the townhouse. She awoke at 12:37 a.m. to a soft moaning coming from Anna's room. Anna's light was still on, and the glow from it spilled out around the seams of the door and out into the hall.

She paused a moment, listening and then whispered her name. "Anna?" There was no response. She spoke her name again. This time she didn't wait for a response, but carefully pushed the door open to find the young woman sprawled out on the bed. Her body was heaped in a messy tangle with the thick, tufted comforter as though she had been fighting an imaginary foe.

"Anna?" she asked again in a soft, concerned voice.

The young woman tossed fitfully at the sound of her name, but was apparently asleep.

Mary Jane walked quietly over to the bedside and sat ever so softly on the edge. For just a moment, the bedsprings creaked with the added weight, and Mary Jane held her breath, hoping the young woman wouldn't wake up. Satisfied she wouldn't, Mary Jane slowly began to stroke Anna's thick tangle of black curls while whispering a soothing mantra, "It's okay dear, everything's going to be okay." In her mind she wondered if it really would be. She had been so careful, so meticulous in her departure from her previous life.

For a year she had worked to build a safe haven for Anna, assuming a new identity and secreting away reserves of cash in hopes of this very day arriving, when Anna could be free, as she deserved to be. But she couldn't help but wonder about one tiny slip that could cost them everything.

Anna moaned again, and Mary Jane began to gently rub her back. A few minutes passed and Anna seemed to settle into a deeper, more restful sleep. Kissing her own hand, Mary Jane applied it to the young woman's temple before quietly removing herself from the room. Whatever had roused her from her sleep would have to wait until tomorrow.

Taking one more look at Anna's petite, prone figure, a concerned smile pinched Mary Jane's round face. Then she turned out the light and returned quietly to her own waiting bed, oblivious to the dangers gathering outside.

CHAPTER 6

GRADY'S PAST

At precisely 2:00 a.m. Grady called off the hunt. Exhausted and fairly confident nothing else would happen beyond the windows of 3345, he began his long drive home to his work in progress. The 1890s bungalow he was remodeling himself was just a half-mile removed from the Mississippi River in St. Paul.

Grady was all of 32, a young man who seemed to have fallen into a rut early in life. A promising, yet grunt-like, undercover career with the FBI had been dashed at the age of 29. He had moved on to the only line of investigative work that would take someone with such a short, muddy history.

For the most part, Grady hated what he did. Approximately 90% of his current work found him following adulterous husbands and wives around with a DSLR and a telephoto zoom, snapping compromising photographs. They were filthy little assignments, a far cry from the six years he had spent working undercover, making drug busts and occasionally helping track foreign agents operating in the Twin Cities.

Recruited right out of the halls of the University of St. Thomas, after receiving his B.A. in Criminal Sciences with a minor in psychology, Grady had been assigned to the local Bureau. There, his role in several high-profile regional busts had pushed his stock through the roof. Then, just as he was about to be reassigned at a national level, something happened that would turn his life upside down.

He could recall the details like it was yesterday. And as he sped along the nearly deserted corridors of highway 394 toward the I-94 junction, tucked under the looming expanse of Minneapolis skyline, he began to relive his misfortune all over again.

It began on a snowy New Year's Eve, almost four years ago. Grady had been indulging at his favorite Irish bar . . . O'Gara's. It was a busy, multi-roomed establishment, located on Snelling Avenue, on the streets of old St. Paul. The pub offered several venues including a traditional Irish pub, a quaint piano bar and modern dance hall named O'Gara's garage. On this particular night, Grady found himself in the long narrow pub, a place he frequented often, ever since his college days. Proud of his Irish heritage, he felt at home there, and he spent several New Year's Eves in attendance. It was an occasion not to be missed if one could manage, rivaled only by the St. Patrick's Day celebrations.

The night of the incident, Grady had been attempting to carry on a conversation with a bartender he had gotten to know quite well. The man's name was Flynn and he had a thick Irish accent to boot. But as the midnight hour approached, the two friends found conversation difficult, as the din within the small Irish pub rose to a rowdy-loud level. Tired of trying to speak over the noise and in-between the constant drink requests Flynn had been receiving from other patrons, both men had finally given up. Instead Grady sipped the head off his third Guinness Stout of the night and began the enjoyable task of people watching.

Alone with no date to speak of this year, Grady had decided he would duck out just before the clock struck twelve. He was generally comfortable with himself, but with it being New Year's and all, he would prefer to avoid any awkward feelings once the sea of people paired off with their partners, or recent acquaintances, for a drunken midnight kiss.

At approximately 11:45 p.m., with his beer only half empty, Grady decided it was time. Just as he was about to get up and leave, a regular, sitting to his right, whom Grady knew only as Shawn, suddenly tottered off his barstool and crashed awkwardly to the floor. Grady watched, amused, as the drunken man picked himself up and brushed himself off. He even allowed a smirk to cross his face as Shawn deposited all the change from his pocket on the bar as a gratuity for Flynn's expert service. It couldn't have amounted to more than 65 cents, Grady guessed. Giving an awkward wave and a drunken grin, Shawn stumbled his way through the throng of people and out into the snowy night.

With the brief entertaining interlude over, Grady began to maneuver the black leather bomber he had been sitting on out from underneath him. It was difficult, as the crowd was thick, and it took quite a balancing effort before he successfully retrieved the coat and slid it over his broad shoulders.

Giving an appreciative nod to Flynn along with his own generous ten-dollar tip, Grady slipped a foot to the sticky floor—now sporting a shiny coat of spilt beer—just as someone from behind touched him gently on the shoulder. Before he could even turn to see who it was, a lovely vision, with long, straight dyed-blond hair, hopped spryly onto the stool recently vacated by Shawn.

"Hey, Grady," she said with a perky smile, and a slightly noticeable alcohol-induced slur.

The touch on the shoulder and the greeting caught Grady by surprise as he found himself gazing into the bright green eyes of a woman he found vaguely familiar. He smiled quizzically, returning her friendly greeting. "Hello," he replied with the feigned enthusiasm of someone trying to hide the fact that he had no clue who she might be. Still stumped, he added with a hint of embarrassment. "Do I know you?"

Ignoring his question at first, the pretty young woman simply replied, "I've been trying to get a seat by you for the last two hours. I noticed you from across the room and had to talk to you before you left." Glancing at his coat she added, "You were leaving, weren't you?"

Grady gazed at her, scanning her pretty face before peeking at her slight yet curvy figure, all in hopes of unearthing any clue that might spark his foggy memory.

"Oh my god," the woman said shocked, "you really don't know who I am, do you? I thought you were just playing with me. It's Nancy," she offered. Yet there was still no recognition from Grady. "Nancy Anderson," she finally elaborated with a bit of a perturbed huff.

It was then the light flicked on in Grady's beer-fogged mind and fond memories flooded back to him like a two-minute film clip set in extreme fast forward. Speechless, he now realized his mistake. They had dated before, for almost a year when both attended St. Thomas. But life's differing ambitions had gotten in the way of something more lasting.

She had been pretty then, but now she looked stunning. Her hair had been darker in college and she had generally worn glasses coupled with thick baggy sweaters—a studious but sexy look that Nancy had pulled off well. Now her eyes glimmered, no longer obscured behind specs. Her hair, longer and more lustrous than ever before, was tucked softly behind each ear, spilling from there in a silky wave before it came to rest just above the noticeable curve of her figure. "Of course! How have you been?" he said with genuine sincerity mixed with a hint of shame.

His early departure now forgotten, the pair fell into an engaging conversation, reliving their brief past as a couple, before catching up on a few highlights of the years they had missed in between. As they reminisced and shared, it seemed with each passing moment the crowd noise became louder and louder. Barely able to hear, Nancy seized an opportunity. Gently placing her hand on Grady's knee, she steadied herself to lean in and catch his every word. The subtle move gave more roundness to her figure and in that instant Grady felt the same old wave of desire wash over him.

Minutes passed and Grady was telling Nancy about his work with the FBI when they were suddenly interrupted by a rousing chorus of 10, 9, 8, 7 . . . Nancy leaned in even closer, her pressure on Grady's knee more intense, her head inclined to one side as she positioned her lips so close they brushed Grady's ear. "Hold that thought," she breathed.

With each word Grady could feel the soft puff of her warm breath on his neck, mixed with the gentle sweep of her hair as it tickled his cheek. The crowd continued . . . 5, 4, 3 . . . with Nancy now pulling back just a bit. The move brought her face to within a few inches of Grady's, and there she gazed fondly into his olive green eyes as a sensual smile creased her lips. The crowd shouted 1, but neither Grady nor Nancy joined in the fray. Each was now totally oblivious to the chorus of "Happy New Year!" from the rowdy crowd around them. Instead their mouths met in a soft and tender kiss punctuated by a little flick of Nancy's tongue across Grady's parted lips.

Nancy pulled back from their moment—her eyes beaming, her face spread in a broad, flushed smile. She wanted to ask him something, but the crowd was too loud for words. Instead, she simply reached out and took Grady's hand. A look did all the asking and Grady's eyes answered a silent yes. Then slowly Nancy led him past the gradually settling crowd, out the door, and into a swirl of white fluffy snow.

CHAPTER 7

THE KID

Sinking into the plush overstuffed aisle seat of his first class accommodations, the one Northwoods insiders nicknamed The Kid pulled his navy blue ball cap down low and rested his blood-shot eyes. He was extremely tired, his mind weary from dealing with the Curt situation and the evening's prior events. It had taken a lot out of him, an unavoidable side effect of his skill set and the drugs he used to enhance it. It was this skill set that had, in his eyes, earned him the legendary label of "Fifth Seed" of Northwoods—a label born of mystery and paranoia—striking fear into the hearts of many at the institute. No outsiders knew his true identity, and that was the way The Kid liked it.

The call last night had come in shortly after he returned to his hotel room near Ghirardelli Square, in the heart of the San Francisco's wharf district. It was well past midnight and he had just been preparing to go to bed when the phone rang. Answering on the second ring a familiar voice began speaking without so much as a greeting. "You done with your dalliance in the Bay?"

"Yeah. Curt's gone, the Fourth Seed has been dealt with, if that's what you're asking," came The Kid's emotionless reply.

"Good," the caller's voice came back, "for we are close on number one and we may need you."

"The First Seed . . . Anna?" The Kid inquired with a mix of excitement and fear rising in his voice.

"Yes. I thought you might be interested. For the time being, you are only backup if the original plan fails."

"What plan? I was under the impression she was mine to deal with," The Kid shot back, a hint of anger rising in his voice.

"Yes, but you insisted on your little Bay excursion first, even though we thought it wasn't a top priority. You know Curt was never a threat like the others. Ultimately, we can't afford to lose her," the caller explained.

"You take her down now and you'll screw up everything I just worked for out here. I know we can use her, she'll lead us directly to Seeds Two and Three . . . Joe and Trent."

"I understand your concerns, but right now we need to get a handle on the situation, and if we have to, I'm sorry, we will do what is necessary."

Controlling his emotions now, The Kid spoke once more. "I understand, just tell me when and where."

"Your departure is at 5:30 p.m.—unfortunately it was the first available on such short notice. The particulars have all been taken care of. Your ticket and instructions will be waiting for you at the hotel's front counter in the morning. Get some sleep—you'll need it." These last instructions were followed with an abrupt click and the line went dead.

In the hours following the call, The Kid could hardly contain his anger, though it was mixed with a strange longing. Contrary to instructions, he slept little the prior evening. Even now as his body was being hurled through the air at nearly 600 miles per hour, he couldn't fully relax. Anna's disappearance came as an intense disappointment to him. He couldn't care less about the others. But she was different. And it appeared he needed to again convince Northwoods Anna still had a use—that she was more valuable alive than dead. The only way he could ensure that was to take his case to the top. He just hoped he wasn't too late.

"Sir?" a soft voice suddenly came from his right.

The Kid lifted his cap and opened his eyes to see a lovely young flight attendant hovering over him. She was in her mid to late twenties with voluminous sapphire eyes, sculpted diamond-shaped face, and dirty blond hair pulled back into a tight ponytail.

"Would you care for a drink?" she asked with a perkiness that indicated she was probably new to the job, and the years of miles, constant travel, and rude passengers had not jaded the genuineness of her rehearsed greeting.

Looking the attendant directly in the eyes, he read her like an open book. Almost instantly he could sense she found him attractive. "A glass of water is all, thank you." He replied directly.

For a moment the flight attendant blushed before awkwardly excusing herself. As she turned back down the aisle, The Kid smiled to himself, taking in her trim figure as she hurried off to retrieve the water he'd use to down his next course of drugs. In his warped mind, he knew exactly what she'd been thinking when her face redden. Passionate images of their bodies intertwined in the airplane restroom . . . private thoughts she assumed were all her own. And why wouldn't he know? After all, he'd suggested them to her with his own mind.

CHAPTER 8

FIRST SIGHT

Operating on only three hours of restless sleep, Grady had returned to the townhouse the next morning just in time to see Mary Jane's silver-gray Gallant pull out of the garage. Its headlights sliced through the early morning darkness as she apparently headed off to work. As far as he could tell she was the only one in the car.

Letting her go, Grady set up shop for about an hour. He settled in again in one of the visitor's parking spaces tucked in the center of the ring of townhouses that surrounded him. He was hoping against all hope to catch a glimpse of Anna before dawn, but he was not in luck and chose to leave just before the first sliver of sun peered over the black-shingled peaks of the row homes to his east.

Grady was careful not to spend too much time in the lot during daylight hours, as he thought he'd be too conspicuous to nosy neighbors when the sun was up. Instead, he decided to preoccupy himself today with following up on loose ends from other cases—tracking down scumbag clients who wouldn't pay and digging into a pet project that was truly pro bono.

Now, just after 5:30 p.m. Grady rolled his Explorer back into the townhouse complex lot to await Mary Jane's return. On the passenger seat next to him was the same notepad in which he scrawled last night's notes, as well as observations he had made regarding Mary Jane's departure that morning.

The first entry under the day's date read: Mary Jane Departure . . . 6:13 a.m . . . . appeared to be alone. Followed by *NSA* . . . his short hand for "no suspicious activity," and then his log-out at 7:11 a.m. He logged in again at 5:34 p.m. tonight. Anticipating the obvious he notated "Mary Jane's arrival" and left the time entry blank.

Setting his log down, he again retrieved Anna's file from the seat. This time he left all contents packed away, removing only the photo of Anna. He told himself he wanted to familiarize himself with her face, just in case she had changed her appearance, but in reality, he had looked at it so much, he could see her perfectly when he closed his eyes—virtually no detail had gone unnoticed.

From the picture, Anna was quite a pretty young lady with an undercurrent of Hispanic features. Her eyes were a deep moody brown and her long hair tumbled in gently curling waves of silky black as it perfectly framed her slender, delicately structured face. Oddly enough, Grady never would have guessed from looking at Anna's smiling picture that she had a not-so-pleasant past.

There was something that bothered him about the photo—it seemed dated for some reason, and he guessed it was why he kept going back to it. Beyond all of his feelings that her stormy history didn't fit the face, he couldn't help feeling that the photo just wasn't current. It was a vague sense, almost a knowing in his mind—without the proof to back it up. Resigned to calling it a mystery he set the photo back down and began to watch and wait.

Time ticked away, and cars came and went from the lot—each time Grady tried his best to keep a low profile—but none of the cars were the silver-gray Gallant he waited for. The townhouse before him remained quiet for the next two hours, with no indications anyone was at home. Grady would have loved to get a closer look, but the residence was quite inaccessible without him being any more conspicuous than he already was. The home sat in the middle of five adjoined townhouses, which offered few interior views from the front. There only appeared to be a bedroom window up on the second story, and a slim window on the lower level situated just to the left and forward of the main entry. Grady assumed this window was in the kitchen.

He had a good idea of the rear layout as well. A risky, late-night trip around the back of the complex the evening before had revealed a main floor sliding glass door off a concrete apron that served as a patio. Above the glass door, a long row of four consecutive windows marched along the narrow width of the townhouse. These likely belonged to a second floor master bedroom. Other than that, any prolonged window peeping would certainly be alarming to any neighbors whose own homes backed up to the rear of Mary Jane's complex.

Finally, at 7:23 p.m. a pair of headlights flicked through the dusky evening and shone briefly into his car interior. Grady slouched down again, watching intently as the lights slowed. It was then that he saw it—a slim crack of light glowing down by where the garage door met the pavement. "Bingo" he said with excitement as the garage door rose, and Mary Jane's car turned into the driveway. Moments later, he could just make out the slightly plump figure of the woman he believed to be Mary Jane slipping from the car and into the house as the garage door slowly made its descent.

Moments later the kitchen window glowed to life as lights came on inside. Grady guessed that Mary Jane was beginning to make herself at home, settling in for another uneventful evening. It was there, at that very moment he made up his mind. He couldn't risk another hour in the lot before someone in the complex called the police about the suspicious metallic blue Explorer and its driver just hanging out. Anna or no Anna, Grady decided he had to have a face-to-face with Mary Jane. Perhaps she might be helpful if he mentioned Anna's father was looking for her.

Uncertain why, Grady allowed fifteen minutes to pass before he opened the door to his SUV to get out. *Was it nerves?* He wondered. As he exited the Explorer's overhead light remained unlit, the bulb purposefully removed to prevent any snooping eyes from seeing too far inside the car. Closing the door softly, he covered ten paces toward the townhouse door before he stopped dead in his tracks. There, to his utter surprise, Grady saw the thin sliver of light suddenly appear and then grow larger as the garage door went back up. "Damn it," he swore under his breath.

Quickly he turned on his heels and raced back to the Explorer, shutting the door just as the Gallant in the garage roared to life. His own keys in the ignition, Grady readied himself to follow the car. Would there be two inside this time? He hoped. Yet again, he faced disappointment. With one eye on the car Grady picked up his cell phone and placed a call, spoke a few quick instructions and disconnected the call. Tonight he had brought backup, and an investigator's hunch told him to stay with the townhouse.

Setting the phone back on the seat, Grady watched the Gallant's reverse lights as they lit a glowing path down the short driveway and then flashed off as the car set into drive. Seconds later the car's running lights disappeared around the corner of a row of townhouses and sped out of sight.

But at that moment, Grady was no longer looking intently at the car. Was it a trick his mind was playing on him or did the light cast through the kitchen window just flash off? Someone was home! Trying to temper his enthusiasm, Grady decided to wait another ten minutes, just in case Mary Jane returned unexpectedly. "Could she be inside?" he wondered aloud.

The time passed dreadfully slowly. Finally, Grady summoned up his nerve once again and retraced his steps to the front door. His heart was racing oddly in anticipation as his long legs carried him across the service drive and up the walkway at a brisk pace. He passed the now-dark kitchen window and paused on the dimly lit stoop. There, he rehearsed his role, playing it back in his mind for a few seconds before pressing the doorbell firmly.

Waiting, he tapped his toe anxiously, wondering who would be on the other side of the door when it finally opened. He heard footsteps, some shuffling by the door and then the overhead light burst on above him. The sudden light gave him a little jump and he quickly attempted to settle his nerves with a long deep breath.

"Who is it?" a soft, wary voice asked.

"Townhouse management, Miss. Could I have a word?"

There was an unnaturally long pause, and Grady thought whoever was inside was unconvinced. But he heard the familiar sound of a deadbolt turning and the door slowly began to open.

CHAPTER 9

THE DECEIT

Anna said goodbye to Mary Jane as she walked to the door. She was a short plump, woman with shoulder-length dyed-blond hair. Her eyes, now tinged brown by her contacts, were so warm and friendly they made Anna feel safe and secure. Mary Jane was the closest thing Anna had to a mother in this world and she loved her like one.

"Sure you don't want to come?" Mary Jane offered one last time as she held the garage door open.

Anna hesitated before reluctantly waving off the invitation. She hated seeing Mary Jane leave. Every morning she went to work Anna felt alone, isolated and scared, feelings that had only been compounded by her dream last night. She spent her days like a hermit, tucked into the couch with any book or magazine she could digest. Every time the phone rang or a car door slammed outside she jumped. This was no way to live. But what else could she do?

In any event, Mary Jane was just going out to pick up Chinese and perhaps a movie. A half hour max, she'd promised.

Watching the door close Anna wished she wouldn't leave. They had spoke only briefly about Anna's dream last night. Exhausted, Anna had slept in, and Mary Jane had been reluctant to wake her, deciding it was best to let her sleep. They had talked once today by phone, but both were unwilling to get into details. What little Anna offered had clearly upset Mary Jane, who promised they would make new plans for their future tonight, after dinner. Perhaps they would move on together, to another city and try to more thoroughly disappear.

Now Anna suddenly wanted to talk, to let it all out, but Mary Jane was long gone. So instead, she set the book she had been reading down on the coffee table and made a trip to the fridge. She retrieved a can of Diet Coke and closed the door. If asked, she wouldn't have even remembered turning off the kitchen light as she made her way back to the sofa, preparing to lose herself in another hundred or so pages of *Les Misérables*.

It was only a few minutes later that she was surprised by the soft scraping of footsteps outside the front door. They paused for a moment, and Anna anxiously held her breath. Then the doorbell rang—the resonating sound sent Anna bolt upright. She'd let it go, she thought . . . pretend no one was home. But something willed her up out of her seat and over to the door.

Pausing, she gathered herself, before peering through the small peephole where her eyes took in the shadowy figure of a man. She couldn't tell what he looked like at all, so she found the switch for the outdoor light and turned it on.

Through the distorted image of the peephole she could make out what appeared to be a man in his early thirties wearing a mildly wrinkled cotton dress shirt that he left untucked, a tasteful tie loosened around his neck, and a faded pair of blue jeans. He was tall, about six-two, with strong, broad shoulders and an unpolished handsomeness, thanks to a square jaw and a slightly crooked nose that appeared to have been broken at least once. His nearly straight, sandy-brown hair had just a trace of ginger in it—and he wore it unkempt and a little too long, Anna thought, as it danced into his olive green eyes—the very same eyes that now twinkled at her as a pleasant smile creased his face. *Harmless?* She wondered.

"Who is it?" Anna finally called out.

"Townhouse management, Miss. Could I have a word?"

Anna stepped back and eyed the door. Closing her eyes she concentrated, replaying the light in the stranger's eyes and the tone of his voice back in her head. She thought she felt warmth and friendliness, but there wasn't anything she could truly grasp onto without searching his eyes face to face. After all, they were windows to the soul, someone once said.

Damn, she thought, furious with herself. *Now he knows someone's home.* Still unsure why she was doing it, Anna decided to open the door. If he were in any way connected with Northwoods, she felt in her heart that she would sense it. Carefully she unlocked the deadbolt, reached down and turned the knob, slowly pulling the door open.

The man stood there smiling, his captivating eyes brightening up with his friendly, almost surprised grin. After a long pregnant pause his words came out in a rushed tumble. "Pardon me. I'm David Sloan from the townhouse management office. I'm really sorry to bother you, Miss . . . ah . . . Miss Flannigan is it? But there have been some break-ins around the complex as of late and we've been going door to door to inform our residents of the problem. So, if it's okay by you, we'd like to take a look at your windows and check the integrity of the locks. Apparently that's how they've been getting in."

Anna let the man's words wash over her and sink in, her eyes constantly glued to his, her mind trying to peer into his. She had ignored his question about her identity, although his rush of sentences had barely given her a chance to correct him even if she had wanted to.

Instead she watched him, with words and images flashing into her own thoughts. *She was right!* At first she felt his surprise—about what she could not tell. Then suddenly there was a hint of innocent attraction, and then a flicker of embarrassment on his part. Anna blushed with him, and quickly tried to get a handle on her own thoughts. *What was it that was there, in those deep eyes . . . friendliness, compassion? Yes both were there, but behind that . . . what was it? Not danger but . . . ?* She concentrated harder. Then a word sparked in her mind, lighting up like a neon sign . . . *deceit!*

If she could have she would have slammed the door on him, but somehow he had managed his way into the entry. Suddenly . . . hopelessly . . . she felt trapped.

CHAPTER 10

THE OBSERVER

Across the lot, in another townhouse, a shadow gazed through the unlit windows of its second story bedroom, quietly observing Grady as he stepped from his SUV. The unit he was in was supposed to be vacant, but he was quite adept at picking locks, and this particular one had failed within seconds of trying. Inside, he found the home's facilities to be more than adequate, providing the perfect view of townhouse number 3345, and the ideal perch from which to observe Mr. Grady Hamilton during his stakeout.

Through his night vision scope, the watcher could clearly see his prey, the tall casually dressed gentleman bathed in a shroud of light, tinged an eerie green by the scope's precision optics. Momentarily, the man lowered his eyepiece, and picked up a very specific Sig Sauer P229 Equinox he had set on the windowsill. With his gloved hands he checked the ammo, flipped off the safety and began mentally collecting himself for his next task. Two even breaths brought his heartbeat under control before he finally returned the scope to his eye.

Seconds later he found Grady's figure again, just as he rang the doorbell. Unconsciously, the watcher and Grady took a deep anxious breath together as they waited for the door to open. The watcher had no clue if Anna was there, but he too hoped that she answered the door. If she did, he was prepared to act quickly, for who knew how long Grady and Anna would be together. And for his plan to work, they had to be.

Moments later, the door opened and just beyond the muscular build of Grady, the watcher could distinctly see a slim, familiar figure. He immediately identified her as Anna. His suspicions confirmed, the man tensed to turn and make his way to the front door, but something in his mind told him to wait another second or two. He knew Grady was quite skilled, for he had succeeded in finding Anna where Northwoods had failed. Something in the back of his mind was telling himself that Grady would succeed in gaining entry to the home. After all, his instructions were to convince Anna to call her father, and he couldn't very well do that from the doorway.

Anxiously, the watcher waited, observing the pair as they exchanged formalities, hoping against all hope that his instincts were right. The watcher knew, if he missed this opportunity, there wouldn't likely be another and it would open the door for The Kid to go to work. He was counting on Grady's need to be thorough as much as he was counting on Anna to allow this stranger in. It was a gamble, particularly with Anna's unique gifts, but if the two stepped inside together his task would be that much easier. Then he saw it. Grady began edging slowly into the open door before it closed gently behind him.

In a flash the watcher turned from the window, racing quickly out of the room and down the stairs. As he went, he visualized the kills in his mind, as he had done so many times before. Just a quick trip across the lot under the cover of darkness would have him at the door—no more than 30 seconds. Then he'd burst in upon the two. He could already see the shock on their faces, then the horror consuming their expressions as they realized he had a gun. He always relished that moment of realization, right before death. The watcher knew he'd have to take stock of what he was up against immediately as he entered. The arrangement of the kills would have to be precise. Control of the situation was a necessity.

The first task would be to wait for Mary Jane to return, so unfortunately he would have hostages, if only for the moment. Then, when Mary Jane entered he'd drop her at the garage door. Anna would scream—that was a certainty, so he'd turn and take her out next, no matter where she was. Then the final bullet would be saved for Grady. This shot would require a bit more tact but he was certainly capable of pulling it off.

Finalizing the details in his mind, the dark figure suddenly found himself at the front door of the borrowed townhouse. Again, breathing evenly, he centered himself for his next leg across the parking lot and the job that awaited him behind the doors of 3345.

Deliberately, he grasped the front doorknob, turned it and pulled the door wide. As he did his hand flexed uncomfortably in the tight restrictive glove. The movement stretched the supple leather to its seams. The undue pressure on his hand momentarily registered in his mind as he walked slowly out into the night. Yes, the gloves he wore were intentionally a size too small . . . but they had to be. After all, the gun and the gloves were Grady's.

And Mitch Patterson, the very man who only two short weeks ago had passed himself off as Bruce Jenkins, was always a step ahead of his prey. He had to be, if he was going to make this look at all like a double-murder, suicide.

CHAPTER 11

THE DANCE

Grady stood momentarily transfixed in the doorway, somewhat surprised to actually find himself standing face to face with Anna. But he was even more surprised at how strikingly beautiful and mature she seemed . . . more so than her photo ever could have suggested. She stood about five-foot nine—her dark, black hair falling in soft silky tendrils that brushed her face and spilled to her shoulders in relaxed curls. And those voluminous eyes—more deep and dramatic a brown than he'd imagined—with amazingly long lashes that licked up in elegant arcs and flickered softly as she offered a smile.

She wore just a light brush of makeup, though she appeared not to need it, and a long, close-fitting charcoal sweater paired with heavily distressed navy jeans. The entire outfit was so simple, and yet perfectly highlighted the beautiful contours of her body. Her appearance as a whole alluded more to a woman well into her early twenties rather than one of seventeen.

Like a young boy, Grady blushed, and thought for the briefest moment that he saw her face redden a bit as well. Looking suddenly away, Grady forced himself to remember why he was here. He actually had what he needed. She was here. That was about it. His job was almost done. Yet he had to press himself to finish. If he could, he was supposed to get her to call her father. That was it . . . simple . . . yet as he looked at her now, he thought the task impossible.

So instead of the 'Your father misses you' speech he had rehearsed so many times, he found himself ad-libbing. Keeping to his townhouse management ruse, he began in about break-ins and such. Then for some reason, simply on impulse, he added something about looking at window locks.

What the hell was that? he'd thought to himself. *Window locks? She's here . . . either tell her why you're here or go . . . case closed.* But deep down inside he knew he had to know more of this young woman's story. For one, the hours he had spent poring over her bio, her photo and the depth behind the eyes somehow had endeared her to him. But also, there was an inherent mystery to Anna, Grady felt—something her father wasn't telling him—and Grady aimed to uncover it. So he pressed on not for his client's sake, but for his own sake. Unconsciously Grady eased himself through the doorway and into the home, without ever really being asked. At the same moment, Anna backed away, actually letting him in. Was it an unconscious gesture of comfort? Perhaps.

It was only then he thought he saw a flash of fear cross her eyes, and he couldn't help feeling he had blown it. But now that he was inside the townhouse he had committed himself. He had to follow through and see where this face to face would take him. He hoped he'd been seeing things in her expression, but somehow he didn't think so.

"You mind if I just take a quick look around? At the windows, that is," he added almost as an afterthought, in a lame effort to keep up the ruse.

Anna backed away some more, now seemingly composed. "No, not at all," she offered with a half smile that was nowhere near as intoxicating as her first. "But if you don't mind, I have laundry to attend to upstairs."

For a brief moment, before she turned to go, her eyes focused on him, boring deep into his own eyes, searching in a way that made him feel open and vulnerable. Grady desperately wanted her to stay and talk to him and he quickly tried to think up a reason for her to remain. He wanted to know so much. He wanted to know about her and why she ran away. What had her life been like? He couldn't imagine this woman before him ever having drug problems, much less being diagnosed with mental illness.

In the end all that came out of his mouth was his honesty. "Please don't go just yet."

Anna stopped in her tracks with her back turned toward Grady, yet she made no move to turn around. Slowly a tear fell from one of her eyes, followed by another and another. She knew why he was here. They had sent him. She thought if she could get upstairs she might escape—maybe drop from a window and run away—but she knew he wouldn't let her go.

Her back still turned she finally replied. "Why, so you can send me back?"

Grady's heart sank at her words, muffled by a gentle sob. She knew why he was here. He knew he'd never get her to call her father, but he could call him right now, tell him exactly where she was, she wasn't going anywhere. The woman who stood before him was utterly defeated, and Grady hated himself for doing that do her. "I'd like to talk," Grady offered soothingly.

Anna turned, showing her tears to him. "About what?" she replied. "There's nothing to tell." Then mustering up her nerve she asked the question. "Did you kill him?"

Grady looked blankly back at Anna, now terribly confused. "Kill who?" he asked incredulously.

"Curt!" she screamed at him as if he should have known. "You killed him didn't you . . . all of you bastards killed him."

"Anna, listen," he said softly. "I'm not sure what you're talking about, but whatever you're messed up in? I promise, I can help."

Anna eyed Grady carefully. Her emotions were clouding her senses now, and her instincts at the moment were way off. Still, she could read something in those eyes of his. Something was there that nagged at her, but what? Frustrated and sad, she blurted out, "Oh for Christ's sake, just get it over with. I'll go—take me back to Northwoods. Or were you sent to kill me, too?"

It suddenly dawned on Grady. She thought he was here to take her away. She thought Northwoods had sent him. And she was obviously distraught and perhaps a bit delusional.

He forced a gentle smile, trying to calm her down and soothe her fears. He needed to set things straight, and the only way to do it was through honesty. "Anna, they didn't send me, your father did. Your mother's very sick . . ." but he stopped his sentence there. For Anna was no longer looking at him, instead she was fixated on something behind him. And suddenly the sadness that consumed those big brown eyes switched instantly to primal fear.

CHAPTER 12

UNINVITED

A steady pace across the lot carried Mitch to the front door of 3345 in a matter of seconds. He chose to walk, to arouse less suspicion. Few people who saw him would ever give a man in jeans and a black leather coat making his way leisurely through a parking lot a second glance. But if he were to run, curious eyes were more likely to follow him all the way to his destination.

It turned out there wasn't a soul out and about as he made his trek. He thought briefly about the windows that surrounded him, wondering if someone might be following his movements from the security of other townhouses. But he quickly put it out of his mind. From his knowledge of the townhouse unit he had occupied, only the spare bedroom window offered a good view of the front, while the kitchen windows in each unit actually looked sideways at the entryways and walls of protruding garages.

Pausing, he listened for voices within, anything that might give a hint to where Anna and Grady stood. He could just make out the muffled noises of what he assumed to be conversation. It sounded like it was well inside the home, but he couldn't be sure. Perhaps it was even the TV.

His heart was now racing, and again he attempted to get his nerves under control, to little effect. This was, after all, the moment of no return and he reveled in the anticipation of it. This is what he would

41

look back on when it was all over. He loved the adrenaline rush that fed him. He loved the ever-present danger of being caught and the fact that every now and then he cheated his own death.

Mitch reached for the knob, and slowly began to give it a turn. Unlocked he thought to himself . . . this was good. Now it was decision time. Should he burst in or enter slowly in stealth? Again, listening to the voices from within, he went with the assumption they were not directly inside the entryway. In addition, the conversation seemed continuous, and had taken on a somewhat charged tone. He decided on stealth; perhaps they might not even notice him as he entered.

From his coat pocket he pulled out a black knit ski mask, and taking one more look around to make sure nobody was watching, he pulled it over his head. Again Mitch tried the knob. This time he turned it ever so slowly to its full release position, until his slight forward pressure caused the door to move just slightly inward. Finally, as quietly as he could manage, he walked the door open and stepped silently inside.

CHAPTER 13

HATCHING A PLAN

The fear in Anna's eyes was all consuming and sent a long, slow shiver down the length of Grady's spine. Realizing something was happening behind him, he began to turn when a firm, deliberate voice came from somewhere near the front door, "I suggest you don't do that . . . or I might have to shoot you."

Instantly Grady froze, every muscle in his body tensed as a flood of fear-induced adrenaline shocked his system, coursing through his body with every quickened beat of his heart. For a brief moment he considered his fight-or-flight alternatives, but decided against both for the time being.

"Why don't you just have a seat?" the intruder asked, in an almost mockingly kind voice.

Grady looked back at Anna for confirmation, as if silently asking whether the man had a gun. Sadly, she just nodded her head yes.

"I said have a seat." The voice commanded, catching the non-verbal cues between the two. "Right now on the couch, sitting on your hands."

Terribly confused, Grady didn't move, keeping his own eyes locked on Anna's, which were currently staring down the gunman. Then, for a fraction of a second her gaze flicked off the intruder and quickly locked on Grady's, as if to convey a meaning to him. And somehow, inexplicably, Grady knew the intruder wasn't intending to let them live.

"Move!" the man spoke more forcefully, and this time Grady and Anna did as they were told. Anna went first, gently easing herself into a powder blue couch that faced the rear of the townhouse and the sliding glass doors to the patio outside. She flopped down in a folded-over heap, placing her weary head gently into her hands.

Grady fell in behind, slowly following Anna, but taking his time to maneuver sideways between the couch and a large wooden coffee table. His slow, deliberate progress let him steal a fleeting glance at the man now holding them captive, and he didn't really like what he saw.

The first thing that registered in Grady's mind was that this man was massive. If he had to guess, he would have placed him at six-foot three or four. The man's chest was big and broad, and his neck was incredibly thick. At the moment, Grady had him positioned just inside the entryway, past the kitchen, but not quite into the living room. A black mask concealed any recognizable features of the intruder's head or face, yet something about him seemed oddly familiar.

Now, taking his seat close to Anna, Grady could see she was trembling quite visibly. And again Grady received a strange sense that Anna was convinced both of them were about to die.

"That's better." The man spoke again, sounding pleased the pair was now fully seated, in a position that gave them no view or advantage over him. "Now we'll just wait for the lady of the house to return. Do you think that's best, Anna?"

The words had barely issued from the stranger and Grady saw Anna's fists clench into the cushions of the couch. They held momentarily, as if she were fighting an urge to leap off the couch and strangle the man, before her hands finally relaxed and she sobbed a single word. "No."

Desperately wanting to offer some kind of comfort, Grady slid his hand across the couch, his palm open as a gesture of kindness and sympathy. Looking down with tears flooding her eyes, Anna gazed at Grady's hand oddly, as if suddenly realizing she had him all wrong. She placed her hand gently into his, where he offered a reassuring squeeze. The gesture seemed to help, and Anna began to pull her emotions back under control before releasing Grady's hand back to him.

Grady fully understood that Anna was terrified . . . in all honesty he was afraid, too. And it couldn't help matters that Anna was wrestling with the idea that Mary Jane would be brought into this mess. Yet ironically, Grady was silently relieved that whatever was going to take place would have to wait for her. This obviously gave him some time—valuable time he would need to think and plan his next move—if he had one.

Grady began to take in his surroundings, looking for something that might offer a way out. To his despair, he found the room to be terribly bare. There seemed to be no heavy objects—at least within his reach—that he could use or manufacture into a weapon. The heavy, hardwood coffee table in front of him supported a few cork coasters and a small wooden tray filled with potpourri, but they would be of little use. In the far corner sat a TV. It appeared to be an old 27" tube type, resting on a wooden console with stereo equipment nestled behind glass doors. But again, there seemed to be nothing he could get his hands on to mount an offensive.

For the longest while, the masked man behind them remained quiet, aside from some very soft rustling indicating he might be moving. And in an odd sort of way, Grady mused about those silly movies where the killer tells his intended victims all about his master plans, only to see them escape and use the information against him.

Alas, this was real life, and the stranger was offering no verbal clues. But at the moment, some non-verbal clues were coming in loud and clear. Currently, Grady could make out the occasional tapping of what he guessed was the butt of a gun on some surface. Listening closely, he found the sound to be thick and resonant, as though he were tapping on solid wood instead of the more clipped, higher pitch that might be expected if the tapping were done on the Formica kitchen countertops.

This bit of information probably placed the intruder closer now, as though he had taken a seat at the small round table situated behind the couch. It also indicated the man was probably a little nervous himself. Trying anything, Grady threw his weight back into the couch's cushions, hoping to bring the man into his periphery, but all the movement did was rock the cheap, lightweight couch a bit.

Still grappling with the situation, Grady's mind suddenly began to wrap around a plan. He slowly sat forward again, waiting about 30 seconds before throwing his back into the cushions once more. The move brought a quick response from their captor. "Sit still!"

Grady obliged gladly, noting exactly where the voice had come from. He now had the makings of a plan. Eyeing the coffee table just in front of his knees, he guessed that the piece was crafted from solid wood, most likely oak. Inclining his head to the side slightly, he again noted the substantial round legs the table rose up on, each sunk deeply into the carpet pile. From what he saw, Grady had a hunch it too would do nicely for his scheme.

Now all he had to do was wait for Mary Jane. Based on a handful of sounds and a faint reflection of the room he could just make out in the sliding glass door, Grady had the intruder located almost directly behind them, seated at the dining table. Which meant their captor would have to stand and turn his back to them to either shoot or subdue Mary Jane as she entered from the garage.

The only question that remained was how could he get Anna off of the couch? Unfortunately, it would be integral to his plan. Grady turned his head slightly toward Anna, wondering if he could somehow tip her off to what he wanted her to do, but she wasn't looking his way. At least she had stopped trembling, and her sobs were either silent or had faded away. What Grady didn't realize was that Anna was hatching a desperate plan of her own.

CHAPTER 14

ANNA'S MOVE

Ever so slowly, Anna began to recompose herself. Terribly confused, she wondered about the man sitting next to her. Who was he, and what did he really want? She knew, at least, that he was misinformed. His mention of her father and mother was proof enough of that. Anna's parents had died tragically in a car accident when she was only 5 years old. She'd lived in state-run homes until Northwoods had picked her up. To her, that meant he couldn't be connected—at least not directly with Northwoods. But he had definitely been looking for her. *Why? Who had sent him? Could she trust him?* These were questions she desperately wanted answered.

For the moment she had to put those thoughts aside. Right now, Mary Jane was her main concern. Anna had made up her mind that if she were going to be returned to Northwoods, she would rather die—and if she could help it, she wasn't going to drag Mary Jane down with her.

In her mind, Anna began keeping careful track of time. Mary Jane had said she would return in a half hour. She had spent five, maybe ten minutes alone before the first man showed, and she guessed she had spent another five talking to him before the second arrived. And that man had been here for at least another five minutes. In total, best guess, Mary Jane had been away for twenty minutes, tops.

CHAPTER 15

GRADY'S GAMBLE

As Grady fell over backwards, tumbling with the couch, he heard the gun go off and the glass door explode, followed by a dull thud as the back of the couch smashed into the legs of the gunman. For a fleeting moment Grady could see him, his masked face so close, before the man hopped backwards, lost his balance, and disappeared from view. Grady heard a sharp smack, like the sound of a head hitting drywall, before his own back slammed hard into the cushions of the couch as it met the unyielding floor.

Staring up at the ceiling, but still sitting on the couch, Grady could hear the gunman just behind him on the floor, scrambling to get to his feet. Before he could, Grady somersaulted off the couch and brought his knees down to meet what he thought would be carpet. Instead they found the other man's chest crashing into flesh and bone with a sickening thud.

Grady heard the masked man gasp for air and he knew he had injured him—how badly he was about to find out. Not wasting a minute, Grady scrambled to turn his body to face the man he now lay on top of. In a second he'd found his masked face, the knit cap pushed slightly askew, so that the eyeholes didn't match up exactly right with the eyes. For the moment the advantage was his.

Drawing back his arm and clenching his fist, he drove his best punch into the man's skull, connecting solidly with his left cheekbone. The man grunted in pain as Grady drove another fist deep into the softness of the intruder's stomach. But the man's knee came up hard, catching Grady squarely between his legs and he rolled off to one side, writhing in agony.

Both men now sufficiently weakened rose to their feet, facing each other amid a heap of overturned furniture. Grady noticed the gun was no longer in his attacker's hands, and his eyes immediately searched for it on the ground. Thinking Grady was off guard, the other man lunged, but Grady was ready and deftly sidestepped him, driving the masked man to one side and onto one of the protruding legs of the now-overturned dining table.

Again, Grady backed away, waiting for the intruder to turn on him, while keeping one eye on the ground in hopes of spotting the lost gun. Once again the man in the mask faced him. His eyes reflecting his full hate and anger. Grady unconsciously positioned himself, his back facing the entry, ready for another attack. Again the man bore down on him. Grady moved to the side once more, throwing a jab at the man's gut as he passed. The punch found its target, but without full force, as the intruder shot a forearm into Grady's face on the way by.

Recovering from the surprise blow, Grady turned to face his attacker, only to be caught off guard by a perfectly placed uppercut. The punch connected square with his jaw, snapping his head around violently and Grady immediately felt his knees wobble before collapsing in a heap to the floor. There, with his head turned awkwardly to one side, Grady's vision began to tunnel. Desperately he tried to hold onto consciousness. If he couldn't he was dead, but his body wouldn't move. Tensing, he waited for the man to strike another blow or for his brain to just go to sleep. He could feel the man hovering over him yet he was helpless to do anything. He was losing the battle, his mind shutting down.

"You messed up Grady," the man said exhausted, kneeling very close to his prone figure. Then, just before Grady blacked out, he distinctly heard the low whine of sirens as they made their rapid approach from somewhere off in the distance.

CHAPTER 16

ON THE RUN

Mary Jane brought her car to a screeching halt just to the east of a pair of tennis courts—their towering chain-linked walls just a thin web of shadow hanging in the night. From that dark void she could just make out the outline of Anna racing madly toward the car. Before she even got to the curb, Mary Jane lurched across the passenger seat and flung the door wide, tossing bags of Chinese food out the door to make room for Anna. Quickly Anna threw herself into the empty bucket seat and slammed the door—the Gallant's tires already peeling away a thin film of sand and dirt coating the blacktopped road.

"Thank God I gave you that cell phone," Mary Jane exclaimed as she pulled a wild U-turn, heading back down the drive toward the main access road serving the townhouses. She didn't say it, but she was even more grateful for their planning. Anticipating such a need, Mary Jane had set them up with phones and arranged a predetermined rendezvous by the townhouse's tennis courts should anything ever go wrong—and tonight things certainly had.

"What the hell happened back there?" Mary Jane blurted out.

"Not now. Just drive," Anna said shakily. "Please, just drive . . . just get me out of here . . . please get me out of here."

Mary Jane obliged, concentrating on the road in front of her. Luckily, she had been on her way back when Anna called and only two minutes had elapsed before she was there to pick up her up. But right now, her biggest concern was a tail. Anna had told Mary Jane enough on the phone to scare the hell out of her, and she was afraid whoever had shot at Anna had been watching them for a while. *Would they be looking closely for her car?*

As they left the townhouse complex and accessed the main road, Mary Jane glared warily at a car sitting in the lot of a city park directly across the street. To her immense relief she could just make out the slender figure of a man nearby as he walked his dog. A quick check of her mirrors told her all else was okay. There were no signs of headlights following from the lot or approaching in any direction as the Gallant picked up speed and raced away.

Yet, as the car crested a long gentle grade, Mary Jane was surprised to see a police cruiser with its lights spinning and sirens blaring as it sped by in the opposite direction. Instinctively she pulled off the road to let it pass—turning to watch it go. After it flew by Mary Jane whispered a breathless *thank heavens*, desperately trying to settle her nerves. Not thinking, it took Anna's frantic scream, *What are you doing!* to get Mary Jane to put the car back in drive and speed off.

At the first set of streetlights Mary Jane turned left, then revved the car through three more lights before she crossed the bridge to highway 494. Turning left after the bridge she accessed the southbound ramp and floored it, reaching 70 mph before the car's tires even thumped over the seam separating the blacktop ramp from the highway's smooth concrete surface.

More than ten minutes passed without a word between the two, as their car passed over highway 394 spreading off into the distance to the east and west. It wasn't until the road bent to the east that finally Anna spoke in a wavering voice. "So . . . where are we heading?"

"Rochester." Mary Jane replied pensively.

Anna paused a moment, as if thinking it over and then finally asked, "What's there?"

"A friend . . ." said Mary Jane, apparently not wishing to elaborate right now.

CHAPTER 17

THE FRAME UP

G rady woke with his face buried into the rough, scratchy pile of a light tan carpet. For a moment he forgot where he was, but the loud blare of sirens outside and the sight of overturned furniture brought it all back to him quickly. He couldn't have been out long. Perhaps less than a minute, he guessed, recalling that he had heard sirens just before he'd lost consciousness. The sirens were much closer now, virtually on top of the house, but still the place wasn't yet swarming with cops.

He rose gingerly, trying to hold his throbbing head as steady as he could. As far as he could tell, the masked man was gone. Pushing himself into a sitting position, he noted with surprise that his hands were now gloved. He eyed them coldly, finding them oddly familiar. They were the ones the gunman wore, that was for sure—but they appeared to be an awful lot like a pair he owned. The fit was certainly right.

Glancing around he focused on the overturned couch. The back, which now rested on the floor was tilted slightly askew, as though it was resting on something. On hands and knees he crawled over to it, just as he heard the familiar report of car doors slamming outside. The sirens had stopped now, which meant the police would be knocking on—or knocking down—the door soon.

Grady had a bad feeling as he lifted the couch to reveal the shiny glint of something metal underneath. Holding the couch up with one arm, he grasped the object, retrieving a gun. Letting the couch fall back into place he brought the gun up closer to his face to inspect it more thoroughly. It too looked familiar. It certainly was the same model he used—a Sig Sauer P229 Equinox. Turning it over in his gloved hands he found the serial number. He had his own memorized for identification purposes, and he compared this gun's etched numbers to the ones he held locked away in his head.

He didn't have to go past the first few digits to realize it was going to be an exact match. From outside he heard footsteps approaching. A series of images flashed through his mind: his gun, his gloves, the shot taken at Anna, the exploded glass door, no trace of another intruder and only one witness who didn't want to be found. Factoring in his own past, he added up the score. Sure, there wasn't a body this time, but everything pointed to Grady as the culprit. He had been set up. He knew the evidence was more than enough to detain him, and most likely enough to put him away for a few years unless someone could corroborate his story.

A knock came at the door. "Open up! Police!"

Not hesitating for an instant, Grady leapt to his feet. As he did, his head began to swim and for a moment he thought he would lose his balance. Sheer determination was all that prevented him from collapsing back into a heap. His first step was slow and wobbly, his second more true, and by his third he was gaining speed. When he reached the shattered glass door he propelled himself through the jagged hole, curled up in a tight bundle to avoid catching on any hanging shards of glass.

In mid air, he heard the thick thud of a foot into a doorjamb and he knew they were coming in. Grady's feet led, landing in grass just beyond the concrete patio as he heard the front door swing violently in with a bang. Not looking back, he tucked and rolled to one side, forcing down the bile and vomit that wanted to rise from his stomach at impact.

Instantly he rose into a crouch, looking left, then right, sweeping the darkness with his eyes to see if the police had come around back. No signs. This was good. It probably meant they were treating this as a domestic disturbance. Whoever called it in may not have been sure if they heard a gunshot or not. The usual police response would be to send a cruiser or two to first check it out.

Making a snap decision, Grady flanked out left, racing as fast as he could down the backyard corridor of townhouses. At the last unit, he looked left into the space between the last townhouse in his row and the next row of townhouses meeting at a right angle. From his vantage point he could see only a sliver of the parking lot but no sign of the police. Opting to skip the lot for now, he raced across the grassy opening and slipped around back of the next row of townhouses. Sprinting, he made it to the last unit in this row in less than fifteen seconds.

Now more cautiously, he crept around the rear corner and made his way along the side of the building to the front. Peering into the parking lot he could see one police cruiser parked right in front of the walkway to 3345. The distant sound of another set of sirens led Grady to believe backup was on the way.

He checked for any sign of the authorities, but saw none. He guessed if there were two officers, both were probably still inside taking in the scene and searching rooms, or perhaps out back investigating the likely exit point. Only fifty paces away, Grady's Ford Explorer sat. It wasn't too late to go back into the house and try to explain the truth of the situation. He could easily say he had been trying to chase down the actual gunman, but he wasn't about to gamble on it.

Making up his mind, he walked slowly around the corner of the townhouse that had provided him cover. He kept his pace casual, hoping not to draw the attention of all the residents he knew were glued to any window that would give them a view of the excitement. Acting like a gawker himself, he even paused as he opened his SUV's door, gazing interestedly at the police cruiser.

He knew he was playing a dangerous game, balancing the desire to flee quickly and the need to look as unassuming as possible. After counting to ten in his head, he slipped quietly behind the steering wheel and closed the door. Moments later he was driving out of the lot, accessing the service road. To the left was a quick exit, but he feared the police backup would enter from there. And from his prior visits, he knew if he took a right he could wind his way through a maze of more townhouses before exiting on a less-used local street.

Signaling his turn, he chose the right and ascended a small hill. He had barely traveled fifty feet when he saw in his rearview mirror the next set of whirling lights turn into the lot he had just exited. Once again, Grady was a fugitive.

CHAPTER 18

ROAD TO ROCHESTER

A nna sat back and allowed herself to be mesmerized by the headlights flying by in the opposite lanes, hoping to clear her mind of all thoughts for just a little while. But Mary Jane, desperate for information, still seemed to want to keep the conversation rolling.

"Hey you over there," Mary Jane teased softly, "I really need to know what went on back there. You know we still have barely spoken about your dream last night. Can you open up to me, please?"

Anna shifted uneasily in her seat, reluctant at first to talk, but finally giving in. "Alright," she sighed, "but none of your psychology mind games . . . I'll tell you what happened . . . period. Tomorrow we can psychoanalyze it all."

Mary Jane agreed, so Anna filled her in as best she could. Starting with her dream last night, she explained her vision . . . of Curt and his ordeal on the bridge, before relating his terrifying plunge into the San Francisco Bay. When Anna mentioned the voice . . . The Fifth Seed . . . she saw Mary Jane's face turn ashen, although for the moment, she uttered not a word.

Seizing upon the silence, Anna moved on to the events of this evening, describing in great detail the first man and his unexpected arrival, before elaborating on the ploy he used to get into the house and the misinformation he had given about her parents. Not pausing a moment, she moved straight to the second man's arrival, the gun he held and her conviction that his plan was to murder them all. Sidestepping the reasoning for her plan of escape, Anna then detailed everything up to and after the shot was fired, before she finally drifted into an uneasy thoughtfulness.

Glancing sideways at Anna, Mary Jane let everything sink in. It was a lot to absorb and she had to resist her strong instincts to delve deeper into its overall meaning. Instead, she just breathed a heavy sigh before offering a few comforting words. "I'm proud of you; that was a brave thing you did back there."

Anna grinned self-consciously. She was thankful Mary Jane didn't admonish her for the chances she had taken. She knew Mary Jane generally respected her hypersensitive instincts, but sometimes Mary Jane could slip unknowingly into her mother's role, momentarily forgetting whom she was dealing with.

Gazing out the window, Anna realized she had talked longer than expected, and the city's lights had faded from view. Their car currently raced down a darkened strip of highway 52, crowded in on either side by vast stretches of farmland. She looked up just in time to glimpse a very large billboard advertising a popular restaurant called Little Oscars. Her stomach rolled at the thought of food, and she realized with the Chinese food tossed out the car door, neither had eaten tonight. A restaurant wouldn't do, but perhaps some chips and a soda at a gas station would help.

"How about a stop for snacks?" Anna said changing the subject, "then I want to hear the story about how you became a Flannigan. You know you've never told me."

Mary Jane sighed. "We do need gas, and I need to make a call, preferably from a pay phone, but I still want to talk more about this stuff. So far you've only told me what happened, and none of your thoughts."

"Nope, you first . . . that's the deal." Anna said, not wanting to talk anymore. Her brain was tired.

Unconsciously checking her speed, Mary Jane used the pause to think of a counter-argument, but eventually decided to give in. "Okay, there's a place coming up here just two miles ahead. I guess we can stop there."

The gas station was deserted, and Anna offered to fill the gas tank while Mary Jane went about the task of making her call. It was only the fourth time Anna had used a gas pump in her life—all in the last month, and Anna reflected on this odd side effect of living most of her life at the will and whim of others.

Finishing up, Mary Jane returned with some snacks, a couple of soft drinks, and a receipt for the gas. Moments later they were back on the road and Anna drank thirstily from her 16-oz. bottle of Cherry Pepsi. The sugary drink tasted great and the bag of chips was starting to settle her stomach. Ever so slowly she began to feel more herself again. Looking over at Mary Jane, she found her noticeably quiet. "Who'd you call?"

"That friend I mentioned earlier."

"Are we welcome?" Anna asked curiously.

Mary Jane's solemn face broke into a happy but fleeting smile, as if her mind had just touched on a fond memory. "Always," she said. "I just wanted to forewarn him of our arrival."

Anna's curiosity was piqued. "Him?"

Catching her implied meaning instantly, Mary Jane cut it short. "It's not like that."

Though wanting to delve deeper, Anna decided to drop it for now. She supposed she would find out about *him* soon enough. Instead, she took another tack, verbally nudging Mary Jane. "Tell me . . ."

"What?" Mary Jane inquired.

"You know. "Anna said, nudging Mary Jane once more. "You promised."

"Oh I suppose I did." Mary Jane didn't like telling stories, particularly when they were about her. She would much rather listen and support. It was the psychologist in her.

"Well you know about Paul of course."

Anna just nodded. She knew Paul had been Mary Jane's husband, long before Anna knew her. She also knew he had been an officer in one of the military services, but she had forgotten which branch. He had died many years ago in the line of duty.

"Yes, go on."

"Flannigan was his mother's maiden name."

"Oh, but how did you . . ." Anna tried to interrupt, but Mary Jane cut her off.

"I'm getting there. Anyway, long before I left Northwoods I vowed I would get you and as many of the other patients out as I could. As you know, we talked about it long before I was dismissed. That's why I gave you our friend's name in Grafton. Of course, you found her, and then she directed you to a go-between here in the Twin Cities who could lead you to me."

Disgusted, Anna sighed. "Obviously, that's how I found you. Tell me something I don't know."

"Be patient, dear," Mary Jane chided. "Anyway. Ever since I realized what Northwoods was really about, I wanted to get out . . . get you out . . . and everyone else that I could. The best way to do that was to expose what they were doing. You might be surprised to know I had been working on gathering evidence to release to the press just before I was dismissed."

"You never told me that," Anna said, mildly surprised.

"That's why I told you to listen." Mary Jane laughed. "Anyway, I was dismissed, but not for the reasons you think. Everyone at Northwoods was told I was let go due to rules violations regarding the patients. To be honest, they would have overlooked those, because they ultimately had all the control. Rather, someone found out what I was up to."

Confused, Anna tried to grasp the concept. "I can't believe they would let you just walk out of Northwoods with all that information. I can't believe they let you . . ." Anna's voice trailed off. She didn't want to say the last word that came to mind. But she didn't have to—Mary Jane finished it for her.

"Live? Well, I guess they knew they had me over a barrel, so to speak."

"How so?"

"Well, before they even told me they were letting me go, they confiscated everything in my office, broke into my house, destroyed all my computer files and dug up every scrap of evidence I had on them and destroyed it all."

"But everything you knew . . . surely you could have gone to . . ."

Mary Jane interrupted before Anna could finish. "To the press? No. The press would need evidence and I was left with nothing."

"Yes, but the police?"

"No." Mary Jane said sadly. "No matter what, no matter how much evidence I did or didn't have," her voice beginning to break, "they had you."

Immediately Anna got the meaning. Northwoods had threatened Mary Jane using her as a pawn.

Mary Jane glanced over at Anna and saw the expression on her face and knew what she was thinking. "Yes, they would have killed you."

"So you left," Anna said with a slight sob.

"Yes, and they watched. For the first few weeks I had a constant and obvious shadow. They wanted me to know they were watching. Then, over time, they watched less, or perhaps they watched more carefully. But their point was made. I was always looking over my shoulder and it drove me crazy."

"So you changed your name?" Anna offered, trying to fill in the pieces in her mind.

"Yes, but not in the traditional sense. After visiting a few dive bars and pretending to drink way too much, I got in touch with a guy who could get me a fake birth certificate. I kept my first name, and chose Paul's mother's name as my last. She was always such a strong woman, and I was proud to have it."

"But how did you manage the switch without Northwoods knowing?"

"The birth certificate was obviously a back-room type of transaction, with people who were careful not to draw attention to themselves. So that part, once I had made the right contacts, was relatively easy. Then I picked a time when I thought they weren't watching and went to the airport. At the last minute, I bought a round trip ticket with Mary Jane Henderson's credit card to Paris, raced to the gate and was the last one to board."

"Amazing." Anna marveled proudly at her "adoptive" mother.

"Quite." Mary Jane shot back, indulging Anna. "So, I stayed only part of a night, holed up in an obscure hotel. There, I cut my hair, dyed it from black to blond, switched from glasses to brown tinted contacts and changed my clothes. I left the hotel that same night by a back door, not bothering to check out. My seven-night stay was already prepaid by credit card. I caught a cab to Charles De Gaulle airport and purchased a one-way ticket back to the Twin Cities with cash and the new passport I had obtained from my friends at the bar."

"You went to all that trouble. So how do you think they found me . . . or us, I guess?"

"I'm not sure. I have all new credit cards, a new license . . . everything. Basically, I'm a completely different person. I do still have a cash card in my old name. I used it occasionally to slowly draw out my life's savings. Although each time I used it I would drive four hours in a different direction, stop at a cash machine and perform the transaction. I was that paranoid. If somehow Northwoods managed to obtained those ATM records, they wouldn't point them anywhere near me."

Anna was perplexed, but she felt Mary Jane was holding something back. "Anything else?"

Mary Jane's eyes remained fixed on the road ahead, contemplating her lone mistake. "There's one other possibility, but I always assumed it was so remote, nobody would discover it."

"What was it?" Anna asked gently, the tone of her voice implying whatever it was, she would never blame Mary Jane for any mistake she might have made.

"I was in a restaurant. Mary Jane said almost sadly. "It was an old favorite of mine, The Uptown Café. I went there, missing my old life, and my old haunts, and never thought it would be a problem. I mean, I looked so different, and the place is dark and always packed. Who'd see me? I thought."

That day I had just given the waitress one of my new credit cards. But while she was processing it, an old colleague of mine, Abby, spotted me. We had gone there together before, so I guess it wasn't that odd to see her. She came over to talk, I was flustered, and wanted to get away. I did my best to excuse myself and eventually did."

"I can't see how that would be a problem." Anna offered sympathetically.

"But it was." Mary Jane replied. "You see, I had forgotten my credit card with the waitress, and just as I was turning to leave the waitress called out my name . . . my new name. Well, Abby . . . when she heard my last name was Flannigan, of course pressed me mercilessly for details . . . asking if I had remarried. I didn't know what to do, so I said yes, and basically ran."

"What a fluke." Anna said, shaking her head, unsure of what to say.

"Yes, it certainly was. Still, if someone discovered my mistake, they were very thorough." Mary Jane said, now suddenly pausing, as if something clicked in her mind. "You know I've been thinking. You said the first man that arrived at the townhouse had no clue your parents were deceased, correct?"

"True."

Still formulating the idea, Mary Jane went on. "I'd say that means he can't be directly connected to Northwoods."

"Yes, but what does that mean?" Anna asked, now suddenly feeling very exhausted.

"It means there is someone else who knows about you, and wants to find you. The question is, is he friend or foe? Do you have any more thoughts on him?" Mary Jane inquired.

Sly Anna thought, weighing the question, realizing Mary Jane had just managed to switch the conversation back to her. Yet as their car crested a hill, slowly revealing the tiny twinkling lights of a city spread out in the near distance, Anna prepared to lie, betraying the strange feelings she was beginning to develop about the stranger who first came to the door. She simply said, "No, I guess I'll have to sleep on it."

"Good thought." Mary Jane said, letting it go for the time being. "We should be safe here . . . we've just made it to Rochester."

CHAPTER 19

GOING HOME

After a couple beers to help gather himself at the Medina Ballroom, one of his favorite west-side establishments, Grady eventually set out for home. Searching his rearview mirror, through sheets of rain that had begun to fall, Grady looked for some sign of a tail. Nothing seemed out of the ordinary. Suddenly he was beginning to regret his decision to flee the scene of a crime.

As he drove, Anna's face filtered through his mind. He couldn't figure out what was going on. He had so many unanswered questions about her, Mary Jane, Northwoods, and now the man who had tried to kill them. He was being set up, but why? He was almost certain the man who had come to his home only a month ago was not Anna's father. It all went back to Anna's face, didn't it? The face of a woman in her early twenties, rather than the seventeen Mr. Jenkins had described. How could a father make that mistake . . . or better yet, why would he lie? It was for this reason Grady had the sinking feeling Anna's father, or whoever he really was, had intended to set Grady up for the deaths of Mary Jane and Anna. And he had strong suspicions the man in the mask tonight was none other than Mr. Jenkins.

His mind reeling, he decided he was too tired to rehash it all—he desperately needed sleep. But first he had to get home and check the place out. Someone had broken in and taken his gun and gloves. *Was anything else missing?* He was doing it again. He couldn't put any answers together right now, so he tried to force it all out of his mind.

For a few minutes it worked, as he let himself be lulled by the rhythmic plink of a cold September rain off his windshield. Even then, Grady's sleep-deprived mind wouldn't give it a rest. Strangely, is was a bright yellow cab that flew by him in the passing lane, that allowed his mind to finally let go, only to dredge up painful memories of the night that turned his life upside down.

The pair left the bar together shortly after midnight that New Year's Eve. Nancy was squeezing his arm so tight that Grady thought he might lose circulation in it. Both a bit tipsy, they had called a cab and waited for it patiently outside in the cold as the snow drifted down around them. Their cab came extremely quickly for New Year's Eve—although in retrospect, Grady wondered if it had been theirs, or one some other poor patron had called.

After a short discussion about your house or mine, Grady gave the driver his address and they endured the next ten minutes in an anxious, awkward sort of silence. Once at his home, Grady tipped the driver generously before leading Nancy up the walk and inside. There, they hastily shed their coats and shoes before falling eagerly into each other's arms. Their lips met passionately with the kiss they wished they could have had at O'Gara's, but had felt too ashamed. It was long and slow, tongues gently probing willing lips and hands exploring bodies that were once so familiar to them. Grady couldn't help feeling as if they had never existed apart.

The next few minutes were spent awkwardly grasping at buckles, straps and buttons as they freed each other from their garments. A purse tossed here, a sock over there, and underwear shimmied out of and discarded on the floor. That night, they made love twice, once right there on the couch and again in Grady's bed before falling asleep, exhausted and fulfilled, in each other's arms.

It was a wonderful evening punctuated by Grady's own dreams of Nancy, back when they were so young, imagining they had never lost touch, and had lived every night like this one. His tough, impenetrable exterior, hardened by

years with the FBI, fell away to reveal the vulnerable man he really was . . .
one who wanted to find love.

The next morning Grady awoke all alone, the indentation of Nancy's
head still pressed into the pillow beside him. He breathed deeply and savored
her perfume that hung like a sweet melody in the air. Still in his boxers,
Grady got up expecting to find Nancy in the shower, and perhaps rekindle
the passion they had shared last night. But the shower was not on, and
Nancy was not there. He wrapped himself in a robe and went downstairs
hoping to find her raiding his fridge, but just as suddenly as she had slipped
back into his life she had gone.

Grady took his mind off cruise control just in time to catch his
Cretin/Vandalia exit. Still in a fog he drove south on Cretin, with the
University of St. Thomas campus spreading out to his left. He then took
a right onto Riverwood Place, west toward the Mississippi river. After a
few more mindless turns, he found himself on Montrose, driving half a
block down before parallel parking the car in front of his house.

He stepped softly out into the darkened rain-slicked street, the
showers appearing to have paused if only for a moment. His Explorer
was parked just a few feet from a dim pool of light cast by a nearby
lamppost—the glowing oversized lantern tucked under one of the
massive oaks that lined the way. Grady took one last look around, yet
there was still no sign of a tail, or the police.

Tired and discouraged he made his way to his front door. Before
opening it, he did a quick check of the lock and the surrounding
doorframe. All seemed to be intact. If someone had entered through his
front door they were very skilled, for there were no overt signs of forced
entry.

Using his key he unlocked the deadbolt and stepped warily inside.

CHAPTER 20

BEN

A light rain began to fall as Mary Jane and Anna pulled up to an elegant Tudor home nestled high on a wooded hill, occupying a ten-acre lot just to the west of Rochester. Their drive into town had taken them past a huge, brilliantly lit convent perched upon a hill to the east, and Anna marveled at its sprawling beauty. Then, just past the convent, once again to the east, Anna caught a brief glimpse of the downtown skyline dominated by the imposing presence of the Mayo Clinic. She had heard about the renowned medical facility but had never seen it. She wondered about its vast research resources and what they could glean about her unique abilities.

Outside the stately home the front lights were on, and Anna guessed they were in anticipation of their arrival. No sooner had the pair hopped out of the car than a gentle old man with a shock of white hair and a cane stepped out on the stoop to greet them. Racing raindrops, Anna and Mary Jane sped up the walkway to the front door of 9511 Forest Hills Road. There they huddled near the gentleman awaiting introductions.

"Ben, I'd like you to meet Anna." Mary Jane said first.

The man who looked to be in his seventies, stood about 5 foot 9 inches tall and carried himself with a slight—but noticeable—stoop. Ben gave Anna a warm smile and took her hand in his, giving it a gentle squeeze. "I've heard so much about you, Miss Anna. If Mary Jane's stories are half-true, you are a remarkable young woman." A flash of lightning lit up the night sky just as Ben finished his sentence and he gave a wary glance to the heavens. "We should get in before it really comes down," he offered politely, his words punctuated by the low, distant rumble of thunder.

Once inside, Ben saw them to his study and let them sink into a pair of tall leather wing chairs before he spoke again. "May I get you something—soda, or perhaps some coffee?"

"Would you by chance have a beer?" Anna asked politely.

Ben gave Mary Jane a sideways glance, which Mary Jane assumed to be a silent question to which she answered. "Yes, she's of age . . . actually into her mid-twenties, but don't press it any more, for age is truly a woman's secret."

"My, my," Ben mumbled somewhat to himself. "And you Mary Jane, what can I find for you?"

"I'll have the same, if you don't mind."

Without another word Ben ambled off to another part of the house to retrieve the drinks. In the meantime, Mary Jane filled Anna in on the story of Dr. Benjamin F. Olson. She explained that for years Ben had been her mentor. She had first met him at a seminar in her early years at the University of Minnesota. He had come from the Mayo Clinic to speak to those in attendance about the powers of the mind, its benefits in healing and the theoretical emergence of a sixth sense as part of the natural evolution of human beings.

After the seminar, Mary Jane had approached Dr. Benjamin with a question about one of his theories and proposed an extrapolation of it. Mary Jane recalled with mild humor his response to her question and suggestion. *"My dear, that discussion could last for hours,"* he'd exclaimed with a smile.

At the moment, Mary Jane thought he was simply brushing her off, but instead he suggested they get a cup of coffee together and dive into the subject more thoroughly. Ben was enthralled with Mary Jane's own insights and Mary Jane loved picking the brain of a premiere authority on brain chemistry as it applies to cognitive thinking. Instantly a friendship and fellowship was formed, and Mary Jane had called upon Ben many times over the years to toss a question or idea his way. She finished her story just as Ben arrived with the drinks, ending with a warning offered in the softest of whispers, "I've never told Ben about your full abilities, and nothing about Northwoods and its issues."

Upon his arrival, Ben caught the tail end of the whisper and playfully offered his own two cents. "Keeping secrets, are we?"

Anna smiled lightly at Ben's jibe, yet at the same time she was processing Mary Jane's words. She realized Mary Jane was not about to bring Ben into the middle of her troubles. Anna reflected that it must have taken an awful lot for Mary Jane just to come here tonight and impose on a friend.

Mary Jane and Anna enjoyed their beer, and Ben joined them with a brandy Manhattan of his own, as the lightning and thunder continued to play in chorus outside the huge picture window, which lent a dramatic view of the water-soaked street and the gathering storm out front. After a bit of light conversation and a brief interlude into some medical dialog that was way over Anna's head, the three said their goodnights and headed upstairs.

"I hope the accommodations are acceptable," Ben said genuinely as they crested the long flight. "Anna, you may sleep in my daughter's old room—you can just follow me. She is 33 now, and uses it only when she comes to visit. Mary Jane, the guest room is all set up. It has been a while, but I presume you still know where it is."

"Yes, thank you so much." Mary Jane responded with utmost sincerity, then she turned down the hallway and headed in the opposite direction.

Anna followed Ben's slow gait toward her accommodations for the evening. As they came to Ben's daughter's room, Anna heard the door to Mary Jane's room shut with a quiet click. Pausing, almost as if waiting for the sound of the closing door, Ben turned abruptly toward Anna, catching her momentarily off guard. "She's quite a woman, isn't she?"

"Yes, she is." Anna replied with admiration.

"Never could lie to me though." Ben chuckled to himself.

Anna just looked at the man, a bit bewildered.

"You're in some sort of trouble, aren't you?" he went on.

Unwilling to give up their secret without Mary Jane's approval, Anna simply said nothing.

"Ah, that's okay. You are respecting Mary Jane's wishes. But we'll talk more about it tomorrow. She thinks I'm too old but my instincts are as ripe as if I were 23 years and 2 months." He said plucking Anna's exact age from the air. "The age fits, doesn't it?"

Anna looked into the man's hard gray eyes and saw a light twinkle in them as he gave her a knowing look. Anna stood there dumbfounded, wondering how this kind old man who had just met her had somehow plucked her exact age out of the air. And this thought so consumed her she didn't even notice Ben had left her side and already begun his journey down the hall to his room.

As he reached his own doorway, without turning to face her, Ben called out in an odd tone. "Sweet dreams, my dear."

Anna just stood in her doorway utterly perplexed, her mind chewing on his last words. She knew Mary Jane hadn't told Ben her age or the full extent of her abilities. But his knowing look and twinkling eyes told her he knew so much more.

The thought pulled at a thread of an idea that was forming in her mind. Was it possible Ben was like her? Anna knew she and the other seeds were not the only ones in the world who possessed unique abilities, and she knew others of lesser ability had come before them—well before them—living in the real world playing their own secretive part in history. It had even been rumored that Hitler had tried to surround himself with such visionaries.

Resigned to the fact she wasn't going to solve the mystery tonight, Anna went to bed pondering the possibility. Was Ben what Northwoods termed a "natural" too?

CHAPTER 21

PICKING UP THE PIECES

Entering his home Grady reached for his Sig Sauer P229 Equinox, tucked in the back of his pants, and instinctively switched off the safety. For the moment, he was happy to have it back, though he'd never known it was gone until tonight. Since his days with the Bureau he rarely carried, although he possessed a license to do so.

Now just inside his foyer, his eyes swept from right to left across the living room, taking the room in segments, the muzzle of his gun always following his gaze in precise unison. Thankfully the room was clean. From off in the kitchen his phone rang suddenly, causing Grady's tightly wound nerves to tense involuntarily, but he made no move to answer it. Instead he let it ring, sweeping room after room in his house, checking all possible hiding spots before he finally allowed himself to relax.

The house was empty, as he had expected. The person who had broken into his house to take his gun and steal his gloves certainly couldn't still be there. But his nerves were still frayed. For now, a cursory check indicated nothing was missing. His files seemed neat and in order, and his computer sat as it always did, occupying the far left corner of his desk. The phone rang again, now actually the third time since he had started his sweep. Someone really wanted to get a hold of him. Sliding over to his desk he picked up the receiver and said hello.

"Where the hell have you been?" the caller said immediately into Grady's ear. "I've been trying to reach you all night."

73

Grady instantly recognized Tom Hanson's voice and realized he had forgotten all about him. On occasion, Grady would use his good friend Tom as his backup on stakeouts. He was an old acquaintance, and sometimes he liked to see a little action for a nominal fee. Tonight, Grady had stationed Tom out in the park across from the townhouse complex and told him to put a tail on Mary Jane's Gallant, should she leave and Grady couldn't follow.

"I'm sorry, I'd been detained." Grady said apologetically as he heard the soft pant of Tom's golden retriever Molly, breathing heavily somewhere near the receiver. "Where are you guys?" he continued, including Molly in his question.

"I have to tell you Grady, you owe me on this one."

"Why?" Grady replied, his curiosity now piqued.

"I got your Gallant." Tom said triumphantly. "Thought you might like that. And it picked up a passenger on the way."

"You're not serious!"

"Yes, I am. And it's way the hell down in Rochester," Tom added, trying to sound perturbed.

"Damn, I do owe you. If you only knew what I've been through on this one."

"Yeah, well, I followed your lady off to pick up some Chinese," Tom began, "and then the video store, and finally back to the townhouse. You know, just like you asked me to. Anyway. When we got back, I figured she was in for the night, so I tried you on your cell phone to see if we should split, but you must have had it off. So Molly and me, we just waited in the park where we always did."

"And?" Grady asked anxiously.

"Well, Molly had to go, so I took her out of the car and let her do her business. Meanwhile, Molly's all finished, and we're heading back to the car, and here comes your Gallant again, tires blazing a trail out of the complex. So, not being able to raise you, I figured we should follow. Hadn't seen the other girl at this point, you know. I have to tell you, I almost turned around when I saw the cops storming back your way.

"My God," was all Grady could manage.

"Yeah, it gets better. So the Gallant makes a stop halfway to Rochester. And to my surprise two people get out. The older lady makes a call and this new one, a younger girl, starts pumping gas. Couldn't exactly tell . . . it was dark, of course. Then the next thing I know we're just outside of Rochester and they pull up to this house parked on one huge friggin' lot. It's so big I can't even see any neighbors."

"Do you think they ever spotted you?" Grady asked.

"No, don't think so," Tom went on. "I passed by as they pulled up to the house and drove down a ways. There are three or four more homes down the road before it dead-ends, so I drove back and pulled the car up close enough so I could see the Gallant still sitting there. I waited a few minutes . . . then rolled back. Right now I'm staked out toward the start of the road, just within view of the driveway entrance, but there are so many damn trees between the house and me, there's no way they'd know I'm here. With the dead end and all, no way anyone's leaving without us knowing, too. So hey, you still want me and Molly to hang?"

"If you can, that would be great," Grady said with a hint of apology in his voice. "I have a couple of things to attend to here, and I will be down to relieve you tonight. That okay with you?"

"Not a problem, bud." Tom said, following up with a few more details and directions to the house, before adding. "Hey Grady, you might want to check your cell, I tried raising you on it several times tonight, but it went right to voice mail. Keep it on in case I need to update you."

"Sure thing, Tom," Grady said, ending the call with a sincere, "Thanks."

Both men hung up and Grady grabbed his phone from his pocket. Sure enough, it was off. Grady guessed he must have turned it off before he went into the townhouse. He activated his phone and booted up his computer at the same time, listening to three of Tom's messages as the 27-inch iMac began to whir to life. There was something he wanted to check before he made his trip to Rochester—it was a hunch he had.

It took five minutes to set up the program. It was a device a programmer friend of his had devised that logged every keystroke anyone made on the computer. As a list of keystrokes came up, Grady instantly recognized there were many that definitely occurred in a block of time he wasn't home. He highlighted a string and moved his cursor over to a key on the screen marked PLAY. Instantly the computer took over and began to repeat every step in triple time that someone else had performed.

Grady watched mesmerized as the computer screen ran through each executed keystroke, following the trail of some unknown assailant on his computer's files. Then, near the end of the string of commands, the computer glitched momentarily, just before it produced a text box on the screen. The message read UNABLE TO PERFORM COMMAND, FILE ENTITLED "CASE 01248; ANNA JENKINS" DELETED. DO YOU WISH TO CONTINUE? YES/NO?

Grady glared at the screen. His hunch had been confirmed. Violently he punched the power button on his keyboard, ignoring the screen prompt asking ARE YOU SURE YOU WANT TO SHUT DOWN YOUR COMPUTER. Someone was playing with his life and he didn't like it. Just then, at 1:17 in the morning, the doorbell rang.

CHAPTER 22

NORTHWOODS

D r. Allan Hauser paced anxiously across his newly acquired hand-loomed Persian rug—its tight intricate weave concealing a small section of the room's high-polish hardwood floors. The lavishly decorated office occupied a full third of the top floor at Northwoods and the floor-to-ceiling windows offered Allan an exquisite view of the beautiful grounds, a crystalline lake and the hillsides surrounding it.

Yet tonight, only occasionally would he pause to peer pensively through the impeccably clear panes that he required be washed weekly, inside and out. At this very moment, as he gazed through the spotless glass, his eyes fell first upon the brightly illuminated pathways snaking through the well-manicured lawn below. Then, almost as a reflex, his eyes shifted up past the shadowy branches outside his windows, their leafy forms perfectly framing his line of sight. Of course, at 1:00 a.m. the lake, the distant trees and the encroaching hills were merely a dense void of irregular black shapes, but his mind's eye automatically filled in what he knew to be there.

Tonight of all nights he was particularly troubled. Mitch, his director of security and one of his more valuable assets, had just reported in. His communiqué had not arrived directly, which could leave a troublesome trail. But suffice it to say the not-so-sketchy details of the evening as it had unfolded in the Twin Cities had filtered their way back to him.

"What a mess," he exclaimed to the empty leather wingchairs in his office. What was supposed to be a neat and tidy bundle of three deaths, pinned on Mr. Hamilton, had turned into an utter fiasco. Not only had Anna escaped, most likely along with Mary Jane, but also the haphazard attempt by Mitch to pin the shreds of their unraveling plan onto Grady had suddenly dissolved. Now, the one man Mitch had sold to Allan as the ideal solution to one of the four escaped Seeds could now become the lose cannon in this ugly scenario.

Mulling over the details, Allan was convinced Grady was now well aware of a plot to frame him. It certainly gave explanation as to why he chose to run once the authorities showed. Otherwise, why wouldn't he have stayed put and related all that had happened to the police? No, Mr. Hamilton knew he was being implicated in the events, and that alone would force Grady to pursue the matter further in an attempt to clear his name. This was something Allan definitely could not afford—especially not at a moment in the project when things were going so well.

The experiments down on sub-level 3 were currently ahead of schedule. The project had recently moved into a new phase, marking a new era in which the four original Seeds, or natural borns, were becoming increasingly obsolete. Their escape had been unexpected. But it provided an opportunity to quietly eliminate each before they could do damage. Allan's top man, Mitch, assured him that he would keep it clean and discreet, attributing their deaths to suicides, acts of God and other such events, where the shadow of implication could never fall on Northwoods.

It was why The Kid was so valuable right now. He had apparently handled the particularly complicated issue of Curt in San Francisco without incident—already neutralizing one Seed. Perhaps he might be useful in tonight's aftermath, trying to track down Anna and Mary Jane, but Allan wasn't certain he was ready to go down that road. The Kid had a soft spot for Anna, and if he were involved he would almost certainly insist that steps be taken to try to spare her life.

Then of course if he opted to use The Kid, there was the question of what to do with Mitch—the two didn't get along very well. Mitch actually considered The Kid to be a horrific freak of nature, and would most likely try to work against him. There were others to consider, including the loose thread Mr. Hamilton posed. Perhaps Mitch could be assigned to handle that little project. For now, an anonymous call to the Minneapolis police department had tipped them off to a suspicious SUV parked in the townhouse lot tonight. Allan hoped for the moment that a little police involvement might slow Grady down. He was sure more would have to be done in that regard, but it was a start.

For the time being Allan decided to table all assignments. Right now, The Kid had been re-routed to Northwoods after landing in the Twin Cities; in fact he was due to arrive at any moment. As for Mitch, he had been ordered to temporarily stand down until tonight's dust settled. Perhaps things would be clearer in the light of day.

Just as Allan was about to retire for the evening, one of the lines on his phone began to flash. Immediately the voice of his secretary came over the intercom. "Dr. Hauser, you have an incoming call. I've taken the liberty of routing it to line three." For a moment, Allan just stared at the phone, watching as the line winked five times and then flashed off. As long as he worked his secretary Lara worked, and she was extremely efficient, and paid well for these inconveniences, as well as her loyalties. What he liked most about her was that she possessed impeccable instincts. Her routing of a call to line three was a signal that meant a sensitive call was inbound. Ignoring his desk phone for the moment, he produced a jail-broken iPhone from his suit's inside breast pocket and waited for Lara to work out the connection.

Ten seconds later the call came through and he touched the on-screen icon to retrieve the call.

"Dr. Hauser," he answered in a serious tone.

A voice on the other end introduced himself, and Allan's face registered an expression of mild surprise. The caller continued speaking, not giving Allan any chance to offer back a greeting. For the longest time Allan just listened with piqued interest, nodding his head appreciatively. "I see, and I'm very grateful for the information. I will have someone pick up the package tomorrow. Say about 9 a.m.?"

The caller spoke a few more words, and Allan responded in kind. "Good, good, I will see to it. Goodnight to you, too."

Allan turned off the phone but didn't return it to his pocket. Again he found himself staring out of his windows, but in a much better mood. In fact, he was quite delighted with the caller's news. Using the same phone, he made two quick calls of his own before finally depositing it back in his breast pocket with a tired, but satisfied, sigh. Perhaps tomorrow would be a better day after all.

CHAPTER 23

SEEING IS BELIEVING

Anna's dream started like all of her others—a mix of unrelated thoughts spilling from her unconsciousness and clouding her sleep until they began to pull together, like threads of a spider web linking together in vast complexities. From an outsider's view her dreams could be described as a magnificent ballet of visions, spun into unison by a powerful mind. Yet to Anna, they were a nightmare, a blurring of the past, future, and present into a unified reality she wished she had never been a part of.

Then in an instant, through a rippling of waves rendered in disorganized multi-faceted colors, a single image slowly began to resolve in her mind. The vision started deep within a gray-walled room, dark and cold, with tiled floors spattered in thick viscous droplets of blood. She stood there, so real in her mind, her tennis shoes staining with tiny specks of crimson as she slowly strode down the length of the long, narrow room. At the far end as she approached, Anna could make out the shimmer of polished steel. Boxes, each lined one on top of the other and rammed flush into the far wall.

She reached out, her long delicate fingers brushing their frigid surfaces. The touch to her, like fingernails on a chalkboard, sent chills racing a ticklish trail down her spine. Then in a blur a shiny handle, like that found on an old car door, materialized from nowhere. Before she knew what she was doing, her hand had clasped the lever releasing the mechanism that opened the long metal drawer with a loud click-clank. As if on its own, the drawer began to slide out toward her, carried on well-oiled rollers that moved without even a whisper's touch.

Another loud click, and the drawer became fully extended, locking solidly into place. Yet she couldn't see its contents. Her eyes were still shielded by the front of the massive drawer—protruding as if pulled from an oversized filing cabinet. Some deep part of her tried to prevent her next move, but her mind willed her body on—sidling around to the side to view what she knew was contained within.

There, a white sheet lay, draped lightly across an eerily silent figure. Looking up to the far end she could just make out the familiar lines of a shrouded face. Those curves and indentations, giving way to a broad, well-built torso as it slipped softly into the vague outlines of two legs cloaked beneath. Closest to Anna were the feet and she suddenly realized one was exposed. The white drape had been pulled back just enough to reveal an oddly twisted bare ankle and a set of five blue toes. Around one of the toes, Anna noticed a slim band of white elastic cord, gently constricting the pale digit, with a manila-hued tag attached. Reaching out she turned the slip of paper over revealing the name she knew so well. Written in ink as red as blood were the letters that spelled only his first name: Curt. The space for the last name had been left blank, and Anna wrestled with its meaning.

Then in a flash, her vision momentarily whited out, returning with Trent and Joe, standing beside her. Here were the second and third seeds, each somber and stone-faced, as they gazed sadly at their fallen friend. Anna now knew why she had been brought here—in an instant it became clear. She, the first seed, was here for them—so they could know—so they could see. Trent and Joe needed to see with their own eyes the horror of their common past, their separate present and their own horrifying futures—unless they took action—unless they all pulled together. Today, they were here to pay tribute to the fallen fourth seed.

From her vision Anna could distinctly see both young men and each appeared to be well. Yet she sensed something else. It was something dark and evil just beyond their somber faces, a foreboding of horrible things to come. Grasping deep into her subconscious, she desperately tried to see where they were, but no landmarks stood out—no points of reference were there to grab hold of. For now, she knew that at least temporarily they were safe.

Then, suddenly the cadaver drawer slammed in, rocketing with a speed and force so furious it splintered the shiny silver wall that held it, collapsing Anna's vision with it. The fragments fell in a slow tumble like mirrored glass exploding before her eyes—each tiny shard, hanging and falling inexplicably at once in a shimmering cascade that drizzled down to a pristine white tile floor.

Expecting to wake up, instead Anna found herself crouched on hands and knees as a foot violently kicked up from out of nowhere, grazing her cheek. She fell back now, laying face up, staring at an unblemished white ceiling raised over white padded walls.

Gently she touched her face where the foot had landed, tracing her fingers over what she guessed was a split lip. Putting her hand in front of her face, her fingers returned sticky with new blood. Anna winced as the salty-tasting liquid seeped slowly into her mouth as the cut bled out.

Hearing a door close, Anna gathered herself and sat up, gazing at the walls of pure white. She knew full well where she was. She stood and instantly her view revolved, though her feet never moved an inch. She was now facing that awful door, the one padded in tufted quilts of fabric-covered foam with that little window, crisscrossed with wire, where evil people watched and sometimes laughed at her agony. But Anna knew where the real observations took place, beyond the mirrored expanse that nearly took up the length of one wall.

Anna was in The Room. It was a place where Northwoods locked the naturals up, sometimes for experiments . . . sometimes for solitary confinement. And Anna couldn't stand the thought, or imagine the possibilities that this vision meant. Still she was helpless, and for now she simply waited until this horrid dream ran its course.

What could have been hours passed in mere seconds, as the door opened again and two faceless orderlies entered The Room. Grabbing her roughly, the pair forced her into a white chair that seemed to have just appeared in the very center of the space. They strapped Anna in against her struggling protests and went about the task of setting up an I.V. In that moment, Anna's eyes gazed sadly up at the clear bag now dripping drugs in a steady trickle into her veins.

Desperately she tried to fight off the narcotics but they consumed her—enveloped her completely—and ever so slowly relaxed her muscles as her senses began to heighten. The scent of something like almonds and horrible body odor stung her nose, her fingertips felt as if they were on fire, and the light within the room scorched her eyes. The door opened once more, and in wheeled a familiar man, securely strapped to the metal frame of a medical gurney. Tilting her own seat up, the orderlies sat them face-to-face and Anna instantly recognized the other prisoner as Grady.

Somewhere in her sleeping mind, Anna searched for how she had come by his name. He had never told her his real name, but in an instant as their eyes linked she knew she was right—and now strangely she knew so much more about him. She knew he was kind and good and never a willing part of this . . . and she could sense he cared deeply for her.

His mouth had been gagged and his body severely beaten but his eyes were still strong. *It was what she would come to love about him, wasn't it?* Now face to face, just a few feet separating their bound bodies, a voice cloaked in medical whites spoke at Anna in fluent French. She recognized the words instantly—after all, she had mastered ten languages and was learning several others. It was part of her talents, just one of the many Northwoods found fascinating.

The voice was asking her—no, commanding her—to tell them all Grady knew—to divulge the secrets they had shared and those Grady might have told. Afraid the drugs could make her do as they wished, Anna shut her eyes to Grady's soul, refusing him with all her might. She knew this man was dead once they had what they wanted.

The instant her eyes closed her mind wrapped around a hand—the hand of one of her restrainers—and it rose up intending a vicious blow. Anna tensed, waiting for the impact; she could sense the hand accelerating downward a fraction of a second before the heavy blow landed. Yet, to her amazement, there was no pain, just a sudden and intense quiet.

Far off in the distance, Anna heard a bird singing a sweet song mingling with the rustle of wind through the trees, and the distant lapping of water on a sandy beach. She was afraid to open her eyes, but gradually she did, bringing into focus a beautiful landscape of manicured grasses, towering oak, hickory nut and pine trees and a serene lake. Her white chair had been traded in for an Adirondack crafted of natural teak. While most would find the view calming, she again knew it all too well. She had sat there many a time, crying softly as she was now, longing for freedom she felt would never come.

From behind, a hand touched her on the shoulder and she looked back to see who it was, but the person was a faceless blur—yet she knew what this vision represented. For good or ill, this person was her future.

CHAPTER 24

DISTURBING MELODY

The door opened and a thin shaft of ethereal light split the darkened office of Dr. Allan Hauser. The man himself strode silently from his immense attached bathroom, complete with Jacuzzi, sauna, and lounge. It was late, and it had been more than a long day, but it was finally over, and tomorrow might bring better news, and perhaps even closure with the girl Anna.

Closing the bathroom door the office quickly receded into almost complete darkness. The lights from the grounds, seeping through the office windows, gave just enough form to the furnishings to maneuver around. Striding by his desk he reached into a leather catchall where he kept the keys to his Jaguar, but his fingers grasped air.

Mid-stride, he stopped abruptly and turned around, wondering where he might have misplaced them. But a jangling sound behind him caused him to abandon the search.

"Looking for these?" a voice nearer the windows said softly. Startled, the doctor whirled to face the intruder. For a moment, his nerves shaken, he thought about the gun he kept in his desk.

"Didn't frighten you, did I?" the voice asked.

"What the hell are you doing here at an hour like this?" Allan snapped at the silhouetted form slung low in one of his wingback leather chairs.

"Couldn't sleep, so I thought I would pay you a visit. Figured you'd be working."

"You should be home. Your home, back in the Twin Cities," he clarified.

"Why? What's there for me? Everything is here, isn't it? This place is what it's all about. You of all people should know that."

Allan sighed. "There's nothing for you here. In fact, it's dangerous."

"Why? They're all gone—except for maybe one. Aren't they?"

"Still. It's not safe."

"For God's sake. I've been in and around this hellhole practically my entire life. What's the harm?"

"You know I've never liked you being here. I've always tried to protect you."

"More like keep things from me. Everything I know is from what I've dug up."

"Why are you here?"

"Somebody has to look out for you. And I think you are about to make a mistake. A very big mistake."

"What do you know?" Allan asked perturbed.

"More than you want me to. You know you can't keep things from me."

"Must we always play these games? Just talk to me."

"Seems to me your life has been about playing games with other people's lives. From my standpoint, how do you think that makes me feel?"

"We've been over this before. What more can I tell you?"

"The truth."

Allan shifted his weight uneasily, considering the request before giving his final answer. "It's late. Too late."

"I figured as much." Slowly the figure rose and approached the doctor.

"Here, I took this from your desk. Didn't want you shooting me by accident."

Allan took the gun from the slender hand that held it and simply stared at it in disbelief. "What would your mother have said?" He spoke after an unnaturally long pause.

"I don't know, I only knew her for a few years. And you, after all, were married to her . . . so you tell me, smartass." And with that, the petite figure turned and strode from the room.

Dr. Hauser watched his 23-year-old daughter walk away from him. For a moment, he felt like a terrible father and widower. What would his wife have thought? He wanted to believe she would have come over to his side . . . understood all the good coming from the research he was doing. Surely she would have been able to see her way to his side.

But as he watched his daughter slowly close the door behind her, he couldn't help but remark how similar she was in appearance and personality to her mother. And as such, he had his serious doubts.

CHAPTER 25

TIPPED OFF

The police entered Grady's home at precisely 1:18 a.m. They did not arrive by force; instead, Grady allowed them in. Wary of raising any more suspicions he had chosen, at least for the time being, to cooperate.

"Mr. Hamilton?" the taller cop asked a question with a statement.

"Yes, that's me."

"Sorry to bother you at such a late hour," the shorter cop conceded, "but there was an incident involving a shooting up in Maple Grove tonight." The cop paused, waiting for Grady's reaction.

"I see" Grady replied, trying to feign the appropriate amount of surprise and confusion until he discovered where the men were leading with their questioning. "But I guess I don't understand how this concerns me?"

"Well, sir," the shorter cop began, "we received an anonymous tip that your vehicle may have been parked in the lot near the residence and was seen leaving shortly after the shooting."

Pausing as if to consider the statement, Grady watched as the taller cop removed his hat and, completely uninvited, began to slowly walk around his living room, casually looking here and there as if he was about to buy the place. Turning back to the shorter officer, Grady decided it best not to overtly deny that his Explorer could have been there, so he followed up with a question of his own. "You said an anonymous tip?"

"Ah, yes sir, we haven't been able to track down the person who phoned it in."

"And so how much faith would you put in a caller who can't even come forward?" Grady prodded.

"Sir, that's not of your concern. Although it *is* of our concern as to whether you were in Maple Grove this evening, somewhere in the vicinity of the Bass Lake townhomes. It's a simple question. Can you answer it?"

Before speaking, Grady glanced back at the taller man. He had just finished poking around some bookshelves and was now nudging magazines about on the surface of his coffee table. Returning again to the other officer Grady replied, "It is of my concern, if people are going to go around wrongly implicating me by placing me at crime scenes I had no part in."

The short cop sighed. "Sir, does that mean you deny being in Maple Grove this evening and deny being anywhere near the Bass Lake townhomes?"

Grady felt his anger rise and he made no attempt to conceal it. "It means what it means. I'm upset you disturbed me at one-thirty in the morning to tell me that someone, whom you cannot even identify, can't even read a damn license plate number. You are wasting my time with this nonsense."

Grady's terse response finally roused the interest of the taller cop and he immediately stopped nosing about Grady's magazines and turned toward the conversation. "Mr. Hamilton, do you own a gun?" he asked pointedly.

"Yes."

"May we see it?" the tall cop inquired.

Grady knew he was in trouble. The only thing he could do was to try to buy some time. Considering his answer carefully, his only viable response now seemed to be one that almost certainly indicated he had something to hide. "Do you gentlemen have a warrant?"

The taller officer sighed, "Our records indicate you own a Sig Sauer P229."

"That's correct." Grady confirmed, anxiety taking the place of his anger. "Now, is there something else you wish to tell me?"

"Not at the moment sir," the officer stated as he returned to the front door. "We have yet to recover any slugs from the crime scene. Please understand we are simply trying to follow up on all leads. As you might know from your days as a federal agent . . ." the man paused momentarily for effect, but failing to get a response from Grady he continued. "An anonymous call gets you nowhere in courts. But when we find the slug, if it should match up to a Sig Sauer P229, you can be damn sure we will be back—with that warrant."

The warning well-taken, Grady was relieved. They weren't about to arrest him, and they had no warrant to search his house. It was a sliver of opportunity and he was going to take it and run the distance with it. "I understand, gentlemen," Grady offered more politely, trying to save face. "My apologies if I was rude, but considering the time of night . . ."

"We might understand," the tall cop said flatly, cutting Grady off in mid-sentence. "But under the circumstances let me tell you how I see things. You are still fully dressed, so we obviously didn't wake you this evening. You have a cut on your right hand and a slightly blackened eye that tells me you were probably in a fight tonight. Add all that up, along with your evasive answers, refusal to produce your weapon and just being an overall smart-ass, I have a pretty good feeling we'll be back tonight. I suggest you get as much sleep as you can."

"Good night, gentlemen." Grady replied, in a tone indicating the conversation was over. For the moment, both men turned to exit and Grady quickly closed the door behind them. From a small window he watched them as they crossed the street and climbed into their black and white. They stayed there for the next five minutes, probably calling in to dispatch to check to see if the slug had been found and a warrant issued for Grady's gun. But thankfully, they eventually drove away.

Racing upstairs, Grady pulled a duffel bag out from under his bed and began to stuff extra ammo, surveillance equipment, extra cash and a few other essentials into the black nylon bag. He knew it wouldn't take long for the authorities to find the slug. He was surprised they hadn't found it yet. It had to be out there somewhere, and when it turned up Grady knew he wouldn't be free to track down Anna.

Hurrying downstairs again he went into his office and retrieved his gun and his phone from his desk, then slipped on a coat and took inventory of everything. On a last minute whim he took out a pad of paper and scribbled out a long note and placed it carefully in Anna's paper file. Then he went to his basement and located exactly what he was looking for along one of the cold concrete walls. Pulling away the face of a loose cinderblock, he tucked the entire file into the space behind and then wedged the face of the cinderblock back in place.

Satisfied, he made his way back upstairs to the back door. Moments later he stepped outside into his fenced yard. The night was cool and lightning flashed from a storm building to the south as Grady hopped the wooden barrier separating his yard from the alley behind.

Landing softly in shadows, he took a moment to look left and right for any sign of surveillance. Confident they weren't keeping an eye on the alley, Grady crossed over to the other side of the narrow strip of blacktop running between the homes and produced a key from his pocket. Quietly, he opened his neighbor's garage, slipped inside and flicked on the overhead light, illuminating a restored 1967 Ford Mustang parked next to a new blue Chevy truck. The Mustang was his, a gift from his father before he passed away. Grady—having only a single car garage—paid his neighbor well to store it for him.

In minutes he was in the car, started the engine and was making his way down the alley. Turning right, he drove by his street to see if his suspicions were right. Obeying a stop sign there, he used the opportunity to take a closer look back toward his house, more than half a block down Montrose. It was difficult to see, but just as he pulled away, something caught his eye. It was the faint but definite glow of a cigarette tip burning slowly in the dark void of what Grady assumed to be an unmarked police car.

Clearing the intersection, Grady gently revved the smooth rebuilt V8 engine and began the long trip to Rochester alone.

CHAPTER 26

WHAT'S IN THE PAST

The last time the police knocked on Grady's door had been almost four years ago. And as Grady drove down highway 52 on his way to Rochester, the recent visit from the boys in blue brought one of his life's most painful memories back like a raging flood.

It was January 3rd, and it had been a full two days since Nancy had left his bed sometime in the middle of the night. Grady wondered if he might receive a phone call from her explaining why she had left so suddenly, but none had come and he didn't know how to get in touch with her.

The day they came, Grady had just finished vacuuming his house when the doorbell rang. The police invited themselves in and introduced each other before asking him if he had recently come in contact with a Nancy McAndrews. Surprised by the last name, Grady responded in the only way he could, asking if Nancy O'Neil was one and the same. After a quick check, the police confirmed his suspicions, indicating the name Grady had given had been Nancy's maiden name.

Shocked to discover she was married, Grady was even more troubled by the fact that her husband had returned home two days early from an ice-fishing trip up north only to find his wife missing. After checking with her friends, her husband called the police and they immediately started looking into Nancy's mysterious disappearance. It wasn't difficult to track her back to Grady. Friends Nancy had been with New Year's Eve had informed police about their visit to O'Gara's, and that Nancy had left with a man without so much as a word to them.

Putting that information to good use, the police found Nancy's car still parked down a side street near the bar, apparently just as she had left it that New Year's Eve. The cops interviewed Flynn, the bartender, and after some threats of obstruction of justice, Flynn gave them Grady's name and admitted to seeing him leave with a woman fitting Nancy's general description.

After that, it wasn't hard to find Grady's home, where Grady confirmed everything the police had learned up to that point. He acknowledged that he had left with Nancy that night, but insisted she had never told him she was married. In addition, Grady informed the police that he and Nancy had been romantic in college and that they had spent at least part of an evening together. Grady wondered if the officers believed him when he went on to explain that Nancy had left sometime in the middle of the night without his knowing—but ultimately Grady didn't care because it was the truth.

The officers, momentarily satisfied with his story, thanked Grady for his cooperation, and excused themselves from his home—letting him know before they left that they would be in touch. It took only an hour for them to return, this time armed with a warrant to search the premises.

When Grady heard their news, his knees went weak and he sunk despondently onto his couch. Through a choke of tears and emotion, Grady listened as they explained that just that morning, only a block and a half away, a jogger found Nancy. She had been badly beaten, her lifeless body unceremoniously dumped over a snow bank just off a walking path down by the Old River Road.

Grady's eyes were tearing now as he continued to drive, not even sure if he knew what hurt most: the loss of someone he could have loved, or the sequence of events that unfolded in the aftermath, ripping his entire life in two. He wondered if he would ever feel comfortable and whole in a relationship again. He had dated little since then, and the dates he had always seemed to end badly. Few women wanted to be around someone who was suspected of something so heinous, and Grady wouldn't hide the fact that he had been a suspect in a yet unsolved murder case. Even so, those he dated who found it in their hearts to believe in him—and try to get close—found Grady's heart to be distant and distracted.

It was all still too painful. Worse than the sorrow was the immense anger Grady felt over the entire issue. And as the police tried desperately to pin it on him, Grady could begin to feel that anger build. His only outlet was to use his spare time to dig into Nancy's death—it was really why he had chosen to become a private investigator in the aftermath. It was the only option that gave him flexibility in his schedule, some access to law enforcement officials, and still let him carry a gun when need be.

At the moment, Grady again found himself pondering the true identity of Nancy's killer. The culprit had never been caught, and probably never would be, but Grady was slowly narrowing his own list of suspects.

Reaching for his CD case, Grady found the one that seemed to fit the mood. It was by Nickleback, and he slipped it into the new stereo system he'd recently installed in the Mustang and punched up track five.

As the thick, throaty guitar riffs cranked through his sound system, and the lead singer's raspy voice cut through, Grady sang along as part of his own therapeutic ritual.

"And I-I-I-I want . . . to rip his heeeeart out . . . just for hurting you . . . yes I do."

CHAPTER 27

Rochester

A soft rap on Tom's car window woke him from a light sleep and he shot up, instantly wide-awake.

"Christ," he said, seeing the face leering through the window at him. "You scared the shit out of me!"

Outside, Grady just laughed. The expression on Tom's face was priceless, and though he couldn't exactly hear what Tom was saying through the closed window, he could tell it was laced with expletives. After a long drive down, during which he had purposefully stoked his own anger in an effort to release some pent-up frustrations, a little levity was exactly what Grady needed.

Shaking his head, Tom turned the key halfway in the ignition and rolled the driver's window down. "What do you mean, sneaking up on me like that. If I had a heart condition, I'd be dead right now," he jabbed, giving Grady a weary smile.

Grady smiled back, a silent gesture between the two that there were no hard feelings. "What's the deal up ahead?" he asked more seriously, nodding toward the house just a little further up the hill where Anna now stayed. "Or have you been asleep this whole time?"

Tom glanced at the digital display on his dash, noting it was now about 3:30 a.m. "So I slept a little, couldn't have been out more than an hour, and I figured they weren't going anywhere."

"As far as I can tell, they haven't. Car's still there." Grady offered.

"So you've been up that way already, I take it?"

"Yep, I've been here about a half hour." Grady commented. "Saw your car as I drove in. I wanted to check some things out up the road, so I let you sleep. I did look in on you at least to make sure you weren't dead, but I could hear your snoring coming right through the windows, so I figured you were fine." Grady joked. "Which reminds me, are you going to let me in or do I have to freeze my ass off out here?"

"Sorry, you got it," Tom said, hitting another button, releasing all the door locks.

Grady jogged around to the other side of Tom's car, giving a brief look at the night sky above before he slid in. The rain had brought a cool front with it, and although the showers had ended, the swirling shadow of dark clouds overhead certainly didn't rule out the possibility another wave might come. Inside the car Tom's dog, Molly, greeted Grady happily. She was a good dog who rarely barked, and she had immediately recognized Grady as he approached Tom's car a few minutes ago. She seemed to be thoroughly enjoying their road trip.

"You never told me what the deal was with things up ahead?" Grady inquired getting settled in his seat.

Tom looked out the window, pausing as if he were playing back his hours of surveillance in his head before he answered. "Not much more than I told you last. I made a few trips up the road on foot to make sure nothing changed . . . and as far as I can tell it hasn't. Lights were all still out, except for the one left on in the entry and the car hadn't budged, so I figured, unless they were going to make a cross-country trek through the woods in a thunderstorm, they're all still there."

"Good. Any idea whose house it is?" Grady asked, not really expecting an answer.

"Mailbox says Dr. Benjamin F. Olson." Tom answered with a smug smile. "If I had one of those fancy iPhones like you, I could have probably accessed a bio on him—that's assuming he's listed on the Mayo Clinic's website. I'd guess that's probably where he works. Anyhow, as you can see, my resources are limited to just me and Molly."

"Thanks," Grady laughed, "I guess I can take it from here, if you two want to hit the road."

"What do you think, girl?" Tom asked his dog.

Molly just wagged her tail enthusiastically. "She says we'll stay," Tom interpreted for Grady. "If that's alright with you? Besides, it would be easier to drive home in the light of day. Less likely to nod off, I suppose."

"Thanks, I appreciate it, but you don't have to do this," Grady added gratefully.

"Nope, we're in, just tell us what you want us to do."

"Alright, then first thing I want is for you to get some sleep. I'll keep watch. I figure sometime before dawn, I'll wake you and drive my car up past the house and hoof it back so I can take up position across the street. It's an undeveloped lot with a lot of trees so I think I can find good cover to keep an eye on the house. At that point, I'll send you and Molly down where the road forms a T. Take a right, which will take you up a hill toward another development. I've already checked that out. Just for reference, a left would take you back to the main road you came in on. Once up the hill double back and park about a hundred yards from where the roads intersect. You're my eyes if anyone comes or goes. Got it?"

"Got it. Just one question, though," Tom added. "What the hell are you messed up in?"

Grady looked somberly back at his tall, lanky friend, his face framed with a short stubbly goatee and a buzz cut that either hid or accentuated his receding hairline, depending on how you looked at it. Speaking sincerely, he replied, "It's better if you don't know, my friend . . . it's just better that you don't know."

Twenty minutes passed and Tom and Molly had quickly returned to their sleepy ways. Grady should have been extremely tired as well, but he had a mildly disturbing thought that was keeping him awake. For some reason Dr. Benjamin Olson's name sounded familiar, but he couldn't place it exactly. He tried looking up the name on his iPhone, but he was in a dead spot for coverage. He thought about hiking back up toward the house to see if reception improved higher on the hill but decided against it. Instead, he spent the next two hours listening to Tom and Molly's chorus of snoring. Eventually, he let the doctor's name and the elusive connection go, and looked quietly out the windows at the darkened forms of the towering trees that surrounded them. It was odd, but right now he felt unusually calm. Perhaps it was the company.

Finally 5:30 a.m. rolled around, marked by the pre-dawn light that was just beginning to seep into the horizon to the east, and Grady decided it was time. Waking Tom, a bit more respectfully this time, Grady let his friend slowly gather his senses before he reviewed their instructions. Grady hopped out of Tom's car, crossing Forest Hills Road to where he had parked his own car facing the opposite direction. Allowing Tom and Molly to turn around first, Grady pulled away from the curb, managed a U-turn himself and headed back uphill past the house.

As he crawled by, with his headlights extinguished, Grady noted no new lights were glowing from within Dr. Benjamin's home. This was a good thing. Then, once past the house, Grady proceeded a quarter mile along finding the intersecting drive he had already staked out on his earlier trip down Forest Hills Road.

It was barely a path really; more or less tire tracks that led back into the thick woods. The tire marks were probably left by developers, staking out new construction sights, or perhaps from hunters who poached off of other people's land. Grady turned his Mustang off the road, accessing the trail, his low-riding car now bouncing and lurching in the ruts, even bottoming out a few times, before he felt he was deep enough. Here, he wouldn't have to worry about some over-observant neighbor calling in a suspicious vehicle parked along a deserted stretch of road.

Satisfied with his location, Grady exited his car, still cloaked in the early-morning darkness. Heading around back, he opened his trunk and began digging in it. First he retrieved a pair of compact binoculars, then a small flashlight and finally more ammo for his gun, hoping he wouldn't be needing it. But after last night, he wasn't taking any chances. Then he stashed everything methodically into his coat pockets before heading back down the road, toward Dr. Benjamin J. Olson's stately home and the sleeping occupants within.

CHAPTER 28

UNEXPECTED VISITORS

The car's headlights blazed a pair of smoky trails through patches of thick hanging fog as they raced along the country road near the outskirts of Rochester. Inside the car four well-equipped men had come to get a job done. To them, it was nothing more than that. When Mitch Patterson, or any other of their clients said go, they went. And though time between jobs was often long, what they did paid extremely well for a fraction of a day's work.

This morning, their mission was to neutralize three subjects with quick, clean efficiency and minimal mess. After that, they were to get the hell out. Cleanup was not their job; that's why trailing a couple of miles away, Mitch Patterson and a second team of four were roving the area in a van . . . ready to sanitize the scene if called upon. Yet if they did their job right, the trailing team would have little to do.

The lead man, code-named Alpha, would never let his men know it, but this mission had him worried. Their briefing had been thorough, and the task seemed simple enough, as no violent resistance was anticipated. But Mitch had tied his hands a bit on this one. The order had come down that no deadly force was to be employed unless in extenuating circumstances. As a result, Taser guns had become the first line in the offensive. The lethal blow wouldn't come until the second team, the staging team, arrived.

Alpha knew his men were extremely skilled in all forms of combat, and these stun guns were not unfamiliar tools for them. Yet he was always wary when restrictions were placed on his strike team. He was a firm believer in Murphy's Law, and knew that if something could go wrong, it would. Thorough preparation and the fewest restrictions made for the easiest jobs. This job allowed for neither.

Up ahead the fog began to thin, as the road began to gently rise up into the hills. Moments later, the headlights illuminated a signpost that read *Forest Hills Road.* Slowly the car turned right and began to make its way toward its intended target.

Activating his digitally scrambled two-way headset radio with an ample 5-mile range, Alpha clicked on air and sent his coded message. "Alpha to Cleanup, Stalker team is taking up position. Is Operation Overkill a go?"

Mitch heard the call on his radio and smiled. The call received late last night from Allan at Northwoods had given him a second chance, and this time he wasn't going to blow it. It was the very reason he chose a team for the task at hand. The odds weren't even fair, four armed men to two women and an old man—it was overkill, and to humor himself, he made it the operation's name. Their task: go in and subdue the three subjects. He and the cleanup crew would then swoop in, set the doctor up for an unfortunate accident, then take the girl and Mary Jane off to be disposed of in a way they'd never be found.

Feeling supremely confident, Mitch replied into his radio. "Gotcha Alpha, we're a go. Switching to radio silence, now. Cleanup, over."

From his position up the road Tom saw the lone headlights of a car approaching from a long way off. He watched it closely as it sped through drifts of fog, before it finally slowed at the intersection and made its turn. Grabbing his cell phone, Tom had Grady's number already cued up, so all he had to do was press TALK.

A mile away, Grady sat crouched behind the thick barricade of a massive fallen oak. He was just trying to decide if he was going to observe or confront Mary Jane and Anna at the doctor's home when he felt his phone vibrate. Eyeing the phone's screen he noticed he now had a single bar of reception. Quickly he jabbed ANSWER . . . the call connected and he whispered "Hello" into the receiver.

"You got company, my friend," Tom's anxious voice came through loud and clear. "Pair of headlights coming your way. Keep your head down."

Grady's heart quickened a bit, and he did his best to stay calm. He wasn't expecting company. He hoped it was a neighbor, but who would be coming home at such an early hour? Glancing briefly at the doctor's house, he had only moments ago noticed two lights bursting on beyond the shades of two rooms upstairs. Another followed shortly thereafter downstairs. But as yet, from this distance, he wasn't able to see anyone through the windows.

Assuming nothing had changed inside the home, Grady looked left down Forest Hills Road, waiting for the car to arrive. He saw it approach at a speed he guessed was five miles per hour below the posted limit, and it cruised along as though it wasn't going to stop.

Pulling his binoculars up to his eyes, Grady gazed into the interior of the car. There he could just make out the figures of four passengers. But what made his stomach knot wasn't the fact that there were four people cruising a quiet neighborhood so early in the morning. It was the fact that every last one of them turned their heads to look at the house as they passed by.

Following the taillights now, Grady watched them until they drifted out of sight. He looked back at the house again, wondering if the car would return—betting himself that it would. For a second, he considered racing across the street and banging on the door. But he was sure they wouldn't let him in, even if he did. And he wasn't about to shoot the lock in.

"Damn it" he swore aloud in frustration before he turned back to scan the road in the direction the car had headed. Just then, his phone vibrated again.

"What's the word?" Tom asked excitedly once Grady connected the call.

"They went by, but they were certainly interested in the house." Grady informed him.

"You think they'll be coming back?"

"Shit!" was Grady's only reply as he noticed through his binoculars the car slowly heading his way again. Only this time the headlights were off and his keen eyes noticed they were one man short.

Guessing what Grady saw, Tom simply said, "I'll take that as a yes."

CHAPTER 29

ULTERIOR MOTIVES

Furious, The Kid paced his modestly furnished room situated on Northwoods' second floor. *He had been shut out again, hadn't he?* He had just got word that Mitch and his team had been given the go-ahead, in another attempt to take Anna and Mary Jane out. Both of them were damn close, just south near Rochester, yet here he sat . . . his talents going to waste.

It wasn't right. Northwoods had undeniably told him that if the first plan failed he was in. Now suddenly he's out because some jackass here wanted containment today. If Northwoods was afraid of drawing attention its way, what the hell did they think plugging three people was going to do? It would make damn huge headlines; that's what it would do. How would they even start to go about covering it up? He didn't know, and he really didn't care. He just wanted his shot at Anna.

"God, I'm working with morons," he said aloud as he planted his foot full force into a table, sending it and the items on it flying across his room. Right now he was working his anger, building it in hopes of accomplishing something in the next few minutes that he hoped he wouldn't regret. And he knew that Anna received emotions like anger, intense sadness or sublime joy more easily.

Sure, it was risky. Anna could pick up on too much, or Northwoods could shut him out totally if they ever found out. But he wanted back in the game and he wanted back in now. The Kid had convinced himself that the next shot at Anna was rightfully his, and if Northwoods wasn't going to hold up its end of the bargain then screw'em. He took a swipe at a floor lamp and sent it crashing to the floor, piling it up with the rest of the debris he had tossed about on his rampage.

The Kid was now in a full furry, completely enraged. It was now or never. Heading over to his dresser he took the next course of drugs nearly a full two hours early. Picking up the paper cup he tossed the little pills back into his throat and chased them with a hefty chug of warm Diet Coke.

Like a prizefighter trying to keep his muscles warm, he rotated his shoulders and flexed his neck this way and that as he waited for the drugs to take effect. First they'd hit his stomach—dissolving in seconds—after which they'd be rapidly absorbed into his bloodstream, where they'd finally filter up to his brain, ultimately altering its normal chemistry. As he waited, he began jabbing his finger with a small pin to keep his anger fresh, and he watched blankly as tiny droplets of his own blood began to bubble up on his skin.

Beginning to feel the rush now, he knew the drugs were taking effect. Crossing the room, The Kid sat down on his unmade twin bed. Holding his head in his hands he began to concentrate . . . hard. Even as he did, slim rivers of blood trickled off his punctured finger, flowing down his face like tears. Briskly, he began rocking back and forth to the steady, up-tempo rhythm of his rapidly racing pulse as it throbbed wildly inside his head.

Thinking now only of Anna, he fixated on her image, until a clear picture was obtained. With that image in mind, he attempted to deliver a simple visual: four unidentifiable shadows, each heavily armed and closing in on her. Finally, he ended his message with a single, simple verbal cue. "Run!"

CHAPTER 30

THE SIEGE

Anna woke with a sense of foreboding, and an overwhelming desire to run. And why did the number four keep popping into her head? Four of something . . . four people perhaps? It was tormenting. She couldn't get a handle on it all. There were too many things happening—too many things whirling around her head all at once.

There was last night with the gunman at the townhouse . . . a nightmare in itself. There was the realization about Ben . . . a natural himself? All followed by that awful fragmented dream, seeing Curt lifeless under the sheet, her inevitable return to Northwoods, and the incident with Grady in The Room with its padded white walls. Now—suddenly—she felt as if she were in mortal danger. What was true and what was false was blurring together, overlapping like two different colored paint strokes, forming a new color, an alternate reality.

"Run." The voice said in her head. "Why?" was the question that she asked herself, trying desperately to be rational. The answer was there, somewhere in the recesses of her mind.

From outside, the low rumble of a car caught Anna's ear and instinct told her to investigate. Hopping off the bed she stood near the window, separating the blinds just a smidge for her to see through. Out on the street a dark sedan cruised by toward the dead end and Anna strained her eyes, trying to peer into its dark interior for answers. For a moment, she thought she could see only a driver, but after her eyes adjusted to the light she was almost certain she saw a passenger in the driver's side back seat. "Four," the voice said in her mind again.

Anna didn't need to see the other two men—she knew how many were there. The image outside matched up to an image in her head and a puzzle piece clicked into place. Slowly the car moved on down the street, but now she was certain it would be back. Sprinting out into the hall, she went in search of Mary Jane's room, yet as she passed the top of the stairs Anna stopped dead in her tracks. From down below, she could hear the voices of Mary Jane and Ben engaged in what seemed to be a heated conversation.

Unsure why, she crept down the stairs, like a small child sneaking up to silently witness a fight between parents. At the moment Ben was talking.

"But Mary Jane, I don't understand why you left Northwoods. It was such a perfect opportunity for you."

Sighing Mary Jane replied. "It's a long story Ben, one I really don't want to involve you in. I'm trying to put that part of my life behind me."

Exasperated, Ben shot back, "The girl though Mary Jane, she's obviously a product of their program. What are you doing here with her if you have no connection with them anymore? Did you steal her for your own purposes?" Ben asked, trying halfheartedly to ease the tension.

"Benjamin, I didn't realize you were so well informed about Northwoods. I can't ever recall you telling me you had an interest in Northwoods, outside of the fact that you knew me when I worked there."

By now, Anna had crept low enough on the stairs so she could look back and see Ben and Mary Jane seated across from each other at the kitchen table. From her perspective, she could just make out their animated profiles.

Frowning, Ben gave Mary Jane a quizzical look. "I thought you knew."

"Knew what?" Mary Jane said, regretting the question before she had even finished it.

"Mary Jane, who do you think recommended you to Northwoods? I honestly thought you knew."

Hearing this, Anna nearly fell off the stairs. Her head spun as more pieces fell into place. Gathering her wits, she plunged down the last few steps, turned the corner and stormed into the kitchen. "You bastard," she screamed at Ben. "You're the one. You're the reason they're out there right now!" She said pointing to the front door.

Mary Jane stood up and said "Anna!" in an admonishing tone.

Facing Mary Jane's reproach Anna turned to her and pleaded. "Listen to me, you don't understand, this man you've trusted all your professional life just turned us in. I'm telling you they're out there right now, four men in a car . . . they're coming for us." Anna said shooting Ben a vile look.

Mary Jane just looked at Anna dumbfounded. "I can't believe . . ."

"Just look at him." Anna yelled again, interrupting Mary Jane. "Look at him, it's in his eyes, I can see it from here, he turned us in."

Ben's guilty eyes had betrayed him to Anna, but Mary Jane remained unconvinced. Trying to settle things she said soothingly, "Please just sit down and let's talk about this."

When Ben spoke his words were quiet, not confident as he had been, and Anna could tell they were tinged with a hint of sadness. "I did it for your own good . . . for the greater good. You must understand the research they do is extraordinarily important. Far more so than you might ever imagine."

Mary Jane fell into her seat, a look of utter disbelief and defeat on her face as Anna shot back at Ben. "You old fool, don't you understand? Don't you see, they're not coming to take us away—they're coming to kill us!"

For a moment, Anna just looked helplessly at Ben, hoping for a response she knew would not come. Yet his eyes told his story perfectly. He hadn't known, had he? Nor was he a natural . . . he was just well connected. He really thought Northwoods was just going to come in here, have some breakfast and a cup of coffee, then escort Anna back to Northwoods and everything would be just grand.

"Welcome to the real world . . ." Anna said bitterly. "I'm getting the hell outta here, and I'd suggest you both do the same." With that, she sprinted for the French doors just beyond the kitchen table. Once there she threw them open with a violent shove and then bolted out across the patio, onto the lawn and quickly into the woods beyond. In her mind, as she ran frantically, Anna prayed that Mary Jane would be close behind.

Back inside the house, Mary Jane glared at Ben as she stood to chase after Anna. "How could you?" she said coldly. "How could you?"

Ben opened his mouth to offer a reply, but he was cut off as the front door erupted inward with a loud concussive bang. In seconds, three men stormed through a smoky haze, sweeping the room. The first and third man in covered the room with the muzzles of their semi-automatic weapons, bracketing the second man carrying the Taser. In a flash the black clad trio crossed the entry in formation shouting, "Down, down, down," as they proceeded steadily forward.

Ignoring their commands, Ben rose from his chair, glaring at the men, defiantly saying, "Get the hell out of my house! There's been a horrible mistake and I insist you leave." But he had barely gotten the last word out of his mouth as two electric probes shot out from a small handheld device the second man carried, and 50,000 volts slammed into Ben's body delivering an incapacitating current. For a brief moment he remained standing, shaking uncontrollably, until he crumpled into a heap on the floor.

Mary Jane, already halfway toward the French doors, saw Ben fold and immediately made a decision to keep going. She hit the glass doors running, her hand slamming down on the handle that released them outward and she raced out into the dim light of a new day.

From behind, she heard the men yelling for her to stop; yet she couldn't understand why they hadn't already fired. In a flash she was at the edge of Ben's beautiful raised brick patio where she made a two-foot leap down to the ground, stumbling just a bit as she did.

Behind, Mary Jane could definitely hear at least one man in hot pursuit, and he was still shouting for her to stop as she broke across the tree line that separated the yard from the woods. Two feet into the foliage, a silenced rifle coughed from behind and a searing pain shot through her upper thigh. Instantly her leg went lame just as she bore her full weight down on it for her next stride. Like a wet noodle it gave way beneath her, sending her crashing headlong into a morass of mud, twigs, and leaves.

From Grady's hidden position, he had seen the men enter the doctor's home. Each was clad in black as they stormed out of the car, running in tight formation up the walk, expertly covering themselves to the front, sides, and rear. At the door, Grady watched—unable to do anything just yet—as the men attached some type of device to the lock, stepped back and waited.

The instant the door blew in and the men scrambled inside, Grady made his break. Tearing through the last of the trees, he scrambled out across the street and flew up the front walk, with his Sig Sauer out in front leading the way—his gun poised to sear a hole through anybody who wore a color darker than burgundy. Once at the door Grady tucked himself up against the façade of the house, pausing only moments before he spun around, kicking open a front door that had been left ajar.

Leaping into the foyer, his eyes searched the room for a target. The first came into view just 15 feet away. It was the man with the Taser and Grady had caught him just turning to face Grady's charge. The man's hand instantly dropped the electric shock device, and he reached into his shoulder holster, seeking a more deadly weapon to subdue Grady's threat. But he was much too slow and Grady, without a second thought, sent a single bullet home, right into the temple of the man's forehead.

Moving toward his first kill with incredible speed, Grady glided from entry to kitchen and quickly zeroed in on his second target. The man was in limbo, halfway through the French doors and just turning back to offer his own deadly answer to Grady's unexpected arrival. But that was his mistake, and Grady didn't give him a chance to flinch, dropping the masked man right where he stood with two quick rounds to the upper torso and neck. Instantly the man fell in an awkward heap between the double doors, his body propping them open.

Scanning left then right, Grady immediately swept the kitchen area for the third gunman, yet he only saw a man he assumed was Dr. Benjamin moaning loudly on the floor. Quickly maneuvering himself over the fallen and around the table Grady reached the double doors. Through the glass he spotted the third gunman, who appeared to be racing back from the trees toward the house. Firing two lead shots as cover, Grady leapt headfirst through the slim opening in the double doors. Landing heavily on his stomach and forearms, he then rolled left toward a massive concrete planter as a spray of bullets sailed over his head and hammered into the siding of the house. Coming up in a neat crouch with the concrete planter between he and the assailant, Grady didn't waste any time. Rising from behind his shield he fired two quick rounds that slammed into the man's chest armor, staggering him, until a third bullet found its mark, caving in his front teeth, and slamming back into his throat before rupturing his brain stem and turning the lights off for good.

Pausing cautiously, Grady knew a fourth gunman was out there somewhere, but God only knew where. So far he had only seen the doctor, but there had been no sign of Mary Jane or Anna. Since two of the gunmen had been in pursuit in the yard, he assumed that Anna and Mary Jane must have fled out the back door and into the woods when the shooting started. This in mind, Grady began to make his way in that direction.

Halfway into the yard Grady heard a woman calling out in pain, "Help, whoever you are, please help." Following the voice, he found Mary Jane propped up against a tree applying pressure to her bleeding leg.

Kneeling down he asked. "How bad?"

"Not too." Mary Jane winced. "I'm trying to get the bleeding stopped."

"Where's Anna?" Grady asked anxiously looking around.

Mary Jane hesitated.

"I want to help her!"

Looking back at her leg, and realizing she wasn't going to be of much help to Anna, she relented. "She ran off, in that direction I think," pointing to the southwest, away from any nearby roads and into the thick of the woods.

"Here, take my phone, call for help. I'll be back as soon as I can," Grady said reassuringly. And then he raced off, before slightly adjusting his course in the direction of two distant gunshots.

CHAPTER 31

FLIGHT OR FIGHT

Anna raced wildly through the underbrush. In her mad dash, branches tore at her clothes and scratched unrelentingly at her face. Initially she'd hit the woods at full speed, but her progress had been slowed somewhat, as she was nearly a quarter-mile deep into the dense thicket. Trying to maneuver over and around fallen trees, the tangle of undergrowth was costing her time, yet her urgency was never more evident, for she'd come to the frightening realization she was being stalked.

From behind, Anna could barely discern the sounds of a branch snapping here, the early autumn leaves crunching there, as she bore ever farther south. Her pursuer had been on her so fast she quickly realized he couldn't have come for her through the house—rather he'd swung around the outside of Benjamin's estate in an attempt to cut off any means of escape before the siege on the home took place.

Something like a muffled, throaty cough echoed through the canopy of trees. Simultaneously a two-inch thick branch to Anna's right exploded in a shrapnel of sharp wood fragments that gouged at her face and tangled in her hair. She screamed, throwing up her hands as a makeshift shield, even though the barrage of wood shards ended almost the instant it had occurred. As her hands covered her eyes, Anna lost track of her footing and she caught her toe on a root, sending her sprawling into the rain-muddied ground.

Picking herself up, she stumbled forward as another cough from an air-silenced rifle sent another bullet blazing a hot trail into the ground right where she had fallen only a second ago. Veering left, away from where she guessed the shots were coming, she again tried to put distance between herself and the gunman. Yet with every step she took, she could feel him gaining ground, as if he were slowly reeling her in like a trophy fish.

Desperately wanting to hide, she looked for any concealed spot as she ran, fearful that whoever was on her tail would see where she holed up. Ahead, Anna could just make out a massive tree that lay on its side. Its huge root ball, torn up from the viscous ground, bore clods of thick reddish-black clay clinging to its exposed root system. Reaching the dead wood, she heaved herself up and over. Loose pieces of the rough bark sloughed off with her progress as she scraped awkwardly over its massive round surface. Headfirst, she fell to the ground, her arms and hands spread out before her, desperately trying to break her awkward fall.

Dirty and exhausted, Anna scrambled on hands and knees over to the massive root ball. The fallen tree now acted as a shield between her and her pursuer, and she hoped this break in sight line would prevent him from tracking her to her intended hiding place.

After a hard, muddy crawl she made it to the roots of the upturned tree. Immediately she began pressing herself back into a narrow hollow, where a tangle of the once subterranean roots and rotting wood had parted enough for her to wedge her small frame. The squeeze was tight and as she maneuvered into the crevasse clods of damp earth fell from the roots, clumping in her hair and coating every inch of her body in an oozing slick. Getting an idea, Anna grabbed fistfuls of the muck, pressing more of its cool compress to her face, grinding the dirt and grime into her hair and the pores of her skin, creating makeshift camouflage paint. Thoroughly covered she tried to calm her breathing, to slow her racing heart to wait out the gunman's steady advance. If she were lucky, he would pass right by her.

The man code-named Alpha made every step purposeful. He had been surprised to see a woman charge out the back door of the doctor's house, well before he had been able to swing around back and take up his assigned position in the siege. The plan had been to attack the two points of exit, the front door being the main leverage point, with himself serving to contain anyone who tried to escape out the rear. Seeing Anna flee, Alpha had delivered the go command to the rest of his team a few seconds early, in hopes of containing any further breaks from within. From here on out, the four-man unit was to maintain radio silence, on the off chance someone might be trying to hack into their secure transmissions. Emergency or all clear was the only communication protocol.

Now, with one of the targets breaking through his containment, Alpha's task was to eliminate that risk. He couldn't afford leaving a survivor to tell of the raid, or implicate his team. Deadly force was now on the table.

Using his night vision goggles, Alpha forged a trail in hot pursuit of Anna, his eyes locked in on her fleeing form the entire way. She had about a 200-yard edge at the outset, but that gap had closed considerably. Only moments ago he let off two shots, each narrowly missing his intended target. The effect of those shots had an unexpected consequence, forcing Anna left of his current position, toward a denser portion of the woods, and a natural leafy screen.

Now, as the morning's glow filtered in through the overhanging branches, his night vision goggles were becoming obsolete, their sensitive optics picking up too much light, turning his view into a bright haze. Removing the goggles, he secured them in his waist pack, momentarily regretting the loss of one of his primary advantages.

At the time, the woods were silent, save for the occasional chatter of a squirrel high in the treetops, or a robin singing its last song of the season. In the absence of footsteps, or the occasional snap of a branch up ahead, Alpha surmised that Anna had opted for cover rather than flight. This meant she had to be holed up someplace nearby. Now all that was left was to find her and flush her out, like a pointer nosing out a defenseless pheasant. Should be easy, but he maintained a vigilant edge.

Every so often, he would try to pick up her tracks in the moist ground as he continued to stalk Anna in the direction of her last known position. Unfortunately, since he had made much of the trek using his night vision goggles, using line of sight, he hadn't been tracking Anna on a direct path. Using angles of attack he had been able to make up ground on her, but that currently meant he was off her trail. After a thorough scan of his immediate surroundings, he couldn't identify any footprints in the vicinity. So he moved ahead, hoping to discover fresh signs of her flight as he triangulated in toward her last known position.

Confident his target wasn't going anywhere, Alpha paused, deciding the circumstances dictate he break radio silence and check in on his team. As the leader this was his call. Lowering his microphone into place he spoke, "Alpha to Stalker 1, report in, over." No answer. "Repeat, Alpha to Stalker 1, report in, over." Trying the same with Stalker 2 and 3 he had no luck and the uneasy sense he had before the mission came storming back.

His team of three should have had the situation at the house well under control by now and reactivated their own voice-com devices. Could something have gone terribly wrong, or had it just taken longer to subdue the victims than anticipated? Contemplating a return to the house to check things out, Alpha decided against it, hoping his men would come online sooner than later. And with his primary target still out there somewhere he stuck to his orders to either contain her or take her down.

Moving forward, Alpha thought about the cleanup van still circling out on the roads nearby, wondering what they had inferred from his last transmission. They would know he hadn't been able to raise his men. If it all went wrong the cleanup crew would vacate the area and the trail would end with Alpha's team. No traceable links had been established between his squadron and his employers.

Up ahead, he made out what appeared to be a huge oak that had lost its battle with a recent storm. This was the location he had lost visual contact with Anna. Advancing with caution, he made his way to the center of its trunk and swung his legs over. If he had crossed just a bit farther to the west he would have picked up Anna's tracks, but he ended up missing them completely.

Just over the dead log, off to his right, a massive knot of roots protruded from the tree's base. To his immediate left the tree's extensive branch system exploded in a tangle of branches with dying clutches of brown leaves still clinging to its limbs. Alpha decided that would provide an ideal hiding spot. About to investigate, he was interrupted by the faint but fast tread of footsteps approaching from the north. Slowly he turned, his eyes picking up the dim form of another figure moving rapidly though the thick undergrowth. Raising his semi-automatic rifle, he lined up his target and gently squeezed off a shot.

The gun's silenced firing mechanism caught Grady by surprise, and if not for the bullet nicking a branch on the way to its target, Grady wouldn't be breathing anymore. Instead, the bullet's trajectory was altered just enough that it grazed by his ear, burrowing into the center of a tree just feet from his head.

Collapsing to the ground, Grady found cover behind a ragged stump and looked through the splintered wood in the direction from which the shot had come. From just over the rounded form of the fallen tree, he could see the muzzle of a gun as a bluish flame burst from its tip before evaporating into thin air. This bullet found its mark, taking a grapefruit-size crater out of the opposite side of the stump. Grady was sure that had been a warning shot. It said: *I can't hit you, but I know exactly where you are.*

Taking a deep breath, Grady knew of only one way to make ground and he needed to move immediately before the gunman could reposition. With a full clip, Grady leapt to his feet firing with marksman-like accuracy at the spot he had last seen the muzzle flare. He knew exactly where he was going, and accelerated to the security of a large tree just off to his right. As he got there, a heavy burst of bullets embedded themselves into the other side of the tree, sending more tiny shards of jagged wood raining into the air. Grady was actually happy for the gunman's renewed barrage, as he was able to identify the shooter's location . . . now approximately ten feet farther east of his prior position, closer to the dead tree's leaf canopy, still along the length of the fallen tree's shaft.

Ejecting his old clip, Grady inserted a new one and took in his surroundings. From his present locale, Grady could make out the fallen tree's massive and muddy root ball. His goal: to swing around to that, and expose the gunman's left flank, forcing him from his cover. Emptying half his new clip, Grady sent another barrage of bullets intentionally high, just over the gunman's new position, pinning him down as he sped toward the muddy uprooted trunk.

Arriving safely, he paused for a heartbeat waiting for the return fire, but received none. Then for the briefest moment, something odd tucked back in the tangle of roots gave him pause, but he had little time to take a closer look. Time was of the essence. Counting to three, Grady sprang from a low crouch and barrel-rolled across the ground as his body cleared the protection of the root ball. From the ground he fired two quick bursts up along the full length of the tree-trunk, but they sailed by unobstructed, past the exact spot the gunman had been only moments ago.

Confused, Grady looked up just in time to see his adversary's head appear over the fallen tree. During Grady's maneuverings the man must have jumped back to the other side of the log. Anticipating Grady's move he had tracked back along the length of the tree closer to Grady's position. Now the gunman—using the bulk of the trunk as a shield—swept the muzzle of his rifle over the fallen tree, bringing it around to train his sights on Grady's sprawled form.

It was a small branch, protruding from the log that saved Grady—bent by the sweep of the gun barrel, it snapped back into Alpha's face as he fired, causing his barrage to spray high and wide of the target. The miscue gave Grady the fraction of a second he needed. Again he rolled away from the hail of fire, the thick thud of bullets tearing up the ground nearby, chasing his roll.

With only a split second to spare, Grady stopped on a dime, propped on his side with his gun leveled out in front of him. Firing with precision from a terrible angle, he sent another two quick blasts in the only place he could, and they tore up the rotting bark in front of the gunman's face. It was enough to temporarily blind the man as he dove for cover.

Realizing it was fight or die, Grady needed to take the offensive while he had the chance. Rising to a knee, he unleashed another warning shot over the log as he climbed to his feet and sprinted directly into battle. Instinctually he figured the gunman was now rolling into a new position. Logic would indicate he'd head farther to Grady's right, away from battle and Grady's position. But Grady was beginning to understand the psychology of his attacker and he guessed he would rotate into a more aggressive stance to the left, closer to Grady.

On instinct alone, Grady's feet took him in that direction. Knowing he only had three bullets left he wasted one of them as additional cover fire to keep his prey down. Two more strides and he let off his second to last shot, less than ten strides away from the spot on the log he'd chosen as his focal point. If he guessed wrong and the gunman had flanked out right, he was dead, but with one bullet left, and no time to load a new clip, he had no choice.

Within reach of the log—nearly three seconds since his last warning shot—Grady was sure the gunman wouldn't stay low forever. On cue with Grady's thoughts he saw the man rising, the barrel of his gun coming over first just a few feet left of where Grady had guessed he would be. In full stride, Grady launched himself sideways into the air, his body facing left and his gun leading the way.

From such close proximity, a mere four feet, Grady could see the surprise register in the gunman's eyes, widening behind his black mask. Then, as if in slow motion, he saw him turn to face the unexpected attack, desperately trying to bring his gun around to get off a shot in close quarters. But Grady, now hanging in mid air, his outstretched gun barely a foot from the man's head, pulled back on the trigger and sent a bullet thundering into the base of the man's skull right where it met his thick neck. An inch to the right and the shot would have sailed wide and Grady would have been exposed . . . an easy target. Instead, the round found its intended mark, just behind the gunman's ear, dropping him in his tracks.

Without his hands readied to break his fall, Grady's side crashed onto the top of the fallen tree, the blow compressing his rib cage and forcefully expelling the air from his lungs as he slid over the other side, headfirst to the ground, where he landed harshly beside his victim. Gasping for breath, he rolled onto his back, staring up at the branches overhead, and the lightening sky beyond. He stayed there, not knowing what to think, not being able to think, just trying to breathe.

After what seemed like several minutes he heard movement off somewhere near the uprooted end of the tree and he tensed before his mind told himself he could relax. From his peripheral vision, he could just make out a female figure, clad head to toe in mud, slowly approach. Arriving beside him, she knelt down, her knees sinking into the rain-softened ground near his face. Looking up at her, Grady noticed her dark brown eyes—now a complement to the earthy tones she wore. Reaching out she smiled and gently brushed her fingers through his hair.

"I'm Anna," she whispered tenderly.

"I know." Grady replied, relieved.

CHAPTER 32

UNEASY TRUCE

Tired and dazed, Grady led a mud-soaked Anna cautiously toward Ben's house. Only moments before, the pair had stopped to stand solemnly over the man Grady had just killed. There was no happiness, no pride stemming from the man's death, just an ugly, hollow feeling. He didn't want to see his face, but Grady had to check out a hunch.

Following that, the pair began their journey back to the house, speaking only in intermittent spurts, with Anna wanting to hurry ahead to get to Mary Jane's side. Grady did his best to hold her back. He explained that the gunmen they knew about had been dealt with, and that Mary Jane was injured, but not seriously so. There still remained the outside possibility of danger. His rationalizations worked, and the young woman kept to his right flank where he asked that she stay.

There was still something that nagged at Grady—thus the reason for caution. It was a smoldering fear that there were more men out there, somewhere nearby. It was a possibility he was unwilling to share with Anna, for he guessed if she knew his concerns, she would bolt for the house to try to protect Mary Jane. If that were the case, and Grady's fears were confirmed, there was a good chance they would be racing back into a trap.

Gradually, they closed in on the spot where Grady had left Mary Jane. As they approached, Grady kept his eyes on the house, sweeping the perimeter for any sign of imminent danger.

With Grady's eyes and thoughts elsewhere and the house near, Anna stepped ahead and was the first to come upon the spot where Mary Jane had fallen. What immediately caught her eye was a clump of leaves—sticky, wet, and stained crimson with blood.

Grady, noticing Anna had stopped, brought his gaze to the ground, realizing they had come upon the spot where he'd left Mary Jane perhaps 45 minutes ago. "This is the place," he said. The confusion in his voice registered instantly with Anna.

"What do you mean?" she asked uncomprehending. "Where could she have . . ." but her words trailed off, catching on a knot welling in her throat as she realized the horrific implications. Finally, it was too much for Anna to contain, and before Grady could stop her, she raced into the house.

Once inside, her eyes scanned the vacant home, looking for a trace of her mentor and friend. Frantically Anna called out her name. "Mary Jane!" Then almost desperately, "Mary Jane!" "I can't do this without you." she screamed, her last call ending in a sob. She knew there would be no answer.

From behind her, Grady spoke softly, "That's where the doctor was," nodding his head over to an invisible spot on the floor. "They must have taken him, too."

"Who?" Anna said, tears welling in her eyes. "There were four men! You said you got them all!"

"I don't know. The same people who removed the bodies of the other gunmen I suppose. They were here too, but now they're gone." He replied.

"What now?" Anna whispered desperately.

"We wait."

"Wait for what?" Anna snapped, not understanding.

Grady produced a cell phone in his left hand, and showed it to Anna. "A call. I gave this to Mary Jane just before I ran after you. I had told her to call the police . . . or an ambulance at least."

"How do you know . . . ?" Anna started to ask, stopping herself. She knew how minds worked, even though Grady wasn't a natural, he had the same mechanisms she did. Everyone did—they just weren't as developed as she.

In any event, Grady finished her thought for her. "How do I know they'll call? Just a feeling I have." he said, not filling her in on the full story just yet.

Pausing, Grady waited for more questions from Anna, but she turned from him, arms crossed, and wandered helplessly frustrated into the kitchen. "For now, we have to get out of here." He finally continued. "I just need to make a call of my own." Knowing Anna had shut down temporarily, he didn't wait for agreement. Grady searched the call log on his phone. In a few keystrokes he found Tom's number and seconds later Tom came on the line as Anna paced.

"Thank God, I thought you were dead." were the first words out of Tom's mouth.

"Why do you say that?" Grady asked curiously.

"After I talked to you, maybe five minutes later, I saw a van come racing down the road. Thought maybe it was backup."

"It was." Grady intoned without emotion, making a mental note.

"Anyway, it came roaring back only five minutes later, this time with that sedan we saw before. Only there was just one guy driving. What the hell happened up there, anyway?" Tom asked.

"As far as you know, nothing. Absolutely nothing. You were never here, okay?" Grady said, hoping to protect his friend.

"Why?"

"Just trust me. Go home. I'll call you."

"Okay." Tom replied, just about to hang up.

"Wait a sec, Tom," Grady stopped him. "What did the van say on the side? Could you read it?"

"Yeah, it was something cleaners. American, Unlimited or a word like that."

"Allied?" Grady offered.

"Yeah, how'd you know that?" Tom said, intrigued.

"Just a hunch. Now go home . . . get some sleep. And thanks."

Grady closed out the call on his end and just as he did, the phone began to ring.

While Grady had been on the call to Tom, Anna had made her way over to the kitchen sink. Doing her best to keep calm, she was now going about the process of splashing the mud from her forearms, face and hair. But when the phone rang, she just stopped and stared at Grady—the water still spilling into the sink from the running faucet.

Giving her a look, Grady answered with a tentative, "Hello."

"Hello, Mr. Hamilton." the voice said. "Congratulations on disposing of my team with such efficiency. I'm assuming since you found your phone where we left it you have dispatched of my fourth," referring to the other gunman.

"Yes," came Grady's stone cold reply.

"Remarkable. Is the girl with you as well?"

"No," Grady lied, offering another terse one-word answer.

"I could argue with you but I won't. Let's just say if you aren't already in possession of the young lady, I suggest you find her and deliver a message. We have Mary Jane and we'd like to propose an exchange. I think she would agree to it. Probably jump at it." The voice added, "Mary Jane for the girl."

"Now why in the hell would I do that for you?" Grady replied heatedly.

"Because, we have your life and you want it back."

"You know, go to hell, what's stopping me from going to the cops right now?"

For a moment there was silence on the line, and Grady could almost sense the smile in the caller's voice. "That probably wouldn't work out very well from your standpoint. I'm guessing—you being an ex-Fed and all—you've picked up on a few things. I'm sure you now realize bringing the local police into this would make things a bit more hairy for us. But, nothing we couldn't overcome."

"I'm sorry, but my cell phone battery is getting low. Call me back when I give a damn." Grady said ending the call.

Looking at Anna, he yelled, "Let's go, now!"

"Why?" she said, with an incredulous look.

"Because I just told them we didn't call the cops."

"Why did you do that?" Anna asked bewildered.

"Because I was trying to get information and I screwed up, now let's go. They're still out there and they were wondering what our next move would be. Now they know. We have to move now!"

Grady and Anna ran for the front door. In under a minute they were across the street and back at Grady's car. Inside, Grady gunned the engine and backed his way over the makeshift dirt road and onto pavement, his car wheels squealing down toward the far end of the dead end road.

His phone had already rung twice since they had started off and he knew it wouldn't stop ringing. Rather than listen to it, he rolled down his window and tossed it to the curb.

"What just happened back there?"

Grady looked at Anna with one eye, keeping the other on the road. "They just called my bluff, now I'm calling theirs."

"But the main road's that way!"

"I know what I'm doing. That's exactly where they'll be coming from," he snapped. For a few moments Grady's Mustang reached over 100 miles per hour before he brought it to a skidding halt in front of the orange and white reflective barricades that marked the dead end. Beyond them a row of trees flourished.

Looking left, he saw what he was searching for. "There," he said triumphantly, as he spotted the rutted tire tracks just past the curb, leading around the barricade.

"What?" Anna asked, obviously not seeing what he saw.

"I scouted this earlier in the morning. There's a makeshift road through the trees here. You can't see it, but about fifty yards beyond the growth there's another road—a washed out gravel road, but a road nonetheless."

Grady eased his car forward, rolling its tires up over the curb, to align precisely with the ruts. Again the car was off road, and it bumped and bounced along, bottoming out a few more times before they cleared the trees and pulled out onto the bend of the gravel road.

He took the westbound curve and again gunned the car up to as high a speed as the road would allow. And while he wasn't sure exactly where he was headed he was growing more and more confident they were going to make it safely.

It was two miles before the car's wheels turned south onto blacktop, and Grady edged the speedometer up, nestling it now just below a respectable 65 miles per hour. Sensing Grady was more comfortable Anna spoke again. "Tell me what's going on Grady. Please."

Grady took a deep breath. "Okay . . . I owe you that much. The call was from them, whoever they are."

"Northwoods?"

"If you say so. I don't really know. Perhaps you would know better. Anyway, they have Mary Jane, and probably the doctor, too."

Already knowing the answer, Anna asked sadly. "What do they want?"

"You in exchange."

Anna's eyes searched the vast stretches of rolling farm fields as they rapidly flew by. "Then lets do it."

"You know that's not the answer," Grady said in exasperation. "They'll have you both. And from the amount of gun power they sent after you, they're not going to let either of you live very long. As long as they don't have you, they'll keep her alive as a pawn. I threw our only link to them out the window, so that should buy us time. If they can't contact us, they can't use her against us."

But Anna wasn't ready for reason. "No, I won't accept that!" she hollered back. "Turn the damn car around."

Ignoring her, Grady didn't slow. He knew he was right and he wasn't planning on dying today.

"Then stop the damn car!" Anna yelled. For a moment Grady's foot hesitated over the brake and then returned to the accelerator.

"No. I can't let you do that."

A mile passed and Anna was becoming frantic, her threats toward Grady less veiled, until finally at 60 miles per hour she flung open the passenger door.

Instantly Grady hit the brakes . . . too hard at first . . . and the car fishtailed wildly. Anna in the passenger seat was still wrestling with a half-open door that kept getting flung back at her from the wind washing across the suddenly altered aerodynamics of the speeding car. For a moment, as the car veered, she felt she might be flung into the ditch, but her seatbelt reined her in.

Grady regained control and brought the car to a sudden stop on the gravel shoulder. Immediately Anna unclipped the belt and sprang from the car. As soon as her feet hit ground she began sprinting back in the opposite direction.

Grady climbed out from behind the wheel and rested an elbow on the roof of the Mustang. He watched her for a second, wondering if he should let her go or chase after her. But the decision ultimately was an easy one—considering she was dead if she made it back to the house.

So he gave chase. She was a fast and graceful runner, but Grady was well conditioned from his days with the Bureau. A quarter mile from the car he was within reach, and he could sense Anna knew he wasn't going to let her go. She slowed gradually until she came to a complete stop—breathing in quick, heavy gasps. Grady remained behind, his own breathing labored, and uncertain of what to say that hadn't already been said.

But Anna simply turned to him and unexpectedly folded herself into his arms. She cried hard into his shoulder, and they remained that way for a while. Grady gently stroked her hair, telling her repeatedly it would all work out.

Finally, she broke free and without a word began to walk back to the car. Grady followed silently as well, afraid to speak, for fear she might change her mind. But Anna didn't, and by the time they were both buckled back behind the engine of the Mustang, her tears had dried into stains on her cheeks, although her eyes remained lost and distant.

Grady started up the car and pulled away. Ten minutes passed as Grady began negotiating his way through the countryside, on his way to a place he felt they could be safe for a while. It was at a fork in the road, in the midst of Grady's momentary uncertainty about which direction to head that Anna finally broke the silence.

"Why did you throw the phone out?" she asked in a soft voice.

"Huh?" was all Grady could manage; surprised she was even talking at this point.

"The phone," she restated, as though it were the issue that had been troubling her for so long.

Laughing at himself and his foolishness, Grady replied, "Plausible deniability I guess. I told them I was having phone problems, so I made the phone problems real. I don't know . . . I was in a panic. I guess I figured if they can't reach us, then they can't hold anything over our heads."

For a moment, Anna just considered the information. Slowly her mind was coming back online—trying to weigh any and all options available to them. "What about the police?"

Grady let a rueful smile cross his face. "I thought of that. Back there," referring to the doctor's home, "I thought it was an option."

"But?" Anna prodded.

"That first call I made. It was to a friend of mine, staked out in the area. His name is Tom. Actually he's how I found you down here. He was helping me watch Mary Jane's townhouse. Anyway, to answer your question, he said he saw a van drive by that had the name Allied Cleaners on it."

"So?" Anna said, knowing an answer would have come even if she hadn't asked.

Grady paused, trying to process the reality of it. "It's a long story, but I was a federal agent back when. Just a lowly private investigator now, but that's another story. In any event, there were a few times we called in teams of special ops to handle messy national affairs. You know, when we wanted to trample the Constitution in hopes of a higher good." Grady tried smirking at his joke, but Anna wasn't ready for mood lightening.

"Anyway," he went on clearing his throat, "Allied Cleaners was a front for one of the teams that came in and could make evidence disappear or perhaps even stage a crime scene. We used it when we would take down drug traffickers and such, just beyond the letter of the law."

"So how'd they get involved here?" Anna asked, pulling her knees up onto the seat and wrapping them in her arms.

Watching the road carefully, Grady waited for a car to speed by in the opposite direction. His eyes followed it in his rear view mirror until it was out of sight before he answered. "Here's what I think happened, and maybe you can help me shed light on it."

Going back to the beginning Grady gave her his theory. "The initial team of four storm into Ben's house. Three up the gut, one around back. Special ops guys, based on a neck tattoo I saw on that last one. Anyway, their backup team, The Cleaners and a guy I'll call the Field Commander, were probably monitoring the situation remotely. Their job is to clean up after the brute force and sanitize the scene. But when things went bad they swooped in to retrieve the leftovers and wash the dishes."

"So why weren't they just waiting to ambush us at the house after we came back out of the woods? We must have been out there thirty to forty minutes, tops. Why clean up and run?"

"When I got my phone back, I checked my outgoing log. Mary Jane did manage one outgoing call. It appears she tried to make contact with someone, but the connection only lasted a few seconds—and it definitely wasn't to 9-1-1."

"I'm guessing she saved us. She used her call as a threat with her abductors to get them to clear the area, and convinced them to avoid a possible showdown with the police. Beyond that, I can't think of any other reason as to why we didn't face an unwelcoming committee the second we were within sight of the doctor's house."

"You have to understand these special ops. By their nature, they are loners . . . secretive types. If they had to, they could handle the cops if they showed up, but they'd rather not. And the last thing they'd want to be doing is putting a few bullets in us to shut us up, just as a few local sheriffs hit the scene. So they split until they could confirm Mary Jane's story."

The mud in Anna's hair was beginning to dry and she was now trying to comb her hands through it to release the mats of thick clay. Doing so, she dislodged a spec about the size of a pea and it flicked across the car and hit Grady on his cheek. Flinching, Grady kept driving, trying to suppress a smirk, as an embarrassed Anna dug in the glove compartment for a tissue.

"You seem to have all the answers," Anna said, producing a crumpled McDonald's napkin, "so tell me, why did it matter so much that you told them you hadn't called the police, when they still couldn't be sure if Mary Jane had?"

Watching Anna out of the corner of his eye, he saw her discreetly wet the napkin against her tongue before she leaned over and gently applied it to the smudge on his face. "You ask a lot of questions," he said more than distracted now as she tended to him. "I guess I was assuming that the men in the van were probably already working the chains of command, back to the police office. I'm figuring by the time they got a hold of us they had already dismissed Mary Jane's bluff. Now all they were waiting for was to find out what our next move was . . . and as I already said I screwed that one up."

Anna sat back in her seat, tucking the dirty napkin in a side door pocket. "What would they have done if the local authorities had shown up?"

Sighing, Grady seemed weary of the twenty questions, but he answered nonetheless. "Depends. If everything was under control, they'd simply say the doctor was involved in federal matters and it was an issue of national security or some other cover."

"And if everything wasn't . . . under control?" she inquired, although she was sure she knew the answer.

"They'd be dead, too."

"So you're saying the government might be wrapped up in all of this?" she asked so softly, it was probably more a question to her than Grady.

But he answered her anyway. "Loosely . . . yes, but I'm guessing you already knew that."

Anna looked somberly back out the window. At that very moment Grady would have loved to have been able to read her thoughts. Finally she replied, "Yes, I guess I did."

CHAPTER 33

THE CLEANUP

The Allied Cleaners van rested for the second time that morning in the closed garage of Ben's Rochester home. It had already arrived and departed while Grady and Anna sleuthed around in the woods, and returned mere moments after Grady and Anna had dashed madly from the premises. It was this fact that Mitch was having the most difficulty with. For the second time in less than 24 hours he had failed to contain the two—a fact that sent him into a temporary rage.

Agitated and desperately trying to get a handle on his emotions, Mitch stopped pacing and sat down next to Mary Jane—both uncomfortably seated on a narrow bench that unfolded from the van wall. The cleanup crew of four, who were currently working the crime scene inside and out, had briefly seen to Mary Jane's wound, and at the very least succeeded in stopping most of the bleeding.

The pain was still difficult to bear, but luckily the shot hadn't hit bone. Rather, the small caliber round had passed cleanly through flesh and muscle. There was a ghastly exit wound, but with the right attention it would likely heal into an ugly scar.

Mitch kept a gun on Mary Jane the entire time, but her eyes were trained on Benjamin. At the moment, he was stretched out, still unconscious on another foldout bench, situated opposite her and Mitch. After carting Ben from the house, the cleanup crew had checked the old man's vitals, discovering a weak and thready pulse. Offering little in the way of treatment, they simply hooked the man up to a heart monitor and left him.

Anxiously, Mary Jane watched the tiny blip on an overhead display indicating an irregular rhythm. She guessed Ben had suffered a heart attack, and knew that without immediate treatment he was in grave danger. Then, as if knowing her worst fears, the monitor blip slowed dangerously, activating a piercing alarm—the first signal that Ben was beginning to crash.

"Ben!" Mary Jane screamed as her legs shot up beneath her and she rushed to his side. For the moment, the pain in her thigh was temporarily displaced by the concern for her mentor, but now, resting near Ben, it began to throb.

"Sit back down." Mitch scolded her, "Let him be."

Mary Jane shot Mitch a vile look and spoke through clenched teeth. "You can't just let him die. Call them back in here."

Mitch wore an even expression, his eyes showing no compassion or remorse. "I can and I will. Now sit back down."

"Then you damn well better shoot me because I won't let you do this." Mary Jane screamed at him. Turning away from Mitch, fully expecting a bullet in the back of her head, Mary Jane brought her attention back to Ben and the monitor, preparing to perform CPR if needed. But Mitch wouldn't have it and roughly flung her across the floor of the van.

"I said, let him die," Mitch hissed.

Mary Jane sat legs splayed out in front of her on the floor of the van, gripped by shock and disbelief as Ben's heart monitor continued to issue its piercing alarm. "You're not human," she seethed at Mitch. "The least you can do is let me be by his side."

Mitch mulled her request over for a second before finally relenting, "Oh, very well."

Mary Jane picked herself up off the floor and limped back over to Ben's side. Grasping his hand she squeezed it tight and looked into his frightened eyes. "Don't go," she whispered. "Don't go. I forgive you."

For a brief moment, Ben's eyes flickered across hers, and she saw deep sorrow there. Gently he squeezed Mary Jane's hand and attempted a soft down-turned smile, as if to say, "I'm so sorry." Then the heart monitor flat-lined and he was gone.

Mary Jane sat there for the next few minutes, just looking at the man who had once been like a father to her. Lovingly, she closed his eyes. For the moment, she suppressed any tears for Ben. Now was not the time to show weakness. She promised herself there would come a day that she would be able to openly and respectfully mourn his passing.

Returning to the bench, Mary Jane made a conscious decision not to even glance at Mitch, refusing to give him the satisfaction of seeing her raw unchecked emotions. Instead, she let the hatred and contempt she had for him brew. Favoring her wounded leg, she sat back down, just as the faint sound of voices approached from the house. Seconds later, the cleanup crew entered through the rear of the van.

"You can return him now," Mitch said to one of the men, referring to Ben's now lifeless body. "I assume you have everything set up like we discussed."

The leader of the crew nodded his assent as he and another man picked up the doctor with gloved hands and removed him from the van. With them well on their way, the other two men hopped out and began reloading some of the gear back into the van. The last item they grabbed appeared to be a black body bag, probably the last of the strike force, and they heaved the lifeless form up into the van to place his body where the doctor had just rested.

Watching with dead eyes, Mary Jane took odd satisfaction at the still body laid before her. It also made her well aware there was a vigilante out there who might be able to help Anna. She'd caught Mitch swearing the name Grady several times and she hoped Anna was with him—because, from what she had seen from the morning's aftermath, Grady was quite capable of protecting himself.

Minutes later, after all the men were accounted for, the van's engine roared to life and backed out of the garage, down the drive, and began to race along Forest Hills Drive on its way back to Northwoods. Back inside Ben's home, gas from an open burner on the stovetop was already seeping into every nook and cranny of the house. An hour later, a lamp, set to an automatic timer, would click on. The connection would ignite the fumes and blow the windows before flattening most of the framework. Then the massive fireball would engulf what was left of the wooden house. Evidence erased.

CHAPTER 34

LANESBORO

It had been over an hour since they had last exchanged words, Grady having lost Anna to her own daydreams. During the silence, Grady had come up with a hundred different ways to broach a subject, but all of them seemed trite, and thus had gone unsaid. He tried to keep an eye on his passenger, wondering if she might open up once more. Yet her muddied body remained oddly still, her eyes always fixated out the window, falling on nothing in particular.

In time, Grady's mind wandered away from new topics of conversation to what this young woman could be thinking. He was not necessarily reluctant to interrupt her thoughts, but more afraid to. In any event, Grady knew there would be time for discussion later. He wanted her to feel safe and secure, and the longer he drove the more he felt he was accomplishing that task.

Now, flying past flat fields of corn, Grady's Mustang came upon a thick grove of trees. After a few hundred yards into the growth, the road dropped away and began a steep decent downward to the left. The unending strip of blacktop became more tortuous, bending back on itself as they descended along its sweeping switchbacks carved out of the rocky limestone hills. Below them, the town of Lanesboro could be seen through fleeting gaps in the trees. This small, quiet town was nestled along the banks of the Root River—a river that had carved out this steep, narrow valley so many thousands of years ago.

Halfway down the slope, Grady braked hard, almost missing his destination, before taking the intersecting drive marked by a whitewashed sign with black and gold lettering that read *Bailey's B&B*. The sudden deceleration, and the abrupt turn seemed to snap Anna out of her reverie and she sat up in her seat. "Where are we?" she asked, almost as if waking from a dream.

"Bailey's Bed and Breakfast." Grady replied with a satisfied sigh. "The owners are friends of the family."

"Will they have room?" Anna asked. Considering it was early fall and the leaves were just beginning to change, she couldn't imagine they would have space for a couple of walk-ins—family friends or not.

"Good question." Grady offered. "They keep a full house generally, but they have a couple of new cottages, separate from the main house. In some of my spare time I've been helping them with interior construction on one of them. I was actually due to come out and help finish it up this coming weekend. Still not ready to be rented out, so I'm hoping we can stay there."

Anna nodded thoughtfully as Grady pulled into an open parking spot, just in front of the main entry. "You mind staying here?" he asked as he opened the door to get out. "Right now I think the fewer people who see you the better, for your safety and theirs."

"Sure," Anna said with an uneasy smile, pulling a dried clump of dirt out of her hair and depositing it out the window. "I guess right now especially, I'd make quite an unforgettable impression."

Half out the door, Grady's feet already crunching the gravel, he gave thought to Anna's reply, before pausing to look back at the young woman that had turned his life upside down again. She was a mess, a complete mess, but even in this blemished state, she had a quality about her that was captivating. Offering a half grin back, Grady just shook his head, as if to dislodge the thought, and without another word he shut the car door and strode inside.

It took five minutes before he returned, with a key in his hand. "We're booked for as long as we'd like."

Not sure if she was happy, sad, or indifferent at the moment, Anna just smiled wearily. Grady, realizing he wasn't going to get a response, pulled out of the parking space and headed down a narrow, tree-lined drive. A quarter mile later, past two cottages they finally stopped at a third.

"Numbers one and two are in use," Grady said, making conversation, not certain if she really cared, as they both stepped from the Mustang. "They were built a few years back—but as you can tell this one is brand new."

Anna gazed at the structure, mentally blocking out the piles of framing wood, bundled cardboard and pallets that littered the drive. Without the mess, the unit itself was breathtaking, surrounded on all sides by thick groves of oak, maple, and pine trees. A natural redwood-sided A-frame, it stood high on thick pedestal legs, each graduated into the steep grade of the limestone hill. The front appeared to be virtually all windows, with a narrow wood deck and wrought-iron railing running the length of the facade. On the near side, a flight of stairs led to a heavy rust-red oak door where Grady let them in under the overhanging canopy of an Autumn Blaze maple.

Anna found the interior to be even more magnificent. The small-but-open floor plan offered a lofted upper level that rested on raw wood pedestal columns over a full modern kitchen, tiled in red brick, and filling nearly the entire length of the rear wall. A long bar occupied the middle of the cottage, serving to separate the kitchen and the living quarters in front. Along the bar, on the living room side, were four leather-topped bar stools, while an oversized tapestry-woven couch, two leather side chairs and a glass-topped coffee table faced the vast expanse of windows. The impeccably clear panes, complete with manufacturer's stickers, stretched the entire length of the cottage and reached high into the peak of the A-frame, offering a dramatic vista of a forest of trees with sporadic glimpses of the tiny river town below.

"Incredible," Anna said in quiet amazement, finally opening up a bit. "You do very nice work."

"I really only helped," Grady replied, never really very comfortable with compliments.

"Stop. I can tell you're being modest." Anna countered, showing a playful side Grady hadn't yet seen, while continuing to take in the place with all its amenities.

"What's that over there?" Anna asked, directing Grady's attention to a small room framed on two sides in frosted glass block. It was situated in the far rear corner next to the kitchen and below the second floor balcony.

"That's the main-floor bathroom." Grady answered politely. "It's designed to take full advantage of the light from the front windows, yet still offer . . . ahem . . . some modicum of privacy."

"I see," Anna said appreciatively, genuinely taking interest in Grady's answer. "Where's that door go to on the far end?" she asked again, becoming more open and curious.

"That leads outside." Grady answered promptly, happy to have her attention. "The front deck wraps around the opposite side and there's a hot tub out there. We put it on the side . . . this time for privacy from the neighbors. But it offers a great view of the town at night."

"So you did have a big hand in the design, didn't you?" Anna said, picking up on some of Grady's unintended verbal cues. "But what I can't understand is why it's not available yet . . . what could be left to be done?"

Grady grinned at Anna's persistence. "I guess to answer your first question. The design . . . yes . . . it's partly mine. I conceived the layout and an architect finessed it. I also helped out with some of the interior framing, finishing, and details. It's a hobby, I guess."

"Normally I'd say your talents are wasted," Anna offered sincerely, "but I've seen firsthand what you do for a full-time job."

Uneasy again, Grady continued on. "Okay . . . well . . . I guess to answer your second question. Why it's not available? The flooring in the bathroom needs to be put in. It's actually going to be pieced flagstone, but the shipment was delayed. Ironically, when I spoke with Mr. Bailey a few minutes ago, he told me the truck arrived just yesterday. Satisfied?"

Anna nodded her approval, her eyes wandering up to the rafters and back into the second floor loft.

Following her gaze, Grady seized an opportunity to clarify something. "You'll be sleeping upstairs in the loft," he said, directing Anna toward a spiral staircase on the near side leading to the sleeping quarters. There's a smaller second bath up there as well with a shower, but the shower hasn't been tiled yet. "I'll take the couch as long as we're here . . . no arguments, please."

"Got it." Anna said unfazed. "So now what?"

"I was afraid you'd ask that." Grady said quite seriously. "I need to go back to the main house, make some calls and talk some more with Mr. Bailey. Why don't you sit tight and make yourself at home. You can even take a shower in the main bath if you want—towels should be in the linen closet right next to the bathroom. I'll also try to borrow some food, fresh clothes and something to drink while I'm out. Then, when I get back . . . say an hour . . . we need to sit down and talk."

Managing a warm smile, Anna gently touched Grady on the arm and replied with a genuine show of emotion. "Thanks."

CHAPTER 35

SETTLING IN

Anna found some new towels, just where Grady said they would be, and a thick terry cloth robe neatly folded on one of the shelves. Still dirty and grimy from the day's events, she desperately needed a shower and set about the task of getting cleaned up. The shower felt incredible, and for the time being it rejuvenated her, body and soul. She stayed there soaking for nearly a half hour, just letting the water wash away her worries along with the red clay dirt.

Once finished, she eyed the mud-caked clothes she had heaped on the exposed subflooring of the bathroom and decided against putting them back on. Instead, she wrapped herself in the robe and returned to the shower. Turning the water back on she retrieved her clothes before retracing her steps to the steaming shower. She tossed the garments into the shower, hoping the hot water would wash them clean.

Finished, she went to the mirror and took in her reflection. Her hair hung down around her face in straggly wet ribbons and she noted with a hint of distain that her face looked worn and haggard. She had bags under her eyes and small cuts and abrasions all over her skin—the result of branches lashing her in the face during her flight through the woods. Even so, she could have looked worse for what she had gone through.

Resigned that there was little else she could do to spruce herself up with limited resources, Anna left the bathroom and retired to the couch. As she wandered through the empty cottage, she wondered why she was even concerned about her appearance. She thought she knew the answer, but was frustrated with the thought all the same. Grady was certainly kind, and genuine, and had taken her safety into his hands. But she knew so little about him. For all she knew he could be turning her in right now.

Back at the main house, Grady met once more with Mr. Bailey in a small cramped office. Mr. Bailey was a hearty soul who had just turned 59. He and his wife had been close friends of Grady's parents before Grady's father had died, and the couple had just recently retired. Opening a bed and breakfast had always been a dream of theirs and they quickly jumped on an opportunity when this place presented itself.

"So what's going on, lad?" Mr. Bailey asked, eyeing Grady like a foster father.

"Trust me, John. You don't want to know." Grady felt like he had been saying that a lot lately.

Knowing Grady's background, Mr. Bailey just shrugged. "Alright, but who've you got cooped up in the cabin anyway? And why'd you need some of Elizabeth's clothes? You got a new girlfriend?" he asked with a chuckle, attempting to dig while lightening the mood.

Sighing, Grady replied. "I supposed you have to know something. She's a friend, and she's in some trouble. She just needs a place to stay and sort things out. That's all."

"So why is it that I can't tell anyone you're here?" John asked, puzzled. "What'd you say . . . even if your Mom calls I haven't seen you? Now come on, kiddo, what's really going on here?"

"John, I said she's in trouble . . . someone's trying to find her. If they can find me, they can find her, so nobody knows. Am I clear?" Grady cautioned sternly, wanting the matter dropped.

"Okay . . . clear." John replied, a bit discouraged. "I won't even tell Elizabeth, unless I have to."

"That'd be great." Grady said, his tone more appreciative. "And thanks for the food and clothes . . . I owe you."

"Don't mention it." John replied a little flatly, apparently hurting over being kept out of the loop. "If you still need to use the phone, you know where it is. I'll leave you alone. You can see yourself out when you're done."

Watching John leave, Grady grabbed the cordless off his desk and dialed a phone number from memory. The phone rang six times before someone finally picked up.

"Yeah." Tom's voice came through on the other end.

A wave of relief washed over Grady. He was deathly concerned that Tom might have hung around, or perhaps nosed around the doctor's house even after Grady told him to go home. "Thank God you're home safe."

"Hey there, I could say the same to you, buddy . . . but I'm guessing you're not home, are you?"

"No . . . and I can't give details. I just wanted to make sure you went home when I told you to."

The line was silent for a second, before Tom spoke again. "Well I can't lie to you there . . . I didn't. I stayed put and saw that same van come back. It left again about an hour later—got its plate numbers and everything. Then I waited about a half hour before I thought it was safe to do a drive by. Even parked way down the street to do a little nosing around outside the house with Molly. But she had other ideas. A white tail rabbit popped up nearby and Molly took off after it. Took me a half hour to get her back to the car. Good thing, too." Tom paused for effect.

"Alright . . . I'll bite, why?" Grady asked, exasperated, not really wanting to play games right now.

Again Tom paused for effect. "Whole damn house blew up," he said, delivering his punch line so that it had the most shock effect.

Now it was Grady's turn to be silent.

"Surprised you with that one, huh?" Tom's voice cracked back over a bad connection. "Figured I would call the cops, tell them what I knew if I hadn't heard from you by sundown. It was one hell of an inferno."

"You haven't called the police yet?" Grady asked.

"Nope. It's your deal now. I'll do what you want me to."

"Good, hold off for now. You're my ace in the hole." Grady said, his wheels turning furiously. "They don't know you exist and I want to keep it that way if I can. These are dangerous people and I don't want you involved if you don't have to be." Grady said, considering his next move. "And Tom . . ."

"Yeah."

"If you don't hear from me for any time over 48 hours straight, I want you to go to my house . . . you know how to get in. You'll have to do some searching, but I left a file there tucked behind a loose cinderblock. Once you have that file, go to the press with it and what you know, then go to the cops and do the same. Tell them both everything. Understand?"

"You bet . . . clock's ticking buddy." Tom replied and hung up.

CHAPTER 36

Cottage Talk

Grady entered the cottage carrying a shopping bag under each arm, one filled with food, the other stuffed with a day's worth of clothing for each of them. Hearing Grady enter, Anna shot up nervously from her comfortable spot on the couch, and Grady saw, to his own embarrassment, that she was dressed only in a short white robe.

"I have a few things for you," he said trying not to look directly at her as he set the bags on the counter. "There's a change of clothes in the one," he added, gesturing to it as he took the other bag to the far counter and began putting the food away.

"It's not perfect, but there's a Lanesboro sweatshirt and some sweatpants that Mr. Bailey was kind enough to steal from his wife. He mentioned if we wanted to go out tomorrow there's a small clothing shop in town."

"Thank you," Anna replied appreciatively, as she approached the counter and began pulling garments from the bag. She was comfortable in the robe, but she sensed Grady's own discomfort and decided it was best she change.

"The last two items in the bag are for me. I held off on asking for undergarments. I really didn't think it was appropriate."

"That's alright Grady. For now, I've salvaged what I was wearing. I'll go put these on."

When Anna returned from the bathroom, Grady had just finished putting the things away and he gratefully noticed she was wearing Elizabeth's clothes. The large sweatshirt hung cartoonishly on Anna's slight frame, and the sweatpants were cinched as tightly as they could around her waist, yet they still looked as if they would fall right off of her. But at least Grady felt he could look at her without feeling immodest.

"Are you going to change?" Anna asked politely as she approached the counter.

"Later. Right now I'd like to have a beer and just sit and talk. Of course, if that's okay with you. Would you like one?" He inquired, referring to the beer.

"Sure, bartender, what do you have?" she asked as she hopped up on a barstool across from him, trying to ease some of the tension in the air.

"Not much choice, only Pabst Blue Ribbon. Sorry."

"That's just what I was going to ask for," she replied with a grin.

Grady fetched another beer from the fridge, opened it and handed it to Anna over the bar. "I might as well play this bartender thing for all it's worth. Why don't you tell me about yourself."

Anna thought a moment before replying. "Ah, that's a loaded question. Where would you like me to start?"

"Start where it gets interesting," Grady suggested.

Anna paused, weighing her response carefully, before deciding that if Grady was truly going to help, he needed to know some things about her. "Well. At its most clinical . . . I'm the daughter of two loving but misguided parents who possessed inordinately high IQs. I was planned—if you will—to see if they could produce offspring that would surpass their own mental limits. To put it bluntly, I was their home-grown experiment."

Grady wasn't quite expecting such a pointed start to their conversation, and his face showed it for a moment before he could come up with a reply. "And the result of that test?"

"Tough to say exactly." Anna said honestly as she sipped her beer. "At what's called a resting, everyday level, I am told I'm approximately my parents' equal, no better, no worse. Although my IQ is still high."

"But . . . ?" Grady interjected, anticipating she had a *but* up her sleeve.

"But," Anna continued, taking his prompt. "I have moments . . . documented moments . . . that my IQ spikes off the charts. These spikes have been associated with dramatically increased brain activity." Grady shifted his body weight, and looked as if he was going to speak, but Anna decided to continue on. "You see, while most people use about ten percent of their brain at its most active levels, I have been studied with brain activities reaching as high as seventy-nine percent."

Grady set his drink down with a thud, at a loss for what to say next. The thought of someone possessing that type of cognitive ability struck him as impossible. Then again, there had to be some sort of explanation for the intense government interest he'd witnessed today. By the amount of force alone, Grady knew Anna had someone high up scared.

"So, what occurs with this increased activity?" he asked, reserving judgment for the moment.

Anna eyed Grady. She knew she had him enthralled but not convinced, although she liked that he appeared genuinely interested. Smiling, she delivered her next sentence as tactfully as she could, wondering if her answer would ultimately convince him that she was a complete nutcase.

"At times nothing . . . at times I can receive other people's thoughts . . . other times I can see what might happen in the future," she offered, shrugging as if she'd just told him she could talk while drinking water.

Grady's mouth dropped a bit, and he wanted to say something but held back.

"Anyway, those are the highlights," Anna continued, afraid she might be losing him. "I can also read, write, and speak ten different languages fluently. Of course there are others like me who have slightly varied skill sets."

"Others?" Grady asked just before swallowing a quarter of his beer in a couple gulps.

"Yes. I thought maybe you knew there were others. Particularly when you showed up at my doorstep that night. I thought maybe you had been sent by Northwoods."

"Actually I may have been, unwittingly." Grady noted, happy to have something to share, other than the sense of disbelief he was feeling.

Anna gazed at Grady's eyes, knowing what he said to be true. "Yes, I think you were their dupe . . . I'm sorry to say. I knew when you mentioned my father that you couldn't be directly linked to them . . . Northwoods, that is. You see; my father and my mother are dead. Have been for some time. Anyone directly linked to Northwoods would have known that. So I'm left with the only logical conclusion, that they chose you to locate me, either once they ran into their own dead ends or from the start to set you up."

"Sounds reasonable. So what about the others?"

"Well, there are four, perhaps five, that I know of. That is including myself. Over the years there have been lesser Naturals, but they never really made it in the program."

"Naturals?" Grady asked for clarification.

"I'm sorry. I'm getting ahead of myself." Anna apologized. "You see Naturals is Northwood's term for offspring produced in a natural way but resulting in someone like myself. We've also been assigned Seed numbers based on when we entered the program. I'm the first Seed. Anyway, these other Naturals and I escaped from Northwoods several weeks ago. We decided to split up shortly after our escape—mostly to confuse Northwoods. The others chose their own paths and I set off to find Mary Jane, which generally brings you up to date."

"I see," Grady said, still trying to process it all. "You mentioned a possible fifth?"

Anna breathed out through her nose, seeming frustrated . . . almost flustered. "Yes, I've never met him or her myself . . . as far as I know. I've only heard about this person. They call him—I'll use *him* for simplicity—The Fifth Seed. If the rumors roaming about Northwoods are true, he has an even more advanced skill set than any of the other four. There are some who believe that Northwoods created this myth or legend to keep the other four Naturals on edge. You see, as long as we assumed there was another Natural cooperating with Northwoods, who could somehow link into our own thoughts, we might not try to be deceptive. If he does exist—and I believe he does—he must be very powerful for the other Naturals to never have slipped into his thoughts and uncovered his identity."

Grady leaned in on the counter, fully engrossed. "So where are the others now? I'd imagine Northwoods is trying to contain them as desperately as they tried to contain you."

Anna felt a twinge of pain as she thought for the first time in a while about Curt. With no better way to handle the issue she simply blurted out. "One of them is dead."

Grady reached across the counter and touched Anna's hand. "I'm sorry."

"His name was Curt." Anna said with a choke of emotion. "I saw him in one of the visionary dreams I have. From what I can tell, he committed suicide." Taking a few moments to compose herself, Anna continued. "As for the other two, I don't know where they are. Last I knew they were safe. They've come to me in my dreams, but less often, as if they are distant. The odd thing is that they are always together."

"Why is that odd?"

"When we split up, we all agreed to go our different ways. I guess it was our way of attempting to preserve at least one from the group. It's much harder to contain four random individuals than a group of four, wouldn't you think?" Anna asked, looking for approval.

"I'd say yes," Grady replied supportively.

"I don't know, I guess we were hoping that one of us would survive to tell our story someday. I seem to be the communication link between us all. The others have similar abilities, but not quite as advanced in that area as mine. For some reason God has blessed me with being the connection—the one that can see and receive the other Naturals across great distances. Sounds odd, kind of unreal, doesn't it?"

Grady contemplated the question, one he wasn't sure he was completely prepared to answer just yet. In the end, what came out was unscripted and honest.

"You know Anna, if someone came to me and told me exactly what you've told me so far, I'd tell them to go jump in a lake. But I don't know . . . here I am with you, and I can't help but want to believe you. You say it and it sounds completely implausible, yet when I look in your eyes it somehow feels real. I don't know why."

Grady shifted uneasily before he delivered his next sentence, although his gaze never left Anna's deep and wondering brown eyes. "What I'm trying to say here is that I believe in you."

Anna smiled warmly. "I know you do, Grady that's what I . . ." But her voice trailed off before she could finish her sentence, perhaps saved for another time . . . another moment.

For a few seconds, an awkward silence hung in the air, before Grady chose to switch subjects. "Can I buy you another beer?"

Anna tilted her bottle and looked at the last few swallows she had left as if considering his offer. "Sure, but let's go sit where we can take in the view. Bring mine over to the couch. I'll be right back, I just have to check on the clothes I'm washing out."

Grady returned to the fridge and got two more ice cold Pabsts. He wandered slowly over to the windows—gazing down at the quiet little town below. He wondered what it was about Anna that made him feel so at ease one moment, and so tongue-tied the next—and he grappled with that thought for a while. He didn't realize it, but he must have been standing there for a while.

"You like the view?" Anna's sweet voice washed over him from close behind.

He turned to see she had gotten rid of her oversized sweatshirt and had on a more fitted, white Pink Floyd T-shirt, likely left over from a day when Elizabeth was several sizes smaller, and just a bit hipper. The short shirt's hem barely skimmed over the same sweatpants which were now tightly cinched with a length of black rope Anna had discovered

150

somewhere—possibly left over from the construction. The overall look returned the gentle curves to Anna's pretty figure.

"No offense to the Baileys, but I was swimming in the sweatshirt." Anna said. "The T-shirt is a little better. I discovered it hiding in the bottom of the bag under the clothes Mr. Bailey left for you. Maybe he was trying to get rid of it without his wife knowing" Anna laughed. "The rope I found in the bathroom, so I decided to put it to good use."

"Much better," Grady complimented her. "And yes, I like the view," he said, finally answering her question . . . although neither of them was quite sure which view they were talking about.

"Me too," Anna said, coming to Grady's side, taking her cold beer gently from his hand. She turned to the window, and Grady followed her cue—each looking back down into the picturesque valley. "How do you think she's doing?" Anna asked pensively.

"Mary Jane?" Grady guessed.

"Yes," came Anna's uncertain reply.

In a show of compassion Grady reached out and put his arm around Anna, pulling her in under his broad shoulder. "You'll have to tell me more about her when the time is right. But from briefly knowing you, and how strong you are, and how strong she's made you, I'm guessing she's a pretty remarkable and resourceful woman."

"I hope so, Grady. I really hope so."

CHAPTER 37

UNHAPPY RETURNS

Mary Jane sat in a small windowless room somewhere in the bowels of Northwoods. The furnishings consisted of a twin bed set into a far corner, covered with scratchy, polyester bed linens. Next to the bed was a flimsy particleboard nightstand with absolutely nothing on it, while an overhead light with a metal enclosure cast its caged shadow across the filthy floor. The floor must have been tiled some years ago in a retro black and white checkerboard, but the white tiles had since yellowed to an unsightly tea-stained hue. With her shoes and socks confiscated, Mary Jane did her best to keep her feet off the bitterly cold floor.

Upon arrival, she had received further medical care for her wound. It wasn't much, barely amounting to a thorough cleaning, suturing, and redressing of the affected site, but at least it was clean. After her brief treatment she had been offered a tasteless turkey sandwich to eat, with plenty of water to help her rehydrate. In addition, the staff had placed her on a routine course of antibiotics to help prevent infection.

To Mary Jane, even the modest care she was being given was good news. It meant two things in her mind. First, they weren't trying to kill her . . . yet. And second, Anna had most likely gotten away. Why else would Northwoods go to the trouble of healing her? If they had recaptured Anna they wouldn't need her, Mary Jane told herself.

Just as Mary Jane was working through this in her head, the door to her tiny cell swung in with a gentle gust of air, and her old boss, Dr. Allan Hauser, entered. He stood about five-foot nine and wore a white lab coat, with smallish squared-off spectacles framing his square, angular face. Just over his thin lip he grew a furry, graying mustache with subtle auburn hints, and Mary Jane figured it was to make up for the hair he was losing on his head.

She knew the doctor well from her prior work here, and in the early years had developed a fairly good personal relationship with him. Of course, all of that was well in the past. Allan smiled—like a physician visiting his next patient—as he strode into the room. "Welcome back," he said without a hint of sincerity in his deep, throaty voice—one that seemed out of place for a short, thin man. "You've had quite an adventure, from what I hear."

Mary Jane said nothing. Instead, she just glared back at Allan, his mocking pleasantries only serving to infuriate her. So she bit her lip in an effort to hold back.

"Not in the mood to talk, are we?" Allan inquired as he ran the tips of his fingers across his mustache—a little tick he had developed when he was lost in deep thought, or desired a dramatic pause. The moment over, he dropped his hand to his side and let out a deliberate sigh. "You really ought to be more cooperative," he said, still trying to achieve a measure of civility. "I must tell you, we are very close to finding Anna, and things might go better for her if you choose to be cooperative."

"Why? So you can kill me off just like you did Benjamin?" Mary Jane asked, still keeping her tone even, burying her deep-seated anger.

Almost instantly the fake smile Allan wore fell off his face, and he let his true emotions surface. "Do you know who you're dealing with?" He yelled, baring his coffee-stained teeth. "We can make life modestly unpleasant for you, or we can make it extremely painful. Your choice."

"I don't give a damn about anything you want me to do, or what you may or may not do to me. You never understood and you never will. This is all about Anna and her safety . . . it's not about me anymore . . .

it's not even about you. Why couldn't you have just let her walk out that door? You know and I know we couldn't touch this place."

"No! You never understood." Allan seethed back at Mary Jane. "This place is everything . . . it's not the individuals . . . it's the end goal. That's where the value lies, for every goddamn person out there," he said, sweeping his arms in a gesture that implied more than Northwoods itself. "Anna's just an experiment that has gotten out of control and become a liability. She's the beginning, not the end. And if you believe someone like her can't make all this come crashing down someday . . . you're more hopeless than I thought!"

"Christ, you're insane," Mary Jane said, almost in disbelief.

"You're wrong . . . the world's going insane. Just look at 9/11. What the hell are we supposed to do to protect our freedom, our way of life, our position of superiority? I'm doing my part to ensure that. What the hell are you doing?"

"I'm working to bury bastards like you." Mary Jane yelled, finally caving into her emotions. "Do what you want to me, I'm not afraid of your threats."

Suddenly the doctor shot forward, moving in quickly to stoop over Mary Jane. Placing his ugly mug uncomfortably close, delivering his next words with such intensity that Mary Jane could feel miniscule droplets of his spit pelting her. "Oh, you should be Mary . . . you really should."

Standing upright, he turned to leave, but thought better of it, wanting to add one more coal to the fire. When he turned back his face was more composed and serious. "One way or another you'll tell us what you know. You'll tell us if you know where Anna may have gone. You'll give us the names of anybody you've leaked information to. And you'll tell us anything you know regarding the whereabouts of the other two Seeds. And since I'm not one for suspense—as I'm sure you've already guessed—once we're through with you . . . you'll die."

Allan again turned on his heels to leave, but this time it was Mary Jane who stopped him. Getting up from her bed, showing no favoritism for her injured leg, she shot her own verbal volley to the man's back. "You lied," she said with a tremble in her voice. "You have no clue where

Anna is, do you? Otherwise you wouldn't be here threatening me. But that doesn't really matter now, does it? Because either way you know I'll never lead you to her."

The doctor tensed but never turned to face her. Instead, he let her have her say before continuing out the door without another word.

Shaking from the encounter, Mary Jane fell back into her bed and stared blankly at the ceiling. She was walking a dangerous line. She knew she held a secret that Northwoods wanted. At the moment, she had no clue where Anna was, but in a little over a week's time she was certain where Anna would be. Mary Jane knew where they all would be . . . Anna had broken the covenant between the Naturals. She had told Mary about the rendezvous. *How would she protect that secret and her own life?* At the moment she hadn't a clue.

As she contemplated it all, gazing into the white ceiling light, its bright glow abruptly extinguished, and Mary Jane was immersed in total blackness. "Let the mind games begin," she whispered softly to herself.

CHAPTER 38

THE DEVIL'S DEAL

Allan stormed into The Kid's room, throwing the door open with such violence that it slammed against the wall and ricocheted back toward his face, his hands just catching the swinging metal door before it had a chance to bloody his beak-like nose.

The Kid sat quietly in his chair, watching calmly as the doctor entered. "Can I help you?" he asked with an amused grin.

Allan glared at The Kid. He was sitting so laid-back and innocent in his chair with that damn blue baseball cap he always wore. Right now it infuriated him, but he didn't know exactly why. "Hell yes . . . you're back in."

The Kid's eyes lit up. It was what he anticipated. His message must have gotten through to Anna, which meant she had probably escaped. It would explain the doctor's mood. "What may I do to be of service?" he asked with mock politeness.

The doctor seemed to be settling down just a little bit, moderating his anger and focusing on the task at hand. "Two things," he said. "First I need you to try to hitchhike off of Anna's dreams. Perhaps they will give us some clue as to where she is, or where the other two have gone."

"You understand the dangers of that?" The Kid asked, mildly surprised at the request.

"To hell with the dangers. Just do it."

The Kid contemplated the request. "Okay, but just so you understand, we have gone to great lengths to conceal my identity from her. Trying to hitchhike off her dreams might put all those efforts to waste."

Exasperated, Allan shot back. "What the hell did I just tell you? Make it happen."

Seeing an opportunity, The Kid couldn't resist. "Fine. But what's in it for me?"

"What? You want Anna alive?" Allan asked rhetorically. "Sure, whatever, it's done."

The Kid grinned at his quick victory, deciding to push his luck and add another contingency. "Good, and this time, I want to be there when you make a play for her."

Allan hesitated, running through the complications of such a prospect, but finally relented. "Done. Anything else before I leave?" He asked sarcastically.

"You said there was a second item, or had you misspoken?"

Flustered and furious at being played, Allan needed to put The Kid in his place. "Don't be a smartass," he bit back. "You need us and you know it."

The Kid nodded, realizing he was perhaps being a little too cocky with the doctor.

Seeing that The Kid understood, Allan continued. "Yes, there is one more thing. While Mitch and his crew may have botched another play for Anna, they did succeed in obtaining Mary Jane, and our cleanup crew seems to have managed to "neatly" dispose of any evidence that may have been left behind. I need you to read her, get into her thoughts and tell us anything she is withholding."

"That could be tricky. She served as a therapist here for a long time. As you know, many of them have developed their own techniques to lock us out," The Kid cautioned.

Allan stared at The Kid for a few seconds, wondering if he was making a grave mistake by bringing him in. "You leave the softening up to me, okay?" Allan said, finally responding to The Kid's concerns. "Her weakness is the girl and vise-versa . . . so maybe there is something there that we can use to our advantage. I'll have to think about that. If not, pain is always a good motivator."

CHAPTER 39

ANNA'S SECRET

G rady and Anna spoke at length about Mary Jane, with Grady asking all sorts of questions about her research and her relationship with Anna. Anna did her best to fill Grady in, helping him understand just how much Mary Jane meant to her. Based on Anna's description, Grady hoped he might someday be fortunate enough to meet this remarkable woman.

Noticing he was sucking air from his beer bottle, the last drops long gone, Grady suggested that they take a little break. Retiring to the kitchen, they made themselves a sandwich from the food Grady had pilfered from the main house; then Grady thought it best to leave Anna alone with her thoughts for a while. As she set about the task of trying to settle in and relax on the couch, Grady took the opportunity to shower and change.

Twenty minutes later he came back out, dressed in Mr. Bailey's sweatshirt and a pair of jeans, about four inches too large in the waist. His own belt did the cinching, and he looked almost as ridiculous as Anna had in Elizabeth's clothes. Refreshed though, and ready to resume their conversation, Grady returned to the couch only to discover Anna sound asleep.

Not in the least bit interested in disturbing her, he went back to the refrigerator and popped open a can of Coke. With that done, he softly eased his way out the two French doors that led to the long, magnificent cedar deck running across the full face of the cottage.

He sat there for almost two hours, watching as darkness fell and lights in the town below began to glow like bright stars dotting the landscape. If you asked him what he had thought about during that time, he couldn't have told you—only what he was thinking in the moment. Such was his tired mind that it meandered from one topic to the next with little rhyme or reason. As a result, he felt he'd gotten no closer to solving their problems.

Checking his watch, he realized it was nearly 7:30, just as the songbirds perched in the nearby trees began bidding farewell to the day, and perhaps a season. After all, it was mid-September, and a cool chill hung in the air, signaling the end of Minnesota warmth. He wondered if he should go check on Anna. She had been sleeping a while and he desperately wanted her company. But he thought better of it, deciding her rest was more important than assuaging his loneliness.

Another fifteen minutes passed, much like the last, before he finally decided to get out of the comfy Adirondack chair to go back for another beer. He half rose when the whispery creek of the French doors signaled someone was stepping outside, onto the deck.

"Don't get up," Anna said with the slight hint of a yawn, moving over to the second, empty Adirondack just to the right of Grady. "I brought you one already," she added, holding up the beer.

"How did you . . . ?" Grady began, but considering their earlier conversation decided not to ask.

"Don't be silly," she said as she eased down into her own seat, anticipating not only his question, but also his conclusion. "I just guessed about the beer. I need more to go on than that. Generally I need to see someone's eyes to actually read them. I guess I also watch their body language and try to pick up on cues others could easily pick up on, but just don't recognize."

"Sorry, I guess I'm rambling on," Anna apologized as she handed Grady the beer.

"No, don't apologize" Grady said accepting the drink. "Could you read me now?" he asked. "I mean with me sitting here face-to-face with you . . . could you tell me what I'm thinking?"

"Perhaps," she said honestly. "Perhaps not. You have to understand that extreme emotions are easiest to read while simple thoughts that are on other people's minds would require deep concentration, an intense state of relaxed consciousness or maybe even drugs."

"Drugs?" Grady asked with concerned interest.

Anna half smiled. "Yes, unfortunately Northwoods used us as guinea pigs. In addition to the isolation, emotional abuse and institutionalization, in the latter years, Northwoods also employed drugs in an attempt to boost our skill set. They tested all kinds on us. Couldn't even begin to tell you them all. But for some reason, drug cocktails that induced intense relaxation and increased brain function seemed to work out for them the best. I guess you'd say the state they tried to have us reach was almost a mirror of sleep . . . only conscious."

"What about addictions?" Grady asked, again implying concern.

Anna sighed. "That was a problem. Curt had difficulties with it . . . the others too, to a lesser degree. In the beginning Curt was misguided. He tried to cooperate with Northwoods, accepting the drugs and participating in their tests without question. They put him in their own form of drug treatment a few times to bring him back, which was mildly successful. But then they would just start pumping him with different drugs and the cycle would repeat. Eventually he began to resent Northwoods just like the rest of us, but he was hooked. When we escaped he said he was clean, but I don't know. Especially considering . . ." but Anna's voice trailed off, unable to finish her sentence.

"What about you?"

Anna smiled at the question, not minding Grady's interest or concern in the least. "I never wanted to cooperate. I always resisted, so they had to force drugs on me. For me, they were truly horrible experiences . . . ones I never wanted to repeat if you get my meaning. So, as a result, I associated the drugs with bad feelings . . . unhappy times.

I'm guessing that's why I never had a problem like Curt. It was never fun, for lack of a better word."

Grady wasn't sure what to say. He didn't want to push Anna into more disturbing topics if she didn't want to discuss them right now. He was guessing she might have had enough of this line of questioning.

As the conversation lagged once more, a hawk screeched high overhead in the darkness. The sound seemed to create a connection in Anna's mind.

"You know, we could learn a lot from animals."

"What do you mean?" Grady said, glad that Anna was directing the conversation where she'd like it to go.

"Well, let's take your everyday housedog for example. The one everyone refers to as a dumb animal. But even they, in all their silly, loveable ways, are remarkable. They have the ability to sense danger, smell fear and read the slightest changes in posturing. As humans we all have, or had, similar abilities, it's just that somewhere, somehow along the line of evolution we began relying more on verbal skills and less on our natural instincts. As a result, many of those skills were pushed to the back . . . some may have even simply faded away."

"Is this how you read people?"

Anna thought for a moment about her reply. "Sure, it's part of it. I'd call what I can do an extension of those suppressed skills. My ability to read people could be a part of our natural evolution, or a freakish glitch, like a frog that's born with five legs."

"I'd never call it freakish. Let's say unique." Grady said supportively before switching the topic slightly. "So you never took the bait before . . . can you tell me what I'm thinking?"

Laughing, Anna said, "So now you're testing me huh . . . don't trust me, do you?"

A hurt look flashed across Grady's face. "That's not what I meant," he said genuinely.

"Oh, Grady," Anna soothed, "it was just a joke. If you're game, let's try it—although I'm not promising anything in this light," she said, glancing briefly up at a nearly full moon above, nestled in just beyond the shadowy limbs of the overhanging trees.

"It would help if you thought of something intensely emotional," she instructed, "perhaps an extremely happy or sublimely sad time in your life."

Thinking hard, Grady gazed up at the stars as if trying to come up with something, but Anna quickly scolded him. "You have to look into my eyes, buddy, or this isn't gonna work."

Grady's eyes quickly came back down to earth, locating and latching onto Anna's own beautiful pools of deep and mysterious brown. Again the eyes . . . incredible, he thought, flickering with such life and intensity . . . particularly with the moonlight glinting off just so. Forgetting his task, Grady found for a moment, all he could think of was this vision before him. She was so unlike Nancy, but somehow Anna reminded him of her. Not the features, or the personality, but the feelings of closeness and connection—that for the first time since Nancy's death, someone else was starting to touch his heart.

Watching Anna's own eyes intently, Grady noticed a look of interested curiosity, mixed with glint of hope, as if something Anna had seen had made her very happy. Then quickly the look faded into a frown, and her whole being took on the appearance of abject sadness. Finally, she turned away, looking down the long neck of her fresh beer.

Unable to look at Grady, she asked quietly. "Who is Nancy?"

Grady nearly spilt his beer, hearing Anna say Nancy's name, and he looked at her in stunned silence. Grasping for words, he ended up choosing the only thing that came to mind. "An old flame."

Anna turned back to Grady, and resumed eye contact. "How did she die?"

Even more shocked, Grady was left speechless. He had said he believed all that Anna had told him about herself, but to be faced with the reality, he was completely caught off-guard. Finally he got himself together to answer the question. "She was beaten to death."

"And you were accused." Anna added sadly. "I guess it's my turn to be sorry, Grady."

"No, no . . ." Grady pleaded with her. "It's alright. Don't be sorry, it's a part of my past that I deal with as best I can."

Keeping eye contact, Anna said, "I know you didn't do it, if that helps at all," her voice even and unwavering.

Grady wanted to reach out and touch Anna, but he thought better of it. "That means a lot to me," he said instead. "You know, even with my closest friends I can tell that, as much as they want to believe in me, there's always that sliver of doubt behind their eyes. But with you . . . I mean . . . anyway, it means a lot to me."

Anna smiled appreciatively. "Can you do me a favor?"

"Name it."

"Will you tell me about her . . . about you . . . just the two of us here, acting like two normal people?" she asked. "Please, no more mind games tonight."

"Sure," Grady replied respectfully. And with that, Grady began from the beginning—starting with how he and Nancy had met in college.

Nearly an hour passed before he finished the story, and Anna had listened, completely engrossed in his tale, asking few questions and letting Grady lead the conversation where he may. "That's it," he said. "Not much else to tell. "They never found her killer, and I am, as far as I know, still a suspect. They never had enough evidence to bring me to trial."

"Thank you for telling me," Anna said sincerely. "Are there any other suspects that you know of?"

"I have my own suspicions, but I'm not sure if the police ever followed up on them," Grady said, sighing heavily.

"Someday you'll have to tell me," Anna offered, not wanting to put Grady through any more. "But it seems to be getting late and I'm dying to take a soak in the hot tub. Is it working?" she asked.

"Yes," Grady said, now suddenly apprehensive. "We turned it on the other weekend, shocked the system and even used it ourselves. It should be ready to go."

Hearing that, Anna stood slowly, her eyes fixed on Grady as if considering something. "I'd invite you in, but I don't have any . . ." her voice trailed off, not wanting to finish the sentence.

Grady was mildly relieved. "I understand." He said. "I'm very tired and will probably just lay down. You know where the towels are, and the control knob is on the sidewall. If you have any questions . . . well . . . ask before you get in." Grady said with smile.

"Thank you for today," Anna said kindly, adding, "and thank you for tonight." With that said she turned to the French doors to go.

"Anna." Grady called out, stopping her just as she grasped the door handle.

Not wanting to turn back, she simply asked, "Yes?" half expecting a request she wasn't sure she could deny, but for all the wrong reasons.

"Your father—excuse me—the man who posed as your father . . . he said you were seventeen? How . . ."

With her hand clutching the doorknob and her forehead resting softly against the windowpane, in some mix of relief and regret, Anna smiled to herself. "I'm 24," she said finishing his sentence, rounding up just a few months. "He lied to you because legally when I turned eighteen a real father shouldn't have been able to keep me privately institutionalized. Unless I was a threat to society—otherwise, I'd be able to do as I wished. As far as I know, Northwoods kept us all at a perpetual seventeen on their records."

"Is that all?" she asked.

"That's it I guess."

"Good night, Grady," she said softly.

"Good night Anna," he answered back, kicking himself for letting her walk away.

CHAPTER 40

REGRETS

Anna eased herself slowly into the churning waters, still wearing the T-shirt from Elizabeth. It was concealing enough for a private dip in the hot tub, though she wouldn't care to be discovered in it. She figured she wouldn't need it tomorrow, since she had checked the clothes she had washed out and they were drying nicely.

In the hot tub, she leaned her head back and let the warm, bubbling fray soothe her neck and wet the long curly tips of her black hair. She thought for a while about Grady, admonishing herself briefly for the way she teased him at the end of their conversation. She had done it in part to get a read on him. Get his reaction. Yet, she found herself disappointed to see the relief on his face when she didn't ask him into the hot tub.

She wondered if 24 was too young for him. He certainly made a point to find out her age. She guessed Grady to be in his early thirties, perhaps only 32. That seemed to be the number that kept floating around her head, so she went with that assumption. Eight years difference wasn't bad at all, she thought, allowing herself a little satisfaction.

Anna lifted her arms to the surface of the foaming water, and waved them back and forth, soaking in the heat. As she did, she glanced around at the dark tree limbs that impinged on the raised deck. It was quite beautiful here, and she felt as if she never wanted to leave. But she knew that wasn't possible.

Again she thought of Mary Jane, and instantly became upset with herself for her enjoyment over the last few hours. Here she was flirting with a man she had basically just met today, relaxing in a hot tub while Mary Jane was probably holed up in a cell somewhere at Northwoods.

Suddenly Anna felt extremely depressed, and vestiges of self-hatred began to bubble inside her. "What would Mary Jane think? What would she say to you right now?" she scolded herself. For a moment, she pondered that thought, looking up at the stars in the night sky as if they might offer an answer.

In her mind, Anna imagined Mary Jane speaking to her, letting her know she was okay and not to worry . . . telling her that she deserved to be free . . . that with or without her, Anna had to finish what they had set out to do. To destroy Northwoods . . . expose it for all it was.

"But how?" Anna whispered to the soft night breeze, imagining the wind carrying her question to her adoptive mother and friend. "But how?"

At the same moment, Grady was lying uncomfortably on the sofa. He had found an extra sheet and blanket in a closet upstairs in the loft, and had converted the cushions into his bed. Right now his eyes were gazing up at the lofted inside peak of the cottage. As he followed the slow revolution of a ceiling fan suspended from the wooden rafters he thought sleep might never come.

He worried about Anna, and if the mild flirting that happened today was the right thing. Life had become so complicated, and to add that to the mix could just make a huge mess. She was 24, and he had just turned 32, so age really wasn't an issue. After all, his grandma and grandpa were ten years apart when they married at the young ages of 21 and 31. Both he and Anna were now several years past that. So what was it that bothered him?

For a moment, he imagined her outside, alone in the hot tub and wondered about the possibilities. But he quickly put them out of his mind. For now, they had to figure out what to do next. They couldn't stay here forever, though the thought seemed nice right now. Still, even simple lives had to move on, and for both of them, the future was so much more complicated.

He knew he had to find a way to extract Mary Jane from Northwood's grip, and he knew he couldn't rest until Anna could live her life the way she chose. Yet, the fact that at some level, the Federal Government seemed to be wrapped up in all of this made him wonder if it would ever be possible.

It felt odd that he had once been a player, that he had once held a government position with the FBI. It seemed so long ago. Yet the day he was let go also felt as if it were yesterday. He remembered the day, and always would.

Grady's direct superior had called him in just a week after Nancy's body had been recovered. They'd put him on temporary leave, which turned out to be permanent. His director told him it was not his choice, and orders had come down from above. Grady often wondered if it had been a cop-out, but he guessed he would never be sure.

Though Grady vehemently insisted he was innocent, his director said even the appearance of impropriety could give the Bureau a black eye. And given other public relations fiascos the agency had recently had with the media, they had to offer the appearance of cleaning house, ousting the bad apples.

Before leaving his superior's office, the man had told him he would be fully reinstated once Grady had been cleared of all suspicion of wrongdoing. Although, since the case had never been brought to trial and Grady was the primary suspect, the Bureau chose to cut ties with him after six months.

It had been the end of his life as he knew it; the loss of Nancy, the loss of his job, and the loss of many friendships that were tied to his life's work.

Now, Anna seemed to have rekindled some of his spirit . . . rejuvenated him. But the obvious complexities of a relationship, under their current circumstances, made his head swim.

As he wrestled with these issues, the side door to the hot-tub deck opened slowly and Anna stepped through, once again wrapped up in the thick embrace of the terry-cloth robe. She crossed the room silently, on light tiptoes, and then made her way up the spiral stairs into the loft. A light turned on briefly, and then was extinguished. And there, in the still darkness of the cottage, both Anna and Grady wrestled with sleep.

CHAPTER 41

TRENT AND JOE

D rifting off into a deep REM sleep, Anna began to dream again. It began with her and Grady—returning to the cottage in simpler times—laughing, sharing, and enjoying each other's closeness. In her unconscious mind she imagined they were free to discover their feelings for each other, slowly and romantically without care, touring the town below by day and making love by night.

Yet as they walked hand-in-hand along a cobbled street, between their exploration of shops and greeting cheerful merchants, two familiar figures stepped suddenly from the shadows of a dark alley and Grady instantly vanished. Now, instead of being in this peaceful midwestern town, she was in a city she did not recognize.

Above, old architectural structures seemed to lick at the vanilla sky, and she watched as the two men—Trent and Joe—wandered down the milling streets of this foreign town, oblivious to her presence. After several blocks, they turned down a narrow alley, through an open arched gateway and into a courtyard. There, they entered what appeared to be a lobby and were lost to the shadows. The sign above the door read in French script, L'Hotel something, but she couldn't make it out, the letters a frustrating blur.

Both young men looked safe, happy and in good health. As they entered the hotel, her mind willed itself to follow them inside, but something stopped her. Apparently this was all she was going to be allowed to see. But there was something else, something that made her hold the vision for a second longer. It was an odd presence that she could not explain. It seemed dark and ominous, and it blotted out any sunlight that filtered into this tiny French garden.

The darkness closed in, obscuring her surroundings until they became foggy shadows dissolving into blackness. There she floated, suspended in the murk, as a feeling of dread and doom filled her soul. She wanted to scream . . . to run . . . to flee from this horrendous feeling, but she was helpless.

From out of the blackness, an arm reached through as if parting a pair of silky curtains. The hand vaguely familiar and safe—perhaps it was Grady's. Contemplating the meaning, she reached for the disembodied hand, its palm outstretched as if bidding her to hold on and follow. As she grasped it, the fingers closed on hers so tightly it hurt and Anna gripped back with equal force, as the inky vision about her began to rotate violently around the arm.

Anna was being sucked through, as if caught in the unrelenting gravitational pull of a black hole. She closed her eyes and held on for her life, waiting for the dizzying spin to end. Eventually the feeling ebbed and there seemed to be a sense of incredible peacefulness and calm about her. Realizing her eyes were still closed, she slowly parted her eyelids, like a child frightened by a horror film, wanting to see but not wanting to see at the same time.

Her vision slowly resolved upon a place of brilliant white light as she still gripped the hand that led her here. Turning, she gazed up, looking to the face that was there, afraid of what she might see, hoping she was right and it would be Grady's. The person's features were diffused by a halo of light as intense as the midday sun. Searching hard, her eyes adjusted to the glow, as an image gradually began to emerge. And as Anna recognized the figure, her anxieties were supplanted by a feeling of sublime joy.

Trying to hold the picture in her mind, she didn't want to let it go. She needed to know more, to understand what the appearance meant, but like sand being carried away by the currents of a stream, the image began to filter away, grain by tiny grain.

CHAPTER 42

THE NEXT MORNING

Anna awoke to the aroma of fresh brewed hazelnut coffee, the distinct scent teasing her nose. From down below, she could hear Grady moving about, making preparations for the day. Sliding out of bed, she made her way over to the dresser mirror and began straightening the robe she had slept in, carefully readjusting the belt that had loosened in her sleep. She quickly ran her hands through her matted curls, returning some of the body that had been lost to the plump feather pillows. Mildly satisfied with her appearance, she crossed the wood floors in her bare feet and headed downstairs.

She was happier today. Her dream had boosted her spirits, and made her wonder if things might turn out better than she had hoped.

"Good morning." Grady said brightly as Anna approached the kitchen, noticing she was again wearing the robe. It seemed to bother him less today.

Anna smiled warmly, returning his greeting. "Good morning. Is that hazelnut coffee I smell?"

"I take it you'd like a cup. Black okay?" he asked. "I forgot to get cream and sugar on my trip to the house yesterday, so . . ."

"Black's perfect," Anna answered, her eyes bright and alive.

Grady busied himself, getting a mug from the cupboard and pouring her a cup. Returning to her, he found Anna had once again taken a seat on the other side of the counter. Grady seemed to notice the difference in her mood. "You appear to be in better spirits today."

Anna wasn't sure she was ready to tell Grady about her dream just yet. She wanted to mull it over in her head a while longer so she simply replied with a shrug. "It's a new day."

Grady sensed she wasn't telling him something, but he was reluctant to press her, so he let it go.

"So, what's the plan?" Anna inquired.

Breathing out heavily, Grady thought for a moment before answering. "Mr. Bailey . . . John . . . said he would bring breakfast by from the house at 8:30. It's 7:30 now so we have a while. I thought after breakfast we could freshen up and then head into town, buy some clothes and other essentials. But from there, I'm not sure. I'd like to make a few phone calls, but not from here. I have a few friends left who are in a position to help, but making contact with them could be risky, possibly revealing our location."

Anna nodded thoughtfully. "Does that mean we'll have to leave here soon?"

"Probably. Either way, I'd rather not draw the Baileys too far into this mess. They're good people and I'd hate to get them in any trouble."

Picking up her cup of coffee, Anna sighed, "I guess I'll hop in the shower then, and see if my other clothes have dried off. That is, unless you wanted to go first."

"No, you go ahead. I'm going to run down to the house to see if I can't get a newspaper. I was hoping to see if yesterday's events in Rochester made the paper. It will give me a read on how effectively Northwoods was in managing to cover things up. At some point we have to formulate a plan of action, and the more I know about how intertwined Northwoods is with the Feds, the better. It could dictate how we go about trying to free Mary Jane and in the process, expose Northwoods. I'm guessing one more night here, then we'll move. To where and how, I don't know yet."

"Grady?" Anna asked, momentarily putting off a shower.

"Yes?"

Pausing, as if unsure how to phrase her next question without causing too many questions, Anna finally just asked him outright. "Do you happen to have a passport?"

"Not with me. Why?" he asked, an odd look crossing his face.

Anna smiled evasively. "It's a hunch I have that I need to tell you about—but not now. I've got to think about it some more."

"Do *you* have a passport?" Grady asked, throwing the question back at Anna.

"No," she said flatly, "but it's something you might want to think about."

"I'll see what I can do. Now go take that shower before the day's already over." Eying Anna skeptically, he added, "I'm guessing it's going to be busier than I anticipated."

At the main house, Grady bought the *Rochester Post Bulletin* and the *Minneapolis Star Tribune* from a couple of vending machines outside. He went inside, found Mr. Bailey and asked if he could use his phone one more time. Once again Mr. Bailey obliged, leading Grady to his office before leaving him alone to his phone call.

"You can reset the clock again, buddy," Grady said as Tom picked up the phone. "Then I've got a couple of favors to ask if you're up to it. If you agree, I'll call you back later today with a final go ahead."

"Anything." Tom offered without hesitation. "Shoot."

"Good," Grady said, satisfied. "I may need you to go into my house and retrieve something for me. The police may be watching, so sneak in the back. If that's a problem tell me."

"A little cat burglary," Tom laughed. "I think I can manage."

"Perfect." Grady said, ignoring Tom's apparent amusement. "Use your key, the one I gave you when you watched my house. Let yourself in and then head to the basement. Remember that file I told you about, the one behind the cinderblock?"

"Yeah."

"Grab that whole file, but ignore the note I left for you. Don't toss it . . . just keep it. The plan still holds: if you don't hear from me for 48 hours, follow what I say in the letter to a T."

"Okay Grady, once I have the file then what?" Tom asked impatiently.

"Right . . . next go to my dresser upstairs and get my passport out of the top drawer, then go back down to my computer and log on. It's password AL076BT. Do a global search for Bill Atkins. Once you find the name, you'll come across several ways to discreetly get in touch with him. You'll have to contact him, meet him ASAP, and get him that photo of Anna in the file. Tell him I sent you and you need a passport made like it was yesterday. It's for Anna, but have him give her my last name and address."

Tom considered a probing comment but thought better of it, instead waiting for more instructions.

"Hey, and Tom," Grady continued. "He's a snitch, so if you do this for me, watch yourself, but he should be able to get what we need without too much trouble. Also, since it's a rush job, you'll need at least five to seven hundred fifty in cash, maybe more up front, but you know I'm good for it. That sound okay?"

"Of course," Tom said happy to help. "I'll wait for your go-ahead," and then both men hung up.

Back at the cottage, Grady remained inside the car. Opening the *Post Bulletin* first, he read the lead story of the front page before he swapped it out for the *Star Tribune*. The story was a lesser item, covered in regional news, but it contained basically the same info. Finally he looked further and found a tiny two-paragraph article he had been hoping to find. It wasn't good news. Tom would have his work cut out for him.

Refolding both papers carefully, he exposed the stories he wanted on top, then re-tucked them under his arm before carefully balancing the sack of food the Baileys had prepared for them and headed inside.

When he got there, Anna looked fresh, clean, and neatly dressed in her newly washed clothes, sipping hot coffee at the counter. Grady greeted her and plopped the bag of food in front of her. He let her unpack the freshly baked pastries and two servings of eggs benedict from the foam to-go cartons as he split the last of the coffee between their two cups, started a fresh pot, and gathered silverware.

Anna watched as Grady finished his tasks and returned to the other side of the marble counter. He was unusually quiet and she began to wonder if she had done something to upset him. For a moment, she thought the chemistry that energized the room last night might have been lost.

Saying nothing, as Anna began to eat her food, Grady picked up one of the newspapers and plopped it in front of her. "Take a look," he said, giving no hint as to what she was reading.

Anna took another sip of her coffee and peered over her cup at the front page of the *Rochester Post Bulletin*. As she began to read, her eyes widened, and she looked back to Grady for answers.

"Sorry, I should have told you yesterday, but I thought you needed a break," Grady apologized.

Anna looked back at the paper, still in shock, scanning the text as Grady began to summarize what he had already read. "They blew up the doctor's house. I wasn't sure, but I was afraid of it—Benjamin was still inside when it went up."

Anna kept reading, hoping she wouldn't find another name listed among the dead, but Grady saved her the time. "He was the only one inside. Mary Jane wasn't there; I'm guessing we've been right all along and she's at least safe for now back at Northwoods."

Relieved Anna eyes returned to Grady's. "What does this mean?"

"The cause of the explosion is still under investigation. But the initial speculation is a gas leak. Unofficially it's an accident. There's a possibility they might find some bullets in the wreckage, but they won't look that closely once they attribute it to the leak. The cleanup crew probably collected most of them, and those that weren't found probably melted from the heat. If we were hoping for Northwoods to make a mistake and open the door for us, they sure closed it damn fast."

Now Anna knew why Grady was so quiet and frustrated, although deep down she was relieved he wasn't upset with her. Not knowing exactly what to say, she offered her own apology. "I'm sorry."

Grady didn't respond; instead, he dropped the *Star Tribune* down in front of Anna with the smaller article showing this time, but this one he didn't even give her the chance to read. "This is a follow-up to a story that must have run yesterday. It's about the shooting at Mary Jane's. The police apparently have a suspect, but aren't releasing any names. I'm guessing the suspect is me."

Anna looked at Grady with questioning eyes.

"You didn't know this," Grady said, "but the gunman who held us that night was using my gloves and my gun. I figure he wanted to frame me for . . ." his voice trailed off, unable to say the last few words, letting Anna fill in the blanks.

"Anyway," he continued, "I got the gun and gloves back before the police arrived, but someone called the cops and tipped them that my vehicle had been spotted in the lot. The cops showed up at my place two nights ago, asking a bunch of questions. They were particularly interested in my gun."

Grady paused for a breath, watching Anna closely as she digested the new information. "I'm guessing they've already searched my place pretty thoroughly, and might even be waiting for me to return."

Anna looked crestfallen and Grady knew she was taking on blame that she shouldn't. He was being his usual coarse self when it came to casework. Softening his tone, he reached out to her, saying, "It's going to be okay. I figured this would happen. But you need to know, I've got a guy waiting to break into my house. He's a good friend and he'll pull a picture of you for a fake passport, and collect mine. But before I send him into the lion's den, I need to know something from you."

"What?" Anna asked apprehensively.

"Where are we going?"

Anna smiled shyly at Grady, "France."

CHAPTER 43

On The Town

The sun reached high in the clear blue sky as Grady and Anna walked along the quaint sidewalks of Lanesboro. There, they meandered in and out of small shops as they purchased everything they would need for the next leg of their trip, including several days' worth of clothing, a second-hand suitcase, makeup, and toiletries. Grady always kept a generous amount of cash in his wallet for emergencies, but they were running through his reserves at a rapid rate. He had several credit cards, but he was reluctant to use them, for fear they might leave an electronic trail others could follow.

"We're going to have to find an alternate source of cash," Grady finally said as they meandered lazily off to the next shop.

"That's alright for now. I think I'm almost done. How about you?" Anna asked slipping her arm into the crook of his, the first real contact they had had all morning.

"I was thinking more for the trip . . . but I'm happy to hear your spree is almost at an end," he said, nodding toward the heavy shopping bags he was carrying for her. "I'd hate to see the damage you could do at the Mall of America," he added with a chuckle.

"You're impossible, you know that?" she said in an obviously false huff.

Not thinking, Grady replied. "Well, at least you'll have something else to wear beside that robe."

Anna slipped her arm out of Grady's and stopped dead in her tracks, letting him take another two paces before he suddenly realized Anna wasn't going to follow. Turning, back to her, Grady knew he had said the wrong thing.

With a genuinely hurt look on her face she asked, "What the hell was wrong with the robe?"

Blushing now, Grady tried to make up for his mistake. "It was uh . . . it's, how would you say . . ." he stammered, but never finished his thought.

It was enough though, and Anna felt a bit of smug satisfaction at his unease. She knew what he was struggling with, and he didn't really know how to say it without further embarrassing himself.

Then in his own mock perturbed way, he said, "For heaven's sake, just come on. You know what I mean."

"Yes, but I'd like to hear you say it." She jabbed, quickly making up the lost paces between them to relock arms.

Changing the subject now, Anna mentioned. "I never asked. Did you get hold of Tom?"

"Yeah, I gave him the go-ahead, and told him I would be in touch later. I hope I'm not putting him in any real danger, though," he added seriously.

"I can't see you doing that to a good friend." Anna interjected, trying to ease Grady's conscience.

"I hope you're right."

"Say, what does Tom do for a living, anyway?" Anna inquired curiously. "Why is it that he can tackle these little projects for you on a Thursday afternoon?"

Grady glanced sideways at Anna with a broad smile, relishing the words before he spoke them. "He's a thief."

Anna let out a sweet little laugh. "Seriously?"

"Yes, seriously. He's *reformed*, of course," Grady said, not really sure if the last part was true. "I met him when I was with the FBI . . . the early years . . . and he offered information for a price back then. I guess we just kind of clicked. He's been a friend ever since."

Intrigued, Anna explored the subject some more. "If he's reformed, how does he make a living now?"

"People like me hire him when they need odd jobs done. That's about as much as I know." Looking around, Grady added, "I think we passed that shop you wanted to go to."

Anna turned to Grady, her arm still clinging to his. "I know, but it's a beautiful day for a walk, and we can catch it on the way back."

Agreeing, they made a quick detour to the car to drop off their bags before they set off. For a while, neither of them brought up the events of the past or their uncertain future. Instead they got to know each other, living in the moment, letting their feet take them on an adventure much milder than those of the past few days.

Their long stroll took them down by the river where they watched the ducks dip and bob along with the current. They wandered over an old railway bridge, now converted for foot traffic, before wandering into a gorgeous park steeped with walls of towering limestone on one side and the Root River on the other.

They walked together simply enjoying the sights and each other's company, until the sun ticked just past two o'clock in the sky and they both decided it was probably time to go. On their way back to town, Grady asked something that had been on his mind since their morning conversation.

"So you think Joe and Trent are in France? What makes you think that?"

Anna knew the question would be asked sooner or later and had her answer ready—she simply told the truth. "It came to me in a dream."

"I see," Grady said out of interest, and not so much disbelief. "Do we know where in France?"

For a while, Anna had released Grady's arm, but now she matched his steps stride for stride with his and took it. "I'm guessing Paris—the architecture seems to fit. Trent also told me a while back his mother was French, his father American. Apparently he was born in Paris, so it might follow that he wanted to return someday. But if you must know the truth, mostly I'm going on instinct."

Grady wasn't concerned about following Anna's instincts, which so far seemed to be very in tune. But he still had a few more questions he needed answered before he committed to an overseas excursion—a trip that for various reasons could be fraught with danger. "Are you sure this is where you want to go? I guess what I'm trying to say is, will meeting up with these two get us any further ahead in terms of Northwoods and Mary Jane?"

Anna sighed, wondering if making the trip was an exercise in futility, but deep down she felt it was the right thing to do. "Everything I know, everything I can understand seems to be telling me that this thing won't get resolved until the three of us are back together. Good or bad, that's the way I think it has to happen."

"Fair enough," Grady said, apparently satisfied.

Hearing Grady's answer, Anna thought she should feel better than she did. But she didn't. She was still keeping something from him and she struggled mightily with it. She wondered if she should tell Grady the group was supposed to meet back in the states in about a week. But if he knew that, he might try to talk her out of the trip to France—and instead await Trent and Joe's return. Anna feared that by that time it might be too late. She also wondered with Trent and Joe already together—and Curt gone—if they would even bother to make the trip back. No, she thought to herself, for now she would keep the group's sworn secret.

Arriving back in town, Grady excused himself, reminding Anna he wanted to make those phone calls he had mentioned earlier in the morning. Apparently not wanting company, he suggested Anna go ahead and take a look through the last shop.

Not really wanting him to go, she watched as he made his way across the street to an old fashioned pay phone, insert several coins and start dialing, before she turned to walk the half block down, entering the small boutique they had seen earlier. The old wooden door tripped a small bell as it swung in, and a tall woman smiled broadly at her, offering a friendly "hello."

Returning the greeting politely, Anna began perusing the small, cluttered shop. It was filled with jellies and jams made from fruits harvested around the area, as well as several bays of old antiques and a wall of local memorabilia. At the far end of the store, two small circular racks supported a collage of mismatched clothing in assorted styles and sizes. "Are these secondhand?" She asked over the rack to the clerk who was reading a novel.

Looking up from her paperback, the clerk responded with another smile. "Gently used is what we like to call them."

Anna wasn't fond of used clothes, but she decided to take a look anyway in an attempt to pass the time. To her surprise, she discovered a vintage brown sundress adrift with tiny peach blossoms, dotted with sprays of red florals. It stood out from all the other clothes, and to her luck, it was just her size. Curious, she pulled the hanger off the rack and held it up, appraising herself in a nearby mirror. The breezy empire-waisted rayon dress had thin spaghetti straps, gently v'ed neckline and a side slit along one leg, running from its knee-skimming hem up several inches of thigh. Compared to the jeans, T-shirts and jacket she had bought so far, it added just the right amount of femininity to her quickly assembled wardrobe.

Using some money Grady had given her, she paid the clerk and thanked her graciously. As she was about to turn to head out the door Anna paused, deciding to ask a question.

Hearing her request, the helpful clerk responded. "You can find what you want just a couple doors down. They're a souvenir shop, so they don't have a huge selection, but you could try."

Anna thanked her again and went out the door with her purchase. Looking back toward where she had left Grady, she could just make out his sturdy figure leaning against the pole supporting the payphone. Guessing she had a little time to spare, she turned in the opposite direction, walking another two shops down before ducking inside. Not wanting to waste any time, she asked another young girl behind the counter to direct her to what she was looking for.

Five minutes later, Anna was back on the street, heading happily to where she had left Grady.

He had just hung up as he saw her approaching. "Found something else, did you?"

"Yes, but it's a surprise, so no peeking." Anna warned playfully before asking, "You find anything out on the phone?"

Grady shook his head. "Nope, I got hold of a guy I knew from the Bureau who I think I can trust. I tried to pick his brain about Northwoods and Allied Cleaners, but he either didn't know anything or was being tight-lipped. Either way, I got zilch."

Squinting into the sun that was just beginning to fall from the sky behind Grady, Anna asked, with hope in her voice, "Anything new from Tom?"

Shaking his head, Grady replied, "I didn't try. I'm guessing he's pretty busy right about now."

CHAPTER 44

BREAKING AND ENTERING

By 2 p.m., Tom had already finished a brief meeting with an acquaintance of his, calling in a favor he had been owed. Right now he and Molly could be found nearing the end of a brisk walk around a very specific part of the Merriam Park neighborhood. Tom wasn't really thrilled with what he had seen on their jaunt. Using Molly as his cover, he had walked her once along Grady's street and then through the alley, checking out the competition. What he discovered were two unmarked police units watching the home—one out in front and the other parked on Laurel Avenue watching a portion of the alley and Grady's back entrance.

What concerned him even more was a house just across the way and a couple of doors down from Grady's. Like many of the homes in this neighborhood, it had been converted into apartments for off-campus students attending the University of St. Thomas. A sign out front advertised that there were apartments available for rent. If Feds were involved in the hunt for Grady, Tom guessed that's where they would be holed up, with a full complement of electronic surveillance equipment.

The other wild card in the equation appeared to be a man Tom and Molly had passed twice. He seemed to be wandering the neighborhood, chain smoking cigarettes, with no apparent destination. From his appearance, if he had to guess, Tom would have said he was a Fed and not a cop. That only steeled his hunch that the apartment across the street was the bird's nest for some more unwelcome company.

Two blocks north of Grady's home, Tom returned to his parked car and let Molly inside. Immediately she lay down on the back seat, panting up a storm. Tom rolled down the windows for her, making sure she had enough air.

Moving to the front passenger door, Tom took off his green windshirt and wide brimmed golf hat. Tossing them on the seat, he retrieved a black baseball cap, black windbreaker and gray nylon sweats and changed into them. Not bothering to change out of his jeans, he slid the lightweight pants up over his New Balance running shoes and right over his jeans. He hoped the change of clothes might throw anyone off who might have already seen him. Tom shut the door, telling Molly through the window that he would be right back.

His plan was still developing in his mind as he walked down to the intersection of Montrose Place and Dayton Avenue and turned west—and it would change as the situation dictated. But he knew where the watchers were, and he was visually triangulating their fields of view in his mind. His goal: find the dead spots in their surveillance and maneuver through them.

As he approached the alley, Tom saw his wandering Fed friend again, turning the corner off Otis Avenue, just a half a block up, heading directly toward him. Casually, Tom crossed to the other side of Dayton Avenue, breaking out into a light jog, hoping to offer the appearance of a runner out for a little exercise—perhaps headed to the River Road just a block west—to run along the high, scenic banks of the mighty Mississippi.

Both men passed on opposite sides of the road, barely giving either a second look. Continuing with his ruse, Tom ran about an eighth of a mile before finally deciding it was safe to backtrack. Reaching the entrance to the alley, he peered around a tall privacy fence and down the length of the back street. To his relief he saw the man he had just passed at the opposite end of the drive. Seconds later the man turned left onto Laurel Avenue and drifted out of sight.

Resuming a light jog, Tom paced himself as he entered the alley, keeping an eye out for new surprises, but there were none. It wasn't long before he found the spot he wanted, slowing to a stop. From his earlier pass through the alley, he knew that the cops parked on Laurel had a great view of Grady's garage, back fence, and the gate that offered Grady access to the alley. But where the cops were currently parked, rows of garages obscured their view of the full length of the alley itself.

Tom guessed that where he stood now was about ten feet outside their field of view. Walking back at an angle, keeping his ten-foot buffer intact, he intersected the fence of Grady's next-door-neighbor just to the west. Looking right then left to ensure all was clear, Tom listened for voices that might indicate someone was in the yard he was about to enter. Hearing none, he pulled himself up and over the tall wooden barrier, dropping softly down in a mossy garden patch on the other side.

The yard was deserted and he moved quickly across it to his right until he reached the fence that Grady and his neighbor shared. Looking at an angle over the top, Tom picked out the peak of Grady's garage, aligning himself so that it would be in-between himself and the cop car as he crossed over. Satisfied he would be out of view, Tom scrambled deftly over it.

Safely inside Grady's yard, he took a moment to look around. Seeing nothing out of the ordinary, and confident with the privacy fence acting as his cover, he made his way to Grady's back door. Searching the doorframe and door, he saw what he didn't want to see. It was in relatively plain view, positioned up high: a tiny metal wire that rested against a small metal plate. The design was such that if the door were opened the wire would lose contact with the plate and sound a silent alarm, to whoever had placed the device there. Tom knew this wasn't the work of the cops—rather, it reeked of the Feds handiwork.

Eyeing the alarm, Tom pulled a black device, about the size of a matchbox, from one of his coat pockets. From it, two narrow but relatively long insulated wires protruded. On one wire was an alligator clip, on the other the frayed ends of exposed wire showed. Carefully he attached the clip to the wire contact on the door.

Letting it dangle, he pulled a small roll of electrical tape from another pocket and ripped off a 1-inch strip. He took the frayed wire ends and taped them to the metal contact plate. Checking his connections once more, Tom again let the device dangle and retrieved Grady's house key. Inserting the key in the lock, he gave it a turn until the mechanism clicked.

Breathing evenly, Tom hoped he was ready for this, figuring if the house was alarmed, it was also probably bugged. Hidden video surveillance wasn't out of the question either. With little choice but to go forward, he decided speed, not stealth, was his only option, for if there were cameras it would be impossible to defeat them without raising the alarm. Once again, Tom grasped the black box—his thumb finding the tiny switch set into its case as his other hand slowly rotated the knob—careful not to push in just yet.

"One, two, three," he said to himself as he slid the door open, at the same time flicking the switch to open the circuit on the black box. His timing had to be precise, as any increased or decreased load on the circuit would result in triggering the silent alarm. Though he'd never know for sure, the power flow dipped briefly, but within the mechanism's tolerable limits and for now, no one was wise to his presence.

Inside, Tom knew Grady's home layout well and he slid across the tiled kitchen floor through an arched opening before immediately turning right into Grady's office. As he did, a camera mounted in an overhead kitchen light fixture captured his fleeting image.

A tiny transmitter relayed his progress in real time, back across the street to the apartments. The video feed popped up on a monitor, showing Tom's shadowy outline as he crossed the kitchen, but for the moment, in the absence of an audible alarm, his initial progress was missed.

Digging in the top drawer, Tom's image showed up again in the apartment, this time on a second monitor, as he located Grady's passport and pocketed it quickly. Though the angle didn't reveal exactly what Tom had gathered, his lingering image was noticed, and instantly a silent alarm was raised as two federal investigators delivered a message to the police. All began to converge instantaneously on Grady's home.

With the passport in hand, Tom raced back out of Grady's office and back into the kitchen. Finding the door he wanted, he flung it open and descended the flight of unfinished wood stairs, finding himself in a cold, damp basement. Getting his bearings, he flicked on a small flashlight and located what he assumed was the north-facing wall.

He shone the light on the cinderblock, looking for cracks, or missing chunks of concrete. The first spot he tried was a dead end and he swore to himself out loud. But the second block yielded results. As fast as his fingers could, he tore the face of the loose block away, revealing a manila folder stuffed inside the cramped hiding space. Unzipping his jacket half way, he didn't bother to check the file's contents—he simply stuffed it inside.

It was then that he heard the first telltale sounds that indicated he had been discovered. From upstairs came the squeak of an opening door, then several feet shuffling around as the old home's joists creaked against the men's added weight. Looking for his way out, Tom located a small window up high on the south end of the basement, near the ceiling. It would have to do as his escape route. Finding an old beat-up folding chair, he set it under the window, stood on it and flicked up the window latch. Pushing on the hinged window, it swung up but with nothing to prop it open, it fell instantly back into place. Tom had to keep shoving it open has he hoisted himself up and awkwardly through the small opening.

Landing outside in dry leaves and grass, he scrambled to his feet. He was on the side of Grady's house, facing another privacy fence only three feet away. Clawing his way up and over it, he landed hard on the other side and swore silently to himself. Picking himself up, he crossed the length of two more yards, hopping each fence as he came to it. On his final drop to the ground, his shoes hit sidewalk and he instantly realized his mistake. He was now standing on Laurel, the same place the cop car had been staked out. His eyes shot to where he'd last seen the cruiser, and breathed a sigh of great relief when he noticed it was gone—probably up the alley now parked behind Grady's home.

He immediately turned right, knowing he'd have to pass the alley in his flight, but it was better than turning left and passing Montrose and the Fed's nest. As he resumed his nonchalant jogging pace, Tom took a quick glance up the alley and noticed the cops were indeed now blocking Grady's garage—the cruiser's lights flashing. To his relief, both officers appeared to have gone inside Grady's house.

Picking up the pace just a bit, Tom made his second mistake, completely forgetting about the roving man on the street. As he turned onto Otis Avenue, he blew right past the guy who appeared to be racing even more madly in the opposite direction. Afraid to look back, Tom never saw the guy turn, as if considering a protest. But the two were now far apart, and in the end, the federal agent decided he was the same jogger he had seen earlier, and hurried off to offer his assistance in the manhunt currently underway at Grady's house.

Reaching his car only a minute later Tom found Molly, happily wagging her tail in greeting. Taking a moment to look over his shoulder, he was grateful to see he didn't have any company. Quickly, he opened the driver side door and greeted Molly with a quick pat to the head as he let out another huge sigh of relief.

"Piece of cake," he said to Molly as she licked at his sweaty face. Tom was quite happy that he hadn't had to access Grady's computer. That was what the morning's meeting was all about. Tom had some very reliable contacts of his own when it came to work like that. And by calling in a favor or two, the price for Anna's fake passport had been dropped several hundred dollars. It would be top-notch work once Tom got them the photo of Anna in the file he'd just retrieved. Of course, he'd charge Grady the full $750 like Grady had offered. Friendship or no friendship, Tom decided he had just earned it.

CHAPTER 45

ROUSTING MARY JANE

The first interrogation began promptly at 3 p.m. the day after her capture. It came just as Mary Jane had fallen into the first deep sleep of her short captivity. Over the last day the lights in her cell came on and off at irregular intervals, but spaced no longer than an hour apart. The sequence became so varied that it began interrupting her normal biorhythms. Without any reference to outdoor cues or even a clock, it made any sense of real time impossible.

Now, the light fixture over her head bled its bright shade of pure white into her tiny room—its radiance so intense that sleep was a virtual impossibility. Waking at first, unsure where she was, Mary Jane saw three men dressed in sterile medical scrubs and masks storm into the room and roust her roughly from her bed.

An unwilling participant, she made them drag her, with her legs dangling free, her feet scraping across the floor. They tossed her unceremoniously into a modified wheelchair. Moving quickly, two men affixed broad leather straps to bind her wrists and ankles as another man bound a thick black blindfold across her eyes.

Back in darkness, she was pushed out of the room in silence and Mary Jane took the opportunity to make mental notes of her trip. Three rights and a left brought them to what she guessed to be an elevator as she heard the familiar swish of the doors sliding open. With her internal gyroscope, Mary Jane hoped if she ever found herself free, she would at least know where to look for an escape route.

On the ride down, she counted what seemed to be two floors until the doors rolled opened again. It was a fact that confused Mary Jane, as she had assumed her tiny cell was already at the basement level. "How far into the depths of hell does this place really go?" she wondered to herself. If there were two levels below the basement, she'd never been allowed on them when she worked for Northwoods.

Outside the elevator Mary Jane was taken down several more corridors and at least five more turns, until she finally, hopelessly lost track of where she was. At one point her mind had her doubling back from where they'd just come, which made no sense. Now, at the end of what seemed to be another very long hallway, they turned her left and wheeled her into a place that felt quite enclosed, with the acoustics of a small room.

Stopped, one of the orderlies bent down in front of her, removing her blindfold, hovering in front of her for a moment—the face shrouded by a medical mask. She thought she recognized the eyes, now expressing what she perceived to be a sad apology. He removed a syringe from his pocket, as Mary Jane's eyes widened and she struggled against her restraints. Immediately the other two men were at Mary Jane's side, helping to hold her arm still as the orderly in front of her found a vein. In seconds, the clear liquid was released into her bloodstream before the men tidied up and left her alone in the room.

Trying to remain calm, Mary Jane looked around, wondering what drugs they might have given her. In front of her was a broad mirror set into the length of one wall, and she figured it had to be a two-way, with an observation room on the other side. The walls themselves, she noticed, were each padded in bright white—a color that merged almost seamlessly with the ceiling's acoustical tiling—most likely to dampen what Mary Jane figured what would be screams of terror or pain. This was "The Room" Anna had told her about so many times.

To her right, the single door opened as the officious Dr. Allan Hauser strode into the room. Once inside, he rolled a stainless steel stool from one of the corners and promptly seated himself to the front and right of Mary Jane.

"You seem to be doing well," he said to her in an oddly cheerful tone. "I trust our accommodations are adequate?"

Mary Jane said nothing in response, but stared right through him with bitterness and contempt.

Unfazed by her unwillingness to talk, Allan continued. "It's time to see what you know, my friend. There are many things we can do to help you remember. The first you are already experiencing. It's just something to help you relax and remove your inhibitions."

Mary Jane shifted uncomfortably in the chair at the thought.

"Ah, I can see the drugs have you concerned," Allan offered. "Don't worry, we gave you a very low dose, so there shouldn't be any long-term side effects. But you should know, if you'd rather not cooperate, I can easily have them pump you with a dose so massive it will leave you a vegetable by the time I'm through with you."

"You crazy messed-up asshole." Mary Jane yelled at him.

Allan's demeanor changed suddenly, and he got right up into Mary Jane's face. "Listen, I'm being more than fair here," he growled. "You have a choice: either you can tell me what I want to hear, or you can put yourself through such horrible agony you'd have wished I'd reached down your throat and ripped your damn heart out with my bare hands. So sit back and enjoy the ride . . . the drugs should be just about ready to take effect."

With no other means of retaliation, Mary Jane spat into the doctor's face, sending an oozing mass of saliva across his glasses. Furious, Allan rose from his stool with such force it flew across the room and crashed violently into the padded wall as he delivered a vicious backhand to Mary Jane's face. Still fuming, he stormed out of the room as Mary Jane's interrogator walked quietly in to take his place.

From behind the glass, The Kid watched Mary Jane closely. He wished he could be in the room with her, doing the actual interrogations. He would relish it, and bring his own ideas to Northwood's modern version of the torture chamber. But for now, this spot was safer, for him and for her.

CHAPTER 46

NEW BEGINNINGS

After another beer on the deck of the cottage, watching the remainder of the afternoon drift away, Grady left Anna once more. He returned to the main house to check in with Tom, before navigating the winding road back into Lanesboro to pick up a pizza from one of the local take-out establishments.

With the pizza in hand, he entered the cottage looking angry and perplexed and Anna instantly knew he wasn't himself. Coming to his side, she took the pizza from him and asked him what was wrong.

"Tom got the stuff I sent him for," was all he could say at first. But Anna, ushering him to the couch, kept trying to ease more out of him.

Reluctantly, Grady explained what Tom had told him, about the surveillance on his house, the electronic monitoring equipment on his door, and the brush with the authorities as Tom came within a hair's breadth of being caught.

"How could I have done that to him?" Grady said referring to Tom. "He's a friend and I used him. I can't imagine what would have happened if he had been caught. At best he'd be in jail."

Slipping her hand around the back of his neck, Anna began to gently work the knots out of his tense muscles. "You need some rest," she said gently. "Tom's fine, nothing happened, he won't hold it against you."

"I don't know," Grady replied, unconvinced. "I've never heard Tom sound that way. I could tell he was upset at what he saw, frustrated there might have been video cameras in the house, recording him. He said he was more than careful and couldn't figure any other reason they would have known he was there. I hope to God they didn't get a good look at his face."

Grady's eyes remained lost, focused straight ahead on nothing in particular, trying to work the possibilities.

"What were his last words to you?" Anna coaxed.

Grady turned his eyes from whatever he was staring at and looked inquisitively at Anna. "I don't know. Why?"

Anna smiled compassionately, saddened by Grady's anger with himself. "Because it will tell you how he really feels. If he ended the conversation brightly with a friendly goodbye, all will be forgotten. If he withheld a goodbye and just hung up, or gave a monotone response, perhaps he still has issues. Think about it, you're probably angrier with yourself. What did he really say?"

Grady mulled it over. "He said, 'Now you really owe me one, I'll see you tomorrow, buddy'."

Anna looked surprised. "We're going to see him tomorrow?"

Sheepishly, Grady forced a half-smile. "Yeah, I guess I forgot to tell you that. He got most of what we needed from the house and said he would have the rest in his hands by noon tomorrow. So we set up a place to meet. We're going back."

"And then?" she dug.

"We fly to Paris out of Twin Cities International at 6:07 p.m.," Grady answered matter-of-factly. "I had Mr. Bailey set up the flight arrangements for us when I was at the house. He still owes me for some of the work I've done on this place, and he agreed to do this for us in lieu of my traditional payment. I think he knew we were in a pretty big scrape."

"Why's that?"

Laughing a bit at the thought, Grady answered, "He advanced me quite a lot of money . . . said it was for future work on cottage number four."

"I guess we're going, then," Anna said, still not believing they would have to give up this wonderful cottage, and with it any feelings of security.

Noticing Anna's own disposition mellow, Grady eased up a bit more. "We'll be okay, don't worry, everything will turn out fine."

Opening the pizza box she had set on the coffee table, Anna gave Grady a sideways glance. "That's good advice. You should follow it."

Grady had no comment, but Anna was starting to realize he was a complex individual. His history with Nancy had to be dealt with, and she guessed he hadn't. Her death had obviously adversely affected many of his personal and professional relationships. She figured it was why he clung to friends like Tom, who took him for who he was . . . always without question. She suspected it was why Grady seemed so troubled by Tom's run-in earlier today. It was odd that this wonderful human being who sat next to her had found a closer friendship with a thief than the upstanding while-collar friends Anna guessed he had developed earlier in life.

Now, wondering if she should push it, Anna decided to add her last two cents' worth and then leave it be. "When we see Tom tomorrow, really talk to him, then you'll know exactly where you stand."

"Thanks," Grady offered appreciatively. "I'll do that."

Outside, dusk was beginning to descend on their last evening in the cottage, and as they nibbled on the last scraps of pizza, they agreed it was best to leave their problems until tomorrow, and enjoy as much of the evening as they could. Once again they wandered out onto the deck and their view they'd come to love.

Rather than sitting, they eased up to the tall deck railing. There they rested their arms over the wrought-iron railing, a couple of fresh drinks dangling from their fingertips as they leaned over the side. For the longest time, there was a quiet silence between them, as they watched the last rays of the day's sun lick the horizon until the stars above began to emerge from an ever-darkening shade of blue.

At some point Anna leaned gently into Grady and he responded in kind, tucking his arm around her slender waist. It was a moment shared as two people began to not only understand, but to feel comfortable with each other and their closeness.

After a while Anna broke from Grady's grasp, turning to him, her elbow resting on the railing for support. "I bought you something," she said happily, her eyes alive with excitement. "Would you like to see it?"

Not answering, Grady looked at Anna with wonder and admiration, trying to figure out what it might be that had gotten her into this bright mood. But Anna had already turned and was heading inside. "Wait there," she called back to him, as she hurried away.

Anna returned in moments, carrying a dusty purple bag with a combination of script and block letters that read Ellie's Boutique.

"Sorry, I didn't have anything to wrap it with," she explained, handing the bag over.

Grady grasped the twine handles of the short, square bag and opened it up—his eyes laughing before he could get out any words.

"I was thinking you could join me tonight." Anna said as he pulled out a pair of navy blue swim trunks. "I hope they're the right size."

"They're perfect . . . thank you," Grady replied, checking the tag before eyeing her skeptically. "But what about you?"

"It's upstairs." Anna informed him, reassuringly. "Don't worry, I won't make you uncomfortable like I did with the robe. I learned my lesson."

On impulse, Grady looped his arm around Anna's shoulder and hugged her with one arm. But what began as an innocent show of appreciation turned into something more, as they found themselves wrapped in each other's arms, rocking slowly to the tempo of their quickened heartbeats. Finally, Anna eased herself from his strong arms and broke free.

"I'm going to change," she said, in a quiet voice, and once again she turned and disappeared through the doors.

Grady found the intense churning waters of the hot tub to be most invigorating and he lounged there as he waited patiently for Anna. It took her some time, but she finally appeared through the side door, her beautiful curls swept back and gathered by a small elastic hair band she had purchased earlier that day.

The suit she wore was a simple scoop-necked one-piece splayed with a delicate white floral design that rose off a deep purple, almost-black backdrop. As she ascended the three steps that would lead her into the tub, Grady couldn't help but admire her long slender legs that carried her, beautifully accentuated by the high cut thighs of the suit. She was quite stunning.

Smiling modestly, Anna quickly stepped into the frothy mix and submersed herself up to her chest in the bubbling water. "You changed fast," she said, grinning at Grady.

"I guess I did. Should I have waited?"

"No," she answered shaking her head. "Although I wanted to see how the suit fit. You wouldn't mind, would you?" Gesturing for him to stand.

Rolling his eyes a bit, Grady reluctantly rose in the tub, braving a light fall chill that brushed across him with the night's whisper of a breeze.

As Grady emerged from the water Anna noted his broad rounded shoulders and nicely defined, but not over-developed chest. And in that moment she tried to dispel the immodest thoughts that flitted through her head.

Grady made it to his feet, so just the lower hem of his wet, new swimsuit floated on the water. Feeling a little modest, he attempted to make light of the situation, doing a foolish modeling turn before he sunk quickly back into the water, where it was cozy and warm.

Amused, Anna laughed as Grady shivered uncontrollably, before the hot water that enveloped him could take full effect. "Not exactly warm out, is it?"

"Not quite," he answered, with a final uncontrollable shiver. "You did a wonderful job with the suits. Yours fits perfectly . . . I mean . . ." Yet again Grady couldn't finish, finding himself tongue-tied, not exactly sure where the boundaries were with them.

"Thank you, I think. And yours, um . . . well . . . it . . . let me see," she said with a wide grin.

Grady gave her a look. "You're mocking me now, aren't you?"

"Why Grady, I would never do that. Never!"

Hearing Anna's false indignation, Grady tried to think of a witty comeback, but he was at a loss for words. She did that to him often, he reflected. So instead, quite childishly, he swept one of his arms across the surface, splashing Anna with a tidal wave of water.

The deluge soaked Anna, drenching her hair and she screamed in more honest exasperation. Fighting back, she leaned forward, slipping off her underwater seat, letting her knees hit bottom. At the same time she thrust her hands forcefully out in front of her, palms together, pushing across the water's surface. The movement sent a wave of retaliation cascading into Grady's surprised face, which Anna followed with smaller, less precisely aimed splashes. Caught up, Grady returned volley, leaving his own seat to send more water back Anna's way as now a warm misty spray clouded them, flying in every direction.

Somehow, in their rough-and-tumble struggles, Grady managed to lock up one of Anna's wrists, and she promptly tied up his free hand with hers. And as a stalemate ensued, with the displaced water running slowly off their bodies, they moved silently closer, inch-by-inch until there was no more space to give, and they finally gave up their holds to embrace in a long, tender kiss.

Breaking lips for a moment, both Grady and Anna gazed awkwardly into the other's eyes, and Anna couldn't help but offer a breathless surrender. "You win."

Collapsing back into the tub, now on the same seat, Anna and Grady snuggled together, her head resting gently on his chest, rising up and down with his heavy breaths. An hour passed like that—the two only parting twice for a chilly trip inside to refresh their beverages. First Grady, and then Anna, and each took silent pleasure in watching the other move.

As they relaxed there, letting their minds wander aimlessly, enjoying the night in all its natural wonder, Anna thought she could sense something from Grady. It was something forming deep inside his mind, and it didn't surprise herself how easily she agreed. Tired and ready for sleep, Anna rose out of the water and bent over Grady. Reaching down she placed both hands on his face and brought it up to meet hers. Sharing only their second kiss of the night, Grady responded by wrapping her up at the waist, as he brought Anna gently into him, their wet bodies pressing heavily against each other.

Both knew, to continue tonight would be wrong and rushing things, given all that had happened. And to rush things for the sake of an uncertain tomorrow would be to admit they might not make it through the next few days together. Neither was ready to consider defeat. Each wanted to believe in a future that held promise and possibility—nothing more.

Separating, they whispered reluctant good nights and retreated to their own beds in cottage number three.

CHAPTER 47

Silent Invitation

At some point, in the middle of the night, Anna awoke in a feverish sweat, her dreams tormenting her mercilessly. Suddenly, lying there amidst a pile of sheets she had pulled from their tucks, she felt terribly vulnerable and alone. Needing Grady, but not wanting to need him, she couldn't decide what to do.

Not yet fully resolving her dilemma, she tiptoed down the spiral staircase anyway, back down to the main floor where Grady slept. Downstairs she wandered through alternating bands of light and shadow—the odd pattern cast by the moon's silvery glow as it filtered through the vast stretches of windows.

There, in the dim light, she could barely make out the lean, sturdy form of Grady folded up awkwardly on the cushions of the couch. The spare sheet and blanket he used as covers had been tossed off him in his sleep as he shivered slightly in his boxers and a t-shirt she'd bought for him today. Perhaps he too had been troubled by his own surreal dreams. For a long while Anna just looked at him, standing there in her own close-fitting cotton tee, thinking he appeared terribly cold and uncomfortable resting there.

Again, pondering what she had come to do, she almost turned back, alone to her own bed, thinking herself foolish and impulsive for even coming down. But the thought of returning to an empty bed, to face her dreams alone, prodded her on, forcing pride out the window, at least for now. She moved nearer, much closer to Grady's side as her oddly distorted shadow fell across his sleeping form.

Reaching out, she stroked the hair on the side of his head using the back of her hand, whispering his name. Twice she had to say it, before he awoke with a slight start—his eyes gradually opening to meet her gaze as the sleep-induced cobwebs that clouded his mind slowly dispersed. Finally, a look of happy recognition flickered through his eyes and Anna returned the warm, silent greeting with one of her own. Saying nothing, Anna extended her hand in invitation. Uncertain at first, Grady took it, his eyes fixed on her, questioning—one she answered with her own anxious look that seemed to simply say, *I need you.*

Slowly, still holding Grady's hand, Anna led him off the couch and back upstairs to the king-size bed that awaited them there. Letting his hand fall as they neared, Anna lifted the covers and climbed in, still holding up the edge nearest Grady so he could slip in beside her. Together, Anna stroked Grady's stubbly cheek and gently kissed his firm lips before she rolled over onto her other side, her back now to him.

Happy just to be near her, Grady wrapped himself around Anna, holding her as close as he possibly could. Anna responded by taking the arm Grady had draped over her side, tucking it with both hands into her warm body as she snuggled back into him.

They lay that way for the remainder of the night, each drifting off into a peaceful sleep. And while an eerie, angry darkness settled momentarily into Anna's unconsciousness, it was quickly banished in what Anna would later describe as a frustrated fury. For the rest of the evening her visions didn't dare haunt her again.

CHAPTER 48

FULL FURY

Mary Jane lay awake in her cell, the light above buzzing incessantly, pushing off the sleep her body so desperately needed. The interrogation session earlier in the day had gone badly. What transpired, as a result of her lack of cooperation, had been a mix of physical and emotional abuse and a second injection to try to knock down the walls of her resistance. The effects of the second injection had left her confused and disoriented.

Their questioning centered around three subjects: Mary Jane's role in Anna's escape, where Anna was now, and those Mary Jane may have leaked information about Northwoods to. Finding a safe place within her mind, Mary Jane had holed up. And rather than focus on lies to throw them off Anna's trail, she put all her strength into refusing to answer any questions they threw at her.

Now, trying to fight off the after-effects of the drugs and the dull throbbing emanating from the gunshot wound they'd used against her, Mary Jane focused on laying as still as possible on her cot. Even the slightest movement sent her head swimming, sending waves of nausea coursing through her gut. Knowing Northwoods probably had video monitors trained on her, she refused to break down, refused to show fear.

So she passed much of the time, eyes closed, focusing on Anna. Wondering how she was doing, praying to God that she was safe. Would it be possible this man named Grady could keep her safe? If she knew that answer, if she knew that today Anna would no longer suffer at the hands of Northwoods, she would gladly die for that cause. Yet, faced with the uncertainty of it all, her only choice was to fight for life.

With her eyes still closed, Mary Jane began to pray again, only to be interrupted as someone from outside kicked her door open with a shuddering bang. Forgetting her uneasy state, she reflexively shot straight up in bed. The rapid reaction threw her equilibrium into chaos, and as her eyes opened to a fuzzy blur of a room, it began to spin uncontrollably. Quickly she shut them to the world, trying to regain her center of balance—as bile rose in her stomach.

An irrepressible anger boiled in The Kid's eyes as he burst into Mary Jane's room. He had just tried to hitchhike for a second time that night off of Anna's dreams and had been shut out. All he saw was a foggy vision of Anna, lying in bed in the arms of another. It was enough to send him over the edge. Forget the fact that he had seen earlier where Trent and Joe were hiding. Forget that he knew Anna had plans to go there herself. Yet what he couldn't forget, what he couldn't put out of his mind was the image that played over and over in his head. The image of Anna's trembling lips brushing across another man's.

He wanted to reach out and punish her for her infidelity, but distance and timing made that unrealistic. So he opted for the next best thing. He'd punish the one person he knew she was closest to. Steadying his hate-filled eyes on Mary Jane, he spoke with menace. "Do you know what that bitch is doing while you're suffering here?"

Mary Jane kept her head tucked to her chest, fighting to get herself right, but lost the battle and vomited over the side of the bed onto the tiled floor.

Seeing Mary Jane was in no condition to reply, he kept on. "Hell, I'll tell you: she's shacked up with some guy, that's what. Your innocent little so-called daughter, that little tramp, is getting it on. How's that make you feel?" The Kid sneered.

With her stomach purged, Mary Jane straightened up, lifting her head slightly to take in the ranting stranger. At first he remained a swirling, shadowy blur. But as her watery eyes began to clear, and the room began to steady, she was able to discern a young man's figure coming slowly into focus—his appearance vaguely familiar. Then she saw the syringe tightly gripped in his hand.

"Somebody's got to pay for her sins." The Kid seethed, moving in slowly.

Agonizing fear and intense disbelief overwhelmed Mary Jane as The Kid closed in. As his face came closer, his features resolved, and all she could manage as he prepared to pounce were a few breathless words. "Oh my God, it's you."

CHAPTER 49

THE SILENT VISITOR

The Kid was nearly on top of Mary Jane when he paused. Something, perhaps a muffled sound from out in the hallway stopped him in his tracks. Was it real or only his imagination? Or, was it his conscience playing games with him? He turned to the door, unsure what to do. Then he looked back at Mary Jane, her fearful eyes, that horror of recognition still lingering there. For a moment his fury was forgotten as he tried to reach out and sense who the person was beyond the door. Yes, there was someone, but he couldn't register a face.

This didn't strike him as odd. He generally needed to know who he was reaching into, to visualize the face, particularly from behind closed doors. He assumed it was some orderly, one of the few who had achieved security clearance to cater to this floor. A few names and faces flashed through his consciousness, but there was no connection, and he didn't exactly make it a point to chum around with all the orderlies.

Quickly, he retreated to the door, and stood so that if it opened, he would end up behind it. He thought he could perceive footsteps fading down the dim corridor. Again he reached out but was shut out. For a moment he considered these words, *shut out*, but shook it off.

He turned to Mary Jane. She sat curled in the corner, probably fearful that if she cried out she would interrupt his current distraction and return his attention to her with a renewed vigor.

For now, she need not worry. The Kid's anger was coming back under control as he considered his options. *Would the footsteps return? Could he finish the job without being caught?* Something in him thought not. Even though he could not grasp the face of the stranger in the hall, he could sense the feet. Lighter now, almost on tiptoe, returning from the far reaches down a parallel hallway. Pausing. Waiting. *Waiting for what?* "Who, dammit!" he said to himself.

He had no time to think it all through. His time was almost up. He couldn't risk spending much more time in this wing without being caught. With a regretful bite to his lower lip, he hurried out the door, turning away from the returning footsteps. On his journey to Mary Jane's room he had been cautious to avoid the hallway cameras, stationed sporadically in this labyrinth of subterranean corridors. Having lived here most of his life, he had learned the dead spots in the camera coverage, and learned to time the sweep of the cameras on their motorized pivots. But on his way out, he cared little if his face was seen. After all, when he left the room, Mary Jane was still breathing.

CHAPTER 50

THE GOOD SOLDIER

The first rays of the morning sun danced through the stout rows of pines set high on the eastern ridge of the misty hills, rimming the lake at Northwoods. In the sky, a pair of mallards, one hen and one drake, flew in low formation, buzzing the heads of two men who'd been wandering the gravel paths around the grounds. Passing over, the ducks dove for the water, their webbed feet stretched out in front of them, as they appeared to hover for a moment, hanging in mid-air before setting down.

Allan and Mitch, watched as the mallards' bodies broke the still calm of the water's glassy surface, then turned to continue their conversation in low, conspiratorial tones. They were discussing all that had transpired last night and their next moves regarding the Naturals.

"How's the woman?" Mitch asked, speaking of Mary Jane.

"Not good. We've stabilized her for now, but the overdose someone gave her last night was substantial. Right now I'd say she's got no better than a fifteen percent chance of making it."

"Fabulous." Mitch said sarcastically. "You still trust The Kid after this?"

"Who said it was The Kid?" Allan asked bluntly.

"Damn, Allan. You're talking to your head of security. It's not exactly like we have some huge mystery on our hands. The Kid despises Mary Jane. He had motive. He had opportunity. Case closed."

"Sounds like you're set to hang him."

Mitch considered a different response, but decided on tact. "No, just haul his ass back into line."

"Well, it's not as bad as you might think," Allan said, changing the subject. "Apparently before Mary Jane slipped into her coma, The Kid succeeded in gathering some information. Says he only went to see her to reach into her mind, which is how he now knows where Joe and Trent are. He's pretty confident Anna will show up there soon as well."

"Where?" Mitch asked skeptically.

Sighing, Allen glanced back at the ducks, pausing as if trying to decide if he believed it himself. "Apparently it was a pre-planned rendezvous by the Naturals. Anna was to find Mary Jane and then they were all going to hook up in Europe to live out their lives."

"And you still think The Kid hasn't been holding out on us," Mitch stated sarcastically.

Ignoring the comment, Allan continued. "Anyway, we know Curt won't be showing up, nor will Mary Jane, but there's still a good chance Anna will try to connect with the other two, or The Kid wouldn't be interested."

"Hell, he's a loose canon." Mitch warned, exasperated with his boss. "He could say anything just to get his way, and keep us out of the way."

"I'd thought of that," Allan said after weighing the argument in his head. "But I still go back to the fact that he wants the girl as bad as we do. If he leads us on a wild goose chase to help her slip further away, she only slips further way from him, too."

Mitch still wasn't convinced. He was certain The Kid was holding something back. But in the end he gave into the possibility. "Well, even if he is telling the truth and planning to lead us to her, I still don't think he's the right guy for the job, with all he's done to undermine our mission."

"Don't make me remind you of your own screw-ups," Allan said throwing a verbal punch into Mitch's gut. "You had two tries at the girl and we nearly exposed ourselves with both. At least if The Kid messes up, he won't leave a damn trail of bullet holes and demolished homes for me to deal with."

Taken aback, Mitch weighed his response carefully, deciding not to press the issue. For now he'd have to find his role and bide his time until his next opportunity arose. He took his own turn to change the subject. "So tell me, if it wasn't The Kid last night, then who?"

For a moment, Mitch sensed a vague uneasiness from Allan, and he shifted uncomfortably before giving an answer. "You're probably right about The Kid. I just wanted to give him the benefit of the doubt. Anyway, it's over and there is little we can do. Believe me when I tell you we need him."

Mitch eyed Allan with mistrust. He was never one to give in so easily, even if . . . no, even especially when he was wrong. There was something his boss wasn't telling him. Was it something about The Kid? God only knew why he coddled him so much, even encouraged him to believe he was some big legend of Northwoods. In the end, he figured he wasn't going to get the answers he wanted and left it for another time. "Okay, so what's next?"

Happy to change the subject, Allan filled Mitch in with the remaining details. "The Kid says he has a sense that Anna's somewhere in southeastern Minnesota; he can't get a firm handle on the town. Figures she won't be there long. According to what he read off Mary Jane she'll be heading to France, probably Paris, to check in on Joe and Trent."

Mitch nodded, absorbing the information, trying to play the good soldier right now until he could have the reins removed once again.

Allan looked coolly at his head of security, anticipating something more out of him, but Mitch was done arguing about The Kid. In truth, Allan couldn't dismiss all of Mitch's concerns about The Kid. His worries were well founded, rooted in a history of deceit. The Kid was difficult to trust, but right now he seemed to have the best angle on the whole mess. "Don't worry too much, my friend . . . you're not completely out of the loop. I'd have you follow The Kid's every move, if I didn't think he'd catch wind of you and take off on his own freelance job."

Stooping to pick up a small rock from the path below, Mitch didn't like the sound of where Allan was heading, but had no choice to accept his boss's final wishes.

Watching Mitch rolling the smooth rock between his fingers, Allan continued. "Anyway, since I can't separate you, and I can't have The Kid flying off on his own, you're going with him. Give him a little line, but if there's any sign he's going to put us in jeopardy, reel him in."

"And if I can't?" Mitch asked, exploring his options.

"Then take him out," Allan said with a calm coolness, as though he was ordering a cocktail at a bar.

Mitch tossed the rock up in the air and caught it again in his open palm. "That's a tall order. What's our objective?"

"Same as it always has been since the Naturals escaped and we built our plan. Take them all down without putting the finger on Northwoods. I'm talking accidents here, Mitch, not bullets and bombs."

"The Kid won't like that. You tell him yet?" Mitch asked.

"No, and as you can guess, he's not to know . . . so watch yourself."

Winding up, Mitch took the rock he was palming and side-armed it out in a low spinning trajectory over the water. The stone skipped six times, scattering the pair of mallards into the air on its last hop before sinking into the depths of the lake.

Not bothering to look at Allan this time, Mitch just stared blankly as a new set of ripples spread out, covering the surface of the lake. "You sure know how to ruin what was turning out to be a nice day."

CHAPTER 51

LEAVING LANESBORO

A sharp crack of thunder brought Grady awake and he cringed unconsciously. Moments later, a fiery stroke of lightning zigzagged outside the windows, connecting with some unknown object nearby, followed by a deep, rattling boom that shook the cottage to its pillared foundation. Thinking of Anna, he rolled over to see if she was awake, only to find her side of the bed vacant.

Fear began to cloud over him as he climbed quickly from the bed, listening for some clue as to where she might be. Overhead, a heavy downpour pummeled the roof making it impossible to distinguish any sounds from below. Crossing the loft he found the stairway railing and hurried down the steps, hoping to see her waiting for him at the counter, but the room appeared vacant.

Wondering where to look next, he crossed to the other side, guessing she was in the shower, but the bathroom door stood wide open and was also empty. Just when he was about to cross back to the entry, he saw the main door open and Anna hurry inside out of the heavy deluge. She carried a large golf umbrella, which Grady didn't recall seeing before, and wondered where she might have picked one up. But then he saw the bags of food in her arms.

"You slept in," she said cheerfully, noticing Grady standing in the middle of the room, still in his boxers and T-shirt. She turned to the counter to set the bags down, but stopped herself and looked back at Grady. "You weren't worried about me, where you?"

Grady smiled feebly.

"You were, weren't you?" Anna asked, amused. "Where in heaven's name would I go in this weather?" she teased. "Sit down now . . . the food's on me this morning."

Grady did as directed, taking Anna's normal seat by the counter as she waited on him. Without asking, she brought him a mug full of black coffee from the pot she had already brewed. Then she began setting the food and plates out for them to eat. "I felt like I needed to meet the Baileys and thank them for their hospitality," Anna explained as she worked. "But you weren't up and I didn't want to wake you, so I took it upon myself. I hope that was alright," she said biting her lower lip.

"It's fine. I'm glad you did. I suppose it's safe, now that we're leaving today," Grady offered. "Has it been raining long?"

"Wasn't when I left, but it came up fast. Mr. Bailey gave me the umbrella as a gift . . . said I didn't need to return it."

"I'm guessing he liked you, then?"

Anna paused from her busy work and thought a second. "I couldn't tell. I mean, they're both so nice, I can't imagine them being any other way to anybody. Anyway, they certainly have a soft spot for you, Mr. Hamilton. Mr. Bailey was certainly beaming as he talked about all the work you did on the cottages. Asked me what I thought of them."

"What'd you tell him?"

"The truth . . . that I was dreading leaving."

Grady looked hard at Anna, wondering if he should broach the subject of last night, or if she would bring it up.

"You're wondering about last night," Anna said, a little apprehensively.

Smiling, Grady suggested, "You're uncanny."

Anna beamed. "I'll take that as a compliment . . . I think. But if you must know—and as you've probably already guessed—I had another dream last night."

Grady was intrigued. "And?"

"And, I know where we are going. The place is called the Hotel du Clos Medicis. It's in Paris and as far as I can tell Joe and Trent were there last night. I saw them again but something—call it intuition—tells me they won't be there for long."

"Why not?"

"Something happened in the dream, kind of like what happened in the one I had the night before. It's hard to explain, but I'll get a vision and everything will seem fine, and then a shadow crosses over, like a sheet of dark vellum falling across a full color photograph. It clouds everything and reduces the image to shades of what they once were. When it happens, I can't even begin to describe the feeling that comes with it. It's almost like someone is watching."

Grady sat a little straighter in his chair. "Like who?"

"Don't know," Anna said honestly. "But it scared me." Feeling a bit self-conscious, she added, "That's when I came and got you. I hope I wasn't wrong to do that?"

"Not at all," Grady said with a smile, deciding to leave it at that.

Having finished setting out the homemade blueberry muffins the Baileys had prepared for them, Anna moved around the counter, listening to steady rumbles from the storm moving off into the distance. She slipped behind Grady, still on his stool, and wrapped her arms around his neck, leaning softly into his back. "I enjoyed it too," she whispered into his ear, giving him a kiss on the neck, "but I suppose we'd better eat and pack up if we are going to get back to the Twin Cities and meet Tom."

He too was saddened by the thought of leaving, and replied a bit glumly, "Yes, I suppose you're right."

CHAPTER 52

Paying A Visit

Wearing a pair of heavily stonewashed jeans and a one-size-to-small Keith Urban T-shirt, a lone figure slid down a long narrow corridor, deep in the bowels of Northwoods. She passed intermittently into pools of light that fired the deep red of her flowing waves of hair, before receding into short patches of darkness. Melody wasn't supposed to be here, and she certainly didn't have security clearance, at least on paper. But being the daughter of Allan Hauser had its benefits. If a guard got in her face, she would merely say, "I'm the boss's daughter, take it up with him".

Rarely did a security guard feel like doing this, knowing the wide swings in Melody's father's mood. He hated to be disturbed, particularly about petty things. Although, what she was doing today was not petty, but she had done it before. If a guard did happen to report the abuse of her security clearance, it generally meant a shouting match with her dad. But, as daughters generally do with overprotective but adoring fathers, she usually won.

Up ahead a guard station loomed in one of the bright bands of light. The guard, a heavyset man in his mid-forties, looked up and wasn't surprised. This was good luck. It was Gabe, who had been with Northwoods for twenty years, and had known Melody virtually all of her young life.

"Hey little miss, what are you doing down here?" he said with a genuine smile.

"Came to visit someone, will you let me through?" she asked, with a coy smile that took about six years off her age.

"Your dad know about this visit?" he asked skeptically. "You don't want to get me in trouble after all these years now, do you?"

Melody just kept the smile on. "Of course he doesn't, but that's never stopped me before," her grin now effortlessly transitioning from coy to mischievous.

Gabe sighed. "Your father left strict instructions this time. If I saw you prowling around where you weren't supposed to be, I was to report it to him. Wha'da ya want anyway?"

"Thought I would check in on Mary Jane. You know we were close for a while back when. All you old-timers are like my family."

"Horrible what happened to her." Gabe said, obviously feeling some true measure of grief. "Tried to find out who was on security that night so I could rip into 'em, but your dad sealed that night's records and had the video tapes confiscated. Rumor is he's even keeping the tapes away from Mitch, his head of security. Said the matter was under investigation and punishments would be dealt out. Course, I know all the guards and no one is talking about it. They've all clammed up. Everyone's scared."

A thought crossed Melody's mind, unrelated to the reason for her visit, but she liked Gabe, and trusted him. So she asked. "What do you make of Mary Jane's return to Northwoods? How much do you know?"

Gabe looked conflicted and rubbed his scruffy round face before deciding on an evasive answer. "That's kind of a loaded question with you being the boss's daughter and all."

Melody took mild offense to this and let it show. "You know me, Gabe. I'm not my father's daughter."

Gabe sighed again still uncertain if he should speak his mind. In the end, he went about halfway to meeting her request. "Between you and me, then?"

Melody nodded her head and gave a reassuring smile.

"I don't have all the details, but I think it's not right. All the years she put in. Like you said, she was downright nice to you. Almost like family, you say?"

"So, we are agreed," Melody said, conspiratorially. "How about letting me go see her?"

"Damn, little girl" he said as if about to say no. Finally he just shook his head as though he didn't believe what he was doing. "Head on through . . . room's D-532."

"Thanks Gabe. Just between you and me," she said with a wink.

Under his desk, Gabe pressed a button that allowed a glass door behind him to release with a tiny click and a hiss, and Melody strode on through.

Gabe watched as her mane of red hair bounced against her shoulders with every purposeful stride. It was a visual cue that brought him back to a time when Melody was just eleven, the same beautiful hair framing her cherub-like face, as she played with Anna, Curt, Trent, and Joe. They had been out on the grounds playing a game called Kick the Can. They were fun times . . . easier times. Gabe had been assigned to their security detail. Then something came to him. Something he hadn't thought about in a long time. There had also been one other back then, but damn if Gabe could remember that boy's name. He had disappeared shortly after that. No warning, no explanation. He was just gone—another thing nobody talked about at the time.

Of course that was all back when Melody was allowed to fraternize with the Naturals. At about age 16 her dad pulled the plug. It was when the fun and games for the Naturals turned into business, and their real study and training began.

Now as Melody's tiny figure faded down the hall, Gabe wondered about the girl and those kids, now all gone. He wondered how she felt about their escape. Must be hard for her, he considered, even though her exposure to them was limited.

As her footsteps were cut off by the closing door one thought nagged at him. How in the hell had he gotten wrapped up in all of this himself? Seemed so different years ago. It all seemed good and right. But something changed about the time Melody stopped playing with the other kids, if he was recalling it right.

But that was how it happened for most long-timers at Northwoods. They sucked you in with their rosy-colored vision of the future. By the time anyone saw the forest for the trees, it was really too late to get out.

Mary Jane was an example of that. "Hmmm," he said to himself, "that's just about the right word. An example." For now, he decided to keep quiet, keep his job and in turn his life.

Melody was now well down the hall, following the room number signs posted at the intersection of each hallway. She turned left down one, then right, and finally left again before she reached the corridor to Mary Jane's room. She'd been moved since the attack, into what was the medical wing. In reality it was no different from where she had been, except the room had medical equipment, a nurse appointed to the room, and in the case of Gabe, added security.

Checking the signs one last time to make sure she was where she was supposed to be, Melody looked back down the hall, surprised to see a young man dressed in white scrubs heading straight for her.

Instantly she recognized Drake's narrow face, long gait, and rough curly mop of red hair that bent into his eyes.

"Hey darlin'," he quipped. "What are you doing down in the depths?"

Melody bristled. Yes, there had been a history there. Being roughly the same age, the two had been close for a while. They'd never dated, though Drake had tried several times. He was the son of one of the staffers, a single mom and Northwoods lifer by the name of Becky Slater.

Melody found it odd that he had access to this highly secure wing, at the relatively young age of 25. She wondered if he knew that he would never be allowed to leave now—although Drake had a personality that fit the place. When Melody was seventeen they started hanging out together, but it had taken only a few short weeks of early friendship to see the side of Drake that few knew. Most people loved him, even though he had no life goals. He'd spent most of his time at Northwoods—as far as she knew—and never aspired to go to college, and was known to drink heavily even while on duty. At one point, he had mentioned to her that he knew how to get into the pharmacy at Northwoods, and could get them some drugs that were nothing like normal prescription drugs, describing their mind and vision enhancing qualities in frightening detail. She had just given him a look that said: *You know I'm the daughter of the director?* That always ended any discussion.

It didn't help that Drake wanted to take their relationship from friendship to fondling. He had not been sweet or caring about his intentions. In fact, he had gotten quite rough. Melody felt the only reason she was able to convince him no meant no was when she brought up her dad. She ended their brief friendship immediately—finding out weeks later he had moved on to seducing Anna.

Though Melody had technically been cut off from Anna and the other Naturals, she had her ways—after all, look where she was now. Even though her dad had forbidden her socializing with the Naturals, Melody tracked down Anna and made it a point to fill her in on Drake before their relationship got too serious. It was with that conversation an old friendship between Melody and Anna was rekindled, and Drake ended up losing his shot at both women in less than a month.

He'd been incredibly bitter about it, and his spare time after that day was spent trying to make each of their lives miserable in any way that he could. Melody eventually went off to college, and Anna started dating Curt—another tragedy in itself.

"You going to at least say hi?" Drake asked, trying to fake a smile, breaking Melody out of her thought.

Smiling disingenuously, Melody acknowledged the evil in front of her. "Hey Drake, just off to see Mary Jane."

For a moment, Drake's face flattened, then the smile returned. "What do you want with her?"

Melody felt a small uncomfortable pang deep down, but dismissed it quickly. "Forget it Drake, you wouldn't understand."

"Your dad know you're here?"

"Of course he does," she lied, now just trying to get away.

"I miss having you around here you know, but you're in med school now, aren't you?" he commented almost sincerely.

"Whatever, Drake," Melody said with a wave of her hand as she tried to side-step around him, not wanting to get caught up in his trite attempts at conversation. But Drake moved directly in front of her, blocking her path, so fast that she stumbled into him, her face hitting his overdeveloped chest.

"You know she's no good," Drake said through suddenly clenched teeth. And for the first time since she was seventeen, Melody felt scared to be alone with the man. She wondered if her screams would reach Gabe back at his security desk, but she didn't need to find out.

Drake simply grabbed her by the shoulders and forcibly moved her to the side, stalking past her in a huff.

Halfway down the hall, not bothering to turn back, he called out. "For what it's worth, I'm glad we never dated."

Melody let the insult slide and took a moment to gather herself, straighten her shirt pulled askew by Drake's rough treatment and headed resolutely to Mary Jane's room.

Inside, a monitor was beeping out a heart rate as a respirator chimed in with a slow and steady *swoosh*. Mary Jane lay on a hospital bed, wires trailing from all parts of her body feeding into a variety of other medical devices as an IV dripped life slowly into her veins.

For over an hour she sat there undisturbed, holding the woman's chilly, unmoving hand. Feeling she had pressed her luck far enough Melody rose to leave. But not before leaning over to kiss Mary Jane's forehead and whisper something unintelligible into her ear.

With that, Melody moved over to the life support monitors and began checking vitals. She understood most of it. She was studying to be a doctor, just like her Dad. Yet in her mind, she was going to be so very much unlike her dad. "Cross my heart, hope not to die," she swore to herself.

CHAPTER 53

TOM FOOLERY

It was 1:12 p.m. and they were already late. The drive back to the Twin Cities had taken nearly two and a half hours, and as Grady's Mustang pulled up outside of O'Gara's, he felt a surge of anxiety over returning to this place. He hadn't been back since the night he had met Nancy that fateful New Years Eve, and at one point Grady thought he would never go back. But when Tom suggested it as a place to meet, Grady couldn't think of a way to suggest another spot.

Looking at the sign over the door, Anna gave Grady an odd look and he nodded. "Yes this is the place. I'm not sure why Tom chose it, other than it's near his house. Or maybe it's his way of punishing me for making him break into my house."

Anna gave Grady a disapproving shove, her way of telling Grady he was being foolish. But Grady wasn't so sure. Tom had kind of a sick sense of humor, and he might do something like this for strange reasons. Tom certainly knew the story that connected Grady with the place. Yet in Tom's defense, the bar was never the main topic of the story, and Grady never suggested he had a problem with returning to the bar.

Inside, Grady and Anna wandered down the long, dimly lit room, and there, in a far corner, Grady recognized Tom's tall figure sitting against the back wall, waiting patiently for them. As they approached, he stood to greet them.

"So this is the woman who has caused all this stir," he started in. "It's a pleasure to meet you finally. I'm Tom."

Tom took Anna's hand in his firm grip and shook it as he gestured toward the table with his free hand. "Here, have a seat."

Anna took the chair Tom was offering at the old square table, with Tom on her left and Grady taking a seat on her right. "We really appreciate all you have done for us," Anna said, trying to get things off on the right foot. "Grady told me all about the problems you faced. I guess all I can say is I'm sorry."

Tom held eye contact with Anna, giving Grady a brief look when she mentioned his name. "I have to tell you," he said, turning his focus to Grady, "I was more than a little angry yesterday when we spoke, but the situation was as much my fault as anyone's. You warned me and I knew the situation going in. I'm just glad it worked out."

Looking more relieved, Grady replied. "Thanks. The best part is that you're okay. I never expected it to be that sticky or I never would have asked you to do it."

Tom waved him off. "It's alright . . . and that's enough said on the subject. Now, assuming you both have a plane to catch, let's get down to business. I think you'll be happy with the results," he said, handing over a large manila envelope he had retrieved from a leather bag at the foot of his chair.

Grady took the envelope from Tom and peeked at the contents, without removing them. Inside were two passports along with Anna's picture from Grady's file. "Any problems with hers?" Grady asked, inclining his head toward Anna.

"No, they're as clean as can be without being genuine."

Grady caught a word from Tom he didn't like. "*They're* . . . meaning both?"

With an unpleasant grin, Tom replied in a low tone as if the four barflies who occupied the place today might overhear. "You didn't see what I saw yesterday. If you tried to get out of the country with your own passport you'd be sitting in the federal pen tonight, I'm sure of that. Those guys that were watching your house—they weren't messing around. So I hope you don't mind, but I went ahead and had them falsify one for you, too. Of course, if you prefer, I did retrieve your original."

Grady silently admonished himself, he should have though of that, but now he had another reason to be troubled. Mr. Bailey had already set up their plane reservations—using Grady's real name. If they used the fake passports, their names wouldn't match up to the flight manifest and they wouldn't be able to board.

Seeing Grady's expression, Tom leaned in. "What's on your mind?"

Grady started to explain the situation, but Tom suddenly excused himself in mid-conversation, stepping away to make a call on his phone. As he did, Anna looked apprehensively at Grady, wondering who Tom might be calling. Grady just shrugged, waiting patiently for his return.

When he did, Tom had a satisfied look on his face. "Sorry, my mistake. I didn't realize you'd already have your reservations. I just made a couple calls and you're all set. I managed to get you both on a later flight to London, under your new identities. Unfortunately, I had to make a rash decision. Instead of booking you on a connecting flight to Paris, I rented you a car and would suggest you drive to the Chunnel and use the Eurotunnel Shuttle into France. Figured with your other reservations out there, that by the time you land at Charles de Gaulle you could have a welcoming party. You wouldn't want to chance that. It'll put you back a few hours, but it will be safer."

Grady winced; he didn't like the idea of a delay right now, but Tom was right. "You did the right thing, but you didn't have to go to the trouble." Grady said, resting his hand on Anna's knee, giving it a little squeeze—his way of letting her know everything would be alright.

"Ah hell, call it a honeymoon present . . . for the newlyweds," Tom laughed, not fully realizing the relationship starting to form between Grady and Anna.

Seeing Grady and Anna weren't laughing at his joke, Tom turned toward Anna, his expression more serious. "I have to tell you the truth, Anna, I was all ready to pull Grady aside this afternoon and try to talk some sense into him. I was going to tell him no woman was worth the kind of trouble I witnessed at his house. But after meeting you I can't do that. Something tells me he's made the right choice."

Anna smiled, at a loss for what to say. Instead, her hand slid below the table to find Grady's, still resting on her knee, and she clasped it tightly.

"Just remember, you've got a guardian angel in Grady," Tom continued. "Trust him—he'll always be there for his friends, I promise."

"So you read the file I gave you, and my notes?" Grady asked, trying to get back to business.

"I did," Tom said sheepishly, turning his attention back to Grady. "Curled up with it last night before I went to bed . . . kind of made what I went through yesterday seem like child's play."

"There's more, and someday I'll have to fill you in. For now, take this," Grady said, handing over another sealed envelope. "It's an appendix to the original . . . a few things I've jotted down that might help if you ever need to turn the file over per my earlier instructions. The old standby still goes: 48 hours of no contact, call the press, then the cops. And I forgot to mention—if you hand over the info to the cops, be sure to mention the press has a copy, too. It just might help save your ass."

Tom took the envelope, eyeing it carefully. The fact that Grady had sealed it only piqued his curiosity.

Grady watched as Tom eventually pocketed the new documents in his coat's breast pocket. He knew, even if he told Tom not to open it, he would. So Grady had placed partial payment for Tom's services inside.

"I guess that about wraps it up," Grady said with a sigh.

"Aren't you going to look at the passports?" Tom asked, surprised.

"No, I trust you. If you say they are first rate, then I believe you. You'd have the better eye for it anyway."

"Thanks," Tom replied. "By the way, from now on you two are Mr. and Mrs. Keating. I used the same first names . . . less likely to mess up if you're interviewed at customs. You're traveling on business. When I booked these new flights I had to use my corporate card. You are both now in the antiquities business."

"You have a corp . . ." Grady began, and then just shook his head. Leave it to Tom to have a variety of ways to finance his little projects. A fake corporate card was a laugh, and an antiquities business made Grady wonder if he still didn't do a bit of high stakes thieving on the side.

Tom, realizing Grady wasn't going to finish his question, went on. "Also, at the airport, watch yourselves. Those other tickets you booked are still in the system, the ones with your real names. If the Feds had any reason to believe you might flee the country, they might have issued a watch on the airline manifests. So keep an eye out—they may be all over the terminal waiting for you to try and board that first flight."

"I can't thank you enough." Grady said, standing to leave.

Anna rose with him, sharing her own appreciation and a friendly hug, and Tom seized the opportunity to whisper a little something into her ear.

Almost forgetting, Grady shook Tom's hand and gave him one last set of instructions. "Keep a running tab of the bill and I'll settle up as soon as I can for all of your extra expenses."

"Yeah, thanks." Tom smiled. "Just don't go getting yourself killed."

CHAPTER 54

SETTING THE TRAP

M itch waited anxiously, situated in a secure room of Twin Cities International's VIP lounge. They had caught a break earlier today, and the decision to jet to Paris had been tabled at the last minute. Their 4:30 p.m. flight had been rescheduled for one that departed at 8:32 p.m. The reason: a hunch Mitch had. Calling some well-connected resources, he'd discovered a Grady J. Hamilton was booked on a 6:07 p.m. KLM flight to Paris tonight. And, it seemed more than coincidence that a woman named Anna Hamilton was also scheduled to travel with him.

Now, if all went according to plan, he wouldn't have to lift a finger to rein them in. That task would be handled by airport security, and a team of federal agents taking up their posts in one of the airport's terminals. Mitch was wary of using federal resources too often, as it invited unwelcome scrutiny on Northwoods and its operations. Yet, the opportunity in front of him was too great to pass up—and he couldn't very well set up surveillance in an airport without them.

Looking to his left toward an uncomfortably small couch upholstered in rich mahogany leather, Mitch noticed The Kid had finally dozed off. He had been popping pills ever since they started out from Northwoods that morning and Mitch guessed he was hitting a pretty big low right about now.

As expected, his travel companion hadn't exactly been thrilled about the delay. Still, Mitch found it odd that The Kid eventually accepted their change in plans without too much fuss. He'd even gone so far as to bet Mitch that Anna and Grady would slip through his fingers once more. The thought infuriated Mitch and it made him wonder if The Kid knew something he didn't know.

Frustrated with what he guessed was the answer to his own question, Mitch glanced at his watch, telling him it was just a little past four. It was still early. Momentarily satisfied that little was going to happen in the next hour, he decided he needed a little something to relax. Quietly, so as not wake his travel companion, he made his way out of the room and over to the common area. Bellying up to the bar, he ordered a scotch and water. It wasn't a celebration . . . that would come later. Right now he just needed to settle his nerves.

Grady and Anna entered the terminal separately at about 4:20 p.m. The divided arrival was by design, for two reasons. First, Grady knew if federal agents were searching for them, they would be looking for couples that fit their general description, so individuals might not draw their immediate attention. Second, Grady wanted to pass through security first, that way if he were detained there was still a possibility that Anna could get away undetected.

Anna protested, but in the end Grady won out. For now, she was to act nonchalant, waiting patiently on an open bench, as Grady made his way through the ticketing line. At the counter, the ticketing agent asked him to show his passport and he handed it over, trying to suppress his feelings of anxiety. The woman behind the counter smiled at him and made small talk as she prepared his boarding documents, checked his bag, and returned his passport to him without incident.

Having seen Grady clear the counter, Anna rose and made her way into the ticketing line. Another ten minutes passed and she received her boarding pass as effortlessly as Grady had. Leaving the ticketing area, Anna moved to her right, spotting Grady right where he said he would be—waiting in line to be screened by security.

As planned, Anna waited before going to the end of the long line to wait her turn. According to Grady's instructions, he was to clear the scanners completely before Anna moved again. Trying to casually pass time, she fidgeted around in her purse as if looking for something she'd lost. All the while she kept one eye on Grady.

With a hat tucked low on his forehead, Grady kept his head down as he approached security. Since the events of 9/11, he knew of new facial recognition devices that could pick people out of a crowd and put a name to them almost instantly. He didn't know if this airport had them, or if his face would even be registered in the database, but he wanted to keep a low profile. Either way, there were certainly unseen people tucked behind video monitors, watching every person who passed security and entered the concourses.

Approaching the bag scanners, Grady removed his hat and shoes before setting down a small carry-on he had borrowed from Mr. Bailey on the conveyor belt, watching as his belongings disappeared inside the machine. His heart thumping loudly in his chest, he walked as casually as he could, through the white arch of the metal detector. Careful to have placed any metallic objects in his carry-on, the detector didn't make a peep.

On the other side, the security guard with the wand watched him closely. Trying to be as inconspicuous as possible, Grady made eye contact with the uniformed man, nodding a friendly hello. The guard didn't return the greeting, but at least made no move to detain Grady as he went about retrieving his bag.

Clear of security, Grady glanced back over his shoulder, caught Anna's eye and gave her a nod. Immediately she turned and took her place in line, preparing to go through the process Grady had. As he waited for her, Grady reflected on the ease of the process so far, wondering if the tickets booked under their real names wouldn't be their saving grace. If the Feds and Northwoods had been tipped off to their first set of reservations under Grady's real name, perhaps they would be lulled into a false sense of confidence, simply waiting for someone named Grady J. Hamilton to check in. But Grady and Anna Hamilton would never check in today, and once the authorities realized that, Grady hoped it would be too late.

Looking back at Anna, Grady noticed she was just placing her purse on the conveyor belt, her face remarkably composed. She cleared the metal detector and was just about to get her purse when the guard called her over. Swearing under his breath, Grady caught a slight change in her expression and knew she was frightened.

The guard seemed polite enough, as he wanded Anna from head to ankles, yet just like Grady she had made sure she wasn't carrying a scrap of metal on her. For a moment, the wand screeched as it swung over the button on her jeans, but the guard didn't seem fazed by it and let Anna go.

Grabbing her purse, Anna walked as calmly as she could manage over to Grady, smiling wearily as she slid her hand into his and they began their long walk down the concourse to their gate. "I'm glad that's over," she said, exhaustion in her voice.

Grady squeezed her hand gently, "Me too. But it's not completely over. I checked this flight's information against our prior flight and our new departure gate is actually four gates past our original gate."

Anna looked confused. "What does that mean?"

"It means we have to pass gate 14, the one we would have departed from if we kept our original flight plans. There's a possibility there might be some plain-clothes agents and security watching that gate pretty closely if anyone happened across our first reservation."

Anna's shoulders sagged in disbelief. "I thought we were done."

Stopping Anna in the middle of the concourse Grady looked into her eyes as people began to mill past them. "Not quite . . . soon though," he said. "We'll have to split up here again. Just be calm and we'll be alright."

Anna's eyes were unconvinced, but Grady pressed on. "Perhaps you might want to use the facilities," he said, nodding over to the women's restrooms. Then he reached up and tugged lightly on a wide-brimmed sun hat Anna had been sporting to hide her hair. "I think your hat needs some straightening. Should only take a minute . . . I'll be waiting for you a little past gate 14. Got it?"

Understanding Grady's instructions, Anna wandered into the bathroom, dallying a bit as she checked her hat in the mirror, pulling it down a little lower on her forehead before returning to the concourse. Up ahead, she thought she could still see Grady's head bobbing up and down in the midst of a large crowd. Keeping her eyes on him, she kept an even pace behind him, thinking that if she could somehow keep him in sight, everything would be fine.

So intent was she on Grady that she didn't even realize when she came upon gate 14. Unexpectedly, the man walking directly in front of her veered right on his way to his own gate and Anna plowed into a stationary figure—a tall, elegant gentleman dressed in a sharply tailored dark suit.

"Excuse me," she said with surprise, as she steadied herself, placing her hand briefly on the man's suit coat.

He smiled at her, telling her it was all right, but Anna barely heard the words. Instantly gripped by intense fear, it took every ounce of willpower to prevent her legs from bolting down the concourse in pursuit of Grady. For where her hand had rested, she was sure she felt the outline of a concealed gun, not to mention, the man's kind smile didn't fit with the intense scrutiny she saw behind his eyes.

Begging forgiveness once more, Anna avoided eye contact, hitched up her purse and strode as calmly as she could around the man. Resisting the temptation to look back, she focused straight ahead, desperately trying to pick out Grady once more.

For a moment, the federal agent turned to watch Anna go. Yes, he knew her name. Getting that close to her, it was hard not to miss her. The I.D. on Grady had been almost as easy, for a different set of reasons. For the time being he tucked the information away. Right now he wasn't sure what he was going to do about it.

Safely past gate 15, Anna picked up speed as she saw Grady waiting just ahead. By the time she reached him, she was practically race walking before she fell into his arms. "I think one of them recognized me," she blurted out as they hugged.

Looking back from where they came, Grady replied thoughtfully, "I'm guessing it's okay. I was watching the whole thing. I'm pretty sure he noticed me, too."

Anna broke from Grady, asking a simple, but loaded question. "Why?"

Smiling vaguely, Grady gave his best guess. "He's an old friend. We entered the Bureau together as rookies. We'd been close for a while, but . . ." Grady trailed off.

"Do you think they'll still come for us?"

Grady looked back at where they'd come from only moments before, but his mind was reaching even further back into the past for an answer. Finally, he simply said. "No."

Anna expression was one of disbelief, imagining the man calling in backup as they stood there debating their situation. But she'd heard the conviction in Grady's voice.

"It will be okay," Grady said. "Why don't I buy you a drink?"

Both still a little shaken, Grady led Anna to a concourse bar where they sunk back into the shadows and waited. For the next couple hours they gradually stopped looking over their shoulders and started enjoying each other's company. Finally, the clock over the bar ticked 7:00 p.m.—well past their original departure time—and the first boarding calls for their flight to London began. In the end, nobody came to intercept them, and Grady and Anna boarded their flight to London without delay.

Swearing, Mitch picked up his carry-on and threw it against the wall. It didn't help that The Kid sat there watching him with a huge smirk on his face.

Somehow Grady and Anna had eluded him again. *Had they gotten on a different plane, or caught wind of the security and decided to bag the trip?* He didn't really know. All he knew was that Northwoods had told him to continue on to Paris with The Kid and follow the plan to track down

Trent and Joe. Other assets here in the states would keep an eye out for Grady and Anna. It was a fact that made Mitch even angrier. Even though, deep down Mitch knew if he found Trent and Joe, Anna and Grady would be somewhere close by. But for now he wouldn't admit that to himself. Right now, he wanted to seethe.

CHAPTER 55

STATE OF MIND

"What can I get you to drink?" A polite and slightly anorexic-looking flight attendant asked Grady and Anna. The two had been seated in a row of three on the left side of the KLM Airbus—one of which was thankfully left vacant so they were able to pull up their armrests and stretch out.

Glancing up from a magazine, Grady ordered a Samuel Adams, Anna a Chardonnay, and the flight attendant busied herself filling their orders. When she was done, the woman handed each beverage over before moving brightly on to the next row.

"To France," Grady said, raising his beer in a mock toast. Anna obliged, clinking her plastic glass off his tin before each took a sip of their drinks.

"I need to thank you," Anna said, looking over at Grady. "I'm not sure what I would have done without your help. You've put your life on hold to help me out."

Grady gazed out the window at multitudes of stars twinkling against a dome of deep purple sky, burnt to an orangish-yellow glow in the west where the horizon met the curve of the earth. "Wasn't much of a life," Grady offered, pensively.

Anna reached over and stroked the top of Grady's hand with her fingertips. "I can't promise it's going to get better. In fact, it'll probably get worse."

Turning to Anna, Grady gave her a disapproving look. "You can't be getting pessimistic on me now . . . we'll be fine."

Anna sighed, "There's something you need to know. Something I haven't told you, at least not fully."

Anna had Grady's attention. She always did, but this moment felt different.

"It's the dreams I've been having. There's one that recurs and it's not exactly pleasant." Anna began hesitantly.

Grady knew better than to respond so he let her gather herself for what she wanted to say next.

"The vision I have, is of you and me, and we're . . . well, we're at Northwoods."

Seeing the distress on Anna's face, Grady asked a question he already knew the answer to. "I'm assuming we are not there of our own free will?"

"No," she said bluntly.

"How certain are you that this is really going to happen? Your visions could be wrong, couldn't they?"

"Of course, they could . . . but unless they stop, or change, it's unlikely." Anna answered honestly, weighing her next sentence carefully. "There's one way I can think of to make sure it doesn't happen."

Warily, Grady asked, "How's that?"

"You could leave me. Once we're in London, go home, forget I ever existed and try to rebuild your life," Anna suggested sadly.

His eyes softening, Grady's next words came from the heart. "I think my life may have just started over a few days ago. You don't just walk away from that."

Anna tried to offer a smile, but the corners of her mouth turned down, twitching as she fought off tears. She didn't want to cry . . . not now, not again.

A few minutes passed between them in silence, the only words spoken were from other conversations going on around them, muffled by the constant whir of the jet's engines.

"Anna," Grady finally said with an intended directness. "I need to know something. I need to know everything actually, because right now I can't accept a predetermined future. And if you're so sure this event will happen, I need to know how your mind works—why you see what you do. Then, maybe we can come up with a plan to change it."

Happy to see the fighting spirit still burning in Grady, Anna took strength from him and told him what she knew.

"I guess I'll start at the beginning," she began a bit warily. "But you'll have to tell me if I lose you. It's not your everyday high school physics material."

"Just try me," Grady said. "I actually made it through college physics."

"I didn't mean . . ." Anna began, but thought better of it, preferring not to get sidetracked.

"Grady, there's a theory in the scientific community, which Northwoods is working at the forefront on, that describes our universe in a way few might be able to understand. Some theorize that there isn't a single be-all end-all universe that most people think of, instead there are an infinite number of universes diverging and converging upon each other."

Looking at Grady, she saw that she maybe had lost him already, so she backtracked a bit. "Let me give you an example. Imagine you are at your breakfast table and have just finished your second cup of coffee."

"Alright," Grady said closing his eyes, willing to follow this out to wherever it might take him.

"Good. Now let's say you have a meeting in 30 minutes, and you are trying to decide whether you have enough time for a third cup of coffee. First, let's assume you follow the first two-cup scenario through. You leave the house with plenty of time, drive normally at a modest speed and arrive five minutes early for your meeting. Life goes on as usual. You got me so far?"

"I don't understand how . . ." Grady started to say, but Anna cut him off.

"Just listen," she said a bit impatiently. "Lets call that universe number one. Now lets go back and assume you decided to have that third cup of coffee. We'll call it universe number two. Wanting the extra cup of coffee, you down it fast and realize now you are in danger of being late for your meeting. Rushing out the door, you hop in your car and speed off 10 miles per hour over your normal comfort level. As a result of your rush, you are driving more carelessly than you might normally. Let's say that in your haste you hit a patch of ice, the car skids out of control, it hits a bridge support and you're killed instantly. Questions?" Anna asked lightly as though she had just described a trip to an amusement park.

"No, but I think I should cut out coffee altogether." Grady said jokingly.

"Be serious," Anna chided playfully, knowing full well she had encouraged his reaction. "You see, the multiple universe theory would call these divergent universes—one resulting in your life ongoing, the other veering off as far as possible with the extreme being the end of your life. What I'm getting at here is that every decision we are faced with in life could result in a fracturing off of universes until unimaginably, all possibilities are covered. This is mandated by the base theory that calls for infinite universes, meaning everything is possible and does exist."

Pausing, Anna saw the look in Grady's eyes and knew she had him hooked again.

"Now, let's go back to universe number two—the third cup of coffee scenario." Anna acted like a teacher, directing her student's mind. "Assume you change lanes right before you would have hit that patch of ice, and so your car remains on the road. We'll call this universe number three. Now you hit a few green lights and suddenly you're gaining on the alternate you in universe number one. Perhaps you even made up enough time that you reached your destination only a few minutes behind the other you in universe number one. The meeting in both universes starts at the same time, and suddenly universe one and universe three are virtually identical. Yet prior experiences affect our lives daily, so no matter how closely they come back together, they can never be exactly the same. These are defined now as parallel universes."

Anna cut off her explanation a moment, as the flight attendant came back around and asked if they needed anything else. Both Grady and Anna politely declined before Anna continued.

"Here's where it can get really confusing," Anna said earnestly, "but it relates directly to how Northwoods thinks the Naturals foresee future events. The theory goes on to describe a universe without our traditional concept of time, where each moment in your life is actually a snapshot that exists eternally. For example, your exact moment of birth is an eternal frame in the universe, existing indefinitely. Now imagine these snapshots of all the moments in your life lined up like a deck of cards standing on end, which you can flip through, like a moving picture book to see life in motion . . . as a whole."

Grady nodded thoughtfully, trying hard to digest the information and jump ahead to where he thought Anna might be going with it all.

"Now think of the intervals in-between these pictures, the space that links one moment to the next. In terms of our consciousness, we perceive these intervals to be equal, and a measure of what we call time. For the sake of a visual reference, let's say that each photo card is connected by a piece of elastic that you can stretch out or compress in."

"Time is elastic!" Grady piped in excitedly.

Enjoying Grady's enthusiasm, Anna somewhat confirmed his belief. "Yes, in a way, although the theory holds that time as we know it doesn't truly exist. Anyway, even though the distance between the cards increases or decreases, we still perceive the intervals between to pass in the constant measured amount we define as time."

Seeing the light now, Grady broke in. "You're going to go back to the parallel universes, right?"

"Exactly!" Anna said, proud of her quick study. "Now, let's string out universe number one, the two cups of coffee, with universe three, the three cups of coffee and mark the same chronological moment in each with an X. We'll use the beginning of that hypothetical meeting as our common moment. But why don't we say that some external force has constricted a section of universe number one while universe number three is spread out. Now, if you run each universe side by side, the X's won't align. In fact the moment marked with an X in universe three might sit side by side with a future moment in universe one—perhaps an event two days or even two weeks from now."

Fascinated, Grady wanted to hear more. "I think I know the answer, but I'll ask anyway. How does this tie back to you?"

Anna smiled a bit self-consciously. It all sounded great until she realized it all related back to her, but she continued on. "Northwoods thinks that the Naturals—during peak periods of brain activity—can tap into these parallel universes, briefly glimpsing events from a parallel world, one that converges but never fully joins. The more they have in common with our present experience, the easier they are to see. If a parallel universe is running side-by-side and is constricted compared to ours, the result of what we see is a portion of a slightly altered future. In reality, Northwoods believes it's a skill all humans possess, although on a limited basis—perhaps explaining why many people have sudden feelings of déjà vu."

"It's hard to imagine," Grady said honestly, "but it's fascinating."

"It's a gross oversimplification, of course," Anna added, "but it begins to describe the possible mechanics of a multiple-universe theory and how those universes might interact."

"So what you're saying is that if your visions follow the theory, the events you are glimpsing are not technically events of this universe, but of another eerily similar one?"

"Yes," Anna said cautiously, sensing where he was going with it.

"But that means that there are no guarantees that what you are seeing will come true."

Anna sighed. She figured Grady would try to go there. "Not exactly. Over my time at Northwoods they would track the accuracy of my visions. They actually did this for all of the Naturals."

"And?" Grady asked, not sure he wanted to know the answer.

"My accuracy scores were well over ninety percent . . . about ninety-four percent to be exact." Anna answered sadly. There are also rumors that the mysterious Fifth Seed that I told you about had episodes where his accuracy was over ninety-nine percent."

Anna could see the hope drain from his expression. "But Grady, that's where knowing the future comes in handy. Northwoods tested altering the future using the knowledge they gained from us. With that knowledge they were able to do simple things to change future outcomes, so that the events we foretold only came to fruition about sixty percent of the time."

Grady could sense the circular argument Anna was trying to make and he didn't like it. He grasped her hand in his, and looked her firmly in the eyes—holding her gaze for several seconds before saying, "Anna, I'm not leaving you."

CHAPTER 56

PARTNERS IN CRIME

I
t was well past midnight, but Kyle Brady remained at his small, dark cubicle inside the Minnesota headquarters of the FBI, at 111 Washington Avenue South in downtown Minneapolis. A single reading lamp and the glow of his computer monitor shed barely enough light to read by. In front of him, he had spread out the file on Grady J. Hamilton. The paperwork inside detailed his expulsion from the FBI, the case against him in the Nancy Broder murder and the most recent addition—the growing case linking him with an attempted townhouse shooting in Maple Grove.

Kyle was familiar with most of it, but the events at the townhouse were new to him. Digging further into the papers, he discovered, based on an anonymous tip, that police had questioned Grady a few nights ago concerning the shooting. Kyle also found it interesting that the owner of the townhouse, Mary Jane Flannigan, had mysteriously disappeared.

The file itself offered few clues about who Mary Jane was, or leads on her possible whereabouts, although some of that might be covered in the missing persons report filed on her behalf. That case was cross-referenced in Grady's file, a file Kyle technically shouldn't be digging into since he wasn't actually assigned to the case.

Reading further, Kyle discovered that after the incident, several of Mary Jane's neighbors had indicated to investigators a young woman had been staying with Mary Jane for the last few weeks, although none seemed to have a clue as to her identity. If this woman existed she had vanished as well.

Flipping a few more pages in the file, Kyle located the evidence log. According to it, a single slug fired from a Sig Sauer P229 Equinox had been retrieved from the base of a ten-foot pine tree out in back of the townhouse. Trajectory analysis suggested the bullet had traveled from inside the townhouse and through a sliding glass door before lodging in the trunk of the tree. The report also indicated Grady possessed a registered Sig Sauer P229 Equinox—although the report did not indicate a ballistics match had been created between the gun and the bullet.

Pausing a moment, Kyle set the file down and rubbed his face. "What the hell have you gotten yourself into this time, Grady?" he said to the empty room. At almost 12:45 in the morning, the Twin Cities FBI field office was deserted and right now Kyle was thankful for that. He wasn't exactly breaking any laws, but there were enough people who would certainly wonder why he had taken such an interest in Grady and this most recent case.

Kyle had known Grady for a long time. In fact, they had entered the FBI at the same time, and had served as partners at one brief point in their ascending careers. It had surprised the hell out of Kyle when he received a call from Grady just a day and a half ago. He recalled Grady had a couple of questions, which Kyle never really let him get to. He had been busy and overstressed that day, and basically brushed Grady off, acting as though his call was an unwelcome intrusion. Something Kyle regretted given the current circumstances.

It really didn't surprise Kyle to see Grady at the airport, just a few hours ago. In fact, he had been brought in specifically to I.D. Grady, since they had known each other so well. Instead, Kyle had let him walk right past him. *Dumb move?* He didn't know.

"Now what to do?" Kyle said to himself again. He had always thought Grady got a raw deal on the Broder investigation . . . losing his job and all. Confident Grady had nothing to do with it, Kyle genuinely felt sorry for the guy. Perhaps that was why he gave Grady the break he did in the airport. Like it or not, he had stuck his neck out for his old friend, and now in retrospect, he needed to justify to himself the *why* of it all.

Lacking answers, he turned back to Grady's file, poring over it once more. Something wasn't making sense and he needed to find out why. Returning to the section about Mary Jane, Kyle decided to dig into her missing persons report. This report he felt comfortable bringing up on the screen.

He had sought out the paper file for Grady from the active cases files, because accessing it on his computer would have created an electronic sign-in that would have connected Kyle and his interest in the case. Right now he felt that was best keep secret.

The file in its paper form was supposed to be signed out as well, but the procedures had become pretty lax. All Kyle had to do was write in the case number on a ledger, log a time out, and sign his name in front of a security guard. But the process had become so routine for everyone over the years, that the guard rarely watched the process closely and it was quite easy for Kyle to enter the number for one of his own active cases instead. He would return the file in the morning with no one the wiser . . . he hoped.

Kyle's monitor now showed a photo of Mary Jane accompanied by a short physical description, and the sketchy details around her disappearance. The first anomaly that hit him was the missing person's report listed Mary Jane as a.k.a. Mary Jane Henderson. Kyle was confident Flannigan was a false identity. He had run a couple of background checks on M.J. Flannigan earlier in the evening, just to familiarize himself with the key players in the mystery, and found the woman's life on the planet seemed to start just a few short months ago. The a.k.a. notation seemed to confirm his hunch.

"What the hell were you doing at this woman's house?" he again asked the empty void of the federal offices. With a new name in hand for Mary Jane, Kyle entered it into a database search and hit the jackpot, as he watched social security, employment, housing, banking, medical and a whole host of other links to records line up on his screen. Kyle picked the employment record link, figuring it would give him the quickest background and history of the woman's life. Every job Mary Jane ever held instantly popped up. He decided to print the document for future reference, and then did the same with her housing record and the missing person's report.

At the printer just steps from his cubical, Kyle retrieved the documents and started scanning them as he walked slowly back to his desk. It was there, standing in the middle of a narrow hall, that something on the employment report caught his eye. The piece of information was buried in Mary Jane's employment history, with the name Northwoods somehow ringing a bell. Kyle recalled the brief conversation he had with Grady. Grady had been trying to ask him if he had any information about Northwoods!

Racing back to his desk, Kyle brought up the search engine again and typed Northwoods into the first field. Moments later a directory with an electronic file bearing a small FBI icon showed up on his screen. Opening it, a page appeared with a brief description of the Northwoods facility. According to the information, the place was a private center for troubled youths. Even though this was little information to go on, the fact the FBI had a file on the place said something. Looking in the lower right-hand side of his computer screen Kyle saw something else that interested him even more. It was a link that read confidential with the words Level 2 Clearance below it.

That was bad luck, for he only had level 4 clearance—the lower the number the greater the access. Unfortunately there was no way he could see the information contained therein without breaking the FBI code and the law. Still, this too was significant, since he didn't know of anyone at his field office with level 2 clearances, except perhaps the Special Agent in Charge. How was Grady linked to this woman Mary Jane? Was he involved in her disappearance? And did it all have something to do with Northwoods, an institution that was either under investigation by the FBI or linked to it in some way? Right now he didn't have any solid answers.

About to close down his computer for the night, Kyle noticed he had failed to scroll down completely through the Northwoods document.

Clicking on the down arrow, new text began to appear. It was a link with a brief description and a date that indicated it was several weeks old. Clicking the link Kyle was taken to the *Minneapolis StarTribune* web site, and the article that followed. Reading quickly, Kyle discovered only a few short weeks ago four patients from the Northwoods treatment center in upstate Minnesota had escaped, their whereabouts unknown. The article went on to talk about the patients in greater detail.

Kyle scanned the four names and found one that stood out like a sore thumb. The name was Anna Jenkins. Wasn't Anna the name of the woman Grady had been traveling with? He knew this from the mission briefing for the airport surveillance assignment. From memory, he knew the briefing had her last name listed as Anna Hamilton . . . but up until this point, Kyle had just assumed Grady had gotten married. Scrolling to the end of the article, Kyle saw four photos of the individuals. Here, Anna looked much younger, but viewing the slightly grainy picture, he knew instantly it was the same woman he had bumped into yesterday.

Suddenly things were getting interesting.

CHAPTER 57

CATCH ME IF YOU CAN

After discovering the links between Grady, Mary Jane and now Anna, and after letting Grady and Anna walk by him at the airport, Kyle knew he had to get more information, which meant he needed to get deeper in a case that clearly his superiors didn't want him directly involved in. Having worked as Grady's partner before, this made sense—yet Kyle had an odd feeling there was more to the Bureau's holding back of information. This case had "national security" written all over it if the Bureau's high-clearance file on Northwoods meant what he thought it did.

It was for this reason he made a trip to the video lab right before he left for the night. What Kyle did on his way out could not only get his bosses on his case for sticking his nose somewhere it shouldn't be, but could get him ousted from the Bureau. He'd basically lifted several important DVDs containing the video surveillance recordings at Grady's house. Somewhere on these discs was footage of a yet-to-be identified intruder who broke in to Grady's house just recently. A notation in Grady's file had tipped Kyle off to the DVDs' existence.

To get the discs, Kyle had to convince Lance, who ran the Bureau's video lab, that he was at least on the periphery of the Grady case. This really wasn't an outright lie, since Kyle had been brought in to canvas the airport. But it was certainly a stretch of the truth. In any event, it wasn't Lance's ass that would be on the line if what Kyle had done

244

were discovered; it would be his own. Without so much as a pointed question, or suspicious undertone, Lance produced copies of the DVDs in question. Since Kyle was checking them out, they had to be a back up copies. The genuine recordings were physical evidence and they weren't leaving the lab without signed release forms, no matter who asked.

At home, and up way too late to make sleep before tomorrow an option, Kyle loaded the last of the five discs he'd received from Lance into his iMac. The disc slid gently into the side of the monitor with a hiss and a whir. Moments later, on the 27 inch widescreen, high-definition display, a small disc-shaped icon appeared. Double-clicking on it Kyle accessed the raw video file titled C5 and dragged it into a folder on his desktop. He opened that folder to reveal the other discs he'd copied to his desktop for quick, easy access. Each copy was titled sequentially, C1, C2, C3, C4 as well as the disc he'd just dropped in the folder: C5.

Clicking on C1, which referenced the first camera, Kyle's computer began loading the QuickTime application and just ten seconds later an image of what appeared to be Grady's front door was displayed in full color.

Selecting the onscreen play button, the still video image flickered to life, but the image remained basically unchanged. Watching the first 40-minutes, Kyle saw nothing unusual, other than a gradual progression in the angle of the sunbeams filtering through the nearby windows across Grady's hardwood floors. Then at 2:46:23, the front door burst in as two federal agents stormed into Grady's house. Yet at least from this angle, there had been no signs of the intruder on the entire tape.

To Kyle's disgust, the angle of camera two showed nothing useful—a shot of Grady's bedroom upstairs. This time, at about 2:46:58, two police officers were the first to enter the frame, but whoever had broken into Grady's house apparently wasn't interested in anything that might be found in the man's bedroom, as he was nowhere to be seen. By this point, Kyle had spent over two hours watching basically nothing but some officers and federal agents pulling maneuvers in a deserted house.

Still, hoping for the best, he selected C3 and hit play. It took nearly 40 minutes before the back door swung slowly inward. Instantly alert, Kyle leaned forward, his face just a foot away from the glowing computer monitor as he began to scrutinize the image. A lone figure, dressed in a dark jogging suit and matching baseball hat flashed so quickly across the screen, Kyle might have missed it had he blinked.

Rewinding, he watched the footage twice more before letting the video run again. With nothing else to see, Kyle reflected on the man he had just seen. The intruder was adept. He kept his hat low and his head down and, since the camera had been mounted high, the shadow of his cap or the cap itself always obscured the man's face.

At about 2:45:14, Kyle saw the same two cops enter cautiously through the back door then disappear from view, but in the remaining fifteen minutes the stranger never appeared again. Kyle knew the man couldn't have left by either the front or back door, and he began to wonder how the guy had escaped.

Anxious about what he might discover, Kyle put off sleep and ran C4 next . . . the footage of Grady's office. Dragging the progress icon below the video display window, Kyle advanced to a point close to where he guessed the man had appeared on the C3 playback. His guess was close, and it took only a minute for the same dark figure to appear in the doorway. The camera angle was a little better—even though the camera was mounted high, probably in an air vent, the angle was longer and not so steep as before, thus Kyle hoped for the best.

Still, the man kept his head down, never once looking up as he dug in a drawer of Grady's desk before retrieving an unidentifiable object. The way the man had positioned himself in front of the drawer, his body blocked any clear view of what he may have pocketed. As quickly as he came, the man in black was back out the office door. Replaying the sequence, pausing and even zooming in at key points, Kyle still found the man's face indiscernible.

Nonetheless, he had gained some valuable information. The man he saw was purposeful and deliberate. He wasted no time, and seemed to know exactly what he was looking for, ruling out that this was a chance robbery caught by some overzealous federal agents. Instead, the man had been sent to do a job—by Grady himself perhaps? Kyle wondered.

Exhausted and on his last option, Kyle accessed the final camera footage, praying he might catch a break. He was disappointed to see it showed what was probably Grady's detached garage. The view was from the inside, again at a high angle, focusing on the right rear of the garage and the service door out the back leading to the yard. There was little light, as there appeared to be only one small window, close to the door on the right wall of the garage. The lack of light in the garage didn't matter much, because the garage door never budged once.

Checking the clock on his computer screen he noticed it was now nearly 5:30 a.m. Having been up all night, he was thankful today was an off day for him. He was tired and ready to call it quits. For the time being, he gave up on the recordings, walked down the hallway and crawled into bed, wondering if he'd made the right decision letting Grady slip by him at the airport.

CHAPTER 58

HIGHER INTERESTS

Allan was pacing. He rarely let his nerves get to him like this, but the early morning meeting he had in five minutes was extraordinarily important. After all, it was what his life's work had been all about. His eyes drifted to a bank of lighted panels attached the far wall of the medical research lab, each holding a still image of a brain scan. On the panels, huge areas of bright reds, oranges, yellows and whites bloomed in different lobes of the brain. They had been carefully labeled, with patient A, B, C and D—each representing a different Natural—as well as a brief description of what the colors represented.

Below the scans, on a long table, sat a set four high-definition computer monitors. These monitors displayed recordings of four other individuals' brain scans. The scans ran real time in steady loops, starting with dark muted colors. After which, a spot would appear and spread, the colors brightening in irregular concentric shapes from red, to orange, then yellow and white—like a thunderstorm bursting forth on a Doppler radar map. In some ways, Allan mused these were like mini-storms erupting across the brain. The purpose of this demonstration was to show how Northwoods was beginning to replicate the brain functions of the Naturals in normal individuals.

For the briefest moment, Allan let his mind stray from his presentation. He wondered how Mitch and The Kid were doing together. He knew from their last contact they had come up empty at the airport, something that didn't surprise Allan. He knew little of Grady, but enough to know the man wouldn't be so reckless as to show up and claim a ticket in his name—it had to be a ruse. But he also guessed Grady would find a way to get Anna over to Europe. So Allan had instructed Mitch and The Kid to travel abroad and reign in his Naturals.

He hoped there would be few questions from his guest about the Naturals' escape. His guest knew a little about the Naturals and the testing but only what Allan chose to divulge. He was certainly wary of sharing too much about the tests. For one, his guest was given information on a need to know basis only. The details were not as important as the broad brushstrokes. In addition, Allan wasn't sure his superior would be able to stomach some of the things he had started doing to the test subjects, all in an effort to advance his research more quickly, to get the results that were demanded of him.

"How would I have made the progress I've made in such short time, though?" he asked himself rhetorically. "Impossible." The time had come that the Naturals could no longer be around. They were getting too old, too uncooperative for his needs. Retaining them forever would be impractical, and sending them off into the world with a polite *sorry for the inconvenience* would be career suicide.

What did it matter in the end if the Naturals had to disappear? They were few and the rewards to the masses were many. If one considered the long-term benefits of his research, the potential savings in lives could be astronomical. But now, the Naturals couldn't be around. They could bring it all crashing down around him. The potential rewards, not only for him, but also for all humankind, were too great. "Yes, it is all worthwhile," he told himself.

Straightening his suit-coat and tie, he took one last deep breath, surveyed the room, and stole a glance at the door to the Environments, where he would conduct the second part of the demonstration. Two members of his guest's security detail and one member of his staff were sweeping that area for so-called threats. But Allan knew his security . . . there were none. Finally he checked his watch. It was time.

Right on cue, his executive assistant opened the door. A sharply dressed man with earpiece tucked behind his left ear strode in. Knowing the room had been thoroughly checked only a few minutes before, the man swept the room with his eyes and gave a nod back toward the door as the guest walked in.

Allan's own assistant recognized the nod and started in. "Welcome to Northwoods. Allow me to present the esteemed Dr. Allan Hauser."

CHAPTER 59

LAST LEG TO LONDON

Outside the window of the massive KLM airbus, the flaps began to extend back and descend to form a gradual arc, the pilot making final preparations for the descent into Heathrow. The effect in the cabin was a noticeable lurch forward as the plane decelerated. Anna, resting on Grady's shoulder, rose up in her seat and clutched his hand.

Unfazed, Grady accepted her moist palm, grasping it reassuringly. In between naps, beverages, and breakfast, Grady and Anna had used the time to get to know each other better. The one thing that amazed Grady about Anna was how much she knew about life outside Northwoods. Having been cloistered within an institute since she was twelve, she knew a remarkable amount about the real world, including air travel, shopping, etiquette in social situations and much more. On the surface, she didn't appear to be naive to the chaos of the real world. So far Anna handled herself as if she had lived in society since birth.

To Grady's surprise, Anna explained that Northwoods spent an inordinate amount of time coaching each Natural about the real world, going so far as to build elaborate sets, making the Naturals role-play with members of the Northwoods staff who acted the part of ticket agents, waitresses, hotel clerks, shop keepers, bank tellers and so forth. Northwoods also encouraged the Naturals to watch movies from an approved list. Grady guessed those movies spent a lot of time depicting real-world situations. He felt this information was significant in some way, making him wonder why Northwoods invested so much time conditioning the Naturals.

The answers in his mind disturbed him. And a new question began to form. "Did Northwoods ask you to role-play using any of the foreign languages you speak?" Grady inquired, not ready to share his theory just yet.

Anna looked at Grady, studying him, wondering where he might be going with the question. "Yes, often," she finally replied. "Why do you ask?"

Grady just shook her off. "Just something I've been pondering. We're going to need to find out what use Northwoods had in mind for you," he added pensively.

Grady was about to ask another question when the plane began to bank slowly to the left. At that moment the captain came over the intercom to announce that, due to strong storms in the area, they were expecting heavy turbulence on their descent—so all passengers should return to their seats with safety belts fastened. Grady decided that for the moment his question could wait.

Anna released his hand and went about buckling herself in. Grady had kept his belt loosely buckled, so he took the chance to quietly observe Anna. He couldn't help but note the soft swell of her breasts as she straightened herself up in her seat, and that she had to suck in her breath to fit the belt around her waist. She liked the thing tight.

Anna's hands paused, in mid-buckle, as if something had distracted her attention. Becoming self-conscious, Grady quickly raised his eyes, and found Anna looking at him with a quirky smile. Apparently she had been watching him watch her.

"See something you like?" she asked amused, the ends of the seat belt still held, unconnected, in her hands.

Blushing, Grady gave a half-smirk and tried to change the subject. "Have you flown before?"

"Once," she said matter-of-factly, disappointed he had switched subjects so quickly. She liked teasing him. She also liked the fact that he showed interest in her body, among other things. "I vaguely remember the trip when I was twelve, when a woman came to get me and transfer me to Northwoods. Why do you ask?" She asked, the buckle momentarily forgotten.

"I understand you have had training, but a buckle as tight as you have leads me to believe you may have had a bad experience on a flight before."

Anna sighed. "I can hardly recall specific details, it was so long ago, but I remember it being extremely bumpy, particularly on landing. I guess it stuck with me."

Grady patted her knee reassuringly as lightning strobed outside the window. He was about to say something to ease her stress, when the plane lurched, dropping suddenly before quickly restabilizing.

Anna's knuckles whitened as she clenched her seatbelt more firmly. Pulling her gaze from Grady, she looked down and quickly tried to jam the two ends together. With her nerves getting the best of her, her first try missed, and she was just about to try again when it hit.

For a moment the plane shuddered violently, rising quickly on an updraft before the bottom fell out—the plane plummeting 50 feet in mere seconds. Anna, with her hands still groping the buckle's ends, rose out of her seat, pulling the straps to their limit, slowing her rise slightly. Yet the strain on her fingers was too much and the ends were ripped from her grasp. Her head slammed into the overhead compartment, as Grady grabbed at her legs and tried to haul her back in. By that time the plane was already steadying, the descent halted as Anna slumped back down into her seat with a thud.

All around them, people screamed, drinks spilled and luggage rained down out of overhead bins that had popped open. Several passengers were still in the aisle, about to retake their seat. They too had been tossed in the air, thrown off balance and had even landed on other passengers. A flight attendant sat folded over in the aisle, clutching her head, sobbing softly. From behind there were more wails of anguish and pain. Fearful of another bout of turbulence, Grady grabbed Anna's seat belt and fastened it for her.

With Anna safely belted, he gently sat her upright and looked into her eyes. She was awake, but seemed dazed and she met his gaze with a crooked, ironic half-smile. He embraced her to him as best one could sitting side-by-side, and her arms responded, encircling his waist in a tight hug as she snuggled her head into his shoulder.

A half hour later they were on the ground. Anna declined Grady's offer to get a medic to attend to her head. There was a small cut, and a large bump beginning to form, but Anna understood what extra attention meant. It meant doctors on the ground, questions about their travel, and perhaps even discovery of their false identities. At the very least it meant delay in their quest to find Trent and Joe.

So they waited for those with more severe injuries to be removed from the passenger cabin and then they themselves disembarked to customs without a backwards glance. The trip through customs itself went smoothly. There were no stops, and each gathered their luggage from the carousel and headed to the car rental booth. Tom had reserved a Fiat for them . . . and in less than an hour they were navigating by way of a complimentary map toward Folkestone, the English Channel and the awaiting French countryside beyond.

CHAPTER 60

RIFT

J ust looking at Trent and Joe, one wouldn't have expected that they would be best of friends. Trent had an almost scholarly look to him, with round spectacles, a closely cropped head of thick black hair and a thin, neat appearance. He had the kind of air about him you might expect to observe on Ivy League campuses—and not knowing him, one might have thought him smug.

Joe, on the other hand, was about forty pounds over his ideal body weight. He kept a football player's build, with broad rounded shoulders, a thick neck and the early beginnings of a bulging gut that spoke to years of being well fed, even if it was at Northwoods. His forearms were nearly twice the size of Trent's, and his thighs looked more like tree stumps than appendages. Yet behind the young man's perpetual party-guy smile—a look that sometimes made him appear simple—was a mind like a steel trap. In fact, if any weight was to be given to I.Q. scores, Joe's was a full ten points higher than his best friend's.

Today, the pair found themselves wandering along the banks of the Seine toward one of their last destinations in the city of light—the hallowed aisles of Notre Dame. They almost hadn't made it here . . . to Paris, that is. In a dream that came to both of them only a few nights ago, Anna had shown them the first person to fall in their desperate struggle for freedom. Curt's suicide had hit them both extremely hard, and each young man had strongly considered returning to the States to rejoin Anna.

After long reflection, they both realized that to do so would be a mistake. Their lives had to go on, they needed to find out who they were, and what they could be outside of the shadow of Northwoods. Whether it was another day, a month, or a lifetime of freedom, they had to grasp it while they could. Yes, Curt was dead, but his death could not be at the expense of their living. It may have seemed selfish, but in light of a lifetime's worth of denied freedoms, who could really have blamed them. Still, out of respect, Joe suggested they visit Notre Dame today, to offer up prayers for their fallen friend and to light a candle in his name before they fled Paris.

Just that morning, the pair had decided they couldn't wait around any longer. They had to leave the city first thing in the morning—Anna or no Anna. Even then it might be too late. They knew Anna was coming. In a sense, in their conscious and unconscious dreams, they had told her where they were. Still, they never imagined she'd come, not with it being so close to the rendezvous date back in the States—though Joe and Trent had been seriously considering not even returning for that. Something must have gone horribly wrong to bring Anna here. And that something probably had to do with the person or persons they could feel were following her, or perhaps now even ahead of her.

All around them, as they trod the cobbled paths and traversed the stony arches that spanned the river, they could smell it—a distant danger, a foreboding of doom that would arrive and envelop the city hours before Anna would. It was like nothing either had felt before, and it scared them to death. Both had guessed, rightly or wrongly, that it had to do with The Fifth Seed, which was odd in and of itself. For years they had never felt his presence, could never have even ventured a solid guess as to who he might be. At times they even doubted his existence. Only now they could sense something. *But why?* The answer either could come up with was that The Fifth Seed wanted them to sense him. Whoever was coming after them wanted them running scared.

Nearly an hour later, Trent and Joe wandered into the long raised courtyard stretching out before the majestic façade of Notre Dame. The twin bell towers soared into a hazy blue autumn sky as tourists bustled below and flocks of pigeons scattered in front of their meandering feet.

Some of the visitors snapped photographs while others chatted excitedly, delighted to be in the presence of such a grand and austere sight. Still others lined up near the massive oak doors, waiting their turn to enter and be awed. With neither leading, the two young men headed straight for the entrance, waiting with the others to slip solemnly inside.

As Trent shuffled forward, he took one last glimpse to the rows of stone-carved saints that fronted the structure, and beyond to the multitudes of perched gargoyles that seemed to gaze devilishly back down at him with quiet contempt. A shiver ran down his spine as something disturbing flitted through his mind and he tried to shake the feeling. It was as if a voice . . . no, several voices were warning him not to go in. Enter he did though, taking one last glimpse of the saints lined up above the arched entry.

Joe was watching the rows of saints and gargoyles as well, and with their vacant eyes cast downward, Joe had the odd impression that those eyes were alive, and following him with a vague sense of abject sadness. Now, as the bright morning faded to the dim glow of the cathedral's candlelight, Joe couldn't shake the feeling that today he had made a fateful decision.

Once inside, it took a few moments for their eyes to adjust to the eternal shadows and darkness that pervaded the cathedral. From within the dark realm the sounds of a Gregorian chant reverberated, and the low, resonating tones washed over them, penetrating their souls with cold, eerie effect.

Ahead, dim light from the rose window cascaded to the floor, allowing eyes to adjust to the great cathedral's soaring grandeur. The ceiling, many stories above, rose into a sweeping arch, supported by massive pillars that marched the length of the nave. The pillars processed forward, impinging upon a grand candlelit altar shrouded in shadows and framed by the massive organ pipes that soared into the thick timbered rafters.

For the moment neither of the men could move, as the center of the cathedral remained roped off and the crowd thrust around them paused with uncertainty before slowly understanding the maze-like obstruction in front of them, finally herding themselves along the back of the cathedral to the right. Trent and Joe, not wanting to become a stone in the middle of a powerful river, shuffled off with the rest of the enclave of tourists to try to understand their own reason for coming.

Still too dark to see very well, Trent found himself frustrated as—more times than he could count—someone would bump unceremoniously into him. It happened so often that he found himself occasionally reaching back to check that his wallet was still there. Tourist books he had read warned of ingenious pickpockets even in this hallowed place. Yet, he knew it wasn't the petty thieves he feared. It was the ghosts he felt were there. His real fear was that he might feel a bump and turn to the perpetrator only to discover nobody there.

Time passed, and the crowd, still unwilling to pick up their feet, began to spread out enough that the two could work their way forward toward the middle of the church. Trent and Joe knew that two transepts stretched out like stubby arms to form the cross—the shape in which the cathedral was erected hundreds of years ago. It took a few minutes to get there, but finally in the right transept they discovered that which they were looking for—rows of pillar candles flickering in the darkness, stretching out to span a twenty foot length and tiered upwards to five or so rows deep.

Ahead, several tourists were already in the midst of performing their own sacred rituals, lighting candles or kneeling by a rail and crossing themselves as they offered prayers to the sick or departed. They had decided that Joe would offer the prayer, and he approached the candles ceremoniously, without a word. Church sessions were not exactly available at Northwoods, but through people such as Mary Jane and other kind caregivers, Joe had found his own relationship with God.

From about fifteen feet behind, Trent watched as Joe deposited a small monetary donation before picking up a long thin wooden stick that he lit from another candle. The moment the fire flickered to life, Trent heard the voices. They started so softly that at first he could barely distinguish them from the chants that echoed to the rafters. But as Joe moved flame to unlit wick, the voices began to drown out the lofty strains of the music.

A sweat instantly beaded upon his forehead as the voices rose to the heavens, haunting him. There were so many of them, he could just barely make out that each was saying the same thing, as if in a disorganized round. For the moment, the overlapping voices shrouded any meaningful message that might be there. Transfixed, Trent wanted to yell, or better yet, to grab his friend and flee this place. But he was rooted in his spot, a spectator watching as the candlelight tribute to Curt caught the wick and began to glow to life.

From Trent's perspective the flame he saw grew to full size almost instantaneously and he expected Joe to return at any moment and kneel in prayer. That never happened. Instead his friend began acting oddly, returning the long stick to another candle's flame as if to relight what was already lit. Satisfied, Joe then turned back to Curt's candle and put flame to flame again, almost as if he didn't see that Curt's candle was alight.

Joe repeated the process three more times, and it became so maddening that Trent wanted to scream. It was then the voices, still echoing inside his head, finally began to resolve, slowly sending their ominous message in one common voice. "His candle doesn't light . . . you've lost him . . . his candle doesn't light . . . you've lost him . . . his candle cannot light . . . you lost him."

Trent caught at least part of the meaning. As a Natural he knew of fractured universes, he knew divergent and convergent paths occurred. He even knew in rare instances a Natural could witness the overlap as universes split apart, or in even rarer occurrences witness two universes crashing together. A splitting of universes is what he guessed he was witnessing now. In Joe's reality the candle would not light, yet in Trent's reality the candle lit without complaint.

Trent didn't know what it all meant, but he could guess: he and Joe were splitting, if not physically, at least consciously. Joe's conscious mind was choosing to follow one reality. Perhaps it was the one he would remember and live as his actual life. Trent's mind was choosing to follow another. It was never taught to them this way. But he could feel it. He knew that the universe he followed contained the seeds of freedom, for him and Joe. Yes, it meant a life of fear, a life on the run, always heading in the opposite direction of Northwoods. Joe, on the other hand, had chosen a path entirely more noble and valiant.

CHAPTER 61

MIND GAMES

Allan was near the end of the informational and technical part of the tour. He had walked his primary sponsor through the medical facts and findings behind Northwoods' recent advances, at least those the doctor had wanted put on display. There were some tests that wouldn't necessarily place their work in the best light, so those figures and findings went unmentioned. But for the most part Allan had been sure to be as transparent as possible, to highlight the progress that had been made in a relatively few years.

During the dialogue his guest had some pointed questions, particularly pertaining to the escape of the Naturals and the incident in Rochester. The doctor did his best to gloss over the escape, and while it certainly wasn't ideal, made it very clear it was under control. He also worked to spin the escape as a positive. For one, they were beginning to understand how the Naturals worked within a real world environment, under duress. It had been something they had tried to recreate for years at Northwoods, with limited success. Allan also said that while the initial press of the escape had brought temporary scrutiny to Northwoods, that had faded quickly and the public and the media had moved on to other stories.

As for Rochester, the cleanup had gone better than expected thanks to the unfortunate gas explosion at Ben's home, and there had been no media links back to Northwoods. The case seemed to be shut on an unfortunate accident that had ended the life of an esteemed Mayo Clinic doctor.

Allan's guest seemed to accept his explanations, offering any support the doctor needed to rein in the remaining Naturals. Both agreed the Naturals' time and usefulness was nearing an end, though it was made very clear to Allan there could be no further miscues or Northwoods would be shut down. Allan knew what shutting down the facility meant. It meant another would most likely open up somewhere, under a new guise. The work being done here was just too important not to pursue. For all Allan knew there was perhaps one already operating somewhere in the United States or even overseas. But shut down was a polite way of indicating that no loose ends could be allowed—nobody left to implicate Northwoods' sponsors. Anyone with knowledge of Northwoods' innermost workings, anyone who could not be relocated to a new facility, would most likely fall victim to an unfortunate accident. What was even more certain was there was no way Allan, as the head of a failed facility, would be relocated . . . he'd be dead.

The pair moved out of the primary research lab, where Allan had shown their sponsor extensive results from tests that had been done on ordinary individuals, non-Naturals. After observing the Naturals for years, Northwoods had discovered a wide range of methods that had allowed them to replicate with moderate success the talents of the Naturals in ordinary human beings.

By stimulating various parts of the brain with electrical impulses, advanced relaxation and meditation techniques, as well as various drug cocktails, Northwoods had been able to increase brain activity and function in normal individuals. The most striking result of the tests included enhanced telepathy and an ability to predict outcomes a few seconds into the future.

"Just inside here," Allan said as they approached a secured doorway, "this is my own private entrance into The Environment. I find it isn't conducive to the tests, to be popping in and distracting the participants, so this entrance leads to an observation hall."

His guest stepped through the door, and instantly had the sense of being in the dimly lit corridors of an environmentally designed zoo. To their immediate right were rows of windows that stretched down the corridor, allowing a view into The Environment's many rooms. What struck this high-ranking observer was how different The Environment was from any other part of the tour so far.

In the bowels of Northwoods, everything took on the feeling of a hospital—sterile, plain, and antiseptic. But through the first window there appeared to be a beautifully appointed home, with plush leather wing chairs, tapestry-covered couches and a fireplace with an ornately-carved mantle.

Allan watched his superior closely. The Environment was relatively new and Allan was hoping to see a glimmer of approval in the hard, cold eyes. But his guest simply turned to him expectantly and said, "So what happens here?"

Unfazed, Allan pointed to a couple of people about fifteen feet across the room. "Observe the pair over there," the doctor said nodding. "The one on the left is the administrator, while the other is the patient—the one with the tight-knit stocking cap."

His guest looked across the room and tried to make out what was happening.

"Here, let me turn the monitors on," Allan offered. His finger pressed a touch-screen mounted on a console in front of the window, and a bird's eye view of the pair came up. It appeared as though the administrator had an oversized deck of cards in a stack in front of him. In front of the patient were more cards fanned out on a table, face up. The patient appeared to be thinking hard about something and was passing his hand over the cards in front of him, as if trying to make a decision. Then suddenly his hand shot out and picked a single card from the assortment in front of him.

Once the patient had made the decision, the administrator turned his card over and the two matched. They repeated this process several times with matches turning up every time but once. On the sixth try, his guest turned to Allan, "You brought me here to show me a damn card trick!"

Allan turned to accept the confrontation head on, almost expecting the reaction. "I know it is not the most impressive display, but I wanted to start here. It will help you understand and connect what we discussed back in the lab to real life. You see, under the patient's stocking cap are electrodes placed in direct contact with his skull. We are sending low-level pulses to his brain to stimulate areas that we have found to be key to predictions. Through simple brain stimulation we have increased the success rate to near eighty percent. Follow me and I can show you more."

The official turned and followed the doctor, hoping for Allan's sake the live-action part of the tour got better. Allan led the way, a few more windows down, past similar patient and administrator interactions and environments until they reached a new set of windows that looked into a different sort of room. It was similarly appointed to the previous rooms, but this one was much smaller, with a large LCD computer screen set up in front of the patient, who wore a stocking cap similar to the first. Two administrators stood behind the patient and observed. One looked to have a paper chart of some sort and was taking notes on it, while the other held an electronic tablet that connected to the Internet.

"Here we have a setup similar to the prior room." Allan explained. "For this patient, we have added mind-enhancing drugs with the electronic stimulation. In addition to external stimulation, this patient has several electrodes that have been implanted in direct contact with the brain—not unlike the electrode treatment given to patients who suffer from the debilitating effects of MS.

His guest simply nodded, a little more intrigued now, as Allan again brought up a monitor to view the happenings in the room.

"What you are seeing here is a patient looking at four different stocks on the New York Stock Exchange. The feed is real-time, and not delayed. The task here is for the patient to make predictions about the four stocks presented to him, whether those stocks will go up or down over five-, fifteen- and thirty-minute intervals."

His guest leaned in closer to the window, trying to make out what was on the screen.

"Here, let me help," Allan said as he touched the screen in front of him and the video feed instantly switched to display a chart. "What you can see here are the market predictions of the patient over the last two hours. This graph shows you the accuracy of predictions for the four stocks, over the course of the two hours, under the five-minute prediction timeframe. We picked particularly volatile stocks with heavy trading to increase the difficulty and limit the effects of learning or randomness. As you can see in the five-minute prediction window, the accuracy is seventy-two point four percent."

Touching the screen again, Allan brought up another graph. "And this one shows accuracy over the fifteen-minute timeframe, with overall accuracy right around sixty-one percent."

Finally, touching the screen again, Allan brought up the final graph and explained. "This final graph obviously shows accuracy for the thirty-minute time period. It averages just around fifty percent, which means our window of predictions with this particular patient stimulus model breaks down somewhere past the fifteen-minute mark."

Again, his guest turned to Allan, and again Allan met the steely cold gaze head on. "Seventy percent accuracy! Five minutes! What the hell are you showing me this crap for? I thought you were making significant progress. We're bankrolling you with millions of taxpayer dollars—and from what you showed me these numbers aren't even close to the Naturals."

Allan shifted a bit uncomfortably, but let the rant conclude. He expected it. People didn't understand. He was doing this with normal, everyday people, and the fact that they were getting movement was revolutionary. Trying to keep his calm, he was prepared with something everyone understands . . . money.

"Let me show you something." Touching the screen, Allan switched the view again and displayed a simple bar graph representing the initial investment in the four stocks, two hours ago, and the relative profit or loss associated with those stocks over the past two hours. A final bar graph at the far right showed the same information, in aggregate for the four stocks.

"Based on these tests, I have one individual here at Northwoods making some modest investments in the market. This person is taking the information from our patient and making decisions on what to buy and when to sell. As you can see, we initially invested ten thousand dollars in each stock at the first prediction of even a mild upswing. On average, over two hours of trading, we have been able to better than double our investments simply by playing the micro trends—getting in while the stock is about to bounce, selling when it's about to slide, and reallocating the profit back into the market at key moments in time. Overall, our net return in two hours is north of forty-two thousand dollars—and none of the stocks within the portfolio have done more than move a few points up or down over that time. You see, you don't need to have complete accuracy to achieve success."

Allan's guest just blinked, realizing the mistake. "So who are the people sitting in the chairs? You said the primary issue with the Naturals is that they were never willing participants. How'd you find people willing to let you use them as guinea pigs?"

Allan smiled broadly. "I thought you knew. These are patriots, young men and women who have put country over self—just as a solider does going into battle. They are members of our own military who chose to volunteer to help their country in the newest defense and espionage frontier. You know probably better than I do, there are other countries, China in particular, even France to a lesser degree, making bold forays into predictive sciences and telepathy. Whoever wins that race will control the world's power as well as the future."

"I see," said his guest, wondering momentarily what types of side effects treatments such as these might have. But the doctor was right; it was no different than sending a soldier to the front, to take a bullet so those behind him could gain another five feet of dirt on the battlefield. "So you have shown me the progress you have made on enhancing abilities in normal individuals, but what of the new vein of Naturals we have been funding? The new frontier you promised us, and the funds we allocated revolved around advances in bioengineering?"

Allan shifted uncomfortably; technically they had been quite unsuccessful with bioengineering, with a large sum of his sponsors' funds resulting in little more than abject failure. But he wasn't about to share that information now. Besides, there were other options—other avenues pursued—that could be highlighted if push came to shove. So he opted for a half-truth. "We are too early in their development right now to show you live examples. The two we have are only five right now, but what we have observed in the past year seems to indicate this new breed of Naturals will posses even greater skills than the first seeds or Naturals," the doctor said with rehearsed precision. Nothing he'd said was technically a lie. "I'd prefer to show you those tests another time."

The official eyed Allan suspiciously, wondering if the topic should be pressed, but thought better of it. "I expect to see progress with that soon, as well as with the subjects you have already shown me. I can't imagine that the Chinese are going to be satisfied with card tricks and a few glorified stock brokers."

Allan bit his lip. If the Chinese could find ways to predict the future and severely mess with the world's stock markets they would wield global power, on a scale so significant, it would be unlike anything the world had ever seen. Today, economic warfare and global market superiority were more important than having all the nuclear weapons in the world.

"Which is why I wanted to show you one more arena before we go," Allan said, hoping to finally impress his boss. It was his last card, and he hoped it had the desired impact.

"Very well," the guest said, checking the time, "but make it fast."

Allan led his guest past several more windows before stopping at Environment 8. This room was completely different than the others. It was dark and vast and the observation window looked down on what appeared to be a complex maze of towering gray foam blocks of all shapes and sizes. To the near right a man stood waiting, dressed in what appeared to be full military body armor. He wore a combat helmet, with the latest advancement in night vision goggles strapped over his eyes.

In his hand he held a military-issue semi-automatic rifle, outfitted with a laser scope. In front of him lay the obstacle course.

"The soldier has been supplemented with a similar combination of electro-stimulation and mood altering drugs, as the previous subject you saw. In this case we have modified the stimulation and drug cocktails specifically for combat scenarios. We've heightened his alertness and even his aggression while focusing on improving his predictive capabilities only a few seconds into the future. As you will see, this greatly improves our success percentages."

His guest looked on with great interest now as Allan pressed a button on the console in front of him. Several video monitors glowed to life in front of them, covering various angles of the room below. He pressed another button and spoke into a microphone that allowed him to communicate with the participant and test administrators below.

"Ready for simulation everyone," Allan said, before releasing the button and turning once again to his superior. "As you will see, our soldier below must run the gauntlet—taking out targets as he goes. We actually run the simulation two ways, one where the soldier is asked to anticipate and attack, while during the other we ask the soldier to evade obstacles and use stealth. But it is much more impressive to watch an attack simulation."

"Oh, one more thing before I give the go. The room below is designed to have over ten thousand possible gauntlet configurations. This is the first time our soldier below will have run this particular combination—so there is no chance of memorization."

The guest's eyes flicked over at Allan and then back to the room in front of them, as if to say *get on with it*. Allan reached for the intercom button again.

"Proceed!"

Instantly, the soldier started through the maze as targets began to pop out at him from a wide range of angles. As the gauntlet unfolded it was plain to see the soldier was turning to face and blast the targets a fraction of a second before they even appeared. In one instance, a target popped up behind the soldier, but the soldier had already turned and was firing with deadly accuracy into the body of the foam dummy.

As the test progressed, the pace at which the targets popped up became dizzying—one after the other, with split-seconds in between, but each time the soldier turned to face the threat before it had materialized. The effect was a flashing, strobe-like, chaotic environment that made following the sequence of events from above virtually impossible.

In the end, the soldier stood at the other end of the gauntlet, every target eliminated, and Northwood's primary sponsor simply looking on in amazement. Never before had this person seen a gauntlet run at such a pace, with so many rapid-fire targets—no soldier known today could achieve that kind of result.

Allan again looked at his guest. He knew he had impressed the one person he needed to impress more than any other. He had certainly saved the best for last. He was glad the official had not picked up on the tiny flaw they were trying to fix. The problem was that they'd over-stimulated the soldier's senses to such as degree—to achieve the perfect predictive killing machine—that in all the tests they had run, the soldier also had successfully killed every woman, child and ally he'd faced.

CHAPTER 62

ROAD TO FOLKESTONE

G rady rubbed his eyes tiredly. He had managed only a few
hours sleep on the plane before he had to jump behind
the wheel of their rental and begin the two-hour drive to
Folkestone. It helped little that Anna lay curled up in the passenger seat,
breathing heavily in her deep sleep.

He woke her up occasionally, afraid that the bump on her head
might be more serious than just a thick knot that had brought on
a particularly harsh migraine. He was worried she might have a
concussion, and was wary of letting her sleep for too long.

The last time he woke her, Anna insisted she was okay. She'd had
migraines before, and she was sure this was nothing different. "Besides,"
she had said to him, "I know at least a little of what's in store for us with
my visions and all, and I'm certain I'm not going to be done in by a little
bump on the head."

The comment had made Grady laugh, and he had let her
sleep longer this time. But now he sorely missed the company and
conversation Anna offered. "When is this bloody road going to end?" he
said under his breath

"Reverted to speaking the mother tongue, now have we?" Anna said
dozily from the passenger seat.

"Thought you were asleep," Grady said, grateful to have someone to talk with. He figured a few more minutes and he might have put the Fiat they had rented into the ditch, he was so exhausted.

"My head hurts too much," Anna moaned.

"The medication we bought hasn't helped?" Grady asked politely.

"Some. But still hurts like a bugger," She chided, using her own British word in a feeble attempt to mock Grady. "How far?"

"Not sure exactly, shouldn't be much farther according to the sign I saw a little way back. The Eurotunnel terminal is close."

"Have you had any more dreams in the little rest you've gotten?" he asked hopefully. If Trent and Joe were on the move from Paris, it would be beneficial to skip the city altogether and try to catch up with them in the countryside. It was a small part of the reason they had driven a rental car, rather than hopping the train straight from London to Paris—it offered them more flexibility to change travel plans. The larger concern was that the Paris Eurostar train terminal might also be watched—but it seemed unlikely. Unfortunately, going by car was going to add at least three hours onto their timeframe.

"Oh, little thing you should know," Anna replied, a bit sheepishly. "When I get migraines, I stop seeing things. I'm in the dark just like you. Must be the pain that shuts things down. So until this thing lifts, we're stuck with the last place I know they were."

Grady nodded, taking in this bit of bad news as Anna groaned and sunk her head back into the headrest and tried to get back to sleep.

She didn't have much luck, as about ten minutes later the Fiat decelerated rapidly as they approached the exit to the station that would shuttle them from Folkestone, UK to Calais, France. On the other side they would pick up a car with the steering wheel on the correct side and begin the two-and-a-half-hour trip into Paris.

"So much for sleep," she grumbled.

"You'll need to wake up anyway," Grady said apologetically. "This is a border crossing so we'll need to have our passports checked again."

The impact of those words on Anna was instantaneous—and she bolted upright, opening her eyes wide. The effect of the light on her optic nerves sent a pain boring into the back of her eye sockets and she quickly closed them to the light once more—her head now crying anew for a dark room and a cozy blanket.

CHAPTER 63

DUALITY

Joe watched as the candle before him glowed to life, joining the others in a flickering tribute to the many who had passed. Just about to return, kneel and pray for Curt he caught something out of the corner of his eye. The candle he knew was lit now appeared to have extinguished. His mind wanted to tell him this wasn't true, but his eyes told him otherwise.

Relighting the long stick he returned it to Curt's candle, watching the wick closely as he did. Once again the candle appeared to light without hesitation. Now, watching the flame, he saw it waver, as if touched by a gentle passing breeze, yet the air in the ancient cathedral was deadly still. The flame danced a few times as if trying to remain, then bent sideways and extinguished again.

What gave Joe the most pause were the other candles that surrounded Curt's. They remained untouched by the mysterious breeze. It was almost as if something or someone unseen had laid breath to Curt's candle in particular. Watching the thin trail of smoke that rose from the wick, Joe thought he saw something else. It appeared to be a ghostly image of a burning flame superimposed over the smoldering wick, as if there were two realities there, with only one that could be followed.

He knew full well now he was witnessing the split, where universes sheared off from one another and either flung away from each other

273

in divergent paths, or meandered side-by-side in parallel. Which was happening he did not know. What he thought he knew was that to witness such an event you probably needed two Naturals, one holding to one reality and the other choosing the alternative.

His guess was that Trent was choosing the lit candle, and his own mind seemed to be leading him toward something entirely different. Consciously he thought of Trent to the point he could almost see him standing behind him, feeling Trent's own powerful mind begging Joe to follow his chosen path.

Joe knew if he decided to return to the kneelers and begin praying that once he turned back to the candle it would be lit. He could easily do this, couldn't he? Joe's mind raced, trying to find the underlying meaning in a candle that for some unnerving reason would not remain lit. In the end, all he could sense was this was the path for him. He sensed grave danger ahead and potentially horrible consequences. And he was sure this path would force him to deal once and for all with the demons of Northwoods.

Trent's path, on the other hand, seemed to be one of flight and total abandonment of Anna and any Northwoods resolution. Was it freedom? Yes . . . technically, but at the cost of friendships, solemn bonds and a life spent constantly on the run. Joe didn't fault Trent for his choice . . . he only regretted it. He knew that no matter what, each would remain together physically, at least for the time being. But wouldn't he always know that Trent had chosen to live his consciousness in another reality?

Returning his stick to another flame, he lit it again and put fire back to Curt's dying candle. Again it went out. He repeated the process three more times, until he could hear in his own mind Trent's softly spoken words, "Good luck buddy . . . I love you." The voice vanished into a vacuum of time as the candle remained unlit. Finally Joe turned to see Trent standing in the same spot he had left him . . . only now perhaps a shell of his former self.

Slowly and somberly Joe approached his best friend. Trent wouldn't know fully what just happened. The Trent he knew was somewhere else, being approached by another Joe in a similar fashion. It was over. Life went on. But Joe couldn't help but suddenly feel as if he was alone. It was a thought that made him weak and exhausted. Today, he couldn't help feeling as if he had now lost two of his closest friends.

CHAPTER 64

HOTEL LE CLOS MEDICIS

Two men strode briskly down the Rue Monsieur-Le Prince, their shadows extending well out in advance of their progress as the lazy day transitioned into the cool evening. Mitch was haggard, worn by a long day of travel and the leap forward in time zones.

He knew time was of the essence, and that their quarry, although tantalizingly near, may have already slipped their grasp. The Kid was unusually chummy with him today, asking all kinds of questions, both personal and professional, and the change in his attitude was disarming. The Kid was like a totally different person, and for a moment Mitch wondered what his motives might be. It certainly wasn't to find out how his daughter, Megan, was getting along in college.

At a time like this, Mitch was all business, and tried in vain to shut The Kid up with terse one-word answers, or by completely ignoring his constant questions. Yet as number 56 drew near, and the sign reading Hotel Le Clos Medicis slowly came into view, The Kid's demeanor instantly changed.

"Now what?" he asked matter-of-factly.

Mitch was surprised. He thought The Kid would just go charging through the courtyard and into the lobby to begin a new volley of questions aimed at the clerk. Taking a moment to think, as though he hadn't been considering this very subject since the plane's wheels left

U.S. soil, he finally confided. "You first. I'll wait outside. You're better equipped to get a read on the receptionist."

"Figured that," The Kid said a bit smugly, finally feeling he was getting credit for his unique set of skills. "Ask for them by name?"

"Yeah. Just don't go barging in and blurt it out. Use a little tact. Perhaps a cover story . . . perhaps you're trying to connect with a couple friends from college. And speak French if you can."

"You know the languages are Anna's thing, but I figure I can put together a few sentences that will work," The Kid replied, sarcastically. "Of course I'll speak French. What do you think, I'm a dumb ass?"

There it is, Mitch thought, the true Kid was back. "Just go."

From across the street Mitch watched as The Kid managed traffic, quick-stepping to avoid an on-coming cab before he disappeared into the courtyard.

The courtyard was quaint, with small trees growing up through grated openings in the tiled terrace, traditional French bistro tables dotting the grounds and flowering vines, of a variety The Kid cared not to know about, scrolling their way up the building's old façade.

He entered through a double door, propped open to take full advantage of the cool fall breeze. Inside, the atmosphere transitioned to a light perfumed scent of vanilla that masked the musty underlying currents common with buildings so well aged.

The salon was burgeoning with antiques and a small fire crackled in the hearth. The Kid approached the concierge counter and rang a bell to draw the clerk's attention. The woman was mid-forties, with dark black hair, severely trimmed about two inches off the shoulder. Her dark brown eyes glared up at him through a set of square librarian glasses, complete with a chain for dropping them off her elongated nose.

"Good day, Mademoiselle," he began in impeccable French. To this she offered him a slight, yet grim smile.

"My name is Jean," he offered, lying, "and I am inquiring about two of my friends who are residing here. They invited me to meet them for dinner this evening."

"Their names?" the woman asked curtly.

"Trying to peer over the tall counter into the hand-kept guest registry, he cleared his throat and said, "Trent and Joe."

The woman eyed him skeptically. "You say you are good friends of these two?"

"Ahem, yes." The Kid answered, again clearing this throat. This time he looked the woman in the eyes as he answered. He was trying desperately to get a read on her, and so far it wasn't coming across well. He could tell she was in doubt of his truthfulness—of course most anyone could have read that, but he couldn't tell why. Perhaps it was her spectacles, or perhaps it was her closed manner, but he was at a loss as to what she was thinking, other than the most overt clues. In the end he attributed it to her being French.

While The Kid tried to get a read on her, Mademoiselle seemed to have ignored his last response and was busy digging through some paperwork. This was promising. Perhaps she was digging for a room number. In the meantime The Kid glanced around, wondering if he might just happen to spy Trent and Joe on his own.

Finally the woman looked up at him again, evaluating him once more through those confounded glasses. "If you are such good friends with them. Perhaps you wouldn't mind paying the remainder of their bill. They seem to have left a night early without the courtesy of announcing their intentions—we wouldn't have known, but room service noticed their bags were missing. Not that they had much—a couple of backpacks is all. Still, per our agreement they owe a balance," she said, handing over the bill.

Unsure what to do next, The Kid pulled out his wallet and settled up, swearing under his breath as he did so.

CHAPTER 65

THE STREET RAT

The pair left Notre Dame in uneasy silence. Neither had spoken a word to the other after the candle-lighting ceremony that seemed to have gone horribly wrong. Joe continually stole glances at his friend Trent, wondering if this person, this friend he had known nearly his entire memorable life, was now merely a shell of his former self.

Trent certainly looked no different, but of course that was to be expected. A split in time wouldn't alter appearance, but Joe wondered about the soul. Was his friend still his same old friend—stiff and prudish on the outside, but all heart on the inside? The thought was enough to drive him crazy, and many times, in the minutes after the candle failed to light, Joe felt like confronting his buddy.

In the end, he remained silent. Silent as they strode side-by-side through the dim gloom of the great cathedral. Silent as they emerged in a haze of gray through the elaborately carved front doors—setting off into the radiant amber glow of a slowly dying afternoon sun. As they passed beneath the Portal of The Last Judgment, the figures there, carved in relief, seemed to be arguing over Trent and Joe's future salvation or eternal damnation, as if understanding the gravity of what had just transpired inside.

For a brief moment, Joe stole a final glance back at the great cathedral's entrance—perhaps hoping for an answer from those stone sentinels. None came. No wink, wave or ghostly words of warning. The figures remained frozen in mid-argument—ever silent—as did the two lonely pair of travelers. Lost in their thoughts, the pair crossed over the Seine to *Rive Gauche*, descending the left bank stairs that led down to the stony cobbled pathways, along the mighty river that birthed this historic city.

It was here that an odd smirk spread across Trent's face. Joe noticed and thought it out of sorts for the mood. His friend was obviously thinking of something in which he found great joy and humor. And it was this odd look, in the light of what they just faced back at Notre Dame that began to make Joe's temper boil.

The look remained for at least a minute, and Joe was just about to grab his friend by the shoulder, turn him to his bubbling fury and confront him on the spot in front of God, the river, and the tourists meandering by. But Trent beat him by a fraction of a second.

"So did the candle light or didn't it?"

The phrase was dry, emotionless—perhaps even tinged with a bit of irony, and its effect instantly melted Joe's anger. In one quick motion of unpremeditated joy, he turned to his friend he had just wanted to hit, and gave him an enormous hug.

Passing by, a pretty young French woman with thick auburn hair and smoky hazel eyes stopped mid-stroll and smiled at the sight. A gruff-looking gentleman buried his head to the cobblestones and quickened his pace—obviously feeling uncomfortable at the sight of two men hugging. And a gendarme knocked his police baton against a stone wall and began to whistle.

In those brief seconds, as their hug fell away, Joe began to comprehend something. He took a moment, imagining Trent back at Notre Dame, caught inextricably in his own dilemma of which fractured universe to follow. Joe's most recent assumption was Trent chose an alternate reality . . . one separate from Joe's.

That was not entirely right. The truth was there was really no way to know which path Trent had chosen back in Notre Dame. Because in this now, in this reality, the Trent standing before him could only say he'd chosen to follow this fractured universe. Understanding this, Joe chose not to give his friend's loyalty or dedication another thought. It would be wasted anguish. The important thing was that some version of Trent was here with him, and today they would move on together, to face the "whatever" of their futures.

As he worked to set his mind at ease, some sense of instinct—or perhaps déjà-vu—made Joe glance around. The auburn-haired woman caught his eye and smiled oddly. The gendarme had moved off, rousting some kids from some object they were trying to fish from the river. The gruff-looking man was long gone . . . the click of his heels on the cobbles a distant memory.

But it wasn't these things that interested him . . . although perhaps one should have. It was the ghosts that he was sure were there. It was the figments of the other Joe and Trent, fresh from the cathedral—the boys that had chosen the alternative reality that his eyes now searched for. He half expected they would be there—ghostly, veiled and ethereal—but there nonetheless. Perhaps the pair was now wandering along the opposite side of the river, *Rive Droite*, sharing a similar moment.

His mind's eye could almost see them. There, on the other side, with different people milling about. But there was a common thread. *What was it? Or perhaps who?* His mind focused, his head began to hurt. In a flash he thought he had it.

Quickly he spun on his heels, searching for the one—that someone who he could feel would have been present in either now. But his haste was unnecessary, his worry unfounded. She was still there on the *Rive Gauche*, standing and smiling at him with those smoky hazel eyes.

CHAPTER 66

RESPITE

The small Citroen rolled down the streets of Paris. Cars, small vans and a wealth of taxis veered around the slow-moving car, blaring their horns in frustration. This was actually the second time Grady had driven in Paris, and from his perspective he had gotten much better with time. Even with his FBI training—which required extensive work behind the wheel at high speeds—he was overwhelmed by how disorganized and chaotic the streets of Paris really were. Lanes were ignored, bumpers were hugged to within the merest of inches and the French roundabouts, favored over the traffic-light intersection, were a mind-boggling mass of cars merging and exiting in and out of up to eight converging streets.

After the border crossing, which went without incident, Anna had slept again, still trying to fight off the effects of the migraine. When she awoke, about a half hour from Paris, she told Grady she was feeling a little better and tried to make herself useful. Squinting at a map the rental car company had provided, Anna tried to prepare Grady a half-mile ahead for what to expect. Their teamwork paid off, and Grady began moving, with the rivers of traffic a little better, so that only one in four cars that passed honked their horns. She kept her eye on their destination, helping Grady steer back on course when they got lost, and trying as best she could to divert him around places of interest where traffic seemed to bog down.

About a mile from their destination, Grady started looking for a parking spot. He wanted to be on foot when they approached, to give Anna ample time to sense any hidden dangers, and his keen eyes an opportunity to search crowds for suspicious activity. The one downside was that if needed, there would be no quick get-away. Based on how difficult traffic was to manage, he would rather take his chances on foot.

It took a few minutes but Grady finally found a place to squeeze the car, between a pint-sized Mitsubishi delivery van and an Audi A6 that looked monstrous compared to the other cars on the road.

Anna stepped out, with her hand to her head, but Grady noticed it was more to shade her eyes than an expression of pain. Grady followed and stepped around to the sidewalk to join her, taking her hand for the first time since their high-speed ride under the English Channel.

Anna squeezed his hand tightly, in an expression that said she was glad he was near. "I think we need a rest." Anna said, staring off down the street.

"But don't you think we need to get moving?" Grady asked, not putting much weight behind the words. He too felt that sitting down and collecting their thoughts would be valuable.

"I think we're too late. Trent and Joe won't be at the hotel, but . . ." Her voice trailed off, unsure if she should finish the sentence.

"So your head must be feeling better."

Anna's focus remained distant as each began to slowly walk. "Much, thanks to those two hours of sleep while driving through the countryside . . . it seemed to help."

"So how do you mean we're late? You don't mean . . ."

Anna interrupted him instantly, not wanting him to finish the sentence. "No, I think they are fine for now. I would feel it, even with my aches. But this is more intuition than anything. I'm assuming the others are already here.

"From Northwoods?"

"Almost certainly."

"Then we do need to make some decisions."

283

A couple of blocks later, Grady ushered Anna to a small sidewalk café. They both collapsed into a couple of uncomfortable iron bistro chairs and Anna quickly grabbed the attention of one of the staff.

A young woman strode over with a half smile that broadened a bit when Anna ordered a bottle of wine in flawless French, accent and all.

"Wine, huh?" Grady asked, realizing their little respite might be longer than he'd first anticipated.

"We don't need to finish it, but I could use something to settle myself."

Minutes later the young woman returned with a bottle, wrapped in a towel, nestled in a wicker wine cooler. She uncorked the bottle, offered the cork to Grady who took a gentle whiff and nodded. She poured a splash of the golden Chardonnay into each of their glasses, let them savor the bouquet and taste, then topped off both of their glasses with their nods of assent.

"What's the plan, then?" Anna asked, her attention now fully focused on Grady's eyes.

"I think we still go." They might have left a message for you, some hint as to where they might have gone. "I guess the other option is for you to try to get a read on them again. Might be easier now that we're closer," he added.

"No, you're right. We should go. The migraines could easily hit again. They often come and go, which would leave us with no leads."

"I think we can limit the immediate danger," Grady offered convincingly. "If Northwoods is waiting for us, they won't make a move right off. There would be too many witnesses. My guess is that they will try to follow us, perhaps even expect us to lead them to Trent and Joe. And knowing that, or at least assuming that, we can take steps to shake them after we leave the hotel."

"It's settled, then. We go."

Grady, noticing he was behind with his wine took a rather large gulp and started to rise from the table. But something in Anna's eyes made him wait and he sat back down.

"I need a little more time." She said, her eyes starting to cloud. Grady couldn't help but look at her quizzically.

Recognizing his confusion, she half stood and slid her chair around so that it was directly next to his. Still holding her drink, she laid her head on his shoulder. "I need a little more time with you."

Grady realized what Anna was thinking. The next few hours or next several days might define their future together, for better or for worse. For now, she just wanted to feel him nearby.

They remained that way for an hour, holding hands, slowly sipping wine, and watching people pass who had no idea how dark their next few days together would be.

CHAPTER 67

Prying Eyes

A thick dusk had settled on Paris, and all around streetlights winked on, painting the streets in a soft yellow hue, while café awnings began to glow from within, lit by strands of clear bulbs draped from their supports. Cars continued to race by along the Rue Monsieur-le-Prince, their headlights playing with the shadows as Grady tried to conceal himself in them. He had approached the rue, from the west by way of Rue de Vaugirard, passing Rue de Medicis, which bordered the Jardin du Luxembourg. He recalled the integral part the garden had played in *Les Misérables*, and wondered if the garden might not come into play in their particular drama. Intuition? Perhaps.

Cautious now, he came to a stop on the western-most side of the street, trying to peer into the depths of light and shadow, and the murky charcoal ground in-between. He searched for what he expected to be there. Where, though, was the big question? He pulled a pack of cigarettes from his pocket, bought just for the occasion, and pulled the souvenir ball cap, purchased at the same shop, down closer to his eyes, hoping to better conceal his identity. The one thing he would have really liked to have purchased was a gun to replace the one he had to leave in the States, but the likelihood of finding someone who would sell him one was pretty much non-existent.

He was a horrible smoker, never having picked up the habit. But he knew it would give him a reason to stand near the corner and do nothing. His greatest fear was that whoever might be watching would be keen enough to realize he wasn't inhaling.

It took about half the cigarette to spot his mark. Based on the layout of the street, and from where Grady saw the hotel to be, the man had picked an ideal spot to watch the entrance. He was situated on the other side of the street, facing slightly away from Grady, under an awning reading a newspaper. He had chosen a place where the light was dim, but without sacrificing his view of the hotel.

But that was not what gave him away. It was a bunch of little details, which, when all pulled together, made him the odd person out. For starters, he was obviously American; his attire was subtly out of sorts with the traditional tourist crowd, and out of place on this particular street. In addition, in just a few minutes of observing, his habits were unusual. He continuously exchanged glances at his newspaper with darting looks to the hotel's courtyard, then up and down the street. Again he would return to his newspaper in short bursts that gave little time to delve into any article at any great length. And lastly, the newspaper page never turned. He was expecting someone.

"A magazine would have been a better prop." Grady whispered to himself. At least you could pretend to be looking at ads for only a few seconds at a time.

Armed with this information, Grady instinctively evaluated his own position. Snuffing out his cigarette with the heel of his shoe, Grady backtracked a bit, crossing at the intersection, so as to come at the observer from the same side of the street. Now, for the man to get a good look at Grady, he would have to crane his neck around unnaturally over his right shoulder.

Cautiously, Grady approached again, briefly letting his mind settle on Anna, safely secreted away one block southwest near the Luxembourg Gardens. Grady kept his eyes open for other observers, feeling certain this man was not alone. For the moment he could not spot any additional suspects.

A gaggle of tourists parted in front of Grady and once more the man came into view, this time close enough so he could throw a rock at him and feel relatively good he would hit him. Then something finally clicked; there was something familiar about him. He knew he had seen him before. Grady held his breath and waited for the man to gaze back in his general direction. It took only moments, but when he turned Grady knew him instantly. He was Anna's so-called father, the man who had stood just a few weeks ago in his office and pleaded with Grady to find Anna.

Suddenly he felt too close—positioning or no positioning. This man had made an impression on him, and Grady was sure he had made one on the man. He held his breath again, praying the man's gaze would fall short of where he stood. It took a few agonizing moments, but his eyes did just that before finally returning to his paper to keep up the ruse.

Quickly Grady did an about-face, but steadied himself. Not too quickly, he warned himself—natural gait, casual stroll. Had the man seen him? If so, he would be raising the alarm and others might begin to descend on him. He chanced a final glance back, as he crossed the street, to steady his fears. But Mr. Jenkins, as Grady knew him, was still there searching the streets with one eye while he kept watch of the hotel with the other.

Fifteen minutes later Anna approached from the same route Grady had. Her knees felt weak and her stomach fluttered nervously, but she kept an appearance of outward calm. Her mission was simple: approach the hotel, head straight to the desk, ask a direct question or two and then leave. Grady insisted she not know ahead of time where the watcher was situated. He didn't want her focusing in on him and tipping their hand. He also wanted her to be as naturally nervous and wary as possible. The man watching would expect her to be looking for him.

Anna felt Grady might be holding something back, but she didn't press further and did as he requested. Her eyes searched, and her mind tried to fight through the dull throbbing headache that had come in place of the migraine. Anyone in her position might have sensed the impending danger, but she reached out with all her unique talents, trying to feel anything deeper that might be off-kilter. In particular, her thoughts centered upon The Fifth Seed. But everything that came back was a blank.

Still, cold hard intuition told her he was near, perhaps not on the street, but close enough for discomfort. By now she was halfway to the hotel and she had not been able to spot the watcher. She marveled briefly at Grady's ability and how quickly he had been able to pick up on things, even without her gifts. Then for one very brief moment she felt eyes rest on her—lingering a moment more than casual observance. Slowly and as nonchalantly as she could, Anna turned her head and gazed into the small window of the doorway she had just passed, but no glare, casual glance or otherwise, returned hers.

She took another two steps and paused. An image flickered through her mind. A mere shadow of a person, pressed back against the heavy wood of the door she had just passed. For a moment she considered moving on but something came over her and she turned and approached the door once more. Hesitantly her hand reached for the doorknob, her palm shaking slightly as it hovered inches away.

Impulsively she grasped it, twisting her wrist while she shoved hard against the door, but it was locked and wouldn't budge. For a moment, she had a sense of thousands of hands that reached out to open the door over its years of existence, but it was one of the most recent that made her shudder. It was then that an impossible thought came to her and her head began to throb more viciously.

Releasing her hand slowly, she paused, recomposed herself and turned once more down the street. Self-doubt began to flood her mind as she covered the last thirty yards to the hotel. She knew what she had just done looked horribly suspicious, and she wondered if somehow, due to one silly whim, she had blown Grady's entire plan.

Anna carried on, resolute. All she could do was play it out as they had scripted, and hope for the best.

Down the road, Grady watched the entire sequence of events unfold. He had been following Anna the entire way, about fifty paces behind, scrutinizing her every move, prepared to act as the guardian angel should anything go wrong.

He had just rested his eyes on the Mr. Jenkins impostor when Anna took her detour to the doorway. The watcher's eyes never left her, and Grady's early suspicions were reconfirmed—this man was definitely their mark. From his distance, and through the dark, Grady couldn't tell what the man's reaction had been to Anna trying to open the door, but his focus never faltered. Only after Anna had resumed her stroll toward the hotel did he hazard a glance up and down the street again.

Grady sank deeper into the shadows, knowing the man's eyes were searching for him. In then end, they returned to watch Anna slowly disappear into the courtyard and the hotel beyond.

CHAPTER 68

SOPHIA

Inside the hotel salon, Anna spotted the reservation desk and strode up to the woman behind the counter. She had no way of knowing, but this was the same woman who had attended to a previous visitor who asked many of the same questions she intended to.

Anna smiled as warmly as she could under the circumstances, and her pleasant greeting was returned with a half smile.

"We are full." The woman cut in before Anna could even state her business.

Speaking in flawless French, Anna politely corrected her. "Beg your pardon Mademoiselle, but I am not looking for a vacancy. I was hoping you might be able to help me with something."

The woman eyed Anna skeptically, but let her continue.

"I am looking for two friends of mine . . ."

"Not those boys again," she replied, cutting Anna off with a disgusted huff. "You are the third to inquire."

Third, Anna thought, momentarily thrown off guard. Who else might have been looking for them?

As if anticipating what Anna was thinking, the woman continued. "There is another woman here waiting for them. I told her what I told you. I don't expect them to return—they seem to have packed up and left."

By now Anna was thoroughly confused. "A woman?" She hadn't anticipated that. For a moment, she considered another question, but the woman behind the desk had turned her back on her, busying herself with some paperwork, as if to say the conversation was over.

It was then a particularly feminine French voice called her name from behind. "Anna."

She wheeled on her heels to face the voice. A young woman who looked to be about her age gazed back at her expectantly—though Anna had never seen her before in her life. For a moment, she was struck by her appearance. She was petite; perhaps only five and a half feet tall, with striking blue eyes that filled her small round face. Her clothes appeared slightly too large, bagging in odd places, and quite out of date. If Anna had to have guessed she would have said she was staring at a very attractive gypsy.

"Wh-who are you?"

"My name is Sophia. I am a friend. A friend not unlike you and your, shall I say 'brothers,' Trent and Joe?"

Anna's mouth dropped open, caught completely off-guard by this new twist.

"I met them down by the Seine earlier today. Apparently we share some special talents. You all are in grave danger, if you have not sensed it already."

Anna simply nodded, still in a bit of shock. She was so close.

"I have little time. I must get back to them. For now you and I are safely out of sight, but the men, the followers, they may draw nearer at any moment, and we must not be seen talking."

"But . . ." Anna started in, though Sophia raised a finger to her lips.

Anna thought she was going to say more, but instead she pulled a small satchel out from under her baggy clothes, and slipped it into Anna's hands. "If all goes well we will contact you tonight." Sophia said. "You will be followed, so take care. You have a plan, non?"

"But I'm going with you!" Anna protested, ignoring the question. "I need to see them."

Shaking her head ruefully, Sophia dashed Anna's hopes. "That would be a mistake. At the moment, Joe and Trent are safe. You, on the other hand, have been exposed. You would only bring the danger to them. And I know that is not your intent."

"No," Anna agreed miserably.

"Get rid of your tail and wait for the call—only then will we arrange a meeting. If you think you are still being followed, do not answer the phone. We will keep calling back until . . ." But Sophia didn't have to finish. She would call back until they answered, or until they realized that Anna and Grady were compromised, or dead, in which case someone else would be answering the phone. "Now go."

Anna left the hotel's salon and entered the courtyard. The night seemed colder than before, and a few shades darker as well. She understood Sophia would wait until Anna had cleared out the watchers before she departed the hotel, as though she were a guest. They didn't know about her, and that was how she intended to keep it.

Glancing left, Anna peered into the darkness, hoping to catch a glimpse of Grady, but there were too many people and there was not enough light to pick him out. She paused, as planned, looking left then right, as if undecided what to do. After a long pause she turned right as scripted, heading for the Boulevard St. Michel, turning right onto it and the waiting Luxembourg Gardens.

She kept her pace to a brisk walk and looked around as if to make sure nobody was following her. She knew this would keep whoever was on her tail at a relatively safe distance. When she arrived at the entrance to the garden, her heart sunk. The gates had been closed, and the park appeared to have shut down for the evening.

In a panic, she looked around, hoping to spot Grady through the thinning crowds of people, coming to tell her what to do next—but she knew he wouldn't have had time to get in position.

Now she faced a choice. Back down the quieter Rue de Medicis or straight ahead down the busier Rue St. Michel? On impulse she picked right, hoping she was correct in doing so. She could feel the man who was following her now, closing the distance, though wary in his own right.

Halfway down the street, she knew she had to do something. She was tired, her head hurt and right now she needed to buy time, so she did the unexpected and faced down her pursuer. If it all went bad, at least Trent and Joe could go on, they were safe, and her involvement seemed to only be bringing them closer to danger.

So she turned around, her shoulders slumped in a display of defeat as she saw a lone shadowy figure approach. He stopped, unexpectedly, halfway across the street, and Anna could now see his face clearly. As if judging her posture the man approached now, glancing around occasionally, a thin smile on his lips.

"You done running?" he yelled at Anna.

She didn't respond, instead she glared at Northwood's security director—hate filling her eyes, with tears she couldn't control trickling down her cheeks.

"Where's Grady?" Mitch asked apprehensively.

"He left me. Turned around in London and said it was too much for him. I'm all you get. Just me. It's done. Let the others go—they can't hurt you. You know that."

Mitch glanced around, not exactly believing her story about Grady, but wondering at the same time if it could be true. He continued to move cautiously closer, trying to avoid the inquiring gaze of the few passers-by who remained on the street.

Anna backed up a little, closer to the wall of the gardens.

"Let's talk, Anna. This has gotten out of hand. You've got it all mixed up." His arms spread in an attempted soothing gesture that to Anna only amplified his deceit.

"Go to hell," Anna yelled, and even those around that didn't speak English now stopped to stare. "Tell that to Curt as he rots in his grave. Or Mary Jane—God-knows-what you've done to her by now."

"What do you want?" Mitch asked, trying not to escalate the situation and manage her in. "Curt took his own life. We had nothing to do with that."

"Bullshit Mitch," Anna seethed, spittle flying from her mouth. "The Fifth Seed pushed him to it and you know it."

"We can give you Mary Jane, let you both go live someplace safe. We just need a few assurances."

"And what about Trent and Joe," Anna yelled back, even though the space between them had closed to about twenty yards.

"They'll have to come in, but we can offer the same to them. This has all gotten terribly out of hand, and you know it. It doesn't have to be this way."

"What about the stuff at Mary Jane's house, or the attack in Rochester?" Anna asked, in a tone more fitting to the distance. "What about that?" She almost pleaded.

For just a moment Mitch hesitated, unsure exactly how to approach it. It was in that moment of hesitation that Anna turned and ran.

Mitch swore loudly to himself and took off after her. In a few powerful strides he'd reached a full on sprint and began closing in on her. That's when it hit him. From out of the shadows came a crushing forearm blow, like a linebacker laying out an unsuspecting running back bursting through a gap.

The collision snapped his head sideways, and flung him into the garden wall. For a moment he held onto consciousness, finding himself flat on his back, staring up at the yellow glow of a street lamp. He heard shouts in French, people yelling in alarm as two distinct sets of running feet, one heavy and one light, pounded the pavement and rapidly faded away. Grady had just got his payback.

Several blocks down the road Anna pulled up, her side splitting and head a wreck.

"Stop!" She said breathlessly to Grady, just a pace or two ahead of her. "Just stop."

Grady turned around, his own heart pounding. Retreating a few hesitant paces, he eyed Anna worriedly. He had heard most of Anna's conversation with Mitch and had been biding his time, waiting for the right moment to spring on him. What Anna had said was not part of their plan.

When Grady saw Anna emerge from the hotel, he was supposed to run around the opposite side of the block and follow Anna and Mitch into the Luxembourg Gardens. Inside the gardens and out of public view, Grady would chase down and subdue Mitch, or whoever else might have followed her.

Instead, he caught Anna coming unexpectedly his way. He was just about to meet up with her and find out what went wrong, when she'd turned to her pursuer.

"That wasn't all an act was it? You would have given up back there, wouldn't you?" he asked, without judgment.

"Yes." She breathed hopelessly. "Yes. It's all so wrong. None of it fits anymore. I'm not sure I can take much more."

Grady moved over, standing her up and she released herself into his arms, her chest heaving against his, either from breathlessness or silent sobs, Grady knew not which. He held her until her breathing softened.

Unsure if now was the right time, but needing to know, Grady had to ask. "Trent and Joe? Are they safe? Did they leave word at the desk?"

Anna moved away, holding up the small satchel she'd been given by the gypsy. "No, but they left a Sophia," she said with a grim smile.

Though she had no energy to do so, she told Grady everything that happened minute by minute, omitting the odd feeling she had when she touched the doorknob.

Understanding Anna couldn't bear to do it, Grady opened up the satchel for her and looked inside. The expression that came over his face was a peculiar one mixed with confusion, and Anna's gut sank.

"Don't tell me," she pleaded. "She was a plant, there's no phone, there's a tracer in there and they know exactly where we are?"

"No, the phone is in here," he said appreciatively. "But . . ."

"But what?" Anna asked, now a little exasperated.

Retrieving another object from the satchel, Grady held it up carefully, letting it catch the light cast from a nearby streetlamp. "It appears as if Sophia thought we might need a gun."

CHAPTER 69

DETOUR

A little ways away, The Kid emerged from his hiding spot in the doorway. Though finding Anna was the purpose of the trip, he had experienced an unexpected jolt when he saw her trim figure and flowing hair.

She had looked frightened and alone, with no sign of Grady at her side, though The Kid was sure he was near. For a brief moment his heart mellowed, and he wondered if he had been doing the right thing. But he knew it was too late for that, and a few minutes later he saw Mitch move out.

That was the sign Anna had left the hotel and he was to follow. Out on the street, a ways behind Mitch, The Kid's path took him directly past the Hotel Le Clois Medicis. It happened to be at that exact moment a pretty young gypsy hurried out in the opposite direction. As fate would have it, they brushed by each other and The Kid paused, politely excusing himself before he continued on.

It was then that something hit him . . . part vision, part instinct. Looking back at the girl, he noticed her pace was quick, and she looked cautiously around as she made her way down the street. In a moment of pure intuition, he turned to follow.

CHAPTER 70

MONTMARTRE

A stiff autumn breeze lashed at the faces of the two anxious young men. Their eyes surveyed the whole of Paris spread out below them, flitting here and there in no particular order. To their right, the Eiffel Tower stood tall and resolute, lit from within by the brilliant glow of powerful torchlights and millions of bright glowing bulbs. Off to their left, lay the other end of old Paris anchored by the twin spires of Notre Dame—its own lights softening the inky black of the evening and bringing an ethereal glow to the magnificent edifice. In between lay the rest, including Musée d'Orsay, the old train depot, now converted to a sprawling museum that housed the works of some of the most famous French masters of Impressionist painting. The museum held the ground straight on, rising just on the other side of the murky dark strip that cut a swath through it all—the Seine.

Directly in front of them in the near foreground rose a puzzle of darkened rooftops, layered upon each other in muted shades of charcoal, with no regard for order, until they sank from view down the hillside of Montmartre. The rooftops were littered with antenna aerials and chimneystacks, all jutting harshly into view. The entire effect carved dense, irregular black swaths into the glittering Paris tableaux.

Trent and Joe waited, each anxious for their new acquaintance to return. It felt odd having just met her to be relying so heavily on her. There were the obvious questions of trust, what with her gypsy

298

background. There was also the fact she told them her original intent had been to rob them. It was why she had followed them into Notre Dame. It was also why she was a third witness to a candle that seemed to want to light and not light at the same time. And it was the reason she would have fit into either of Joe's *nows*. *Rive Gauche or Rive Droite*—either way she would have followed them, and probably had, given the implications of universes that ran parallel.

"Too long," Trent muttered to his friend nervously as he curled the collar of a leather bomber jacket to cover his neck.

"Give her some time," Joe offered, secretly sharing his friend's unease. It had been over five hours since they asked Sophia to wait at the hotel in hopes of delivering a message to Anna. Both felt tonight was the night Anna would arrive, and they were almost certain she would visit the hotel they had shared with her in their connected dreams.

"You think we should have trusted her?" Trent asked, referring to Sophia, betraying the doubt in his voice.

"Shut up," Joe admonished. "It's done. And she was all we had," he added more thoughtfully, as he looked up and down the street for any sign of their newfound French friend.

"You're attracted to her, aren't you?" Trent asked.

Perturbed more at the accuracy of his friend's observation than the imposition of the question, Joe shot back. "You talk too much."

"You think?" Trent asked seriously, the hurt showing in his body language.

"Yeah. I think," Joe added, trying to deflect the conversation away from himself.

Trent, gazed out over the city, surveying the lights for a moment, before responding. "Well . . . you're stuck with me, you know."

"Yeah. I know," Joe said, with less frustration. "I shouldn't have got defensive. I couldn't handle this crap without you, you know."

"Goes both ways," Trent admitted, letting the tension ebb away.

"You guys going to kiss?" A voice whispered softly from the step behind them.

"Oh damn!" Joe yelled, turning around to see a beaming Sophia, just inches from their faces.

"Christ." Trent said under his breath, as he jumped about a foot off the step and spun around.

"How in the hell . . . ?" Joe asked Sophia. "You're freaky."

Sophia's lower lip slid out into a mock pout. "You want me to leave? I can," she said mischievously. "But you'll never hear about my lovely interlude with your precious Anna."

"You saw her!" Joe marveled. "What did . . . ?"

But Sophia stopped his question by wrapping her arms around his neck and pressing her lips to his in a long, slow kiss.

"What was that for?" Joe asked, pushing Sophia away, more out of surprise than distaste.

But Sophia thrust her index finger to Joe's lips and shushed him. "I was trying to shut you up. We're not safe here. We should not be discussing such things out in the open."

Trent, still standing from the fright Sophia gave them, watched dumbstruck. "Then let's move," he said, not bothering to disguise is irritation.

Sophia gave Trent a disapproving look. "Mon ami. I said it was not safe here to talk of such things. Too many ears, and I may have been followed. But it does not mean we should waste such a beautiful view. Sit, my new friend. We must have a drink." She said these last words as she produced a bottle of Champagne and three plastic cups from the step behind her.

This time Joe objected. "But if we are being followed?"

"You do not trust me. Non?" Sophia asked, showing hurt feelings that appeared to be genuine. "If I was followed then what are we to do? If we leave now he follows us. If we leave two hours from now . . . what?" She asked, hoping one of the guys would finish the thought.

"He follows us?" Trent said dumbly.

"Exactly!" Sophia exclaimed. "And he will not do anything but watch until you and your precious Anna are reunited. This I know in my heart. Only we must not talk of important things now. There will be plenty of time for that later. For now we must act as if we are three new friends, enjoying the sites of this magnifique city, from one of the most romantic views there is, if you ask me. So we must act the part. To do anything else would arouse suspicion," Sophia added with a laugh.

Joe nodded—clearly captivated by this frail little street charmer. Trent was starting to feel like a third wheel, and his instincts said if he was being stalked by someone out there in the darkness, he should run. But Joe had already settled into a conversation with Sophia, the decision made without him. For a moment Trent tried to reach out into the darkness with his mind, to see if he could feel the presence of someone watching . . . someone like The Fifth Seed. But not knowing the identity or even the face of the person he was trying to reach out to made the task difficult. He tried random faces of those he had met over the years at Northwoods, but still nothing.

"Come, my friend," Sophia prodded, snapping Trent out of his concentration. "Sit. Join us. No business will be conducted tonight until we learn to trust one another. Non?"

Sighing, Trent gave in and settled back on the cold concrete step, but not before shooting a wary eye out into the shadows of the street. Sitting now, but uneasily, Sophia poured him a glass of Champagne and handed it to him with a quirky little grin.

Trent tried to smile back, but it came across only partially sincere. He couldn't help but think there was more of a chill in tonight's air than the temperature warranted. And his mind seemed to wrap around a dark, shadowy figure huddled out where the light from the street lamps couldn't reach—far enough away that Trent's mind touched on just enough to frighten the hell out of him. Was this real or imagination fueled by fear? He couldn't tell.

"Cheers," Sophia said brightly as she raised her cup. As the three clinked plastic she sent a private message to their watcher—letting her thoughts be carried away with the gentle breeze that tussled her long, ragged auburn locks.

CHAPTER 71

CAT AND MOUSE

The Kid watched from the shadows as the trio raised a toast on the steps of Sacre Coeur. He was not happy. He had just spent the last two hours following this little street rat through the seediest depths of Paris. In that time he had found her to be a worthy adversary. She played him like a cat, toying with a mouse in its paws before devouring it. Yet she wanted him here now. Uncertain why, he played the last two hours back in his mind, trying to unlock the answer.

For the first hour The Gypsy took at least five different Metro rides to various parts of the city, sometimes getting off to wander aimlessly around the streets. Occasionally she'd window shop, pausing casually at various small boutiques, while at other times she'd literally steal a bite to eat from a street vendor's cart. Every so often, in maddening form, she'd simply get off the Metro, head to the other side of the tracks and return to the exact same stop she came from.

For a while The Kid thought she was looking for a mark to pickpocket and he wondered if he had been right to follow this girl from the hotel. Perhaps he should have followed Anna, but deep down he knew tonight was not their night. That was left for another time, another place . . . his visions were becoming clearer on that subject. Instinct told him to give the street rat a little more time . . . that Trent and Joe were on the other end of this chase. He'd felt it the moment he'd bumped into her outside the hotel.

302

Then, in the last hour, she had turned it into high gear. Stop after Metro stop, hopping off one, and jumping on another, leaving barely enough time for The Kid to slip onto the underground train. The effort had drawn The Kid closer and closer to her, to the point he was worried for his cover. He had to get close enough to avoid missing a stop, but remain just far enough off to avoid showing too much of his face. At least he knew the street rat was on to him and was trying to lose him, which meant there might be a payoff for him in the end.

It was on the last stop that she got him. She timed it perfectly, hopping a Metro with only seconds to spare. The Kid rushed the train at the last minute—hopping through the doors exactly one section to the rear of where the girl had got on. Breathing heavily, satisfied he'd made it in time, The Kid looked forward through the compartment only to see the gypsy exiting through the same set of doors she'd entered, mere seconds before they'd shut. He'd watched as her slim, lithe body flitted effortlessly between the doors like a ballet dancer gliding across a stage. And for the briefest moments her eyes danced across and locked on The Kid's own defeated expression.

She'd used the ploy not only to lose him, but also to get a better look at her pursuer, and in that instant The Kid knew she was a Natural. It had shown (or was purposefully conveyed to him) through the impish smile she wore, and it only served to fuel his silent fury. Not thinking, The Kid turned to jump off the train and chase after her, only to slam face first into the windows of the closed doors.

As the metro picked up speed he'd searched the stragglers on the platform—trying to get a better look at her—but she had disappeared that fast. All The Kid could do was slump into a nearby seat in defeat. The chase threatened to expose him, though he figured she hadn't gotten the best look at him. Still, he'd need to find her, somehow.

In silence, The Kid endured the ride, imagining what he would do to the street rat if he ran across her again. He'd love to get his hands on that long, slender neck of hers. Three minutes later the train arrived at its next stop and The Kid leapt through the doors the moment they opened, racing to the surface level.

Up on the streets in a dark and seedy part of Paris, he immediately located a taxi pulling up on the opposite side of the street. Anxiously he raced after it, running against traffic, trying to flag it down. If he acted fast enough he might get back to the previous Metro stop and pick up her trail.

But what The Kid saw in that next second stopped him mid tracks. As the door to the taxi had opened, a skinny, young, and familiar girl with ragged auburn hair stepped from the back seat. She'd glanced quickly left and then right before hurrying off into a crowd of people who'd just left a bar and began wandering down the street. Part of him had been shocked, but another part of him felt an odd sense of admiration for the girl's audacity. And as she'd faded into the crowd, moving toward steps cut into the hill of Montmartre, she'd tossed a baiting look over her shoulder, directly at The Kid. It left him standing dumbfounded in the middle of the road, as cars bore down on him, screeching tires and blaring their horns.

Which brought him to where he was now: watching the little street rat, sharing a glass of Champagne with the two people The Kid sought. The very two people The Kid desperately wanted to take down—and if he had the means he would have done it now—but Mitch would not trust him with a gun. The Kid marveled again at the girl. She must know he was still out here watching, yet somehow she was unconcerned. Not only that, she'd convinced both Trent and Joe to stay and have a drink. It was insanity.

He knew what the she was doing. She was still toying with him, sending her own message through her actions tonight. That message was clear: she wasn't afraid of him, and she could get Trent and Joe to learn not to fear him—to trust her. It was an obvious taunt that she was better than he and that she had complete control of the situation. The Kid now knew she could lose him whenever she wanted—but he wasn't so sure she could accomplish it with Trent and Joe in tow. *Why did she want him here now, hiding in the darkness? Was she going to help him?*

As The Kid struggled to come to an understanding, the girl did something totally unexpected, she let him into her thoughts. Apparently she wanted to make an introduction, because he suddenly knew her name: Sophia. The Kid had no intention of returning the favor. But there was another part to the message, and it told him much about her intentions. The message was simple, direct and ominous, and suddenly he felt exposed and vulnerable.

Yet the Kid had one last trick up his sleeve. It was one of his more unique talents, and it afforded him the best hiding spot in the world . . . the very one he'd used to remain hidden from the other Naturals all of his young life.

CHAPTER 72

TOUCHING THE VOID

Unexpectedly Sophia rose up from the steps of Sacre Coeur, shooting her gaze instantly to the right, knocking over a plastic cup of Champagne in the process—the contents pouring in rivulets down the ancient stonework.

"What is it?" Joe said, concerned.

"We must leave immediately," Sophia said, fear and confusion in her voice.

Trent was standing and already heading down the steps—happy to be on the move. It was killing him, sitting around knowing The Fifth Seed might be somewhere out in the darkness. Joe just waited calmly for a better explanation.

"He was there. Then . . . he was . . ." Sophia said struggling for the right words. "Then he was just gone."

Trent paused, anxiously waiting for the other two to move, but Sophia kept her gaze locked on the dark shadows about 200 yards down the street, reaching out with her mind to try to touch the mind of their shadow once more.

"If it's The Fifth Seed we told you about, that's not unusual," Joe said matter-of-factly. "In all our years at Northwoods, we never knew his identity. Never saw his face, and never touched his mind. The closest we ever came was an occasional vague sense of dread and foreboding."

"Yes, but you never looked him in his eyes, did you?" Sophia asked defiantly.

"No," Joe replied honestly.

"I have . . . briefly, yes, but enough to make the connection. It was part of the purpose of the chase . . . to get a look at him . . . to get a peek into the soul of your nemesis . . . to turn the advantage to us. I wanted him to know you did not fear him. Fear is his most powerful ally. Why do you think he has concealed his identity for so long?"

Joe let the words sink in, and he realized she was right. For too many years they had shown fear. It was time to change that. But losing touch, losing the upper hand, losing her own control of the situation had obviously shaken Sophia.

Trent, getting anxious, shouted up to them. "Jeez, maybe he just left or called in some help . . . it's been insanity sitting here waiting for something to happen." He was trying anything to get them to move, to understand the urgency he'd felt all along.

Sophia weighed her options once more, but started rapidly down the steps chasing after Trent. Somewhat reluctantly, Joe got up and followed, spilling what remained in the bottle of Champagne as he rose. The bottle fell to his feet, clanking much too loudly down several steps before shattering on the third bounce. None of the three turned toward the noise, for they were too unnerved and on the move.

"I thought of that." Sophia said as they hastened away. "In fact, I tried to bluff him—to get him to leave with a message of my own. I thought if I *suggested* to him that my two 250-pound brothers were on their way to beat him to a pulp, perhaps that would shake him from our tail." Sophia laughed nervously as she took the lead down the street, away from her last sense of where their follower had been.

"And?" Joe asked, between quick breaths as he ran.

"All I can say is his presence did not fade away gradually, like someone moving further into the distance." Anticipating the next question, she added definitively, "He was not blocking me. I know how that feels."

"Then what happened?" Trent asked anxiously.

"It was the strangest thing . . . as if he just disappeared into thin air. Or, oh damn, what is the word?" Sophia breathed. "The word that pops into my head is *replaced*. That makes no sense. Non?"

As the three ran down the street, Joe pondered it. Trying to think of anything that might explain the experience Sophia just had, but the frightening answer was simply, "No."

"I didn't think so," Sophia said. Her mind still trying to reach behind them to get any sense whether the one the boys feared, the one they called The Fifth Seed, was following. But all she could feel was an empty hole or void.

For a moment, Joe tried to reach out and touch The Fifth Seed with his own mind. He knew Sophia had a better shot than either he or Trent did, because she had seen him, and could visualize him in her mind. But Joe had to try.

For a moment he felt something oddly familiar, something eerily close. But what he felt his mind said was simply not possible.

CHAPTER 73

UNSETTLED

Anna paced across the cramped hotel room they had rented for the night as Grady's eyes followed. He sat on the lousy excuse for a bed and worried for the young woman he'd met only days ago. She was struggling with something, and it wasn't just the call from Trent and Joe that she was anxiously waiting for, as she would have liked him to believe.

Something had happened, something between the time she had walked to the Hotel le Clos Medicis and when he found her on the streets of Paris outside the Luxembourg Gardens confronting the man, until tonight, he'd only known as Anna's father. Something had made her want to give up just a few short hours ago. Grady had the sense it wasn't something Mitch had said to her.

But what? Could it be she was worried about Mary Jane? Could something have changed with her condition? Was she now in even graver danger? Or was Anna still harboring feelings of guilt and self-loathing over the feelings that had been building between she and Grady, while Mary Jane remained captive somewhere in the bowels of Northwoods? Grady guessed not, believing that if Mary Jane were the cause of Anna's current mood she would confide in him.

It seemed more logical Anna sensed something was wrong with Trent and Joe. Grady could see where Anna might not want to say anything to him until she could confirm her feelings, which brought him back to the call that hadn't come in. As they waited, now almost twenty minutes past midnight, Grady considered the pair he had yet to meet.

The way Anna spoke of them, he'd begun to understand who these young men were and what they meant to Anna. Joe was a big-hearted lug with an amazingly sharp mind. Anna described him as a football player with a law degree. She spoke of his love for writing, his romantic poet's heart, and his impressive ability to process vast amounts of information, conflicting messages, and high-pressure situations and make sense of it all.

Trent, on the other hand was a studious-looking sort. Anna had described him as thin and lanky, with a bowl cut and plain features. His round spectacles lending him a Harry Potteresque look. She called him charmingly high-strung, a bit standoffish at times and generally reserved. Of the three other Naturals, Anna suggested she knew the least about Trent because he kept a thin veil up at all times—never really allowing anyone to get too close.

Grady was also beginning to understand subtle differences in terms of their Natural talents. He was surprised to find that each Natural was somewhat unique in this regard. Anna was their glue, the connection, the person who could reach out and touch the minds of others, even over vast distances. She was their link whenever they were separated—able to reach into their thoughts and feelings and occasionally walk with them in their experiences from afar.

In contrast, Trent had the ability to project. An odd twist of their talents, it allowed him to present alternate realities, or lies, to others who tried to view his thoughts. This had led Northwoods to think at one point that he wasn't a strong Natural because his predictions or projections often came up wrong. What few people understood was that Trent could easily decipher the real from a projection—glimpsing a parallel universe that would come close to the here-and-now, but never converge.

Joe was the analytical Natural in the group. His predictions were the most accurate of the four by several percentage points. Many believed it was due to his ability to take multiple stray thoughts, visions and experiences, see the threads of connections, toss out the information that was noise or clutter and come to a sound, reasoned and rational conclusion. Because of his abilities, Northwoods had spent an inordinate amount of time early on trying to understand how his mind worked. That interest faded over time, and led the Naturals to speculate that Northwoods had someone even more talented—the fabled Fifth Seed—who was even more accurate than Joe.

Finally, there was Curt. His abilities were clouded, partially because Northwoods had used his willingness to cooperate, pumping him with more drugs than the others. Still, his early talents indicated an enhanced ability to dig into others minds—to understand their feelings and help influence, guide or even control their decisions. As Northwoods found more complex drug cocktails that artificially simulated and enhanced key parts of Curt's brain, his talents began to drift across those of Anna, Trent and Joe. In short, Northwoods had begun to mold its own Natural.

Watching Anna pace, Grady wondered why Curt's name hadn't come up recently. She had spoken of him often early on, but had mentioned him little in the last few days. He knew Anna was still mourning Curt's death, and that she'd had little time to wrestle with those emotions. But she seemed to be blocking it out now. He wondered if it was a coping mechanism, if she was simply moving through stages of grief, living in denial. In any event, he knew true healing would be able to come only when Anna could put the current events behind her, and find space to deal with her grief.

It didn't help that Curt and Anna had once dated. Grady reflected, with a hint of jealously, how she glowed when she described the good traits of his personality. He'd been the comedian of the group, but what the jokes had hidden were his own insecurities—a need for everyone to like him no matter what. Anna had guessed that was why he, of the four Naturals, had been the most cooperative with Northwoods, offering to help, giving in freely to the tests. Although, it wasn't until Northwoods ramped up their experiments that Curt completely changed.

Grady found it intriguing Northwoods had been a relatively happy place for the Naturals in their younger years. There had been a time the institution treated them with care and respect. True, they studied them and experimented with their incredible minds, but Northwoods once went to great lengths to help them live comfortable, happy lives. In their youth they'd been able to play with the other non-Naturals at the institute. Even in their teens the Naturals were allowed to have social lives and go to school inside the institute. They were taught about the outside world, how things worked, how people behaved.

It was about this time Anna had begun to date. Strangely Northwoods seemed to encourage it. Grady tried to recall the few early romances of her life. She had talked briefly about Drake—the son of one of the workers at Northwoods—and the uncomfortable interest he'd had in her. Then there had been Curt, but his bout with drugs had extinguished that relationship. Anna had mentioned a couple others, but nothing that felt of great significance.

It was during these years, shortly after Mary Jane was brought on, that changes at Northwoods began in force. By the time the Naturals turned eighteen—when each had assumed they would be released—Northwoods completely changed the routine. The Naturals were confined and separated from the rest of the non-Natural population at Northwoods, and the tests—which previously had felt like regular doctor's visits—became intense and uncomfortable sessions. This included the administration of mind-altering drugs, brutal mental interrogations, intrusive physical examinations, mental mind games and forced participation in strange and dramatic role-playing sessions. If any Naturals were uncooperative or rebellious, solitary confinement was the preferred punishment.

It was these changes at Northwoods that apparently brought about severe changes in Curt's personality. Anna described Curt during this tumultuous time as someone who was completely torn. His desire to please, and the early stages of drug addiction kept him in line at Northwoods, and his cooperation resulted in preferential treatment that made him an outcast among the other Naturals, driving a rift into the once close-knit group. Anna tried to convince Trent and Joe that the Curt they all cared for and loved was still in there somewhere, and all he needed was to be free of Northwoods. It was a hard sell; one Trent and Joe never fully bought into, but they'd offered to be more understanding, if only for Anna's sake. It was Anna's own persistence, with Trent and Joe's support, that got Curt to back off the drugs and reconnect with the group, earning him a spot in the escape plans.

Still resting on the hard, lumpy bed, Grady caught Anna's eye as she paused her pacing—but again she looked quickly away. It was almost as if she was ashamed of what he might see in her. For a moment Grady wondered if that was the case, if she was ashamed of what she was thinking . . . what could that be? As he sat there, weighing a question that had been bugging him for a while now, trying like hell to understand Anna's strange and swinging moods, the phone mercifully rang.

CHAPTER 74

ANNA'S ANGUISH

Anna knew she was pacing, and that Grady's eyes were on her. She'd occasionally catch his eye, give him a faint smile and look away. She was starting to come to some conclusions . . . conclusions that on the surface she didn't like, but necessary ones if she truly cared for the man sitting on the bed worrying about her.

She wondered why he didn't ask her the questions on his mind, the ones she knew he had because when she caught his eye, she could read him like an open book. The wonderful and strangely intoxicating man who sat there so concerned about her still understood little about her. Though he accepted her abilities, he forgot she could easily read his thoughts—was even thinking along with him—and sometimes helped him along on his own journey to understanding. She preferred it this way though, because if he asked the questions about what was troubling her, about what was on her mind, she didn't know if she could answer them honestly without breaking down and giving in to him. That would certainly ruin the conviction she was trying to steel in herself tonight.

She had to leave him. As heartbreaking as it may be it was the only way. Her dreams and visions continued to lead her back to a fate too unbearable to imagine. Nothing had changed in the last few days to alter her vision of the future. Nothing they'd done in the past several days had done anything to make her believe the outcome would change. It was why they were in Paris, wasn't it, to try to change the future by getting to Trent and Joe before Northwoods did? Instead it seemed their actions, their pursuit of Trent and Joe, were leading directly toward a horrifying outcome.

The only way Anna felt she could alter their reality was to remove Grady from her life. If he wasn't involved, he couldn't fall into Northwood's grasp. True, she might not succeed in extricating herself from a predestined future, but she was willing to live with that . . . and even die for him. As she paced, she began to firm up her plan. Once the call came in she would pick up the phone, find out where Trent and Joe were, and lie to Grady, giving him a false location . . . anything that might push him in a different direction. In the morning, maybe she would send him on an errand for coffee, and slip away to meet up with Trent and Joe on her own.

The thought tore at her heart. How had she become so attached to this man in so little time? But she knew the answer. She could see ahead, she knew who he was, and who he'd be to her in the most painful and frightening of circumstances, and it made her heart ache. He hardly knew her, but that didn't matter. He cared for her, which was all that mattered to him. To be that man for her—her protector—she felt he would most certainly die. And where was the worth in that?

Pacing still, she turned and caught his eye, and for a moment she feared he was looking inside her, reading her soul and her thoughts. It was unlikely, but possible. Anna knew what the Naturals did was only an intense extension of what other people experience during bouts of déjà vu. The Natural's own talents were a mere extension of their own long buried animal instincts . . . instincts long since set aside in favor of extensive verbal communication. In many ways words had actually become a crutch for the human race, and people had forgotten how to read body language, to smell fear, sense danger and slow things down with their mind. Animals still did this today because they needed those senses, using them in unison to make them infinitely more acute and powerful, culminating in a sixth sense for survival.

Wondering momentarily if Grady was trying to dig into her soul and lay it bare, Anna looked away quickly. She couldn't bring herself to look at him; for if he knew what she was planning to do, he would never let her do it, and she loved him for it. At that moment she wanted him to at least know that. She loved him and always would, no matter what. As she was about to turn and tell him, the phone rang.

CHAPTER 75

THE CALL

Anna put the phone Sophia had given her to her ear before the first ring faded out to the walls of the hotel room. "Allo," she said instinctively.

"You can cut it with the French, Anna," Joe's voice said from the other end.

Breathlessly, afraid to know, she asked anyway. "Are you both okay?"

A chuckle, then a pause, and Anna could feel Joe turning to look at Trent and another—perhaps Sophia—almost as if reconfirming with his eyes what his answer would be. "We're all fine. It's been a hell of a night."

Anna let out her breath in a long sigh of relief. For a moment, Grady misunderstood Anna's reaction for bad news and rose from the bed to comfort her. Seeing Grady rise to approach her, Anna, without thinking turned away from him, burying her ear into the phone, intent on the conversation.

"I'm so glad! I was so worried," Anna said joyfully.

At the sound of her voice, Grady realized his mistake, but not before noticing the unintended slight by Anna, and slouched back down on the bed.

"And you?" Joe asked. "You sound well . . . is all okay?"

"Yes," Anna said quickly. "As good as can be given everything. But these are not conversations for the phone. We must meet. Where are you?"

317

There was a long uneasy pause, and the dread crept back into Anna's mind. "There are complications, Anna. Again, we are all okay. We are staying tonight at Sophia's but we think we're being followed."

"But how!" Anna remarked, her voice rising now with the strain.

"It's a long story, and as you said yourself, this is not a conversation for the phone, but we think it might be The Fifth Seed."

Anna's legs went weak, and her hand began to shake as her trembling voice croaked out the question she knew the answer to. "But when can we meet?"

"I don't know Anna. It has been a while since we have felt his presence, so perhaps we lost him. Or maybe he moved on. But something new happened that none of us have ever experienced before and it means we have to be cautious. It's hard to explain."

"I can't take this Joe. I can't take this." The desperation was back in Anna's voice, now desperately wanting Grady's arms to comfort her, wondering why he didn't come, not realizing the small slight she'd given him only moments earlier. So Grady remained where he was, his pride a little damaged, fearful of upsetting her more—so he simply tried to follow the one-sided conversation through Anna.

"I know Anna. I'm sorry. It's not how we wanted it, either. But if you are safe, and you have not been followed, then I believe Northwoods will leave Trent and I alone for now. As long as they don't know where you are, they will assume we will lead them to you as well. They know we are trying to join. So please do not worry about us. At least for now, I do not feel as if we are in any immediate danger."

"What are you saying?" Anna said, anger clouding her voice.

"Come on, Anna. I'm not saying we won't meet. We just need to be careful. We need a little time to make sure we have lost our tail. Once we are certain, we can join up with you."

"You sound like you already know the place."

"I think I do, but I'm wary of saying too much. It might be best if you and Grady head there before us, and we will contact you when we are on our way."

"You make it sound like it is a long distance. Please just tell me where."

"You already know it, Anna. Do not forget who you are or what you are capable of. I do not have to say such things aloud for you to know them. Remember my face and the place will come to you as if it were there all along."

"But . . ."

"Anna!" Joe admonished. "You need to remember who you are. You are the connection. If we discuss this much more then I fear others will pick up on it."

"Okay," Anna said in a small voice.

"You alright?"

With a sniffle, "Yes."

"Good," Joe said, ignoring the emotion.

"How long?" Anna asked, her voice wavering.

"A day or two at the most. If it takes any longer we will call with a new plan."

"I miss you both. Please hug Trent for me."

"I know Anna. I will."

It took all of Anna's will to say the last word. "Goodbye."

But Joe wouldn't let her hang up just yet. He needed to get something across to her—something of utmost importance. "Oh, and Anna? Once you know the place . . . before you go to bed . . ."

"Yes?" Anna replied warily.

"Close your mind to us and everyone else. Do not reach out to us even out of curiosity. Am I clear?"

Anna couldn't get the words out, so she simply nodded her head as she hung up, sobbing softly as Grady watched, caught between wanting to comfort her and wary of intruding, wondering what to do.

CHAPTER 76

SIZING UP THE SCORE

Sophia left Trent and Joe in her brothers' room as she retired to hers. She lived with her two older siblings in a small second-floor apartment over an Irish-themed pub nestled in the hill of Montmartre. Her brothers' room was available tonight because they happened to be away visiting their mother in the small town of Chinon, in the Loire Valley. Sophia's mother had moved there several years ago to live with her sister shortly after the death of her husband.

Through her open window Sophia could plainly hear some of the crowd from the pub below the apartment, dispersing drunkenly into the night. She shed her clothes for a nightdress, grabbed her phone and slipped out her window onto the fire escape balcony. The long, soft whisper of cloth billowed around her in the autumn breeze. Sitting on one of the metal grate steps, she clutched her knees to her chest and thought about the day, and her next move.

Somewhere out there was the man who had followed her through the city. Trent and Joe referred to him as The Fifth Seed. They had never seen him, but she had. She hoped that would serve as an advantage to them.

She was upset with herself for being so cocky with this Fifth Seed. She had wanted him close for a couple of reasons. One, she wanted to understand her adversary better. She had learned at a young age from her father that fear was a useless emotion, and with their family's street life,

Sophia knew if you felt fear you had no business being in the situation you were in. You needed to control situations and take command of them to make the score.

That was her second reason for drawing The Fifth Seed close. She thought perhaps if she understood him more, understood what he wanted; she could use it to her advantage. After all, she was a street tramp, and her living was made finding situations she could take advantage of—and to do that you needed the upper hand. You needed control. Whether it was picking pockets, stealing from a shop, or conning someone out of their hard-earned money, it was what she was good, perhaps even great, at.

Over the course of her young life, Sophia had used her Natural talents to help her family enjoy an easy life. First working with her mother and father and more recently with her two older brothers after her father passed away. It wasn't an ostentatious life by any means—particularly by French means. A look around the three-room apartment would reinforce that. But it certainly wasn't a hard nine to five working life either.

She was always looking for that big score, and at one point Sophia had wondered if the situation surrounding Trent and Joe might pay out big. She had known Trent and Joe were in trouble—she understood that before she even spoke with them. It was obvious by their subtle actions and movements in Notre Dame. In Sophia's experience trouble meant opportunity. For a time, she had been thinking that those who sought Trent and Joe might pay good money to know their whereabouts. That was another reason she had lured and toyed with The Fifth Seed.

She had known the instant she passed him outside the hotel he would follow. Her only regret was not getting a better look at him—but she feared if she had done that he might gain a deeper understanding of her. So she took him on her wild goose chase across Paris. She could have just led this Fifth Seed directly to Trent and Joe, but then he really wouldn't have needed her, would he? She needed to let him know he was up against someone formidable, someone who was in complete control—and deliver what he so desperately wanted.

Sophia guessed The Fifth Seed didn't necessarily have the kind of monetary resources she would be seeking for such a transaction. After talking to Trent and Joe about their past and why they were on the run, she learned a little about the organization they were running from. Sophia figured any place that would go to the trouble of tracking a couple of mental institute fugitives all the way across the Atlantic . . . well, there just might be a bankroll behind that chase.

That had been the way she had been formulating her plan—right up to the moment she sat on the steps of Sacre Coeur and kissed Joe. It was such a silly impulse, because she wanted to shut him up and the idea just flicked across her mind. That was the beginning of her doubt; after the kiss, her conviction wavered. She wondered if she truly could turn these young men over.

Then when The Fifth Seed called her bluff, and disappeared into thin air, Sophia felt real fear. She understood all at once the dangers behind the playing out of this game, and the horrors ahead for Trent and Joe if their shadows of the past ever caught up with their futures. In that instant she knew she would never be able to gain the upper hand, because for the first time in her life fear left her paralyzed. She was stuck on one side—and for once in her life she felt it just might be the good side. Even with her fear the thought made her happy.

As she was considering turning in for the evening the phone vibrated in her hand. Flipping the phone open she answered as quietly as she could. Her brother's window was open to the fire escape where she sat. The lights were off inside the room, so she assumed Trent and Joe were sound asleep. Still, she was careful not to let her voice carry.

"Hello."

"Hello my friend. It's me, Jack."

"Did you follow him?"

"Non, je regrette. You said a gentleman in a blue ballcap, and he would most likely be watching you on the steps of Sacre Coeur. Oui?"

"Oui," Sophia said dejectedly.

"I arrived a bit later than anticipated. I did see you and two very ugly Americans running down the steps of Sacre Coeur, but no gentleman with a blue baseball cap. Do you have a better description? I could search the streets around your apartment again."

"No, I don't. I never got a really good look at him . . . just the blue baseball cap, pulled low over a pair of dark green eyes."

"Then perhaps I can come over tonight? I would keep you safe."

"Jack," Sophia said with exasperation. "You know that never worked with us. Why must you persist? Besides, I have company."

"You know one can always try." Sophia could perceive the smile in Jack's voice. "For you, I will check the bar below, and the street around your apartment once more, and give you a full report in the morning. But if you will grant me this one request?"

"What?" Sophia asked cautiously.

"I shall give you my full report in person, and you must not change from that lovely little night shift you always wear to bed. For one can always admire, even if one cannot touch."

"Goodbye Jack," Sophia said, and hung up.

Yes, that was another reason why she had lured The Fifth Seed to the steps of Sacre Coeur, and why she had tried to have the boys linger there as long as possible. She had wanted to buy some time to set up a tail on this Fifth Seed using one of her many street friends. Her original plan had been to scare The Fifth Seed back to his hotel for the evening, back into his hole. It was Jack's job to follow him and find out where he was staying and who was running this Paris operation for Northwoods. It was that other person she had wanted to deal with.

But that was then. It was a whole new game now, and she simply wanted to know where her adversary was so she could decide on their next move. The three of them were working blind, and she didn't like it.

Flipping her phone shut, Sophia was just about to head to bed when she heard a noise. Glancing up, she saw a foot emerge from her brothers' room and a dark figure stepped out onto the fire escape.

Sophia held her breath, wondering who it might be, and in some odd sense hoped it would be Joe coming to check on her. To her dismay, it was Trent. As his foot hit the metal grating it creaked with the extra weight, and for a moment Trent thought the whole thing might go crashing down to the street with them on it.

"Is it safe?" he asked warily, one eye on the scaffolding and the other on Sophia, his eyes darting awkwardly to her nightdress, then away.

"We've had many more out here before, so yes, I'd assume so," Sophia said a bit abruptly, cursing her luck that the foot belonged to Trent and not Joe.

"You obviously were hoping for someone else," Trent said with a hint of satisfaction as he read her mind, cursing her secret desires.

"What is it you want?" Sophia snapped, hoping to hurry along whatever brought Trent to her so she could put an end to this dreadful day.

"Who were you talking to on the phone?"

Knowing it was best not to lie to him, she shared part of the truth, hoping it enough to satisfy whatever concerns he might have. "His name is Jack, if you must know. He is a friend, and I was trying to set him up as a tail on the one you call The Fifth Seed. It was why I wanted you and Joe to linger at Sacre Coeur. I was buying time for Jack to get into place."

"And?" Trent asked, watching Sophia's eyes the entire time. To her credit, she never tried to conceal them from him.

"The Fifth Seed vanished before Jack could set up a tail. You were there—you know how that all went down."

Trent searched her eyes, reaching out to see if what she was saying was true. For all his trying, the only conclusion he could come up with was that she was being honest. Perhaps not sharing the full truth, but still being honest.

Sophia waited for more questions, but when none came asked, "Is that all?"

Trent seemed to mellow a bit, as he ran his hand through pencil-straight hair. It seemed to be a nervous twitch, and Sophia made a mental note of it.

"I guess that's it," he said, almost apologetically. With that Trent turned to step back through the window. But he paused, popping his head back out, as if he forgot to say something.

Sophia cringed, thinking to herself, *Now what?*

"Sophia?" he asked.

"Yes?" She made no attempt to hide her frustration.

"Thank you." Trent said sincerely, not wanting to leave her, taking one more moment to admire her figure revealed beneath a nightdress that clung to her curves, pressed by the evening's breeze. "You need to understand, Joe and Anna are my life. I love them to death. I just need to make sure your intentions are . . . well . . ." He stumbled over the word, "sincere."

Sophia was taken aback. She hadn't been expecting that from Trent, and it made her feel bad for her prior intentions.

"You're welcome," Sophia whispered back with a strange softness in her heart.

But the words drifted by an empty window. Trent had already slipped inside.

CHAPTER 77

FALLING HARD

Anna sobbed softly in a chair, her back still turned to Grady in what he wrongly sensed as a sign she wanted to sort through her emotions alone. Grady rose from his chair.

"I need to go make a call," he said with a little more frustration than he wanted his voice to convey, "and I don't feel comfortable making it from here. I'll be right back."

Anna, hearing his voice, turned with tears in her eyes to protest, but he was already at the door. She just looked at him, her eyes catching his momentarily; pleading with him to stay . . . something she couldn't bring her voice to do.

But this time Grady averted his eyes, turned briskly, and walked out the door.

Anna sat there, confused, wondering if Grady had picked up on her earlier intentions to lie to him . . . to abandon him. As she sat there in the room by herself, she felt more alone in the world than she ever had.

She tried to steady herself, to get hold of her emotions that were running completely wild. She wasn't sure how much more she could take. Now, Anna couldn't help but wonder if the one person who remained by her side had simply decided to lie to her and walk away—leaving her alone in Paris. Perhaps Grady finally had had too much. If that were the case, it would be what she wanted for him . . .

to be away from her, and away from danger. Even knowing that, she desperately wanted him to come back.

It was an agonizing half hour before the lock in the door turned and Grady entered. Without a moment's hesitation Anna leapt from the bed and threw herself into his arms. It took a moment, but Grady eventually softened to her embrace and folded her up into his arms, his nose buried in the nape of her neck, breathing in her scent as her soft curls brushed across his lips.

"I thought you left me." Anna sighed, fighting back tears. "I thought you left me."

Grady simply hugged her harder, squeezing her body to his, reveling in the soft swell of her breasts, the quivering muscles of her stomach and the hard, unyielding press of her pelvis against his own.

He kissed her neck as he whispered into her ear "Never." She returned the embrace with a passion that she knew she would regret. But it was honest, it was bare and she needed him to know—no matter what happened in the future—the depths of the feelings building inside her.

Anna's hand reached up and she ran her fingers through the hair along the base of his neck, teasing the waves, making Grady shiver. Tentatively, he slid his hand down the arch of her back, lower and lower, testing every inch until he caressed the roundness that stretched the seams of her jeans. He pulled up gently, squeezing lightly, enjoying the firmness, as Anna let out a soft gasp. In that moment she brought her face around, opened her mouth to his and kissed him deeply . . . more deeply than she had kissed anyone before.

Right there, she melted, her body going loose and fluid and she ground herself into him with a raw, honest desire. He fell back against the door, their lips parting for a few brief seconds as Grady's hand rode up, releasing the hem of her shirt from her pants. She responded raising her arms up, allowing Grady to pull her shirt up around her chest and over her head. He watched with yearning as her hair spilled back, a shower of shiny locks dancing about her bare neck and shoulders.

Hands trembling, Anna fumbled at Grady's jeans, accepting his help as she slid open the zipper and peeled them off him, dropping them to the floor. Grady kicked out of his pants, not wanting to take his eyes off Anna, feeling a little self-conscious as he stood open and awkward in his boxers before they ate up every inch of space between them to intertwine once more.

Bound in each other's embrace, Anna freed her right hand, and slid it down between them, carving out space as it reached lower, until she wedged it between his thighs, gently encouraging him. Another deep kiss elicited a groan from Grady as Anna drew him hard into her before playfully pushing him away to wrestle his shirt over his head. As the shirt came off, Anna's hand returned, this time pressed against Grady's chest, holding him at arms length, allowing her long, thin fingers to dance through the crop of hair there, fingernails tracing the firm, defined contours of his muscles.

Grady took advantage of this brief interlude to drink Anna in with his eyes, relishing every last detail—from the fire in her eyes to the sweep of her hair, to the elegant line of her neck that rode down to her broad shoulders, where two thin ribbons of fabric strained to support a simple white bra that shaped a gentle valley of cleavage. The roundness of her breasts rose over a trim, not-quite-flat stomach that plunged in a gentle arch into her jeans. To him she was awkward and beautiful, vulnerable and powerful all at the same time, and he knew in that instant he couldn't stop this even if he wanted to.

Anna dropped her hand to Grady's, taking it in her own, locking eyes with him as she led him silently over to the unyielding rock of a bed. Anna turned and tore at the sheets and pillows, tossing them all to the base of the bed. She grabbed the mildly surprised Grady and pulled him to her, down into the heap of linens on the floor, taking intense pleasure as she guided his weight down on top of her. As they kissed again, Anna loosened her jeans, allowing Grady to help her slip out of them, to be discarded in a heap. Wrapped together again, Anna's body rose and fell in beautiful rhythm to Grady's own desire.

They remained entangled like that, rolling and writhing on the floor until Grady's exploring hands found the clasp that would release her from the last of her garments. Sensing his difficulty, Anna rolled him over, resting on top of him now as she reached back, unclasping her bra, letting it dangle momentarily off her shoulders, allowing Grady to take brief pleasure in the sight, before she slipped it off and tossed it with the rest of their clothes. Immediately she threw herself onto his chest—her breasts pressing into him hard, her tongue searching once again for his.

There, on the floor they made love . . . at times slowly, savoring every moment . . . at times full of yearning and desire so strong and passionate it felt like neither could hold back. As the night ticked by, everything but themselves was lost and forgotten. Nothing was said about the other Naturals, The Fifth Seed or any future rendezvous. Everything else could wait until morning.

As Anna rolled off Grady and snuggled up next to his side, their hearts beating together in a blissful chest-pounding rhythm, she said the one thing she absolutely had to say to him tonight. "I love you." Before Grady could even respond, she knew his answer, and it made her smile with her whole being. With raw delight, they made love all over again.

CHAPTER 78

THE HANDOFF

The Kid returned at four in the morning to wait outside Sophia's apartment. He had left shortly after the events on the steps of Sacre Coeur, and allowed another to take his place. Yet he hadn't slept much. Instead he used one of his more unique talents, reaching out through the mind of another to keep tabs on his eventual prey. It was easier to let someone else take watch. One who would be harder to sense by the other Naturals.

The person The Kid had chosen to use that evening was of little consequence to him. What mattered was his ability to control and manipulate this other person's mind—to do his bidding as The Kid rested safely nearby. It was this unique talent that he believed earned him the legendary name *Fifth Seed*—a name that struck fear in to the hearts of many at Northwoods. When people spoke of another with powers beyond the other four seeds it was him they mythologized and feared. Of everything in the world, this was most important to him.

The Kid had not gone back to stay with Mitch, for Mitch was lounging halfway across town, and for what The Kid needed to do, he had to be close. Mitch was furious he had not returned to the hotel. He was even more furious he hadn't bothered to check in until just moments ago. The Kid calmly explained he had been indisposed. When he told Mitch he'd discovered where Trent and Joe were staying, Mitch stopped complaining and started asking serious questions, such as, "Where the

330

hell are you?" In The Kid's mind, that was close enough to a serious question. And once Mitch had calmed down he offered to take The Kid's place.

Normally The Kid would have balked at having Mitch take over anything for him. He was convinced under most circumstances Mitch would find a way to screw something up—and so far he had. *Seriously what did Allan see in the guy?* But after the evening's events, The Kid felt like the wheels were in motion toward a predestined future, one he had seen. And the longer he remained close to the other Naturals the more likely he was to jeopardize the future he so desperately wanted.

Yes, there were uncertainties around who might be left standing at the end . . . Grady, Joe or Trent . . . or perhaps any combination of them. His visions had not been completely clear on this point, which told him there was still a little more work for him to do. While his visions continued to indicate a much desired and inevitable meeting alone with Anna, the elimination of Trent, Joe and Grady would only help to more firmly seal that future. All of those things needed to play out in the next several days in France.

The Kid half-hoped when Mitch arrived on the scene he would simply storm into Sophia's apartment and put a bullet in each of them, getting them out of the way. He was tired of the pre-game and wanted the main event to begin. Killing Trent and Joe now, though, would mean they couldn't lead them to Anna. Mitch would never go for that. While The Kid didn't feel like he needed to be led to Anna, he certainly wanted Grady eliminated sooner rather than later. The longer that man lived, and the closer he got to Anna, the more The Kid sensed he might be the one to alter a future The Kid was desperately trying to manipulate to his advantage. He had invested so much time and planning in this outcome—more than Mitch or Allan would ever know.

There was also another personal reason why he wanted Trent and Joe to lead them to Grady and Anna. During the night he had caught glimpses of the new couple, their love growing ever stronger. He hated to replay the details in his mind, because they were particularly sickening. While he'd leave the messy job of taking out Trent and Joe to a so-called expert like Mitch, he had an intense desire to take out Grady himself, making him suffer in the process. He would take great pleasure in telling Anna every gruesome detail before punishing her severely for her infidelity.

At half past four The Kid spotted Mitch walking down the street, ready to take his place on the dark streets in the shadow of Montmartre. Mitch walked up to him in the pre-dawn glow and The Kid stepped out of the shadows to greet him.

"Why the hell do you always wear that stupid cap?" were the first words out of Mitch's mouth.

"Why the hell are you so late?" was The Kid's terse response.

Exasperated, Mitch decided to skip the pleasantries and get down to business. "Okay, just get on with it . . . where are they?"

The Kid nodded toward a point about a block down the street at the entrance to the apartments. "Over there, the door just to the left of the bar entrance."

"Anybody come and go since you've been here?"

"No, they're still in there. I can still feel them, though they are all doing a pretty good job of blocking their thoughts right now. But that still means they're there."

Mitch grunted his acknowledgement.

"You said on the phone the doc was going to get you some back up?" The Kid asked out of curiosity, not seeing anyone who appeared to be with Mitch.

"He's parking the car," Mitch lied. "Why do you ask?"

"Because on the other side of the building there's a fire escape, as well as a rear entrance. Trent and Joe know they are being watched, so they might try to slip out the back or even try to roll through the bar. There might be a way to get into the bar from the apartments and they certainly might try the fire escape. You'll need at least a couple pairs of eyes, unless you suddenly develop the ability to reach out to them and feel their presence."

"Yeah, we should be able to cover it. Go get a rest and come back in a few hours."

"No. I'm done here and they'll be on the move again before I wake up from my nap at Hotel Five Stars," The Kid said with a hint of a sneer.

Mitch shot The Kid a surprised look. "Why do you think they're moving?"

"Because they know they aren't safe. They sensed me last night, but I think I managed to throw them off. The more I hang around, the more likely they are to be on guard. They won't lead you anywhere near Anna if they sense danger. We need to lull them back into a false sense of security and then as soon as they feel safe, they'll rush to Anna."

"Well, what about you? Can't you just try to—what do you call it—hitchhike off her thoughts? That's how you found these guys."

The Kid actually marveled for a second that he and Mitch were having a civil conversation and really wanted to throw a jab at him just to spice things up, but he was too tired now. "I've tried. Lets just say last night she was a bit indisposed. And my guess is right now she is doing everything she can to block me. She's closing down because she knows we're close. But that just means she's blind as well."

"Makes sense I guess," Mitch said. "So what do I do about you if they decide to move on?" Mitch said, jerking his head in the apartment's direction.

"If it's in the city, that's easy; just let me know where you end up. I can meet you any time you think it's safe. If it's outside the city, you said you have another guy showing up a little later? Must mean you have two cars. Send one of them to pick me up, and we'll follow a half hour behind. But, if I get too close again, and they get a sense of me, we'll just scare them off."

"Alright, Kid," Mitch said, hesitating a few awkward seconds before he added a final few words. "And thanks. Hate to admit it, but you did good work last night."

The Kid eyed Mitch for a second to see if he was being sincere. "You know Mitch, that's awfully nice coming from a complete asshole like yourself. And I'd almost take that as a compliment if I didn't honestly believe when this whole thing is said and done, you'll be the first lobbying the doc to off me, too." With that, The Kid headed off to the nearest metro.

Mitch, never wanting to let someone get the last word in, yelled after The Kid. "Get some rest; you'll need it, you little prick."

The Kid kept on walking. It was a lame shot even for Mitch. Right now The Kid had no intention of sleeping, because while he was talking to Mitch a small detail had popped into his head, a little detail from when he had tried to reach out to Anna last night. He wasn't sure why it hadn't struck him before. Perhaps it was the sheer frustration of seeing her in bed with Grady. But the vision had been of her in a robe . . . and on the front of the robe was stitched the name of a hotel.

CHAPTER 79

ON THE MOVE

At 4:13 a.m. Sophia quietly entered her brothers' bedroom. She could hear heavy snoring from the far bed across the room. As her eyes adjusted to the darkness, aided by a thin veil of light coming from the window, she saw the noise came from Trent who'd taken her brother Paul's bed.

She crept forward a little more, closer to her youngest brother Stephan's bed. The shadows here made it difficult to see and her eyes barely made out a figure amidst the lumps of blankets and sheets. She paused, listening for breathing nearby, but could hear none. For some reason her heart was quick, and her palms a bit moist. "It was time, wasn't it?" she thought to herself.

Another step forward and a floorboard creaked, and she froze, because it wasn't her foot that made the noise. She whirled around to face the sound and her small frame slammed into the hard, broad chest of Joe.

Trembling from the fright, she looked up into Joe's face, an expression of apology in her eyes. In a split second Joe spun her back around, as his hand slid up to cover her mouth. In the same movement, he bore the full weight of his heavy build against her and drove her forward, face down into Stephan's bed. As they crumpled together onto the sheets, Joe ensured half of his weight rested on top of Sophia, pinning her down.

Without releasing his hand from her mouth, he whispered, "What are you doing in here?"

Sophia began to mumble and protest through Joe's hand.

"Quietly!" he warned in a low threat, and Sophia nodded her head. After a moment of consideration, Joe slid his hand off of Sophia's mouth, his palm wet with her saliva. At the same time he shifted his weight off her and she slowly turned to him.

Joe expected to see raw anger in her eyes, but was surprised to see only urgency. "We need to move!" she whispered.

"Why? What have you seen?" Joe asked.

"Do I have to say? You are awake. You look like you have not slept either. And you were waiting to ambush anyone who happened to enter the room. You tell me why!"

"Because whoever was out on the street has moved. Am I correct?"

Sophia nodded, her eyes wide and deep. "Did you feel him tonight as well?"

Joe looked over at the window for a long time, past Trent, as if searching with his mind for something he couldn't see. "Yes. For a while it was a hole, a shadow that felt like nothing there. But the feeling was almost . . . I don't know . . ."

"It meant something had to be there . . . the hole. Correct?" Sophia asked gently, completing Joe's thought.

"Yes," Joe stated with conviction. "It was only recently he became stronger—I don't know how to say it any other way, but more whole. That's when the feelings of fear and dread returned."

Sophia's eyes confirmed she had felt it, too. "So what does that mean?"

"I don't know right now. I have some thoughts, but they are only wild guesses. I feel we must reach Anna now more than ever. What I do know is for some reason he has left, not like before where he seemed to simply fade into shadow where he could not be reached. Now, at least temporarily, it feels like he has gone away. Would you agree?"

"Yes," Sophia replied, her eyes locking on Joe's, feeling an odd sense of connection to him—partly because he seemed to genuinely want her opinion. It was another show of trust and bonding, and in that moment Sophia wondered how she ever could have contemplated turning him in to their pursuers for money.

For the first time, Joe realized he was very close to Sophia. To his embarrassment, he noticed she was wearing a slim whisper of a nightdress that had risen a little immodestly up her thighs when she slid to the bed. There was something rough about her, something untamed about her—like few other women he had met. As her ragged hair danced across her bright eyes he was momentarily transfixed.

"We need to go, Joe," Sophia said almost apologetically, snapping him out of his interlude. For the briefest moment, Sophia sensed a regret in the man's eyes. It was just a flash, and it was gone, and his hard, contemplative look returned.

Joe scrambled off the bed, and over to Trent, not hearing Sophia as she let out a sigh filled with regret. Joe began rousing his friend as Sophia picked herself up off the bed and readjusted her nightdress. Trent didn't wake easily, but he finally sat up, rubbing the sleep from his eyes like a young child greeting a parent in the morning.

"What the . . ." Trent said, looking back and forth between Joe, who was now standing over him by the bed, and over to Sophia who had now moved over to the doorway. She was leaning anxiously against the jamb, looking as if she wanted to flee the room.

"He's gone," Joe said, hoping those two simple words would say all he had to. They had their intended effect.

Trent tossed aside the covers and got up, looking again between his friend and Sophia, reading for a moment a bit of blush in Sophia's cheeks. Casting that thought aside momentarily, he refocused. "Well, what are we waiting for? Lets get moving before he comes back."

The three scattered to the corners of the apartment to grab clothes and gather their few belongings. It took five minutes and they met up in the living room. Seeing everyone was ready, Sophia hoisted a small pack over her shoulder and headed for the apartment's front door.

"We should use the fire escape," Trent said, trying to redirect Sophia.

"Non," Sophia said, in a tone that was harsher than she intended.

"It is too exposed. The lamplight from the nearby street hits it because it is high off the ground, but below there are many shadows we can lurk in. The fire escape is also much too noisy for such an early hour. We would draw much attention just trying to climb down."

"But I thought you said he was gone!" Trent shot back, showing more anxiety than he wanted.

"Mon ami . . ." Sophia began, but this time Joe cut her off.

"He is," Joe said more confidently than he felt. "But that does not mean there might not be others out there who may have taken his place. If The Fifth Seed came to find us, my guess is he did not come alone. Our best hope is to slip out now, while they are changing the guard.

Trent shot his friend a glance that indicated he didn't like this at all, but he bit his lip and followed Joe and Sophia out the door. Halfway down the hall, Sophia produced a key from her pocket and opened a locked door. Behind the door was a winding metal staircase that wound its way down to the main floor.

The trio clambered down to the bottom and found themselves in the empty, dark bar. "My friend owns the place." Sophia laughed with a sly smirk. "He trusts me with the keys and asks me only to keep an eye on it when it's closed. He allows me an occasional drink for the trouble."

Neither Trent nor Joe commented. Instead they followed Sophia through a maze of bar stools and swinging doors to a storage room in back, which offered access to a rear service door to accept deliveries. Without making a sound, Sophia slowly released the bolt and eased open the door. It creaked softly on its hinges—the noise making each of them cringe. Instantly the three were slammed hard in the face with the chill of the night.

"Damn, it got cold," Joe whispered, as they stepped out into the shadows of the alley. It was the same alley they would have accessed from the fire escape. In fact the scaffolding, to their immediate left, rose like a spider's web into the night, up the stone walls of the building. Sophia had been right: a streetlight from the street threw a halo of light across the upper reaches of the building, including the fire escape. Down here, the shadows overlapped in layered patterns of dense black and charcoal grays, masking their presence for the time being.

Looking around, the group surveyed their options. Moving to the left would take them directly to the street, which looked to be the fastest means of escape, while the path to the right led deeper into a complex maze of back alleys and shadow. Both Joe and Trent were already leaning left, hoping for a quick exit. It didn't surprise either of them at all when Sophia grabbed both of their hands and said, "Non, come this way."

As the three moved out, one of Mitch's ten new French assets voiced a single phrase into his radio. "They are on the move." It was a phrase that put in motion a complex and well-orchestrated plan of pursuit intent on observing.

So as Sophia led the boys deep into the alleys and underground of nighttime Paris, Mitch and his men followed, far into the dark side of the city—one that doesn't appear in any travel guides.

CHAPTER 80

THE MORNING AFTER

G rady woke with a start . . . gripped with an overwhelming fear Anna had left him in the middle of the night. It might have been his experience with Nancy that made him feel history would inexplicably repeat itself, or perhaps it was something else he was picking up on.

As he rubbed the sleep from his eyes, trying to get a sense of his surroundings, an arm reached out and grabbed him around the neck.

"It's too early to be awake." Anna said in a soft, sleepy voice, pulling him back to the rumpled sheets. She kissed him tenderly, wriggling her robed body under the covers to mold into one with his. As they kissed, Grady felt the weight lift from his chest, letting go of his fears and losing himself in the moment.

"I'm glad you're here." Grady said as they parted, and he instantly regretted the subtle nod to his fears.

Anna caught the subtext, not only in Grady's words, but also in his eyes, which so clearly reflected his deep-seated fears. Suddenly she felt ashamed for her temptation to leave him, although Anna didn't know if last night had changed her feelings in that regard. Awkwardly she tried to cover up a potential lie with a question, "Now where would I go?"

Grady eyed her for a moment, regretting the course of the conversation and the fact it now seemed to have spoiled the morning's mood.

"Nowhere I guess," he said, brushing his lips across hers in a kiss that tried to cover up the mess.

Anna smiled at him, her bright eyes dancing across his, not trying to read him, simply trying to lose herself again in his admiring gaze. She was tired of the mental games her mind always wanted to play, and she made a conscious effort to shut her thoughts down and block it all out.

"Oh, damn!" Anna said, suddenly remembering something.

"What is it?" Grady asked concerned.

"Nothing . . . nothing big. I just forgot to do something Joe asked me to do," she explained vaguely. Anna didn't want to get into it all now. It was too nice being next to Grady, the morning after, and she wanted to savor it for just a little while longer. But she had forgotten Joe's request. He had specifically told her to shut down her mind last night, to close herself off. While she certainly wasn't sending her thoughts out to touch Trent, Joe or even The Fifth Seed from afar last night, she hadn't exactly concentrated on keeping others out. Heightened emotion conveyed most easily to others trying to hitchhike off thoughts, and she'd have to assume last night would be considered one of the higher states of emotion in her life.

Ironically, the thought brought a smile to Anna's face and it had a reassuring effect on Grady. He seemed to accept the explanation for now and appeared equally anxious not to dampen the mood both were trying to carry over from the night before.

Rolling over, Anna tried snuggling her back into Grady, and he obliged, taking her in, wrapping her up in his arms. They lay that way for the next hour—occasionally changing positions or turning their heads to share a gentle kiss. They talked of normal things like how wonderful it would be to return to Paris someday, when they could explore every romantic nuance of this beautiful city. For those precious minutes they pretended someday they could be a couple.

It was Anna who finally brought the fantasies to an end. Not certain how to say it, she decided to just come out with it. "We need to head to Chinon."

"Where?" Grady asked simply.

"It's a small town, as far as I can tell, in the Loire Valley," Anna said uncertainly.

"What's there?" Grady inquired, anticipating the answer.

"At some point Trent and Joe, and perhaps their new friend Sophia from the hotel. But they will meet us there. They have been delayed. Joe said he thinks they might have picked up a tail last night."

Grady rolled to face Anna now, a grim smile spread across his face, not happy their night together was coming to an end, but determined to support her in any way he could. There was a growing part of him that wanted to try to convince her to walk away from her quest, to flee the past and write a new future together. But he knew as long as Trent and Joe were in danger, and as long as Mary Jane was still a captive of Northwoods, the road they were on was set in stone.

Anna told Grady everything Joe had said, nearly word for word. She even shared Joe's suggestion to shut down her mind, along with her fears that last night that was probably the last thing she was doing.

Grady reached out and caressed the nape of her neck, trying to ease her tension and allay her fears. "So, last night—is that what you were thinking about? Things like the address of the hotel we were staying at or the city we plan to visit today?"

Anna blushed mildly, reaching under the covers with both hands to find and test the firmness of his glutes. "I guess you are right, there were a couple of other things on my mind," she teased back, her fears fading away with their playfulness.

Grady kissed her longingly, just as he had last night, making Anna groan inwardly with pleasure. Satisfied with her response, he pulled away. "Anyway, I hope I had your full attention last night," he said, playing up his mock indignation.

The comment brought an image to Anna's mind and it made her laugh out loud.

"What's so funny now?" Grady asked self-consciously.

"Well," Anna said blushing again. "If anyone was trying to hitchhike off of my thoughts, they got an eye-opening show." And with that she kissed Grady back. But it was an until-later kind of kiss as she slipped from beneath the covers and got out of bed. "Anyway, I guess it's time I took a shower."

As she walked across the floor—Grady's eyes riveted on her back—she allowed her robe to slip off of her shoulders, letting it fall just below mid-back. It rested there for a moment, and Anna knew he was watching.

Then to his surprise, she let the robe drop all the way the floor. Grady laughed to himself, all at once admiring her intoxicating mix of vulnerability and spunk.

Then, for a brief moment she paused to look back over her shoulder. "You are coming, aren't you?"

CHAPTER 81

PREDESTINED

The Kid strolled down the streets of Paris, a little hitch in his step, as he wondered what might happen in the coming minutes. After leaving Mitch, he had stopped by a coffee shop to down a double espresso and ask for directions. It took only twenty minutes to arrive at his destination by cab—a quaint Paris neighborhood near the Eiffel Tower, with bistros, cafés and boulangeries dotting the street corners.

It felt romantic, and for a moment he felt a twinge of anger jab at his gut. But he quickly cast those feelings aside. He would let nothing get in the way of his feeling that he and Anna would soon be reunited.

Which brought him to a question that was troubling him. "Why was he here?" Yes, the simple vision of a hotel name on a robe had let him know where Anna and Grady had made love last night. Those details were all too vivid in his mind. But there was nothing else, no sense of what he should do now that he was here, no sense that this was the place he and Anna would reunite—for he knew exactly where that would be, and this Paris arrondissement was far from it. Nor did he feel the urge to go out of his way to follow Grady and Anna if he happened to stumble across them. It would place him too close, for too long . . . and Anna might begin to unravel some of the mysteries, and that would adversely affect his desired version of the future. Right now he actually felt that Mitch following Trent and Joe was the safest way to ensure that future.

344

Odd he had to come all the way to Paris to figure that out. But there was still something unfinished, and he sensed whatever that was had to happen here, on these streets, today, to keep it all moving forward.

It was the reason he had followed Sophia instead of Anna last night, because he felt it wasn't time. It was an informed hunch and he'd learned over time to trust those things his mind chose to reveal to him. The Kid wasn't sure why his mind worked exactly the way it did. Nobody had it completely figured out . . . not even Northwoods who had studied Naturals for years. They had their theories, yet how it all worked didn't matter—but the knowledge that it worked certainly did. Over time The Kid had learned to simply trust his mind, not question it.

Having reached the hotel, he began to walk around the block, waiting for fate. He was on his third trip around when it all aligned. He was just turning the corner, about to trek back down the street in front of the hotel when he saw her, and the vision of her stopped him dead in his tracks.

She was across the street in front of the hotel, her hair bouncing as she strode through the open doors, beneath the hotel's red awning. She paused for a moment, radiant in a pretty brown peach-blossom sundress that hugged her divine curves and showed off just a whisper of her long legs. She was well over one hundred yards away, and she glanced left away from him and then quickly right. Her gaze seemed to go right through him, and for a heart-stopping moment he felt like he had blown it. Yet it was likely his OCD habit of donning a ragged blue ballcap that kept his eyes from hers.

For a breathtaking moment he observed her, until Anna once again glanced left. Exhaling, The Kid realized she was simply trying to decide which way she should set off. With her gaze still away from him, and no sign of Grady, The Kid turned and slipped quickly back around the corner from which he came. He didn't wish to press his luck anymore, although he was dying inside, reminded of how beautiful she was, how totally captivating she could be.

He knew at that moment, that this was the reason for him to come. There was no need to linger or follow, she would come to him now. Somewhat reluctantly he strode back to the nearest Metro station—realizing his time in Paris was over. Mitch wouldn't like it, but The Kid had more important things to do back in the States. It was time for him to prepare a homecoming for Anna, to start planning their future together—away from Northwoods.

CHAPTER 82

Pushed To The Edge

A nna had left Grady in the room to finish getting ready as she went in search of breakfast. Feeling particularly sexy today, she had decided to slip into the sundress she had bought in Lanesboro. It fit perfectly and when Grady saw her in it, he told her all he wanted to do was take it off her . . . very slowly.

Blushing and batting his groping hands away from her, she somehow managed to make it out the door without falling back into bed with him. The feat had taken every ounce of her willpower.

Now, as she rode down in the elevator, she made sure she prepared herself. She'd be out on the streets, looking at landmarks, street signs and shop names and if she left her mind open, these details might be picked up on by The Fifth Seed. She needed to make sure she had closed her mind. It wasn't a hard task, particularly since the Naturals often tried to close themselves off to their captors—which had given Anna plenty of practice. It wasn't foolproof, particularly in close proximity and eye contact made. But from a distance, it was virtually impossible to reach into a properly closed mind.

The elevator door slid open to the lobby, and Anna strode confidently through it. As she reached the front doors, she took a deep breath before walking out under the red hotel canopy to greet a warm and beautiful September day.

Pausing, she tried to get her bearings. She was looking for a boulangerie where she might find a couple fresh pain au chocolates and café noirs. She knew one was just around the corner from the hotel. She had seen it last night when she and Grady had returned from the confrontation with Mitch outside the Luxembourg gardens. But last night she had been distraught, and now she was struggling to recall which direction that might be. She glanced to her left and noticed a local café, but no bakery. She looked right toward an urban market, and then left again.

Still uncertain, she thought about returning to the lobby and asking for directions when something far down in the deep reaches of her mind struck her as out of place, and in that instant her knees went weak, fear gripping at her throat as she tried to breath.

CHAPTER 83

A FATHER'S ANGUISH

It had been the middle of the night in Minnesota when Mitch called in to report they had found Trent and Joe, and were hoping to follow them to Anna and Grady. It was the report the doctor had been waiting for and so had not been frustrated about being awakened at such an hour.

By the sound of it, Mitch had things in hand, and by now should have received the backup support Allan had arranged through the vast network of Northwoods friends. Even The Kid had seemed to be willing to stand down to let Mitch operate, which made the doctor feel they were at least working relatively well together. Allan had to wonder if The Kid had some ulterior motive, knowing something neither he himself nor Mitch knew.

Now, two hours later, the doctor was still awake. He couldn't seem to get his mind to shut down. There was too much on it . . . and too much at stake, yet there was one maddening thing that kept popping back into his head. And it didn't really have anything to do with what was happening in Paris.

It was Mary Jane, now several days since the attack inside Northwoods, and she still lingered in a coma. Allan had since discovered that a lethal dose of one of Northwood's narcotic cocktails had been injected into her IV. The doctor remembered back to the morning after the attack, as he and Mitch stood by the lake. Mitch was sure The Kid had done it. But even then the doctor knew that wasn't the case. He'd known the would-be killer's identity—and it had been eating away at him ever since. He was trying to understand the motive. Every scenario he ran through came back in a way that just didn't add up.

Allan paused, for he had been pacing anxiously about his 5,000 square-foot mansion nestled on fifty acres of wooded land only ten miles from Northwoods. He found himself near the gourmet kitchen he rarely used—though his house staff made good use of it on the rare occasions he was home around mealtime. He could hear the automatic coffeemaker click on, brewing a pot so it was hot and ready for him promptly at 4 a.m., the hour he normally awoke.

The sound rocked him from his spot and he began moving again. His footsteps led him across the cool, bare hardwood floors to his grand foyer with a sweeping staircase. Grasping the cherry wood banister, he began mounting the steps, retracing a route he had completed nearly twenty times tonight.

At the top of the stairs was an antique console table his wife had bought years ago. On it were photos of the family throughout the years. He picked up a polished silver frame and gazed into the unmoving eyes of his wife and asked her a silent question, lifting his eyes to the heavens to see if this time he would get an answer.

Placing his wife's photo back on the console with care, he contemplated the photo that should have been there, the one of his only son. If the photo had been there it would have shown a picture of a young, driven and determined young man, with the same red curly hair of Allan's own youth. It was not to be—too much heartache would be associated with that frame.

Moving left down the hallway his fingers danced over the frame that held the smiling face of his daughter Melody—the girl he loved more than any other, the woman who looked and acted so much like her mother. She was one person he would protect at all costs—and he wondered if she knew this about him.

For the life of him, he couldn't understand why his daughter was back here now. She had such a promising future as a doctor, currently enrolled in medical school at the University of Minnesota—though she could have gone anywhere in the nation. The day the Naturals escaped, she had appeared back at his doorstep, defiantly saying she was staying for a while. He protested, told her she would miss her studies, but she informed him she had not scheduled fall classes, and was taking a semester off to reevaluate her life. Allan had bristled at this—telling her she would waste her life doing anything other than what she was destined to be.

Melody ignored his pleas, telling her father, with a waver in her voice, he needed her more than medicine needed her now. So she stayed. Other fathers might have been able to convince their daughters to change their minds. Other fathers might have closed their doors and said no—you aren't living here. But not Allan. The loss of his wife tore at him, and Melody was his link to her—his embodiment of her. At least that is what he had thought until recently.

His pacing had brought him to the door—the same one he had paused in front of so many times before in the last two hours. He wanted to barge in and confront her—to demand answers. In the end, it was just like every other time tonight. He wanted answers, but was more afraid of the answers he might get. Silently he walked away from Melody's door, leaving the questions hanging in the air. *Why? Why you?*

CHAPTER 84

ROAD TO CHINON

The pastoral French countryside flew by the windows of the little Citroen. Grady drove and Anna again navigated in the passenger seat. Earlier, when Anna had come back from getting breakfast, Grady sensed another change in her mood. It wasn't as obvious as her other mood swings of hers, but her playfulness was gone and she seemed distracted.

Not that they could continue to live in the fantasy world they had escaped to last night, but Grady had at least hoped for some lingering effect. Instead, she was anxious to get going and leave Paris behind, like she was running away from something—or to something. She ate quickly, gulping her coffee, hurrying Grady to do the same. She said she wanted to get to Chinon as fast as they could, in case Trent and Joe had shaken their tail and were on their way. On some level it made sense, but Grady wasn't buying it. He found it unlikely Trent and Joe would set out so quickly, figuring they'd be more careful and purposeful.

Anna's mood mellowed in the car—as if she was relieved to be on the move again, and she slipped her hand underneath Grady's thigh as he drove. It was an odd gesture, but it told him she wanted to keep him close. Absent being able to hold his hand, it kept a connection.

"I forgot to ask," Anna said, the thought coming to her out of the blue. "What call was so important last night that you had to leave the room?"

Grady smiled at the question, because Anna should have guessed the answer by now. "Tom."

Instantly understanding, Anna felt ashamed for having thought of so many less noble reasons as to why Grady had left her so abruptly last night.

"He okay?" Anna asked a bit timidly.

"Yeah, I think so. Nobody's grabbed him in his sleep and taken him away for questioning or anything like that," he said, keeping it light. "He's pretty good at keeping himself on the right side of trouble, if there is such a thing."

Anna laughed at the thought, thinking about the strange bond the two shared, one she'd first witnessed at O'Gara's. "Did you tell him what's happening here?"

"Very little," Grady replied definitively. "Better that way."

Anna understood. Grady didn't want his friend any deeper than he already was.

"I just told him we were relatively safe, hadn't located your friends, but were working on it. And that he could reset the clock." Grady paused, as if struggling to explain something before finally getting the words out. "Anna. About last night."

"Yes," she said, uncertain where Grady was going to go with it.

"I'm sorry I ran out like that. But I got the impression that you wanted to be alone. I let my emotions get the best of me. Anyway, I knew I owed Tom a call or otherwise he might take what he knew to the authorities, so I stepped out to give you some space and get my own head right."

"Would that have been bad?" Anna asked, "Tom going to the authorities, I mean?"

"I keep weighing it in my mind. And I keep coming back to the same answer. I don't know exactly how high or how deep this goes. Based on what happened back in Rochester, I have a pretty good feeling an organization like the CIA, or worse, is involved.

"There's worse?"

"You don't want to know, Anna. The things I heard about while I was at the FBI. The secret organizations like the Black Ops—that's just one of many. Our government . . . or should I say our power hierarchy, is often creative at devising new tools to further national security and their own private agenda."

"Noted," Anna said, not taking the subject further. "Anyway, you were saying?"

"Well, like I said, some group like the CIA is probably involved, but seeing my old friend and partner Kyle back at the airport makes me wonder if the FBI isn't wrapped up in it as well. Since 9/11, the CIA, NSA and FBI technically report to the same head. The idea was that they would share information and collaborate in the higher interests and greater good of the United States. But the fight against global terrorism is about as far as their joint cooperation goes. They often treat the other organizations as rivals, or in some cases, enemies. Given that, if we, or worse, Tom takes what I gave him to someone involved, someone who'd rather sweep it under the rug. Well . . ." Grady paused, not wanting to finish the thought.

Anna did it for him. "He'd get swept under the rug right along with it."

"Exactly," Grady confirmed grimly.

A thought struck Anna. Something that didn't necessarily sit right with Grady's reasoning, or at least he hadn't elaborated on it yet.

"So why have him go to the authorities if he doesn't hear anything from us? Why put the time limit on contact? Either way he'd be in jeopardy."

Grady sighed, trying to understand it himself. "Because I'm trying to buy time, trying to get more information as to who we might be able to trust. If we get caught at some point—as your visions seem to indicate—I wanted an ace in the hole, or even a bargaining chip to hold over Northwood's head to try and stall . . ." but again he let the thought hang. "Anyway, Tom has the most uncanny instinct for self-preservation of anyone I've ever met. If push comes to shove he will find a way to take care of himself. I just don't want to put him in that situation if I don't have to."

Anna understood. Grady would only ask Tom to get involved if the situation were dire. Leaning in toward Grady, she slid her hand a little deeper under his thigh, a subtle gesture that she was concerned about him . . . she was there for him. As she watched him drive, his eyes riveted on some point on the distant road, she couldn't help but think Grady underestimated the loyalty of his friend. If push came to shove, she had a feeling Tom wouldn't give a damn about his life if Grady's were in jeopardy. She realized Grady had lived for so long without friendship or love—since Nancy's death—that true friendship, even love, were foreign to him.

For the first time Anna realized, as much as she still felt she should leave Grady for his own well-being, she knew she never could. It wasn't her mind that told her this . . . it was her heart. Right now, needed her as much as she needed him.

CHAPTER 85

THE FACE

Kyle Brady woke up at 3:30 a.m. with things on his mind. Something wasn't sitting well with him. Foremost was his boneheaded move of letting Grady walk by him in the airport, for no good reason, which is why he was trying to find a good reason after the fact. He wanted at least some nugget of information to help him justify the potentially career-ending move he'd made.

Everything he tried was a dead end. He kept circling back to Northwoods and this mysterious woman Grady was messed up with. And what about Anna? Everything he had read about her escape from Northwoods indicated she was only seventeen. But if this Anna was the one he bumped into at the airport, there was no way she was seventeen . . . more like mid-twenties. He could find no rational reason for the anomaly in age. Who would lie about that, and why?

Then there was Northwoods itself. There was little detailed information about the treatment center other than it was a private institute that catered to the needs of troubled youth of wealthy families. All of that made sense. But what didn't make any sense was why the FBI had a classified file on the institute, one that reached beyond Kyle's clearance level. What in the hell did the government have to do with kids with mental imbalances and chemical addictions?

Then there was the woman's home that Grady apparently shot up . . . Mary Jane Henderson. Her story was interesting in that she was a doctor whose specialty seemed to be dealing with savants. So why would she uproot her promising career to go work with kids, whose most unique talents likely involved pissing off their parents to the point they got themselves institutionalized until they reached legal age.

Nothing was adding up, and it frustrated the hell out of him. Yet what information, loose threads and circumstantial evidence he'd been able to dig up was at least enough to indicate everything here was not as it seemed. To Kyle, that was significant.

Even his attempts at discreetly asking around at work if anyone had run across the name Northwoods over the last few years came up empty. Most of his coworkers looked at him like he was crazy. They immediately asked him why he was asking, and if it was related to something secretive Kyle himself was working on.

He was getting nowhere. Desperate for any kind of a lead, and realizing he wasn't going to be able to go back to sleep before he had to go to work, he walked over to his computer and woke it from its sleep.

He knew what he was going back to: the video clips from the break in at Grady's house. He had made electronic copies from the disk, and saved them to his hard drive. He had isolated the time period of each video, so he was looking at a twenty-minute window of the intrusion at Grady's.

Kyle had no idea what he was going to gain from looking at them again. He'd scrutinized every last frame of the videos and he never found an angle good enough to reveal a face. There wasn't even anything decent enough to extract a partial of the man's face. All Kyle needed was a little slip on a single frame that he could have the lab guys at the local branch blow up and enhance. Still, there was something that drew him back to the camera feeds.

For a moment, his cursor hovered over one of the clips he knew showed the intruder—or at least the top of his head. But he had grown tired of watching the same old thing. Instead he moved the mouse over the C5 feed. This was the garage feed that he hadn't gone back to since the first viewing, because at first blush there wasn't any action on it. He clicked on it anyway because it was the one video he hadn't scoured ten times over for any kind of lead. Right now he could use anything to occupy himself until he had to go to work and think about something other than Grady.

The video loop loaded, and a picture of Grady's garage came up on the screen. Again, he saw Grady's blue Explorer parked there, the door to the detached garage and a window in the far wall of the garage. Through the window he could just make out the top of a fence that must have served as a divider between Grady's yard and his neighbors.

"Looks like you need to paint your fence." Kyle chuckled to himself as he looked at the computer screen.

"Whoa," Kyle said, still looking at the fence, because what seemed to appear at the top of the fence was a black-gloved hand. Kyle leaned in closer. Another hand grasped the top of the fence. For what seemed like an eternity the hands simply remained at the top of the fence. Kyle assumed the person on the other side was being cautious, looking around for anyone who might be watching. "Come on buddy, show yourself to me," Kyle urged the screen.

The hands seemed to grip a little harder, and a black clad figure came into view. First the head, then the torso, and then the legs followed as the man rolled over the top of the fence and dropped to the ground. The entire sequence took less than two seconds. No wonder Kyle had missed it on his original pass.

He moved the time bar at the bottom of the clip back about five seconds and let it play again. When the face came into view, Kyle paused it, and again squinted into the monitor. Slowly, frame-by-frame, he advanced the video. The fact that this video was from a hidden camera, placed in a dark garage, looking across the garage, through a window, out to the bright outdoors, made immediate identification absurd. But that was okay—Kyle now knew what he was looking for. He wanted a frame where he could isolate as much of the eyes, nose, mouth, cheekbones and jawline of the intruder. They were the keys to the photometric and geometric algorithms used in facial recognition software.

On the 37th frame he found the one he wanted. Searching the frames again, directly before and after, he decided this was the best face shot of the entire sequence. He zoomed in; on the first couple of clicks the face seemed to become clearer, but as he moved further in, the image became pixilated and began to break up. There was no way he was going to make an immediate ID.

Kyle wasn't defeated. He couldn't wait for the day to start now. He had his first break—and one more favor to ask of Lance from the lab.

CHAPTER 86

BREAKING IT DOWN

Four state-of-the art 50" monitors spread out in front of Lance. He was working on some routine video analysis from the Minneapolis-St. Paul International Airport, breaking down several feeds and performing IDs on some of the travelers over the past several hours. He wasn't viewing the feeds in real-time—there were people at the airport to do that.

There didn't appear to be any imminent threats associated with these men and one woman. But they had all been searched going through airport security or detained for various reasons. Several had been cleared and allowed to travel, while another had been handed over to airport authorities for having a small amount of narcotics on him.

Lance's job was simply to get a face shot, enhance it, and then run it through a facial recognition database to see if the men had any known aliases, and run an occasional background check. The airport had systems like this as well, but they were designed to make snap judgments in the interests of air and national security. Anything requiring a closer, more in-depth look ended up in Lance's queue. These days there was more than enough for him to work on.

"Need your help again," came a voice from behind him, and Lance, deep in concentration, trying to tease out enough points on a facial profile from a particularly poor angle, jumped in his chair.

Turning to the voice, Lance gave him a piercing glare over his specs resting halfway down his nose. "Damn it, Kyle, you have the softest step of anyone I've ever met."

Kyle laughed—he'd been told that before, surprising a few people in his lifetime. "You have a few seconds for me?"

Lance glanced back at his four monitors and then back at Kyle, "I've got another hundred faces to break down by noon. What do you think?"

Kyle knew it was an exaggeration, but he also knew his friend was knee-deep in work and had been since 9/11. The guy was generally the first at the office in the morning, and often could be found there late into the night, trying to keep up with his workload. Lance had a few assistants, but nobody was better than he was, and he took the lion's share of the volume, particularly any jobs that had a uniquely challenging piece of video. He was legendary in what he could coax out of even the worst video resolution.

"Will just take a second for you." Kyle said, stroking Lance's enormous ego while handing over the garage surveillance disk from Grady's home. He made sure to get it in Lance's hand, as it was less likely for him to turn down the request.

Lance eyed the disk and the label. "Broke all this video down already. Nothing on this one, and the perp on the other disks never gave me a profile to work with. Real pro," he said, handing the disk back to Kyle.

But Kyle wasn't going to take it back and folded his arms across his chest. He knew exactly how to get Lance to put this disk at the top of his queue. "I know you're good buddy, but even the best sometimes make mistakes."

"What'd you find?" Lance shot back skeptically, taking the bait.

"You missed the perp," Kyle said confidently. "You losing your touch?"

Lance gave Kyle a perturbed glare and turned, now in mock reluctance, back to his computer to load the disk into his DVD drive. "I told you I've broken down every second, and the guy never showed up in the garage. It's a dead feed."

Kyle let Lance go to work. He had said all he needed to say to get what he wanted. As the feed came up in the video player, Kyle directed Lance to enter in a precise time code, advancing the video to about ten seconds before the hands appeared on the fence.

"Start it right there," Kyle instructed.

Lance watched the video play, his eyes on the interior of the garage, ready to prove Kyle wrong. A minute passed and Lance turned back to Kyle and asked sarcastically, "How long do I have to watch before something happens?"

"You already missed it." Kyle said, having some fun at his friend's expense.

"Bullshit," Lance said, not so much out of anger but disbelief. But he was already looping back to where Kyle had told him to start the video the first time.

As the feed started up, Kyle offered a hint, "Keep your eyes on the window."

Lance shifted his gaze slightly, and watched the window as instructed and there he was—Grady's intruder. "I'll be damned."

"It's okay, Lance. I only saw it by chance. For some odd reason, when I started it up this morning, I noticed you could see the fence outside the window, and was thinking Grady needed to give it a fresh coat of paint. Pure luck."

But Lance wasn't listening. He was already working to isolate the frame with the best face shot. It took him only half a minute to pick the one, a process that had taken Kyle almost ten minutes. Once he had it, he isolated the face, cropping in on the image, and the picture instantly enlarged and became unrecognizable. His fingers working rapidly, Lance began applying a series of programmed filters. In the simplest terms they read various coloring and tonal qualities of the original image, and began enlarging the image in very small increments. With each fractional enlargement, the program began to sample each individual pixel, evaluate its surrounding pixels and intelligently add new pixels. The new pixels were based on a complex algorithm that factored in over a hundred different variables of the original image. The program applied the same technique to each new successive image generated. Each step in the enlargement was run through complex software that evaluated the enlargement and made corrections along the way.

As the image began to step up, and features began to resolve, Lance turned to Kyle, the excitement of the hunt now in his voice. "You know, I kind of forgot these copies existed. Good thing you had them, because the disks I gave you are the only ones we've got now."

Kyle wasn't sure he had heard Lance right, "What do you mean by that?"

"Huh? Thought you knew, being involved in the case and all."

Kyle winced. He was certainly stretching the truth with Lance about his connection to the case, but he wasn't about to tell him so right now.

"Anyway," Lance continued. "The case was pulled from regional last night. A whole crew came in and cleaned out all of our files. I heard it had been elevated to national. You know, routine bullshit that happens to us all the time. We get a big case, do all the leg work, then someone higher-up swoops in to do the final cleanup and take all the credit."

Kyle stared at him in disbelief. "What do you mean by national? FBI?"

Lance laughed. "Dude, you're asking the wrong guy. Nobody's flashing me any creds. They shook down your boss and he came out of his office with his tail between his legs, telling everyone here to cooperate. Surprised he didn't let you know."

Pausing, Lance turned back to his monitors and whistled through a narrow gap between his two front teeth. "But maybe it's good he didn't because you might have found a crack in the case. Take a look."

Kyle stared at the face now filling one of the monitors. "Hey Lance. Do me a favor?"

"Yeah, I know," Lance cut him off. "Run it through facial recognition. You know that will take some time."

"No buddy," Kyle replied, his voice breaking up, fear creeping in. "I need you to keep this all under wraps. What we've done here. Destroy the disk and forget I ever asked you to look at it."

Lance turned to face his friend, hearing the strain in his voice. "Yeah. Sure thing. Whatever you want. But don't you want to at least find out who this perp is? The face scan will only take a couple hours."

"No need," Kyle answered with disbelief. "I know exactly who that is."

CHAPTER 87

CHINON

Anna and Grady strolled along the banks of the Vienne River. They held hands as they went, both lost in thought as they watched small wooden boats bob and sway on the gentle river current, moored by ropes along the river's rocky edge.

Only twenty feet behind them lay D8, the Quai Charles VII. Beyond the road were small shops, restaurants and hotels set into a rocky spur of land that rose to a high plateau above the river. Atop the plateau was sprawled the massive Château Chinon, built on the site of a Gallo-Roman castrum as a fortified stronghold by Theobald I, Count of Blois in 954. Over the centuries French royalty added on to the edifice . . . the Mill and Boisy Towers in the twelfth century . . . the Dog's Tower in the thirteenth . . . and the Argenton Tower in the fifteenth. In the thirteenth century, Philip II added on the entire westernmost end, called the Fort Coudray. Separated from the rest of the chateau by a dry moat, it housed the famous Coudray tower—adorned with graffiti carved by Templar knights awaiting execution—it had served as temporary residence to Joan of Arc on her fabled visit with Charles VII in 1429.

The Château itself was immense and a significant landmark that could easily be identified, so as Anna walked alongside Grady, she made sure she kept her mind closed. Earlier in the day, she and Grady had found a room just across the Quai Charles VII, in a quaint bed-and-breakfast, with rooms of odd shapes and sizes. Theirs looked out across the road to the lazy river through two sets of French doors that could be swung wide to let the river breezes tussle the sheer French draperies.

After arriving and paying for two nights' stay just to be safe, they left their car behind and footed it into the old city of Chinon, a five-minute walk from their hotel. They toured the cobbled Rue Voltaire, exploring the historic town turned tourist destination—most notably for its massive chateau, but also for its many Loire Valley wineries nearby. They searched for a quiet place to eat, but their combined moods, and long journey had left them wanting solitude rather than a noisy, packed café. They found a small market and purchased some cheese, a bottle of local red wine, crackers and salami to improvise a small picnic. They had everything except a corkscrew, so they had to return to their hotel to beg one from the lady of the manor and her fluffy white dog. With the opener in hand, they headed back along the river and the Quai Charles VII. Up ahead the road intersected with the Rue Carnot and the bridge that would take them to the opposite side of the Vienne River.

The opposite bank looked lazier and seemed to offer a sandy stretch of riverbank, perfect to rest and regroup. As they came to the far edge of bridge, night had just begun to fall, the day's blue sky now transforming to a dusky purple. To their surprise and delight they found a small park bench to sit on as they spread out their dinner and uncorked the wine. As Anna opened up the packages of salami, cheese and crackers, setting it between them on the bench, Grady went about pouring two plastic cups about half full of the full-bodied red and handed one to Anna.

It wasn't until then that each took a moment to look up, across the river and realize the magnificence of the massive fortress on the hill. It was vast and foreboding, with crumbling walls and massive towers that speared into the air. In the early dusk, the outside of the structure was ablaze with lights. The whole appeared to be born out of the treetops that clustered the middle of the hill, forming a dense swath of black shadow. Farther below, the twinkling lights from the shops along the

Quai Charles VII appeared to cut right underneath the trees and the fortress itself.

Anna gasped when she saw it and grabbed Grady's knee with her hand, giving it a gentle squeeze. Equally awed, Grady had never seen anything so majestic, yet at the same time cold and creepy. Both took the next several minutes to consume the view as they sipped their wine and ate hungrily, exchanging little but small talk as they did.

"Do you think they'll call tonight?" Anna asked, after they finished their meal. It had been the question each had been mulling over in their minds since they arrived in Chinon.

"I don't know," Grady answered honestly. "Do you have a feel for it?"

Anna looked troubled, not sure how to answer. "It's been hard, Grady. Knowing they are out there, knowing Mary Jane is still back at Northwoods. While not knowing at the same time."

Grady thought he understood what she meant. "You're still following Joe's advice?"

"Yes," Anna replied with noticeable regret. "You don't understand what it is like to know you can reach out to them, to try to understand how they are, and to have to keep yourself from doing it. It's killing me."

"Been a while since you mentioned Mary Jane," Grady offered. "Before you closed everything out, had you felt anything new there?"

Anna exhaled long and slow. "No, not really. I wish I had. It's harder being so far away from her. But even then, when I tried to reach out I got nothing."

Not wanting to say it, but wanting to know what was on her mind Grady felt he had to ask. "You don't think . . . ?"

"No," Anna said immediately. "If that had happened, I'm certain I would feel it. It just seems as if she is very, very distant . . . inaccessible is the word that seems to fit."

Grady left it at that—his eyes, once fixed on Anna, now returned to the Château Chinon.

"Sometimes I wonder if coming to France was the right decision. Am I supposed to be here? I really don't know. What am I chasing?" Anna asked of herself more than anyone else.

Grady let Anna work through it. He thought it best to let her process her emotions before asking questions that might lead her in any way. He'd come to respect Anna's instincts and he wanted to see if she got to the place she needed to be without coaxing or coaching.

Not getting a response, Anna took Grady's arm, willing him to look at her again.

"I'm not sure I can answer that for you," Grady said, realizing it wasn't the answer she wanted. He knew she wanted him to take control, to make the decision to stay or to leave, to pursue Trent and Joe, or to skip town and try to live a normal life together.

"Why?" Anna said breathlessly.

"Because in all of my heart I know I want to be with you . . . to at least explore the possibility of us. But I don't want to be with you if you always look at me as the one who gave up. The one who said we should walk away. If something happened to Trent, Joe or Mary Jane because of my choice, I'm not sure you'd forgive me. I'm not sure I'd forgive me."

Anna looked crestfallen. "But Grady, do you realize what's on the other end of that? What if I decide to continue down this path, to pursue Trent and Joe and it leads to disaster? What if that very pursuit ends in . . . what if you don't make it . . . much less Trent, Joe or Mary Jane? How do you think I'd feel knowing I made the choice?"

Grady reached out and took her hand in his. "Anna, just because you can see things that may or may not happen in the future does not mean you are responsible for them. You are *NOT* responsible for Curt's death. And you will *NOT* be responsible for anything that happens to me, or any of the others. We all make choices and we all have to live with them. I've made my choice. I'm here with you and will be to the end. Trent and Joe both are doing everything in their power to reconnect with you. You all believe something needs to happen with all of you together to bring this to an end. Correct?"

"Yes." Anna said with conviction.

"Then you have all chosen to come together. Each of you has made an individual choice. I have made an individual choice. Yes, there is risk in that. But we all come accepting that risk. If we didn't we wouldn't be here. But what you have to realize, Anna, is that there are dangerous people after you, and from the looks of it they won't stop. No matter what we do or don't do, you've got to come to grips with the idea that some people's futures may have to be sacrificed to bring down Northwoods."

Anna knew Grady was right, and she watched without another word as he efficiently packed up the food that lay between them. With this task accomplished, Grady pulled her in close to him and she laid her head on his shoulder as they continued to sip on their wine and gaze at the view.

By now the evening had fully settled upon the region, and the lights on the chateau created a play of deep shadow and alternating light that made the structure all the more auspicious. Finishing her wine, Anna stretched out across the bench and placed her head in Grady's lap, and he began to gently stroke her hair.

Directly in front of her, the reflection of the lights from the opposite side of the river danced along the shallow eddies of the current. The effect, along with the wine, lulled her into the far reaches of her mind, and slowly, effortlessly she fell asleep.

Her dream began without shape or context, just a wavering thin, horizontal line of light that began to ripple, and with each ripple, part of the picture resolved, repeating again and again like a plucked guitar string, until the lighted chateau revealed itself to her in her mind. It stood strong and resolute against an angry midnight sky that bubbled and boiled with furious energy.

In the dream Anna wanted so terribly to reach out to Trent and Joe, to share their combined future, and have them help her make sense of her visions, but knew she could not. Yet having dozed off unexpectedly, she'd left an opening for others to slip into her dreams uninvited.

As her mind touched upon the chateau, she tried to dig deeper into what was there and the building storm beyond. Then, like a cork rocketing off a champagne bottle, it came to her. Instantly she knew the chateau itself held the key to their collective futures . . . the coming together of the remaining Naturals. Good, bad or indifferent—it was an essential step in their journey. The message was abundantly clear; what lay beyond the ominous walls was fraught with unimaginable peril.

Her mind might have gone on, trying to dig deeper, but a buzzing against the side of her head coaxed her from her sleep. When she awoke, she was looking up into the admiring eyes of Grady, her head still resting in his lap.

"How long was I out?" she asked groggily.

"Not long, twenty minutes, tops," Grady offered soothingly.

Anna sat up and brushed out her flattened hair with her hand. "And the buzzing?"

"The phone," Grady replied with a laugh as he dug it out of his front pocket. "You were sleeping on it."

Anna woke up quickly, looking at Grady expectantly, at the same time frustrated they had missed the call.

Grady turned on the phone and looked at it in puzzlement. "Looks like they left a text."

Anna snuggled up closer to Grady to get a closer look, while warming herself in their shared body heat. The temps had fallen dramatically since nightfall, from a mid-day high of about seventy-five degrees to what now felt like mid-fifties. "What did they say?" Anna asked with caution.

"They'll join us tomorrow night. They think they have shaken their followers, but want to be certain. They want to meet in the town square at eight." Grady said with a hint of hope.

"I wouldn't be so sure," Anna said grimly.

Grady simply looked at her with surprise. Waiting for her to explain.

"Tell them we need a safer place," Anna said.

Grady again gave her an odd look, before typing. 'Anna says we need a safer place to meet.' He hit send.

Thirty seconds later the reply came back. 'Why?'

"They want to know why," Grady relayed to Anna, before finally deciding to hand her the phone to text her own response.

Thinking carefully a moment, Anna knew what she needed to say. 'Danger! Need more private spot. Must meet as long as possible without interruption. Anyone wants out say so now. I'll understand.'

The response again came almost immediately. 'OK, hold for more details.'

The wait was agonizing. It must have taken a half hour as Anna and Grady huddled together on the bench waiting for the second reply. Finally it came. 'All in. Meet 8pm Chateau Chinon. Call this # at 7 tomorrow. He'll get you in.'

"Is that the reply you were hoping for?" Grady inquired.

Anna was really starting to wonder if Grady wasn't reading her now a bit as well. As she looked back up at the haunting edifice of the chateau, she said, "I hope so."

CHAPTER 88

REFUGE

In Paris, Trent and Joe had holed up after a long day of running at a friend of Sophia's. When they had first set off, Sophia wound them through the back alleys and side streets of the city, taking them through some of the seediest parts of Paris. For two hours they had moved non-stop at a frantic pace, simply trying to outrun any potential pursuit. Once daylight hit they took to the underground, hopping from Metro stop to Metro stop—on one train, off at the next—over to the other side of the platform and back in the opposite direction. They had crisscrossed Paris several times by noon before they finally slowed down.

Trent and Joe fought back all urges to reach out and feel any potential pursuit for fear of exposing themselves and their location. They assumed The Fifth Seed was still out there somewhere, looking for them, waiting for them to make a miscue. Instead they used their eyes, ears and feet to try to detect any followers. They had discovered none. Even Sophia, a seasoned and street-wise Parisian, couldn't detect anything out of the ordinary. If they were followed, the pursuers were good.

The remainder of the day their pace became much more leisurely, walking around the Louvre and Musée d'Orsay, playing the tourist part, all the while scanning the crowds around them for a face they may have seen in the morning on the streets or on the Metro, but nothing stood out. Occasionally a face looked familiar, but that was normal when one had been scrutinizing faces all day. Out of thousands of faces there were bound to be a few that looked familiar or alike. Still, every time they thought they might have spotted someone that could have been present two, three or even four hours earlier, the face was gone after a few minutes and never returned.

Now, they tried to relax in a cramped one-bedroom apartment on the outskirts of Paris. Their plan in the morning was to get up early and spend a few more hours trying to determine if they had picked up a tail, and if nothing seemed out of the ordinary, they would head to Chinon in a borrowed car—again from Sophia's friend. There they would meet up with one of Sophia's brothers in a local bar before the rendezvous in the chateau.

Sophia insisted she would not take them to her aunt's house where her mother was staying—for she did not want to bring danger to her family's doorstep. Her mother had married into the gypsy life and assumed that life of danger—yet her sister, Sophia's aunt, had taken a more fortuitous route in life, studying medicine and marrying the son of a local vineyard owner. In her early life Sophia's aunt had served as town doctor while her husband slowly began to take over the vineyard from his father. After a few years under Sophia's uncle's watch, the vineyards went through some difficult growing seasons and her aunt chose to give up her small practice and help her husband at the vines.

Anna's text had thrown them all for a loop. The mention of danger had them all nervous again, and looking over their shoulders, wondering if anyone could have hung with them all day today, and if so who. Then there was the change in meeting place. Sophia had recommended a public place where they could feel secure, even if someone had managed to follow them that far. Instead, Anna had asked for a quiet, secure place where they wouldn't be interrupted. The group seemed to agree that *interrupted* was a key word, and wondered what Anna knew, or had up her sleeve.

After Anna's text, it had taken a little time to make the arrangements. Sophia had placed a call to her older brother Paul and tried her best to explain the situation without a lot of detail. She relayed they needed a private place to meet in Chinon, that there was a possibility they were being followed, and if they were being followed there was the potential for real danger. They needed a place that was isolated but secure. She knew Paul would do anything to protect his younger sister if she was in any kind of danger, and he had come through.

Paul knew just the place. Their cousin Victor was head of night security at the chateau, and after playing the *it's family* card and offering a few costly future promises to Victor, Paul had secured the arrangements. All that was left was for it to play out tomorrow, and for now they all needed their sleep.

They stretched out on the floor of the apartment's main room. It was large enough only for a small love seat, a dining table and a tiny, barely serviceable kitchen. Much of the furniture had to be pushed aside for them to fit side-by-side, like a row of sardines. The one other room in the apartment was reserved for Sophia's friend, Jack. Just before the lights turned out he emerged from his room and bid his guests good night.

Joe bristled as the slick Frenchman entered the room. Every second Jack was around Sophia he would make rude or suggestive comments to her—and treated Trent and Joe as nuisances that he would only tolerate because Sophia wished him to. Joe really didn't like putting their security in his hands, but their other choices were slim. And as long as Sophia asked, he seemed willing to oblige.

"Good night, my American friends," Jack said with a mock sincerity. "And goodnight, mon cheri," He added in a sing-songy voice to Sophia.

Sophia, to the right of Joe, rose on one elbow and was the only one to offer a reply. "Good night, Jack." Behind the words was a finality that implored him not to say anything more.

But Jack could not help himself and insisted on one more try. "You look so uncomfortable out there, Sophia. There is plenty of room in here with me."

"Go to bed, Jack," Sophia urged, embarrassed now by her friend.

"Very well, but it is a chilly night and I could keep you blissfully warm. If you change your mind . . ." And with that he turned on his heels, and closed his door.

Situated just to the left of Joe, Trent got up and turned off the lights. The day had been particularly long for him. When Joe and Sophia weren't worrying themselves with the possibilities of a tail, they both fell naturally and effortlessly into a kind of relaxed flirtatiousness, which was uncomfortable to be around.

Trent still harbored reservations about Sophia's trustworthiness. It was why he had visited with her on her balcony the previous night: he was trying to gauge her intentions. Having been friends with Joe most of his young life, Trent would do anything and everything to protect him, not just from harm but heartache. Joe was razor smart, but Trent knew he was blinded by infatuation.

Eventually sleep overcame his thoughts, sparing him more feelings of awkwardness. For as his breathing came heavier, signaling a deep sleep, Sophia rolled over and into Joe's welcoming arms and they stole soft, quiet kisses and exploring caresses throughout the night.

Outside Jack's apartment, Mitch was making final surveillance arrangements for the evening with a paired down crew of three men, before he returned to the hotel for his own, much-needed sleep.

The day had gone better than he could have hoped, thanks to a new friend. Shortly after noon he had called off the pursuit of Trent and Joe because of a fortuitous tip from an unexpected informant. A good thing, because the length of the chase this morning had made it more and more likely that Trent, Joe and Sophia might begin to realize they had seen some of his men before—across vastly different parts of the city. Right now, he needed the trio inside Jack's apartment feeling secure enough to lead him to Grady and Anna. That wouldn't happen if they were running scared.

The tip came from a relationship he had struck last night out on the streets in front of Sophia's. He had made a friend, someone who really didn't like having Trent and Joe around Sophia. His only demand was that when they move in to take Trent and Joe they leave Sophia alone. Mitch would do what he needed to, but it was an easy enough lie to the naive Frenchman. In the end, the informant promised to pass along any information he received.

When Sophia called Jack about midday, asking if they could crash at his place for the evening, Jack enthusiastically obliged. As soon as Jack hung up he called Mitch and told him the news. He even let Mitch know he'd offered Sophia and her disgusting American friends the use of his car tomorrow, which Mitch found to be a valuable bit of information.

The fact Trent and Joe were well within sight, and Mitch had almost a full day without having to deal with The Kid put him in high spirits. His mood would turn quickly in another thirty minutes when he realized The Kid had skipped town without telling him where he was going.

As for The Kid's whereabouts, he was currently relaxing on a KLM Airbus somewhere high over Iceland, en route to the United States. He too was quite happy with himself . . . quite confident he had set things in motion to ensure a future that would bring Anna to him. Had he not been so confident—and had he not been so fixated on the figure of a young twenty-year-old exchange student in the seat next to him—he might have been able to focus his mind and pick up on Anna's slipup tonight, during her dream. He might have realized that through Grady's supportive nature, Anna was stronger than she had ever been in the past. She was changing. The way she thought and acted was changing. And she had just made a decision tonight that could put her in gravest danger and threaten his own idyllic version of the future.

For all of them, the next day would change everything.

CHAPTER 89

THE MORNING OF

Anna woke in Grady's arms in their small but elegantly-appointed room of the Hotel Agnes Sorel. Little did she know the name of the hotel had a connection to the events of the evening to come. She inhaled the musky, natural scent of the man next to her and it made her swoon a bit. For a moment, Anna thought about waking him, but was finding joy in this private moment. She studied the early lines of his face, the slightly askew nose (broken on at least one occasion), the thin yet firm lips, and the broad cut of his jaw—early morning stubble drawing a faint shadow across it.

Today was the day she should have left him. After tonight there was no turning back—for either of them. Of that she was certain. But her decision had already been made. If her conviction to leave him had wavered after they'd made love in Paris, it had been totally cast aside after they made love last night. It had been different than the first night, which was raw and out of control. Last night had been tender, sensitive and loving. Now resting here Anna knew somehow it was all changing. She also knew the man laying beside her needed her as much as she needed him.

For a moment her mind turned to Nancy. She thought about that fateful New Year's Eve . . . wondered how Nancy had ever left him . . . how she had ever got up the nerve to walk out and leave him behind. It was a decision that ended in her death. Would Nancy's future have changed had she stayed the night? Lives changed significantly on some of the simplest choices people made. Today, Anna had chosen the man who held her now—and she couldn't help but wonder how it would change her future.

What would she have done if she had left Grady, she wondered? Would she have still tried to connect with Trent and Joe? She knew the answer instantly. No. It would make no sense to try to save Grady and not her other two friends. Anna knew exactly what she would have done. There was a lingering hunch, a weighty feeling starting to form. It was a hunch that seemed to indicate the place to meet The Fifth Seed was not here in France, but back in the States, in a small town bar. It was a bar that held unique significance to her. *Why there?* It was something she couldn't answer.

As she tried to play it out in her mind, Grady woke and saw her looking at him. "You okay," he asked, groggily, with mild concern.

Happy to see him awake, Anna rolled on top of him, softly kissing his forehead, then his eyelids, then his nose and chin. Finally she parted his mouth with hers in a long good morning kiss.

"Lovely," she said.

At about the same hour, Trent, Joe and Sophia were spending more time riding the rails underneath Paris, once more trying to verify whether they had a tail. They wanted to be certain, especially given Anna's warning to them last night of danger, although there seemed to be even less cause for alarm than yesterday. Every trick Sophia used to expose a potential shadow turned up nothing. Trent and Joe had even split up at one point, to travel in exact opposite directions while Sophia waited on the platform to observe everyone who might have hopped either train in pursuit, or looked particularly confused. There just wasn't anyone who seemed to be paying them any undue attention.

An hour later they met up at a predetermined Metro stop. After agreeing nobody could have followed them thus far they had one more trick up their sleeve. This one required timing and they were about an hour early. Sophia went up to the streets to fetch breakfast and left Trent and Joe alone together on the platform.

"You like her, don't you?" Joe said sadly, almost as soon as Sophia had left them.

Trent was taken aback by the sudden comment from his friend and even more by its accuracy. "What do you mean? It's you she's obviously interested in."

"That's not what I asked," Joe offered with a sigh. "Come on . . . we've been friends for how long?"

Trent noticed his large friend didn't look quite so large now. His shoulders were sunken and his posture was slouched, while his face wore an anguished look that said it was killing him he might be hurting his friend. "I can ease off. She told me she thought you were a bit aloof at first, but she's really starting to like you."

"Not in that way." Trent said, with disappointment in his voice that surprised even him, and he instantly regretted it.

"I don't want her to come between us. We could just leave here. Now. Together. Find our own way to Chinon."

Trent seemed to think about it for a moment, again studying his friend. Either way, he and Sophia would never be. Once again Joe, the sensitive one, had picked up on Trent's emotions—on his own attraction to the girl Joe had been groping last night. For a moment, he secretly resented his friend for being so kind, so compassionate, and so right all the time.

"What do you say we get out of here?" Joe encouraged again.

Trent knew what Joe was offering. He was willing to leave a girl he was starting to have feelings for in order to spare the feelings of his best friend. Trent knew Joe would do anything for him . . . even give up his own happiness for him.

"No," Trent said firmly. "It's cool."

Joe looked his friend in the eyes, waiting a few moments to allow him to change his mind. Then he gathered him up into his arms and gave him a big bear hug.

Sophia returned at that very moment, and sensing something personal, held back a few paces.

It was Trent who finally broke the hug, and turned to Sophia. "What do you have for us?" he asked, trying to change the subject and the mood.

Sophia simply handed over the bags of food. "We'll have to share the coffee. I didn't have enough hands to carry three cups and the food."

"It's cool," Trent said in response to Sophia, but his eyes were locked on Joe's. It meant the world to him that his friend would have given it all up for him, and he wanted Joe to know it.

The three ate their pastries as they waited for the next train. They finished just as it pulled up. Hopping aboard, Sophia pulled out her cell phone and sent a quick text that simply said, 'On our way.'

They road the Metro for about twenty more minutes . . . the first few in a kind of awkward silence, before all of them, even Trent, began to loosen up and started talking and even joking around. As they neared their destination they became more focused and subdued. They were about to pull off their last sleight of hand, so if someone was following them on the Metro, they wouldn't be able to follow them in a moment or so.

As the doors opened the trio raced like mad off the train, across the platform and up the stairs. On the street, they searched and found what they were looking for—a small rusty, red Toyota. As they ran to the car, the driver's door flung open and Jack hopped out, flipping the keys to Sophia. Snatching them out of the air, she tossed herself into the driver's seat, offering a hurried thank you to Jack, as Joe and Trent whipped open the rear doors and threw themselves in.

In a second Sophia was gunning the car off the curb and into a sea of traffic six lanes wide. Jack just stood there on the curb until the car was lost from view in the revving swarm of metal, rubber and glass.

"Au revoir, my American friends," he said knowingly. "And until we meet again . . . mon cheri."

CHAPTER 90

Kept Secrets

Melody walked through the upper-level corridors of Northwoods. Since her last visit with Mary Jane, she hadn't pressed her luck trying to visit the underground complex again—though she would have liked to. She didn't want to get any of the guards in more trouble than they might already be. She wanted to keep some kind of peace with her father, because their next heated conversation seemed to be one neither of them wanted to have.

Today, as in every day that she visited the institute, she had a particular destination: Habitat 3, directly below her father's office. It was a visit that both lifted and deadened her spirits. This was her deal with the devil . . . her own father . . . and a large part of the reason she kept coming back to this god-forsaken place. If it hadn't been for what was behind those doors, she would have abandoned her dad long ago, moving on and never looking back. Every day she visited she wanted to run away even more. But it was complicated. Too complicated.

Pausing at the door, she pressed her hand to a palm reader. This was one sensitive area her dad gave her full access to. After all, even though he was a monster, he knew how much this meant to her. A soft hiss around the doorframe and the electromagnetic lock released, air rushing in at the edges. In addition to being highly secure, the airtight seal ensured soundproofing so no noise might escape from the room.

Melody grabbed the handle and entered the habitat. Once inside she pressed a button that resealed the door with a hiss. What she entered felt like a grand and spacious playroom. A large overstuffed purple sofa occupied the middle of the room, with bright orange and yellow beanbag chairs in front of it. All sat in perfect position for a couple of kids to watch a large flat-panel TV mounted to the wall. Toys littered the floor and Melody had to pick up her feet to avoid tripping. Ten feet behind the sofa was a kid-height counter with two children-sized stools tucked underneath the overhang, with a full kitchen for prepping meals just beyond that. On the far side of the room, huge windows soared to the ceiling, providing a fantastic view of the lake—much like her dad's view above.

The room was empty, but Melody could hear voices off in the distance. As she wandered by the counter, she noticed a couple of half-eaten peanut butter and jelly sandwiches, apple wedges and two empty grape juice boxes.

She moved past the counter and came to a low table by the windows. The kitchen table was rarely used—the room's live-in guests preferred the informal counter. She paused for a moment, trying to figure out where the voices were coming from. Her options were left toward the wall with the TV where a door led to two spacious bedrooms, or right past the kitchen table where another door led to a padded exercise room, an art room and the pre-school room. All three rooms were interconnected.

Melody decided the voices were coming from the right, and walked past the kitchen table, her hand mindlessly brushing the hardwood top. As she did, a young woman, also in her mid-twenties, appeared through the doorway, and Melody smiled a silent hello to the nanny—at the same time holding up an index finger to her lips, in a silent conspiratorial *shh*.

The nanny smiled back at her brightly, and as she passed by Melody she whispered instructions. "They're in the exercise room. They'll be happy to see you. I'm just going to clean up their lunches."

Melody nodded her appreciation and began to tiptoe. She wanted to surprise them. The art room was equally as messy and lived-in as the rest of the apartment. It appeared as though the boys had been busy finger-painting this morning, with several new works of art attached to the art board on the wall. Melody admired the messy smudges as she continued her silent quest, before reaching the opposite end of the room and the door that led directly to the exercise room.

Carefully, she peaked around the frame, trying not to make a sound. Twin five-year-old boys with sandy blond hair and matching outfits sat several feet inside, playing together with a Nerf basketball. By their voices and their actions, it looked like they were on the verge of an argument. Just like brothers. Owen, the oldest by twenty minutes, had the ball and was holding it tight. When Melody arrived he was just turning away from his brother Ethan, trying to protect it.

Melody watched with delight. She had seen this game before and it never ceased to fascinate and frighten her at the same time. She kept her eyes on the soft, squishy red ball, clutched tightly in Owen's stubby little fingers. Suddenly his hands collapsed and they were squeezing nothing but thin air—the ball seemed to vanish. This didn't faze Melody . . . she'd seen it before.

Ethan giggled wildly as he watched his brother's frustration, because the ball hadn't gone far. It was now in his hands. He clutched it even more tightly than Owen had. It appeared he also didn't think holding it tightly was going to do the trick, so he rose from his cross-legged crouch and was just about to run away from a very angry Owen. As he turned to flee across the room, the ball vanished through his own fingers.

Ethan's self-satisfied giggles now turned into a playful scream, and he turned around to eye his brother who had the ball firmly in his grasp. "Mine!" Ethan yelled at his brother with a broad grin. Just as he was preparing to charge and tackle his brother and the ball, Melody stepped in.

"Boys!" she said as firmly as she could, with a smile on her face.

Instantly the pair looked up and raced over to greet her. "Auntie Melody!" they screeched in perfect unison.

Melody laughed at them as they charged into to her and she wrapped them both up in a big hug. She wasn't technically their aunt, but now was not the time or the place to correct them—and she ate it up. "Oh, I missed you boys."

"You just saw us yesterday," Owen reminded her, as he hugged her back.

"Yeah, and the day before that," Ethan piped in, also sharing in the group hug. "You're not leaving again for school, are you?"

Melody laughed. "No. No. Like I told you before, I'm here for a while." As Melody stood there with the boys in her arms, her heart broke, and the guilt that ate a little bit of her insides each day took another giant bite. She couldn't stand that these wonderful and spirited little kids were here in this place. They deserved to be normal boys, playing with other kids, in normal schools.

But deep down, Melody knew that these unique boys were not ready for the world . . . and the world was certainly not ready for them.

CHAPTER 91

VEILED THREATS

M elody slipped out of the boys room, having spent a good two hours playing with them in the recreation room, reading them stories and joining in a spirited game of hide-and-seek. They had worn her out, and she thought it best to head home. Before she did, she needed to talk to her father. She wanted to take the boys out for a bit, perhaps have them sleep over at her father's house. He'd let her do it on occasion before, just to get them out of this solitary environment. Ultimately, the risks were low.

She walked back to a bank of elevators to see if she could catch her dad in his office. It was worth a try, anyway. She hoped her father wouldn't bring up the one topic they both had been avoiding. As the doors to the elevator slid open, Melody came face to face with Drake. When he saw her, a sly grin spread across his face.

"Going my way?" he smiled as though trying to be nice.

Get lost, freak, was the thought that came to mind, but what came out was a single perturbed word. "Whatever."

"Come on, I've got something that could change that uptight mood of yours." He dug into his pocket and he produced a couple of small bottles of medication.

Melody glanced at his outstretched palm and saw one of the bottles bore a name on it. It was inscribed *Trent*; below it the label bore the names of the various drugs present in the pills.

"What are you doing with those?" she demanded, as the doors closed and the elevator began to rise. Does my dad . . . ?"

But Drake cut her off quickly with what Melody guessed was a well-rehearsed answer. "He's the one who asked me to run down to the sublevel lab and pull the pills. Just doing him a favor, so don't get on my case."

"Two bottles?" she asked skeptically.

Drake pretended not to hear the question and he stuffed the bottles back in his pocket. But as the elevator reached the top floor, Drake's hand lashed out hitting the button that locked down the doors. His finger locked firmly in place, he backed Melody into a corner. He stood almost a full head taller than her, and his chest bumped up against hers in a blatant attempt at intimidation, glaring down at her with contempt.

"Your dad and I are quite tight these days," he hissed. "He even trusted me recently on an off-site mission. So you can stop pulling the *my daddy* crap because things are changing around here, and I'm gonna be a part of the new order."

Melody summoned all her nerve and shoved him hard in the chest, and Drake stumbled across to the other side of elevator. As he did, his finger fell away from the elevator button, and the doors slid open. Melody thought about darting out and down the hall to her dad's office, but Drake was still too close to the doors, and with the elevator now opened to the corridor, he appeared to be less willing to continue the intimidation.

So he simply backed out of the elevator, his eyes strangely avoiding contact, focused somewhere below Melody's chin. As we went, he breathed a final warning. "It's all changing . . . girl. Get on or get trampled."

As the doors closed, Melody wrapped her arms around herself and shivered—the request of her dad now forgotten. While the elevator descended, she thought about how Drake was changing. He was not the lowly scumbag that few people knew anything about. He was becoming something different . . . something more powerful . . . something quietly dangerous. He obviously knew something she didn't, and he was holding it over her head. If there was one person at Northwoods Melody was starting to fear, it was Drake.

CHAPTER 92

TWIST OF FATE

M itch sat behind the wheel of a small Peugeot van as it raced south from Paris toward the Loire Valley. In the passenger seat sat Henry, commander of a French paramilitary unit Allan had somehow finagled into aiding in the pursuit of Trent and Joe. Mitch wasn't even sure what type of unit he'd been given access to—although based on what he'd observed so far, the men were definitely elite forces. At first he'd assumed they were mercenaries, but these guys were too polished and had weapons too sophisticated to be mercs. He wondered why the French government, or more appropriately, who in the French government, had an interest in this chase. There had been no government in history that ever did favors for another government, unless there was something significant in it for them.

Whatever their motives, it didn't matter to Mitch. What mattered was he had backup to help finish the job once and for all. The one challenge that this partnership did create was leadership confusion. Mitch felt he should be, and was, in charge and went out of his way to test that, often giving the French commander direct orders. Surprisingly, the commander allowed him to take the lead—to a point.

The straw that seemed to finally break the camel's back was quite trivial. It happened after they stopped briefly to gas up and allow Henry's five men to slip out the back of the cramped van and stretch their legs. Henry had driven the first leg, but Mitch kept pressing him about his slow driving and lost time, insisting he be allowed to take the next leg. A fairly senseless argument ensued and after an unnecessary delay, Henry reluctantly turned the keys over to Mitch.

Mitch's desire to rush things was barely warranted. Thanks to the tip from their friend Jack, he'd been able to get a tracking device attached to the car. It had actually been Jack's suggestion. Jack had let Mitch in on the fact that Sophia, Trent, and Joe planned to make their final run into the French countryside in his car. It was a no-brainer for Mitch once he heard that. He had the tracer placed and kept the surveillance off the kids.

Instead of following them through the Metro the entire morning, Mitch and his allies set up shop in the Peugeot, and waited for Jack's car to move. To be safe, the van followed a good fifteen minutes behind the Naturals, using GPS to keep pace. The plan was to lull the Naturals into a false sense of security—get them to stop running so they would lead them to Grady and Anna. So far, it seemed to be working.

Finally on their way, Mitch needed to prove his point that he was a better driver. Making up for lost time, he drove exceedingly fast. They were in the country now, on a single lane road that wound back and forth across the natural terrain of the river valley. By estimates from a GPS expert in the back of the van, they were now almost thirty minutes behind the kids. Mitch wanted to try to close the gap by about half.

With each passing mile he drove more recklessly, passing slower cars in no-passing zones as they climbed hills or sped around hairpin turns. On several occasions Mitch had to dart back in behind the car he'd been trying to pass to avoid a head-on collision. In one particularly hairy case, he needed to gun the accelerator to slip in ahead of a car they'd been passing, avoiding a truck racing at them in the oncoming lane with inches to spare.

As they hit a fairly straight patch of road, Mitch's cell phone rang. Grabbing it off the dash he recognized the number at once and answered.

"Did you know The Kid is back?" Allan asked immediately.

"You gotta be kidding me. I thought he decided to hit the Paris red light district, and not come back," Mitch said, half-joking. "He give you an explanation?"

"Yes, but it was a sack of lies," Allan said without hesitation. "Just not sure what his motive is. I thought I'd call you and see if he had said anything to you before he skipped town."

"No sir. Wish I knew. But I think it makes things simpler out here now."

"How so?"

"Well, we're getting pretty close to the three Naturals." Mitch explained. "Looks like they are probably trying to get together somewhere south of Paris. I still don't know exactly where, but we have a tracer on them. Anyway, if The Kid were here he'd be doing everything in his power to save Anna."

"Yes, that's always been a concern with him."

"Well, not having The Kid here basically eliminates the complication," Mitch suggested.

Allan thought about that before giving his reply. "Just because The Kid isn't right there with you doesn't mean he can't try to influence an outcome . . ."

"Yeah, I know," Mitch answered.

". . . or already know it," Allan continued, almost thinking out loud to himself.

"What do you mean by that?"

"Think about it, Mitch. The Kid left Paris for a reason. The only reason he'd leave Anna behind would be because he's already confident she'll be okay. He knows more than we do. Might want to keep that in mind as you approach."

"Will do, sir," Mitch said. As he hung up the phone he knew who he was going to line up first in his crosshairs. Normally he'd take down the most significant threat in a group with the first bullet. That would be Grady. But Allan's comment just changed his mind. He'd like nothing better than to screw with The Kid's smug attitude. It was time someone took him down a notch. And he knew just how to do it. Mitch's first bullet was reserved for Anna.

As Mitch visualized the kill, a bullet scorching a tunnel through Anna's chest, a tremendous and violent thud rocked the van.

CHAPTER 93

GATHERING STORM

A storm was brewing off to the west, riding in from the ocean—the tall cumulous clouds arching high on the horizon, their tops sheered off by high winds.

Anna walked ahead, down the streets of Chinon, as Grady meandered behind, kicking stones off the cobbles pensively. He wondered how soft he had gotten since his days at the FBI. Was his training still with him? It had been in Rochester—and that gave him some comfort—but what of Anna, just a few paces ahead of him? Had she softened him more? How would he react if her life were on the line? Could he remain detached enough to gain control of a bad situation? He wondered why this was now going through his head.

The call had come only fifteen minutes earlier from Sophia's brother Paul, and they were simply told to walk down this lonely street and wait. Up ahead, Anna paused, allowing Grady to slowly catch up, and as he did, she slipped her hand into his.

"Whatcha thinking about?" she prodded.

"You," he said, eyes cast down, kicking another stone absentmindedly.

Anna gave his hand a squeeze in reassurance. "It'll be alright."

"Yeah," Grady answered, shifting his wary gaze from the ground up to the skies, and then off to the west toward the coming storm. It was 7:30, and with the clouds blotting out the late-day sun, it was already getting dark.

Anna wrapped her arm around his waist and pulled his face to hers with her other hand so he'd look her in the eyes. "You don't have to do this. I can go the rest of the way on my own."

Grady's eyes hardened, and the thought seemed to snap him out of his reverie.

Anna, seeing the answer in his eyes, kissed his lips lightly and said, "Let's go."

They walked another five minutes before they heard footsteps approaching from behind. They both turned and saw a burly, twenty-something young man walking toward them. He was about five-foot ten with slicked-back black hair, a wedge nose, deep-set brown eyes and big bushy eyebrows. It had to be Paul, but the man looked more Italian mafia than French.

As Anna and Grady waited arm-in-arm, the man nodded politely to them, and walked by. For a moment, both thought they had been wrong but as the young man passed, he spoke two words to them in such a low tone they could barely hear.

"Follow me."

Anna and Grady exchanged a glance and fell in behind the man. He led them silently west down Rue Voltaire, to Rue St. Jeanne d'Arc and up the hill toward the chateau. Just before Rue St. Jeanne d' Arc intersected with Rue du Chateau, Paul turned to them and spoke.

"It's almost eight o'clock now. The chateau is just closing. We'll wait here."

Anna and Grady waited for further explanation but apparently that was all Paul was going to say. They stayed for another fifteen minutes, Grady with his arm around Anna as they leaned up against a stone wall. Paul, on the other hand, seemed a bit anxious as he paced back and forth, smoking a cigarette and then another.

Finally, Grady couldn't stand not knowing, he needed some answers. "How are we getting in?"

Paul glared at Grady for a second, almost as if sizing him up before answering. "My cousin Victor is the head of security. I work for him occasionally when I'm visiting my mother and aunt to earn a little extra money."

"What about the other guards?"

Again, Paul looked like he was trying to decide if Grady deserved an answer before he finally shrugged. "Victor will be with us. He's reorganized the shifts so that the two or three men who normally patrol the interior won't show until 10 p.m. We're officially classified in his log as a private tour for special visitors."

Grady nodded. "And the others?"

"Well," Paul said, flicking his cigarette away, the embers sparking in the dusk as it hit the street, "It's a fortress that rises out of rocky cliffs, with twenty-foot walls, and only one way in. That's across a stone bridge that spans a dry moat. There is generally a man stationed at the entry and one to walk the rear perimeter where the land that meets the wall is flat. I can't be sure, but Victor probably will be taking the main entry duty and may have one other man with him for the perimeter."

For some reason what Paul was describing didn't sit well with Grady. He would have felt more comfortable having the full security detail around them. But he understood Victor's position. This was unauthorized and could jeopardize his job. He wouldn't want a lot of people around to who might want to get him in trouble. As Grady thought about it, he wondered what had been offered to Victor to go along with this plan.

With a couple of his questions answered, Grady decided to let the conversation slide, but Paul kept it going. "So, you two married?"

"No," Anna said first. "Why do you ask?"

"No reason I guess. I just was watching you both for a little bit before I approached you. You know, I'm kind of protective of my little sister, and so I wanted to observe you when you weren't on guard. You just seem comfortable together. But I didn't notice any rings."

Anna held up her left hand, displaying her ring finger. "It does look a little bare, doesn't it?"

Paul laughed, sensing the joke behind the comment. "Anyway, you seem like nice people. Sophia really seems to want to help. Which one of you is like her?"

"That would be me," Anna said, almost forgetting Sophia was a Natural too.

Paul simply nodded, feeling he had held up his end of the conversation, and was content to wait the remaining time in silence.

Just past 8:15 p.m. Paul's phone rang once and cut off. Immediately he turned to Grady and Anna and said, "We can go now. My brother Stephan has arrived with Sophia and the two others. They're inside the castle now."

CHAPTER 94

TWIST OF FATE, PART 2

Given the complex and twisted ways in which universes intertwine—the smallest decisions affecting their tortuous path—Mitch had been derailed by one of his own egotistical decisions.

The argument at the gas station with Henry about who would drive the next leg had delayed them by almost five minutes. But as Mitch hopped behind the wheel and sped through the Paris countryside, he slowly began to gain on the phantom Peugeot van in some other universe that had a five-minute head start on him.

Then, just at the fractional moment in time, on a lonely stretch of tree-lined road, as he was about to overtake the phantom van driven by Henry in an alternate reality, a deer leapt from the brush and raced across the road. The large stag reacted a moment to late, seeing the vehicle bearing down on it before it tried to turn and retreat to the safety of the woods. As it did, the twelve-point buck's massive, muscular hindquarters sideswiped the front fender of the van with a loud, sickening thud. Mitch, distracted by Allan's call, had no time to react as the impact rocked the small van, sending it swerving across the road.

Fighting the wheel, Mitch finally regained control and pulled onto the shoulder to a piercing sound of metal scraping metal. He leapt out to inspect the damage, finding the right front fender completely caved into the wheel well. Swearing, he looked down the road, hoping at least to see a deer lying dead on its side, but the damn thing was hopping back into the woods with only a slight limp. He was certain it would live, and if he had more time we would have taken his gun, tracked it down, and shot it.

After heading around to the back of the van to ensure all of his men were okay, Henry came up to inspect the damage with Mitch. The tire had gone flat and would have to be replaced, but before that could be done, he'd need to somehow pry the fender back out so it wouldn't scrape against the spare and damage it, too.

The repairs could take up to an hour, with a crowbar, hammer, and a fresh spare tire, but it would eventually drive again. Yet had Mitch let Henry drive they would have been about three seconds farther down the road, approximately 100 feet or so, meaning the deer would have crossed safely behind them. In that alternate reality Mitch and his crew would only be about twenty minutes behind the Naturals, instead of now being an hour back. That time difference was about to make all the difference.

CHAPTER 95

CHATEAU DU CHINON

Paul set off again, with Grady and Anna in tow. The night had formed around them, aided by the encroaching storm. Overhead the sky was a tableau of contrasts. Directly above, the stars started to emerge, shining brightly in a sea of dark velvet. But just to the west, the black shadows of the storm clouds had blotted out the sky erasing all figments of the stars from view. Every now and then, bright flashes of silent lightning blossomed within the storm body, momentarily illuminating the pillowy churn of air and moisture as it boiled up into the heavens. Occasionally a flash arced a bit closer, hopping from one cloud to the next—the white-hot electric charge cutting a narrow jagged swath through the air before sending low distant rumbles rolling across the countryside.

As Paul turned left off Rue St. Jeanne d' Arc onto Rue du Chateau, the immense fortress appeared now much closer and fully illuminated against the inky night sky. Earlier in the day, Grady and Anna had taken a tour of the chateau, wanting to be familiar with the intricacies of the place and its complex and disorganized layout, just in case there was any trouble tonight. While the chateau looked massive and foreboding in the daylight hours, it wasn't until tonight, with the structure lit up against a turbulent sky, that Grady finally began to appreciate its ominous, looming presence. The three walked the road at a brisk pace, anxious to meet their friends—and in Paul's case his younger sibling.

Just before the chateau the road ended abruptly, falling away to a massive dry moat that created a vast chasm between them and the fortress beyond. Grady wrapped his arm around Anna as they paused to let Paul go ahead and negotiate their way. Out of the shadows a figure appeared from a tourist hut that served as the gateway to the narrow footbridge spanning the moat.

Grady guessed this was Victor, the head of security for the castle, and the pair spoke for only a few seconds before Paul waved them up. Victor had already retreated back into the tourist hut when they caught up to Paul, and Grady assumed the hut served double duty as a security station during the evening hours.

"He said we can go on in," Paul recounted. "Said the rest are waiting in the main courtyard just across the footbridge and beyond *La Tour de l'Horloge*—the clock tower."

Anna and Grady both looked up at the mention of the tower. They knew it well from the tour earlier in the day, and had heard its working bell strike the hour since they had arrived in Chinon. It was a massive six-story, oblong stone edifice that dominated the entrance profile to the chateau, and inside even held a museum dedicated to Joan of Arc. It was here, in this very fortress the young martyr had made her plea to the Dauphine of France, Charles the VII, to rise up against the English and oust them from the country.

As they started across the narrow stone bridge, their eyes still resting upon the clock tower, two quick flashes of lightning rocketed from the clouds, playing out in a zigzag pattern beyond—backlighting the stone structure against the rolling thunderheads. As quickly as the lightning appeared, the night sky returned, blacker than ever.

Anna shivered at the sight, and sought Grady's hand for comfort. Even Paul seemed to be a bit put off by the sinister display, pausing with the lightning flash as it illuminated the tower windows giving the sense of something glowing within the high, empty halls.

After a moment he continued on, "This bridge used to be a drawbridge," making nervous small talk.

"This the only way in?" Anna asked, engaging in the small talk Paul had started, trying to settle her own nerves.

Paul turned to her briefly to give a simple answer. "Yes."

"That's good," Grady said to her in a low voice only she could hear. "If there is only one way in, it will be easier to ensure we are alone."

Anna forced a smile at Grady, trying to imply that she was comforted by the thought, but it broke up into a half grimace. "I was thinking the same thing," she said with a whisper. "But that also means there is only one way out."

Grady nodded. It was a good point, but if Victor and his men could guard the single point of access—which is what castles were designed to create—they wouldn't need an alternate exit strategy.

They had crossed the entire length of the footbridge, and were currently passing through an arched, open corridor cut through the body of the clock tower. For several moments they were in almost complete darkness, the only light coming from up ahead, before eventually they emerged from the tower and entered the chateau grounds. As they moved inside, they appeared to have entered a small sort of grotto impinged on three sides. Directly behind them stood the walls of the clock tower, while to their immediate left the interior wall of the chateau rose thirty feet up into the air—the city of Chinon far below on the other side. To their immediate right, a low stone wall and a grove of mature trees beyond it blocked any view of the larger courtyard they were entering. Their only option was directly ahead, along a path that gradually ramped up over the next fifty meters.

Paul kept moving ahead with new purpose, as gravel and ancient stone shards crunched beneath their feet. Grady could also sense a quickened pace from Anna; perhaps leaving behind some of the dread now that they were in the chateau—finally looking forward to being reunited with Trent and Joe.

It was clear that the great expense to illuminate the exterior of the chateau had not carried over into the interior. Other than a few spotlights aimed up tower shafts, or pointed out windows, the interior of the fortress remained unlit. The tremendous amount of light generated for the exterior provided almost an ethereal, otherworldly ambient amber glow within. As Grady, Anna, and Paul gradually mounted the gravel ramp, three shadowy figures began to resolve on the ever-expanding horizon.

While the figures were backlit, and indiscernible, Anna's heart skipped a happy beat, and she let go of Grady's hand and ran to them. When she reached the group she flew into Trent's open arms, giving him a massive hug that nearly took him off of his feet, before she threw herself into Joe's welcoming clutches. Paul arrived next and grabbed his sister in a quick embrace, taking her completely off-guard. He rarely showed emotion like that, and Sophia realized he somehow sensed the severity of the situation she was in.

Grady was the last to make it up the ramp, respectfully hanging back to give the friends an appropriate amount of privacy and time to reconnect. For a moment he let himself feel a sense of satisfaction. When he had first met Anna, and they had decided they needed to find Trent and Joe, Grady wasn't certain this day would ever come—with all three of them in one place, all in one piece.

After breaking from Joe's bear hug, Anna returned to grab Grady's hand, hurrying him along. "I want you to meet them," she said anxiously, hoping her friends would be accepting of Grady. As they approached the group, Anna slung her arm around Grady's waist and began introductions.

Trent and Joe seemed to appraise Grady in a protective, brotherly sort of way. Having been trained by the FBI, Grady knew if someone was looking you in the eye, you didn't back down, you returned their gaze with confidence and authority. The approach probably turned out to his advantage: with Trent and Joe being Naturals they could instantly read the man and his open intentions.

Joe was the first to approach, and he reached out his hand saying, "It's nice to meet you. We appreciate all you've done for Anna."

Grady took the offered hand and shook it firmly, and was just sharing a few words with Trent when Sophia broke in. Grady had noticed Paul and Sophia remained a little ways off from the group during the brief reunion and even seemed to get into a bit of a heated discussion at one point.

"I'm sorry everyone, but Paul says we need to hurry. The storm is almost upon us, and so whatever we need to do, we must do now."

Everyone looked expectantly at Anna, including Grady. "We need a half hour," Anna said confidently. "Grady, can you get everyone organized?"

Grady stepped forward and was about to give instructions when he heard a noise coming from the darkness, somewhere off to their far right. Instantly he wheeled, pulling his gun, the same one Sophia had left for them back at the Hotel le Clos Medicis.

But Paul quickly stepped forward and placed his hand on Grady's arm. "It's only my brother, Stephan, who brought the others here. He's been checking the grounds."

Lowering the gun, Grady could feel his heart pounding in his chest. He'd forgotten about Sophia's other brother . . . a huge tactical error. Nervous about meeting Anna's friends, he'd failed to assess all variables of a situation before entering it—something that had been drilled into him with his FBI training. The effect put him on guard. It was time to forget about pleasantries, and even his feelings for Anna.

As Stephan joined the group, Grady tried again, explaining the Naturals were going to move further into the fortress to a courtyard at the far west walls called the Fort du Coudray. Grady and Anna had chosen this location because it was separated from the rest of the fortress by another dry moat and stone bridge. This would put two pinched points of access between anyone who might attempt to reach the Naturals, and should ensure they could complete uninterrupted what they were here to do.

Grady sent Stephan back out to check in on Victor, after which he was to retreat back inside the chateau and take up a high-ground position covering the tunnel through the clock tower. Paul would take position by The Dauphine's Apartments, a series of partially ruined dwellings along the front of the chateau, very near the bridge to the far courtyard and the Coudray Tower within. Finally Grady would take up a protective position nearest the Naturals.

As they set out, Sophia spoke up. "You forgot about me. What am I to do?"

Grady was about to answer when Anna broke in. "You're one of us, Sophia. And I think I'm going to need you. From what Joe just told me, you may have some information that could be very useful."

Sophia looked anxious, but was happy to be considered part of their group, which obviously meant she would be staying close to Joe.

It took about ten minutes for everyone to take up their positions—everyone except Stephan, who probably was just reaching Victor's security station. As the four Naturals crossed the bridge and approached the Coudray tower they gathered around Anna expectantly.

Smiling a little self-consciously, Anna described what she wanted them all to do. "A lot has obviously happened over the last few days, and we could spend hours discussing all of the details, but I think there is a better way to go about it."

"What's on your mind!" exclaimed Trent, picking up quickly on what Anna was about to describe.

"Exactly," Anna confirmed. "Sophia, I'll explain it to you since you've never done it, but when we were little kids, we used to play a game called *what's on your mind*. We would all sit in a circle and join hands and try to guess what the other person was thinking. We actually found that when we did this we could share more information and greater detail than we ever could convey in words."

Sophia looked around at her new group of friends, shrugged her shoulders and said, "I'll do whatever you ask."

The four found a soft patch of grass to sit on, away from the worn paths in the center of the courtyard and joined hands. Anna faced west, holding Sophia's hand who faced north, and she in turn held Joe's hand who faced east, looking at Anna, while Trent held Joe and Anna's hand and faced south, looking at Sophia.

Grady watched as the group got settled. His nerves were starting to fray, and he hoped what they were trying to do didn't take long. Anna had told him a little of what she hoped to accomplish and he thought it was worth trying. In fact, if she succeeded, they might be a step closer to figuring out some of Northwood's mysteries. The one thing that could derail it all was if Trent and Joe were wrong and had not been able to shake their tail.

Before Anna got everyone started, she shot a glance up to the sky, and noticed the clouds had moved in. Only a small patch of stars could be seen through the advancing turmoil. And the distant rumbles of thunder were becoming more frequent and pronounced. For a moment she thought of all the people who had gazed upon the stars from this monumental place, for so many centuries. She imagined Joan of Arc herself, on this very spot outside the Coudray Tower—her home while she stayed at the chateau—looking up to the heavens for guidance. After a brief, silent prayer sent to Joan herself for courage, Anna began—trying to forget the horrific fate that eventually befell St. Joan.

"Open your minds," she directed.

"But what about The Fifth Seed?" Trent immediately interrupted.

Anna shot him a warning glance. "We're going to work on that. If he is nearby then he already knows where we are. We can't change that, but we can work as a group to block him from what we see."

Properly admonished, Trent shut up and let Anna continue.

"Again, open your minds. Let your thoughts flow out to the walls of this courtyard and back again. Use those physical walls as your mental walls, raising a barrier to anyone who might want to see."

The group began to focus, visualizing the walls and using them as their minds' fortress—solid, secure and unyielding. "Good," Anna continued. "It's time to remember and recall. Bring back your memories of the not-so-distant past, from the day we left Northwoods forward, to this moment, in this *now*."

Sophia felt a little odd. She had closed her eyes and wasn't really sure what to do, other than follow Anna's calming, guiding voice. But she began to feel a sensation of belonging, of connection, as if she was now a significant part of a larger whole, and it was one of the most wonderful, connected experiences she had felt in her life. Wanting to know if she was doing it right, she opened an eye to glance at the others, and saw that all except Anna had closed their eyes. Anna appeared to be concentrating on each and every one of them, willing their thoughts to come together, to come to her, and Sophia understood without words that Anna was this group's connection.

"You're doing just fine, Sophia," Anna said, reading her thoughts, and Sophia realized that Anna's lips had not moved—the thought had simply been sent to her, and her alone, through their connection. Sophia closed her eyes again, and tried to let go.

In Anna's mind, flashes of the others' thoughts and memories began to play out in her head. They were random at first—disorganized and dizzying—but her sharp, intuitive mind began to sort through the clutter, weeding out the stray thoughts and focusing on the ones she thought mattered. As she did this, she helped guide the other's minds to focus on what she wanted them to bring forward.

An image suddenly came to her. It was one of her own, of Curt, so many days ago, standing on the precipice of the Golden Gate Bridge and his fear lanced into her like a knife. As he jumped, Anna felt herself lurch forward, trying to catch him, and she winced in pain and anguish as his screams faded to the depths of the bay. In her vision she could feel him there, The Fifth Seed, lurking in the darkness . . . watching . . . waiting.

Instantaneously her view revolved, spinning wildly until it centered on Trent and Joe. They were inside Notre Dame. She could hear the chants, the voices, the overwhelming sense of anguish mixed with the bitter smell of fear. She'd been brought here to witness first-hand a candle that would and wouldn't light. And she watched as a world clinging to two impossible realities was torn in two. Her vision spun again, a sickening blur, bringing bile to her throat. Mercifully the world around her settled, focusing on the same scene, replayed through the eyes of an onlooker: Sophia.

But it didn't last long. The image was violently shoved aside by a memory of their escape, as Melody shepherded the four Naturals through the halls toward Northwoods' laundry service and an unsecured door. The words: *Wait here. I'll be back.* Then loud noises, raised voices and a horrifying scream—then terrifying silence.

But the quiet couldn't last. Because Drake threw Trent to the grass, somewhere outside on the Northwoods grounds, just days before their escape. Kicking him in the ribs. Coughing blood. *You're up to something! I know it.* Trent's trembling, sobbing . . . begging—but he'd never tell. Not Drake, not Joe . . . not a soul. Another kick. *Tell me! Tell me! Tell me!* Then a gust of wind.

The train rushes to the platform, blowing papers across the Metro station. Sophia hops on. A menacing dark figure floats through the doors just one section down. A partially formed face leers from beneath a decaying blue ballcap. Just an angry blur. Sophia jumps off the train as Anna lunges through the vision, trying to rip the hat off, but she's being slowly dragged away. Sophia's focus is wavering, uncertain, scared. *I'm sorry.*

Anna tries to let Sophia know it's okay. But it's too late, she's running away . . . terrified. Sophia stumbles down the steps of Sacre Coeur. Chased by a champagne bottle and a hollow black void. Lost, vacant, empty—like nothing she's ever felt before. Watching, Anna shivers. The world has turned bitterly cold, as if there will never be sun again. Joe follows, reaching out, grasping at emptiness, finding something vaguely familiar, yet misshapen and grotesque, and he runs faster.

Then Anna again, facing the door once more. Facing her fears. She can feel eyes on her, dissecting her from the window. But every time she looks they disappear. Only a body pressed up against the door, breathing hard, waiting for her to turn away so he can watch again. He likes to watch. But that's not what concerns her. She knows . . . if she lingers too long . . . the darkness will consume her too.

Nothing makes sense anymore. Nothing seems real. Just a fractured figment of consciousness spread across unlimited realities. Until Grady. Until that night. He brought her back. He brought her purpose. Until that morning when a mysterious watcher out on the street pushes it all out of reach once again.

These thoughts were only the beginning. What the group needed to do now was pull the common threads from each experience and weave them together into a single tapestry of understanding. As she began to focus the group's minds on this new task, a flash of lightning and instantaneous clap of thunder shocked the group and scattered their thoughts.

Grady remained steady even though the lightning strikes were moving closer and closer. During the last clap he barely flinched. He had found his focus, and was holed up in a dark spot near the bridge over the dry moat. He kept his gaze back toward the darkness of the central courtyard, where he could just barely make out Paul keeping watch from the opposite side of the moat. So far neither had spotted anything out of the ordinary.

After the thunderclap, Grady stole a sideways glance back at the group of Naturals, and noticed they had been shaken from their ceremony. Some had opened their eyes and were glancing around at the skies. It had been almost a half hour since they had sat cross-legged in a circle, and they had barely moved since. Grady hoped they were near an end—not only because of the storm, but because he continued to have a growing feeling that Trent and Joe had been followed from Paris. Concerned, Grady looked back into the central courtyard again, his eyes trying to search the shadows beneath the grove of tall, dense trees that had grown up in the center of the fortress.

Desperately, Anna worked to regain the group's attention; they were so close. Only a few minutes more and they might be able to make sense of the threads. It was something the others seemed to sense themselves, as they listened to Anna and tried to refocus. As the first droplets of rain began to pepper the dry ground around them, and lightning continued to flash, it was becoming increasingly difficult for them all to concentrate. Again, Anna repeated the instructions to let their minds flow out to edges of the fortress and back into them again, to erect a wall.

But it was too late. In that instant, Anna felt Grady drawing his gun. Sophia felt her brother rolling behind the partial ruins of a crumbling dwelling wall, and Joe felt Trent's courage as his friend's mind swept out over the courtyard—realizing what was about to happen a fraction of a second before everyone else. Their mental walls were useless—the threat was now inside the ruins of the fortress.

In the next second, a bullet fired and lightning flashed—crashing into a rod atop the Coudray tower—sending a shower of sparks raining down around the Naturals. And as one of their ranks fell, all hell broke loose.

CHAPTER 96

OPENING THE DOOR

Mitch had finally gained the upper hand and kept it, making a snap decision that had paid off. After hitting the deer, it had taken almost an hour to make repairs, but he and the French commandos had managed to make the vehicle serviceable once more. They still had the GPS locator that allowed them to track the Naturals as long as they stayed with Jack's car.

The team rolled into Chinon at about 8:30 and quickly located the beat up Toyota. It was parked along the Rue du Chateau, about 200 meters from the main entrance to the ruins, and there was a moment of indecision, wondering where their adversaries might have gone. There were no hotels in the immediate vicinity in which the Naturals might stay, and no restaurants or bars to be seen—only a few houses and closed shops along the tree-lined way.

As Mitch gazed up at the lights of the chateau, looming over the trees, his hunch told him the chateau was where he would find them. Leading the group down the street, they flanked the paved swath, spreading out, while keeping to the shadows. Mitch and Henry, the French commander, remained together and took a moment to observe the chateau entry. If the Naturals were in there, Mitch and his men were at a distinct disadvantage, for there was only one way in—the front door—and the Naturals knew the lay of the land while his men did not. Mitch also realized that while fortresses were designed to keep attackers out, once a threat was able to penetrate the defenses and achieve a foothold inside, the fortress instantly worked against the dwellers, with any viable means of escape cut off.

After several minutes of watching they had counted two guards—one who patrolled the rear perimeter of the landmark, and one who watched the main entrance. Both wore official government security uniforms and carried semi-automatic weapons by their side.

"They may technically be government-trained officials," Henry said, "but they are mostly locals who are soft and undisciplined. They are designed more to frighten off by appearance than to provide repelling force."

Mitch liked the sound of that, and a plan started to take shape in his mind. He told Henry of his idea and he agreed. In seconds, two French commandos were stalking their way up the street toward the guardhouse. They were expertly trained, and remained virtually invisible in the night, right up until the point they burst into the guard house and subdued Victor. Another contingent had been sent out along the chateau perimeter to do the same to the other guard.

As Mitch and Henry were about to move in, and plan their advance into the chateau, they saw something that caught them off guard. A young, stocky man, dressed in plain clothes, was making his way from the chateau back across the narrow stone bridge. Henry contacted one of his men.

"Commando 3, you have company coming from the chateau."

"I have him, leader," came the instant reply. "We also have confirmation from the guard of six more inside. Sounds like our party. Advise."

The commander thought a moment. For most of the time he had spent with Mitch, he had played the part of loyal French commander, offered in full service to the American while he was in France. The foolish American, with the huge ego, actually believed the French government would allow a foreign agent to operate unhindered on their soil.

In reality, Henry was a cover name, and his role was more complicated, for he was no ordinary military leader—but a permanent attachment to France's own Naturals program. While the American and French governments were allies and the free-world leaders in the study of Naturals—eventually there could only be one. France saw the alliance with the Americans as a way to further their research, and jump ahead of them in the race for supremacy.

What made this particular operation so palatable to the French was that the U.S. government had so completely botched their first attempt at understanding Naturals they were willing to dispose of them. If the U.S. wanted to set their program back by eliminating their progress and starting over, then the French wouldn't stand in their way. They would gladly support them . . . to a degree.

So Henry's standing orders were to eliminate the American Naturals while feigning support for Mitch. The only limits: to minimize exposure of the operation to the French public and avoid collateral damage. He wondered what his superiors would say about shooting up a national monument. But the chateau provided him a situation he could control—keeping it out of the public eye. Henry felt he could keep damage to the centuries-old structure to a minimum, so after weighing it all he made his decision.

"Commando 3, you have authorization to take out the man on the bridge." No more than a second later the silenced semi-automatic rifle of Commando 3 coughed once. Out on the bridge, Stephan staggered briefly, stumbled back and fell over the stone edge to the bottom of the moat.

"There, clean enough," Henry said, half to himself, as he watched the sequence unfold.

Mitch, standing next to him, looked at his French friend with newfound respect for the decisiveness and efficiency of the kill. Now, with the doorway to the chateau wide open, it was time to go into battle . . . together.

CHAPTER 97

BATTLE OF THE CHATEAU

Fire rained down around the Naturals as a peal of thunder rocked the chateau to its rocky foundation, and a single bullet found its mark. Aghast, Anna leapt up and rushed to Trent's side, the shot echoing in her ears, as blood poured from his chest, and rain began to pour down in torrents.

Trent's sacrifice had become his final apology. In the group's shared visions, he'd had the unique privilege of seeing the events of the candle lighting ceremony at Notre Dame from the eyes of others and it had sickened him. Joe and Sophia's memories were a vivid depiction that he'd chosen an alternate reality—and his existence in this here, this now, was nothing more than a shell of an existence.

In one fateful moment, as his mind stretched out to the walls of the chateau, he'd sensed Mitch . . . his gun aimed at Anna's heart . . . and he knew there was only one choice. There was nothing left for him in this world, in this *now*. He'd go on somewhere else. This was their *now* . . . Anna's *now* . . . not his. So Trent stood to fall, throwing himself in front of the bullet intended for Anna.

Joe hurried over to help Anna, grabbing a now limp and lifeless Trent under the arms, dragging him as fast as he could, closer to the side of the Coudray tower. If they could reach those walls, they could find cover, at least for a while.

In the meantime, Grady and Paul began to lay down cover fire into the tree line where they assumed the shot had come from. Grady saw a muzzle flash from a grove close to the dry moat, and he had to will himself not to follow the bullet's path, praying to God it wasn't intended for Anna. Instead he steadied himself for the long shot, virtually impossible for a good marksman at this distance, but he was an expert. Through the rain he lined it up and pulled the trigger, a fraction of a second later he saw a shadow slump to the ground. "One down . . . how many more to go?" he whispered to himself.

At least he had Paul, but the position he held on the other side of the bridge was tenuous at best. Realizing his predicament, Paul fired off two successive shots into the trees as he leapt from his cover and raced across the bridge, with Grady laying down cover to protect his path. Yet even Grady's cover fire could not prevent several more shots from the tree line as Paul traversed the stone bridge—the bullets cratering the sides of the stone walkway sending a spray of deadly stone shards into the air. It seemed like an eternity, but under a hail of fire, Paul came crashing down close to where Grady had taken up new position.

Together, temporarily protected by the four-foot walls of the bridge, they took a moment to glance over at the Naturals huddled at the base of the stone tower, all hovering over Trent. Both men counted off the bystanders in the rain, and accounted for the remaining three. The other bullet intended for them appeared not to have found its mark.

Anna, sensing Grady's eyes on her, looked over at him with concern then back down at Trent. He knew she wanted him by her side, but Grady needed to remain focused and calm, and to think through their limited options.

Paul nudged Grady's arm to get his attention and in his hand he held out two fresh clips for his gun. "I see you have Sophia's gun. It's the same as mine, and judging by how you dropped that guy from the tree line, it's better if you have some of my extras."

Grady sitting on the ground with his back against the masonry simply took the clips and stuffed one into each of his front pockets. "Is there any way out of here, other than over the walls?"

Paul nodded his head, his black hair now plastered to it from the rain. "The Agnès Sorel tunnel."

Grady looked at him, perplexed. "That's the name of the hotel we are staying at," Grady yelled over the wind, rain and thunder now building to a constant roar.

"Yes," Paul yelled back. "She was maid of honour of the Queen of Sicily. It's a long story, but she became the mistress of Charles VII. He had a tunnel constructed so that he might sneak out and visit her. It was ruined, but has since been partially reconstructed during the renovations."

"Where?" Grady said, anxiously.

"I've seen it only once. When I was helping Victor with security, he showed it to me. It's back in the Dauphine's apartments, those partially-reconstructed structures on the other side of the dry moat."

"Damn, I assume something like that would be locked up tight at night." Grady shouted, rising up to cast a wary look at the tree line. The gunmen's weapons had been silent for a few moments, and Grady guessed they were trying to maneuver around to either get a better shot at the Naturals, or stage an assault on their position on the bridge. To do that, Grady knew they'd have to break into the open at some point and leave their cover behind.

"You'd be right," Paul confirmed, but you don't think I'd walk my sister into a dead end do you?" he said with a serious grin. "I'm a street rat, and I always know and plan for my escape. I asked Victor for the key when I spoke to him at the guardhouse. He wasn't thrilled about it but he obliged."

"What did you have over that guy, to get him to go out on a limb for you like that?" Grady asked.

"Nothing," Paul said. "Except that he's crazy about my sister and I told him I would arrange a date with her."

"I thought you were cousins!" Grady yelled back confused, wondering why he was concerned about that now.

Paul smiled a bit slyly. "Cousin is a very loose term among gypsies my friend. We have a thieves' blood oath, nothing more."

In any other circumstances Grady would have laughed, but right now he needed to refocus. He needed to figure out how to move Anna and the rest of the Naturals across an exposed and treacherous expanse between the tower and bridge. Then he needed to usher everyone over the stone bridge and into the Dauphine's apartments. It was then that a horrific thought struck him. He had assumed that the gunmen would need to come out into the open to attack, but the tree line road right up to the dry moat. In the darkness, one could feasibly scramble down the side, through the brush at the bottom of the moat, and up the other side without being seen. If that were the case, everyone over by the tower was in more immediate danger than he thought.

Sharing his fears with Paul, Grady told him to hold his ground and cover him as Grady tried to work his way over to the Coudray tower. But Paul shook his head. "You're the better shot. I'll go." And without letting Grady object, he sprinted off toward his sister.

Caught off guard by Paul's sudden flight, Grady wasn't prepared to provide cover, and a single shot escaped the tree-line, sailing just inches behind Paul's head before lodging in the stone fortress wall, thirty meters behind. Quickly, Grady popped up and placed three evenly timed bullets in the general vicinity of the shooter, keeping any additional shots from getting off. Then he flipped back down as three bullets carved into the top of ancient stone masonry right where he hid. Risking a peek around the corner, he saw Paul had made it safely.

What Paul came upon was not good. Trent was dead, a clean shot to the heart. Anna and Joe were by his side—each clutching a hand as if willing him to come back. Sophia was out of sorts as well, shouting at him from her refuge near Trent, asking if he'd seen their brother Stephan. Paul knew now was not the time to share with her what he knew must be true—there was no way they'd be under fire right now if Stephan were alive. They'd all have time for grieving later, and Paul knew he had to take control of the group and get them away from their dead friend.

"We're not safe here," he yelled to the Naturals. "We have to move, now!" But the three were in shock. Sophia managed to stagger over to him, and Paul let her fall into his body with a sob.

Finally, Anna seemed to wake up to Paul's presence and turned her attention away from Trent to scream over the wind. "Where's Grady?"

"If you come with me . . ."

A huge flash coupled with a thunderclap broke up Paul's words, and he paused to let the rumble pass. "If you come with me," he repeated, "I'll take you to him. We have a way out." Paul didn't want to tell them just yet how precarious that route out would be; right now he just need to give them some hope.

Joe had dropped his dead friend's hand and seemed to come around, and he rose and took Sophia from Paul and hugged her.

"We can't leave Trent here," Anna pleaded. She was sopped head to toe, and her hair hung around her face in ragged tendrils, but there was a fire in her eyes. The water running down her face was not from tears—what Paul saw was pure hatred and anger.

"He's dead," he yelled, rain pelting his face and stinging his eyes. "Joe, talk some sense into her."

"No." Joe shouted hugging Sophia closer to him. "I won't leave him here for them. I'll carry him. I'm strong enough."

Paul just looked at him and shrugged helplessly—if Joe wanted to commit suicide to save a dead friend that was his choice. "Get him ready; give me a second and we will make our break."

Paul pressed his body close to the stone tower and started to edge his way slowly around the curved façade, closest to the grove of trees where the shots had first been fired. He wanted to check on Grady's hunch and see if anyone was moving through the moat. He inched along as far as he dared, hoping he wasn't exposing himself to a fatal shot. Once he felt he could go no farther, he waited, his focus down into the murky depths of the moat.

It seemed to take forever before another lightning flash exploded above him and for a fraction of a second the black void of the moat was lit up like mid-day. In that instant, he saw them—at least three of them, about halfway across the moat. Instinctively Paul dove back around the curved face of the tower back to Sophia and the others, as five rapid-fire shots chased his footsteps around the corner. At the same time, everyone heard Grady exchange fire from his position to the south, chasing muzzle flashes, hoping to get off another deadly shot.

"We've got to go. We're about five minutes from being completely outflanked and exposed."

Joe was already hoisting Trent up over his shoulder and winced noticeably as he did. Anna saw the pain and started toward him, but Joe just shot her a look that said not now, and Anna backed off.

"Okay," Paul yelled. "Anna and Sophia first." He gathered everyone around him and gave directions. "Stay low, run as fast as you can, and angle your path southwest to keep the tower between you and the shooters for as long as possible." Paul waved across at Grady, signaling he was going to start sending people, and Grady popped up and started firing into the woods.

"Go!" Paul yelled, and both women shot off through the rain, slipping and sliding on the wet grass. About halfway there, Anna tackled Sophia to the ground, sensing something, and both crashed into the mud as several rounds soared over their head. They crawled the rest of the way on their stomachs until they finally reached Grady's side.

To her surprise Grady handed Sophia the gun for a moment and lifted Anna up out of the mud and hugged her to him—kissing the top of her head and feeling her breathing against his body. He looked at both women, taking his gun back from Sophia. "Stay low and behind me," he warned. The women obliged, as Grady got ready to provide cover for the next wave. Paul gave a signal, and Grady shot up over the stone wall and placed several more rounds into the woods.

Joe came first, slow and lumbering with Trent's weight on his shoulders and Grady thought he was a goner for sure. To his surprise, Paul set out a few steps behind Joe, stepping directly into the angle of fire and began spraying his last remaining bullets into the trees. Grady did the same, emptying what remained of his clip, and it was enough to keep return fire to a minimum. Finally they were all safely on the bridge, crouched below the wall.

"You were right, Grady," Paul breathed heavily. "They're coming through the moat—three of them—once they make the other side, they can pinch us from both sides on the bridge. We have to keep going."

"Understood," Grady said as he scrambled on hands and knees to the head of the group. "The good news is I'm pretty sure I took out another shooter in the trees. So that makes at least two down, at least three in the moat, and at the very least one living, breathing asshole in the trees, because someone is still shooting. Now everyone follow me and crawl—no heads above the stone's edge. They can't shoot what they can't see."

The entire group moved hand and knee over the bridge, trying to scramble as quickly as they possibly could, yet Grady's biggest fear was when they reached the other end, the gunmen in the trees would have taken up a better position as well and they'd be sitting ducks. Finally they reached the far corner of the bridge, with Joe laboring behind, struggling to take care of Trent.

Grady looked back and pulled Anna close to him. "You need to talk to him, Anna. I understand his loyalty to his friend, but he'll slow us all down and get us killed."

Anna nodded and moved back to Joe. She sat down next to him as Joe clutched Trent close to him. His blood was now all over Joe's clothes and he looked a mess. Anna reached over and stroked Joe's back as he sobbed silently.

"He's still out there, you know. You and he are still out there, together in some other simpler life. You know that?"

Joe simply nodded, a gurgled sob coming from his big frame.

"You know that nothing we do here will bring him back now. All we can do is protect what we have left. Right?"

Joe nodded again, but this time he let it out. "You don't understand, back in Notre Dame. Trent wanted to walk away. He wanted to choose another path, and I didn't want him to. I wanted this path. Or at least I thought I did." And his chest heaved and he sobbed again. "I forced him to . . ."

"No!" Anna yelled louder than she needed to. "You didn't force him into anything. The Trent I know—no disrespect—almost certainly chose the alternate path in Notre Dame. We need to believe it for him. We need to believe it for us."

Anna didn't wait for an answer—she simply turned and crawled her way back up to Grady. She had surprised herself with her conviction, and wondered if Grady was rubbing off on her.

A few moments later Joe crawled his way up to Sophia, without Trent, and she let him snuggle up into her side. The two made an odd couple, with Sophia's petite frame and Joe's build, but they seemed to work together.

Grady surveyed the rag-tag, muddied and bloody group, trying not to look back at Trent resting peacefully in the center of the bridge. "Paul is leading the next flight. He'll go and take up cover first, then the rest of you move out, and I'll bring up the rear."

Anna wanted to protest, but thought better of it. It wasn't time to question—it was time to just to do. Tonight had only solidified that feeling.

Grady popped up once more, shooting every now and then into the trees as Paul raced fifteen meters to take cover behind a crumbling stone wall, another ten to dive behind a stack of new stones waiting to be used in the chateau renovation, and finally ten more to a doorway to the Dauphine's Apartments. Throughout the sequence fire was returned—but only by a single gun—leaving Grady to wonder if the attackers hadn't committed too many men to their rear flank, thereby opening the front door.

Looking at the Anna and the others, he said. "You next."

"There's no way Grady." Anna said. "There's too many of us, too many targets. And one of us is bound to be shot."

Grady looked between her and the trees, and knew she was right. Grady didn't have many more bullets, and they were running out of time. A thought came to him. "You said one of the abilities of a Natural is to implant a false image in someone's mind. To present a false reality."

"That was Trent's talent, Grady," Anna replied. "I'm not nearly as . . ."

419

"I understand Anna, but you have to try."

She nodded, and closed her eyes, sending her thoughts out to the edges of the chateau they wrapped around a dark and shadowy figure, one that felt familiar . . . it had to be Mitch. Focusing on him, she bore deeper, trying to invade his thoughts and his mind. Once she felt she had a connection, she delivered several images of him lying in his own pool of blood. She was trying to scare him into being more cautious than he normally would.

Opening her eyes, Anna didn't wait for Grady to give the command. She took off, with Sophia and Joe following, and Grady laying down more cover. Anna could feel the figure in the trees, crouching away from the triangulated suppression fire coordinated by Grady and Paul. It wasn't until the last few meters a few shots got off, but they were well off target.

With everyone safely inside the Dauphine's Apartments, it was Grady's turn. He stepped up and caught Anna's urging eyes, through the sheets of rain, across the distance. Steeling his will, he placed his last several bullets into the trees as Paul emptied his final clip in cover. But the shots were misplaced. The threat didn't come from the trees. The clock had run out, and the rear guard that had slid through the dry moat, up past the Coudray Tower, had made a rapid last-ditch advance.

In the end, Grady moved out a step too slow—allowing one dark, black-clad figure to roll into view from the opposite end of the bridge. A rapid burst of fire followed, coupled with an angry peal of thunder that rolled in waves across the chateau grounds. And Grady fell heavily into the mud—a round dot of crimson blossoming across his chest as the rain continued to pour down.

CHAPTER 98

THE AGNÈS SOREL TUNNEL

Anna screamed as she saw Grady fall. She tried to race back out the doorway of the Dauphine's Apartments, but Paul's big arms reached out and hauled her back in. As he did, two well-placed shots ricocheted off the stonework of the doorframe, where Anna's head had been only seconds before. Roughly, Paul spun her around, planting her feet back on the ground.

Her eyes darted back to the doorway and the storm outside—over to Joe, his eyes a mask of agony. But those eyes said to her what she had said to him only moments ago. Biting her lip, she turned to face Paul. "Get us out of this hell-hole," she commanded. Nodding solemnly, Paul set off with Anna, Sophia, and Joe following—off into the depths of the apartments, down a narrow stone stairway and into a maze of stone corridors below.

Outside, Mitch stepped cautiously from the cover of the trees. Of the two men who had been left with him, one was dead, and the other wounded from Grady's precision fire. A third had been left to guard the entrance of the chateau to ensure no one came or went.

Through the ravaging wind and steady rain, he approached Grady as another man raced across the bridge, pausing over the fallen man. It was Henry; he looked up at Mitch as he approached Grady with his gun still drawn, his two other men bringing up the rear.

"Get the others," Mitch yelled. "I'll deal with him." Henry paused for a moment, not sure if he should obey those orders, but he waved to his men and they set off after the others into the Dauphine's Apartments.

Mitch could see Grady was still alive. Face down in the mud, his body rose and fell in labored breaths. Now very close—his own gun pointed at the back of Grady's head—Mitch kicked him over with his boot. As he rolled, Grady held his up own gun, pointing it at Mitch's face, hoping Mitch would believe his bluff and back off or perhaps just put him out of his misery. But Grady's strength was fading and the gun simply tumbled from his hand and his arm fell back to his side. It was empty anyway.

"You're a particularly troublesome asshole," Mitch spat. "It's a shame about Trent over there. But you couldn't protect them all, could you? This is bigger than you, Grady . . . I thought you'd have learned that by now. But I admit I underestimated you. Still, one man can't possibly take this all down . . . you know that now.

Grady tried to rise up, to fight back. To let Mitch know he hadn't won . . . not yet. But he collapsed back into the muck. His energy was fading, and the world around him began to tunnel in.

"That leaves Anna and her new friends," Mitch continued, ignoring Grady's feeble attempts to continue his resistance. "They have no way out." And with that, Mitch picked up his boot and drove the heel hard into the bullet wound. Grady screamed out in agony, his body slipping deeper into shock, until he finally, mercifully closed his eyes and let the darkness consume him.

Under the Dauphine's Apartments, Paul was searching frantically for the correct corridor, trying to remember exactly where the tunnel was. They could all hear heavy boot steps on stone, as an untold number of gunmen continued the pursuit. Just about to give up, and give in, Anna moved down a narrow hallway to what appeared to be storage rooms and spotted another stairwell that had been carved out of the very rock the chateau rested on.

"Over here," she whispered, as loudly as she could manage without letting her voice carry too far. Everyone turned and Paul confirmed that it looked like the right place, and they all clambered down another flight of steps. A door at the bottom opened into a long arched and narrow corridor that was no more than five feet high . . . the Agnès Sorel tunnel.

They crouched down and shuffled a little sideways for about a hundred meters, until they came to an immense iron grate with a massive lock. It appeared to open into a dense wall of impenetrable foliage and vines, as if they were about to enter a jungle.

Paul dug in his pocket for the key and pulled it out. Placing it in the lock, he said a silent prayer that it would turn. They could already hear the footsteps getting closer, and soon their pursuers would be on top of them. For a moment, the key wouldn't budge the lock, but Paul applied more pressure and it finally gave. The door swung inward, and Paul led first, pushing through the greenery. To his relief, the wall of plant life folded back like a second gate—which in reality it was. The vines had simply been coaxed to grow across the iron door's latticework, effectively concealing the secret passage from the outside.

Paul hurried everyone past him, and he pulled the main gate shut, turning the key in the lock from the other side. He couldn't have done it any sooner, because as he pulled his hand back through the grating, he saw the first gunman enter the long narrow corridor. Deftly, Paul stepped outside and swung the second gate closed, at the same time pressing the group off to the side, just as three rifle shots raced through the leaves and out into the air.

Anna looked up, the steady rain from the passing storm plinking off of her face and forehead. They were at the base of the massive stone wall that fronted the chateau. The hill fell rapidly down to a street below, and beyond that the houses and shops of Chinon.

"We need a car," Sophia said, her voice fluttering.

Anna didn't like the sound of it, and turned to see what was wrong. It was Joe, and he sat slumped up against the face of the chateau walls, clutching his side. Anna saw the blood. Lots of blood. She'd assumed it had been Trent's but realized there was more than before, and it was spreading. Paul quickly removed his shirt and handed it to Sophia to press against the open wound in Joe's gut.

"I can make it a little farther," Joe said, lifting himself back up. "I just needed to rest."

With even greater urgency the four of them scrambled down the slope. On the streets, Paul got his bearings and lead them further west, closer to the river—their destination: the Hotel Agnes Sorel. There, Anna would retrieve the car keys from her room and they'd begin to set a new plan once they had a car. But Anna knew what her plan was. It was one she realized hadn't changed in the least, despite all of her attempts to alter it.

CHAPTER 99

THE FINAL CONNECTION

Sophia accompanied Anna into the Hotel Agnès Sorel while Paul continued to help Joe tend to his injury. When they entered, the hotel hostess was beside herself over their wet, muddied and bloodstained condition.

Sophia spewed out the first lie that came into her; they had fallen in the river and just needed to clean up. It gave them the space to keep moving and they quickly retrieved the keys to the car, racing back outside to help slide Joe into the passenger seat.

Paul drove at breakneck speed, arriving at his aunt and uncle's winery fifteen minutes later. By that time Joe was slipping in and out of consciousness, and both Paul and Sophia feared their aunt Genevieve, would turn them away immediately. They knew how much the woman despised the lifestyle her sister had subjected her children to. But their worries were unfounded, because when Genevieve saw the injured young man her latent medical instincts kicked in and she began immediately tending to his wounds.

As Genevieve worked, Sophia tried in vain to get a prognosis, but the grim look on her Aunt's face told the whole story. Frustrated and afraid, Sophia kept pressing until an argument ensued.

"Sophia, stop with the questions!" Genevieve scolded. "I need to stabilize this young man, before we take him to a hospital."

"But that's impossible," Sophia pleaded. "We can't go to a hospital. Can't you tell we are in grave danger. There are men—men who did this to Joe—who will come looking for us very soon. They will not ask questions, they will simply kill."

"He will die without hospitalization," Genevieve declared with clinical calm.

"Non! With you he has a chance. Left exposed to our pursuers, he has none!" Sophia shouted, before adding in a softer tone. "We have none."

Paul, who'd overheard the exchange, decided they didn't have time for this, so he said the one thing he knew would get them to listen.

"Stephan is dead," he proclaimed.

"You don't know that!" Sophia shot back, momentarily forgetting her pleas to her aunt so she could face down her brother's shocking interruption.

"I do," Paul said with a cold hardness in his eyes. "And you, Sophia, of all people, should know that better than any of us."

Sophia glared at her brother, unwilling to let herself accept what she knew in her mind was true. She had felt the emptiness, the fresh new hole that Stephan had left in the world, but still she desperately clung to hope.

Genevieve's gaze shifted from Sophia to Paul and finally to her sister, who had dropped to the floor sobbing after Paul's bold proclamation about her other son's death. After a moment, Genevieve brought her gaze back to the young man on the table and something softened in her eyes. Perhaps she'd read the raw passion of new love in her niece—the girl who'd been so hard and unmoving all her life. Perhaps it was Paul's cold, matter-of-fact pronouncement of her nephew Stephan's death. Or perhaps she realized her sister was never much of a mother, and right now her two remaining children needed their aunt. In the end, she simply nodded her acceptance.

"He will die," Genevieve said matter-of-factly. But her words were half-hearted and resigned. "I know a place," she said finally.

It was all Anna and Sophia needed to hear. With Joe's temporary security negotiated, they needed to move again, immediately. Sophia spent the next few moments lingering by Joe's side, telling him in between fits of consciousness how much she cared for him . . . that she would return . . . that they would be together soon. But right now she needed to go and help his friend Anna. Joe simply squeezed her hand as she kissed him on the lips . . . a tender farewell. Then Anna and Sophia fled out the door, Sophia praying, for the first time in ages, that it was not their last kiss.

Paul remained behind to help with Genevieve's plans. He had more friends in the city, and the underground of Chinon, to navigate everything they would need to try to coax Joe from the brink of death. But he also needed to do something else. As futile as it might be, he needed to go out and search for his brother's body—for his mother's sake.

Distraught and afraid, Sophia drove through the night, with Anna in the passenger seat—a sisterly kinship forming between the two, forged out of the chaos at the chateau. Right now Sophia would do anything for this woman, and she knew Anna needed her company and closeness, or she would crack in two. There had been so much weight placed on such a delicate frame, yet Sophia somehow knew there was only more to come for Anna.

Twenty miles away—back at the chateau—the cleanup had already begun. The fortress would remain closed tomorrow or longer. The official reason would be severe damage from the storm. Even then, the locals would talk for the next weeks, months, and even years, swearing they had heard multiple gunshots echoing from within the fortress.

The French authorities would stick to their story, insisting lightning had been the cause, until several local tourists began to turn up deformed bullet fragments and empty shell casings the cleanup crew missed. The revised story had a military training exercise taking place inside the chateau to prepare the country for a variety of possible terrorist scenarios. The story appeased most, but one can still slip into a local bar and hear men and women gossiping about the shootout in Chinon.

As for Mitch, he had been officially handed his departure notice. Henry had arranged transportation for him directly back to Charles de Gaulle airport. He had even gone so far as to place Mitch in temporary custody, and considered making him the fall guy for the massacre at the chateau. Henry had never expected that four kids and a few of their friends could do such damage to his unit, and a national monument. He had expected a quick, efficient mission, and several easy kills. It had been anything but.

Mitch fought it, insisting he be set free to pursue Anna and her friends. But Henry informed him that, being on French soil, the Naturals were no longer an American concern. France and its people could no longer allow a Westerner to call the shots and run unchecked across their country, not after what happened here tonight.

So, as the van pulled out, with Mitch cuffed to a post in the back, he wondered about Anna and where she might be right now. He wondered if the limp, nearly lifeless body of Grady lying next to him on a gurney might be enough to finally flush her out of hiding. Her security blanket was dwindling. Gone were Curt, Trent and most likely Joe, if the bullet Mitch himself had put in him did its job.

As the hours passed, two different vehicles in two different cities pulled into very different French airports. Mitch and Grady had been unceremoniously escorted to the Charles de Gaulle Airport, where a military air transport arranged by the U.S. government awaited them. To get them out of their country, and avoid any further political fallout, the French authorities had expedited their boarding directly off the van and onto the plane. It appeared Mitch would never be welcome in France again.

Sophia and Anna, on the other hand, had driven through the night to arrive at the Marseille Provence Airport. As they pulled into the parking lot, Sophia stuffed a wad of cash into Anna's hands.

"The flight will be expensive," she insisted.

Anna had some money she'd collected from Grady's belongings at the hotel, but she had wondered if it would be enough. Thumbing through the bills Sophia handed over, Anna realized she should now have plenty to get home. "Thank you. I'll pay you back, I promise," Anna said gratefully.

Sophia sighed. "But the money is not the reason I am here with you now, is it?"

Anna eyed Sophia with respect. She had never asked Sophia to drive her all this way, and never would have, given the uncertainty over Joe's condition and her brother Stephan. Sophia had virtually insisted. Anna had hoped they might have one last moment together and Sophia sensed it.

"No," Anna replied, the apology in her voice clear. "I'd like to try one more time . . . to try to connect. It won't be the same as if we had the others, but I need to try to make sense of some of the things we saw in the chateau."

Sophia smiled, understanding Anna was uncomfortable with the request. "Give me your hands," Sophia insisted, and Anna obliged. They sat in the car for the next fifteen minutes, trying to pull back the threads of their previous session with Trent and Joe, until finally Anna let go. For the longest time Anna just sat and stared out the window, a very blank look on her face.

"You should get moving," Sophia prodded, pulling Anna out of her reverie.

As if from a deep sleep, Anna stirred, nodded her head and both women got out of the car. Inside the airport, once the tickets were bought, Anna explained she needed to make a call.

"You can use my cell," Sophia offered.

Digging into her front jeans pocket, she pulled out a slip of paper Grady had given Anna a long time ago. There was a phone number printed on it, to use if she was ever in trouble, if she ever got separated from Grady.

Taking the phone, Anna dialed the number and let it ring. After the fourth a male voice answered. "This is Tom."

"Tom, it's Anna. I don't have the time or energy to go into details, but I'm coming back without Grady." Anna let her words sink in, but to Tom's credit he respected her wishes and didn't ask any questions. "I'm going to need your help in trying to figure out how to get him back. That is, if he is . . ." but she couldn't bring herself to finish the thought.

"I see," Tom said, a little more reserved than Anna expected.

"Everything okay, Tom?"

"Anna, I'll do what I can . . . you know that. Obviously I'm dying inside at what you just told me. Of course I want to know more. But I'm not alone right now. Actually I'm not even at my own house—it's not safe there anymore. When you do get back there's someone here you should probably talk to."

Anna hung up the phone and handed it back to Sophia. "Bad news?"

"I'm not sure. Guess I'll find out when I get back."

With that the two women hugged and said their goodbyes. Anna could sense Sophia was anxious to get back to Chinon, and for her sake, Anna hoped she was returning to better news than she thought she had just gotten from Tom.

As Anna turned to walk through security to board a flight to Amsterdam, where she'd hop a connection to the Twin Cities, Sophia called out to her.

"What did that mean? I saw something with you back in the car when we were holding hands, but I don't understand."

Anna looked at Sophia, so tired. "I don't exactly know myself yet. But I'll be honest with you, it's the last thing I ever expected."

One hour later, both Anna and Grady's flights were taxiing down their respective runways, the wheels of both planes lifting off French soil at almost identical moments in time, which could have been significant . . . if time really mattered at all.

CHAPTER 100

COMPROMISED

T om was waiting for Anna as she cleared customs without incident. There were some anxious moments over the last 24 hours as she tried to make her way back to the Twin Cities. Arriving in Amsterdam, waiting over six hours for a seat on a connecting flight to the States, and finally customs—wondering all the while if Northwoods would reach out and grab her at any point. She traveled using the false identity Tom had obtained for her, and it seemed to be working, meaning either Grady was dead or they hadn't been able to get him to talk.

The final anxious moment was meeting Tom, and as he hugged her ragged, tired body she looked around expectantly for the person who had got to Tom.

"Where is he?" she asked, with an exhaustion and resignation that couldn't be masked.

"Who do you mean?" Tom asked, a little perplexed.

"You mentioned someone I should talk to when I called from France. You sounded guarded on the phone, like someone had compromised you or was coercing you," Anna explained.

"Oh, Kyle," Tom said, with almost a nonchalance. "He's back at his house. I'll take you there now if you're okay with that."

Anna looked at him with surprise in her eyes. "So he's not from the government or police? I just assumed."

Tom looked at his feet and shuffled them a bit self-consciously. "I didn't exactly say that. He's FBI."

"He's trusting you to meet me alone?" Anna asked skeptically, looking around again for someone to swoop in and whisk them both off to some small, cramped interrogation room in the bowels of the airport.

"It's not what you think, Anna." Tom tried to explain. "Oh . . . damn . . . I guess I had the same feelings when he first showed up on my doorstep. But I believe he wants to help if he can. Why don't you just come with me, and you can judge for yourself."

Tired of the circular conversation, Anna simply agreed. She trusted Tom, and if Tom trusted whomever they were going to meet, then she'd go along.

As they walked out of the airport to find Tom's car, he asked one last question. "So if you thought I might be compromised, why did you fly back into the Twin Cities? You could have easily flown into another airport and disappeared."

Anna didn't have to think about the answer, because she had been through it over and over since the events at the chateau, and she had plenty of time to confirm her choice while on the plane. With a chilling soberness she stated the simple, honest truth. "Because I'm done running."

The drive back to Kyle's house took about thirty minutes, to a small split-level home south of the Minnesota River in Savage. Anna had dozed briefly on the way, and Tom found it difficult to wake her once they arrived. When she finally did come to, he gave her a few moments to get her bearings, as the early evening shadows began to settle in outside the car.

"I can tell Kyle you're exhausted and need rest," Tom offered.

But Anna shook her head. "No. We need to keep this moving. Grady could certainly be dead by now, but if he isn't I don't think he has much time. This has to end soon, for better or for worse, and if you think Kyle can help us in any way we need to try."

"Very well," Tom said with concern in his voice. "You ready, then?"

Anna didn't reply. Instead she answered by opening the door and getting out of the car. As Tom approached the house, the door opened and Molly came bounding out, hitting him hard in the chest with her paws before bounding off and greeting Anna.

"Molly!" Tom yelled with disgust, worried that Anna would be in no mood.

But Anna crouched down and tussled the Golden Retriever's ears as Molly thanked her with big licks to her face. "It's okay, Tom," Anna said with a hit of a smile and a half laugh. She's gorgeous. She yours?"

"I forgot you've never met her. Yes, she's all mine."

"And a damn good thing, too," said a good-natured voice from inside the doorway to the house. "She's been tearing up my place since you've been gone."

Anna looked up from petting Molly to see a face she knew instantly. It was the same man she had bumped into in the airport. The same man who had let her and Grady go, when she knew he'd been there to help find them. *What had Grady said about him? They'd been partners before at the FBI?* In that moment, Anna felt like she could trust him with keeping her secret.

"You must be Kyle," she said, straightening up and offering her hand. "Tom says we have a lot to talk about."

CHAPTER 101

The Gates of Hell

An ambulance pulled up to the gates of Northwoods, and the driver leaned over and spoke into an intercom. After identifying himself, and running an ID card through a scanner, the big iron gates swung inward on automatic hinges.

Before the gates had even fully parted, the ambulance was through and the gates immediately started to close again. The driver maneuvered the emergency vehicle down a long, narrow lane lined with a single row of gnarled oak trees on either side. Half a mile up the path the road opened into a circular courtyard.

Mitch hopped out, walked around to the rear doors and swung them wide. Two men dressed in paramedic clothes jumped from the back, carefully removed a wheeled gurney and extended the wheelbase. Once set up, the two men checked the vitals of the man under the white sheet. Everything appeared to be in order, and the drugs that were being slowly dripped into a vein in his arm through an IV ensured he continued to sleep. Soon, the drugs would be cut off, the reality of consciousness would set in, and the pain from the gunshot wound would be used against him in order to try to extract the truth.

Satisfied, the orderlies rolled him up a stone ramp next to a bronzed metal railing, Mitch followed behind, keeping a close eye on his prisoner. If Grady had just chanced to wake up at that moment, he would have gotten his first view of hell on earth. Grady was at Northwoods . . . just like Anna's dream had foretold.

CHAPTER 102

ANNA AND KYLE

Anna and Kyle spoke for hours. She laid everything she knew on the table . . . or almost. She spoke of her years at Northwoods, the other Naturals, the mysterious Fifth Seed, and life before and after Northwoods started using the drugs. She went into detail about their escape, Mary Jane, meeting Grady, Mitch, the incident at Ben's house in Rochester, their escape to Lanesboro and ultimately their attempts to track down Trent and Joe in Paris. Finally she laid out in vivid detail, every excruciating moment of the siege at Chinon. Tom, who listened along, was visibly disturbed when she got to the part about Grady being shot. Kyle simply sat in his chair, drinking a beer and stroking his close-trimmed goatee, which was starting to show signs of gray where he constantly thumbed it.

Anna finished what felt like a regurgitation of every horrible detail of her life. After she finished, Kyle kept stroking his goatee, occasionally running his hands through his wavy mop of reddish brown hair. Anna looked down, studying her feet, waiting for Kyle to say something . . . anything.

But it was Tom who couldn't bear the silence anymore. "Are we going to do anything?" he asked, looking directly at Kyle. "He was your partner. Doesn't that mean anything to you?"

Kyle sighed. "We wouldn't be here if it didn't. I would have turned you in long ago. And I never would have let Grady get by me in the

435

airport. You see, the question isn't about loyalties; the question is can we even do anything?"

"But you're FBI!" Anna shouted, her pent-up frustrations surfacing.

"Now hold on," Kyle started to explain. "I didn't say we wouldn't try. I'm just not sure there is a great way to go about it. Tom showed me the file Grady was gathering on Northwoods, and there is a lot of what you just told me in there. With your witness to the atrocities there is at least a chance that we could get a judge to issue a search warrant for Northwoods."

"I sense a *but* coming," Anna guessed.

"Yes, because there is an equally good chance that a judge would need more facts. Much of what we have against Northwoods is what you, an escaped—and I use this word lightly—mental patient, are saying about your former incarcerator. That goes directly against your credibility. Let's not even go into the abilities you say you and your escaped friends have. Factor that in and most people would consider you insane; not great ground for a witness to stand on.

"But . . . !" Anna began, although Kyle backed her off by raising his hand.

"Tom here told me about you, and says what he knows came directly from Grady and the occasional calls they shared over the last several days. Unless Grady has completely snapped, I'm willing to give you the benefit of the doubt, although I still can't actually fathom it. If I hadn't heard rumors of such mental talents in my circles, there's no way I'd even be giving you the time of day. That said, I had always assumed they were just that . . . rumors. The FBI can be just as rumor-hungry as any workplace . . . perhaps even more-so given the secrets we deal with daily."

Anna eased up and sat back in her chair, curling her legs up under her, allowing Kyle go on.

"Okay, so I already gave you two scenarios if we go to authorities with this. There is an even better chance, based on everything that I have heard, that some faction of our government, and possibly even my own branch of service, is involved. I can tell you the FBI has files on Northwoods that I can't access; the security level is too high. That tells me we are investigating them, we are collaborating with them, or serving as a shell unit—basically acting on orders from above without knowledge—playing the good soldier. No matter what the scenario is, I have a hunch if we went nosing around asking questions, or throwing out accusations, you both would disappear pretty quickly and, at best, my career would be over."

"It's why, I tracked down Tom and brought him here. You see, Tom was an informant for Grady and me a while back—very low-key, off the record stuff. But if I could connect him to Grady, others around the Bureau could, too. Eventually, they'd come calling at Tom's home, if they haven't already."

"So what the hell do we do?" Tom demanded.

"Here's the deal," continued Kyle. "This goes much higher than my regional FBI office. I can tell you when I was brought in to canvas the airport nobody knew anything, other than Grady was implicated in the shooting at Mary Jane's. So I can do a little nosing around tomorrow without too much fear that it will roll up the chain to National. If I can find out who's involved—FBI, CIA or State Department—or better yet who isn't, then we have our path."

"Aren't you concerned that they all might be involved, or that the top is above any of those organizations?" Anna suggested.

"Very possible," Kyle said without having to think about it. "But the likelihood is that one of them is lead and one of them knows nothing about it and is being kept in the dark. These agencies tend not to get along, and often battle over turf and power—although technically they all now report to the same boss since 9/11. If we can find the odd agency out, we can maybe pit it against the others."

"Sounds like it could take a long time," Anna said, almost to herself.

"It could, but it is the only way I can think of to get the right kind of attention on the situation," Kyle replied with regret, realizing even if Grady was still alive, the plan might not be fast enough to save his life.

Anna had heard enough, so she politely excused herself, heading downstairs to the guest room Kyle had set up to get some rest. As she drifted off, she opened her mind wide. She could care less about the consequences, and the possibility Northwoods would track her down in the basement of an FBI agent's home. *Let them come,* she thought.

That night, as her dreams unfolded, her heart soared and ached at the same time—as she realized what she had been coming to suspect. He was alive.

CHAPTER 103

CALLED ON THE CARPET

Kyle arrived at 111 Washington Avenue South at 7 a.m. He was actually about a half hour late to work, for him anyway. Tom had been up, and already taken Molly for her morning walk by the time Kyle got out the door, but Anna was still sleeping, and neither men wanted to disturb her. She'd been through hell and it might not get easier anytime soon.

On the drive into work, Kyle tried to go over all of the details he knew in his head. He barely ever took notes, and stored a tremendous amount of information in the fastest search engine he knew of—the human brain. He loved to organize the information into pieces, and then move those pieces around and try to make them fit. When a couple of pieces locked into place it gave him a rush.

He was moving a few of those pieces around in his head, and starting to come to conclusions around who was leading the Northwoods experiment and who was on the outside. What began to worry him was that it appeared, against precedent, several of the Nation's security agencies could actually be working together. That was unusual, and what it likely meant was that the person calling the shots here was the head of National Security. Rival agencies only cooperated when they were told they had to, and only one man had that power. Not even the president herself could coerce that kind of cooperation.

That left Kyle with few avenues to pursue, but there was possibly one. It was through the man who just happened to appear at his desk right now.

"Sorry sir, I didn't see you there," he explained to his boss and Regional Agent In Charge, Brian Stone.

"Can I have a word with you Kyle?" his boss asked, a half-frown creasing his forehead. "It's about some of the side work and digging you've been doing lately . . . I believe around a place called Northwoods."

Suddenly Kyle realized this was going to go a lot faster than he wanted it to. "Sure," he said, and got up and followed his lanky gray-haired leader into his office. Once inside, his boss stepped around him and closed the door: not a good sign.

"Have a seat," Brian offered, more command than polite gesture. He walked around his desk and settled into his tall leather chair. Leaning back, he began to look at the ceiling as if scrutinizing the tiles and discovering something fascinating up there.

"There are people around here," Brian began, "who are saying you've taken a keen interest in Grady's case. And that you've also been digging around the Northwoods files, asking what people know."

Kyle knew it wouldn't be good to lie to his Agent In Charge. He already knew anyway. "Yes, sir."

His boss took his eyes off the ceiling and leaned forward, resting his forearms on his low-rent metal desk. The leather chair was about all the luxury the American taxpayers could afford—at least for a regional director.

"So what have you found out?" Brian asked with an interest that surprised Kyle. Perhaps this wasn't going to be the lynching he expected.

"I'm not following, sir. Aren't you going to tell me to stop digging around and do my job?"

Brian chuckled. "If you already know that will it do any good for me to tell you?"

Kyle just shook his head. He wasn't about to fall into that trap and give an answer.

"There's a reason you're putting your neck on the line here," Brian went on, "and I want to know what it is. And don't give me any of that crap, that it's all because you two were partners. It might explain a passing interest in the case, but from what I understand, you're running a full-scale investigation on the side, and that means you've got information. You've got a lead."

"Okay. I've got a few minor leads, but why your interest? Why not just shut me down?" Kyle asked, avoiding answers if he could, and asking his own questions to feel out the conversation's ultimate direction. He hoped he wasn't overstepping his bounds. He needed to understand his boss's motives before he could trust him with the information.

Brian sighed, leaned back in his chair again, and put his arms behind his head. It appeared he was struggling with how much he should say. "Well, it helps your case that National is pissing me off right now. First they raided this place and pulled all our files on Grady and our investigation—all without warning. Then they shut us out. Now they've got their undies all bunched up over some copies of the surveillance footage from Grady's house that have gone missing.

Kyle flinched when he heard his boss mention the videos, and he knew that Brian picked up on it. Surprisingly, he showed no interest in pursuing that topic further . . . yet.

"I'll tell you I haven't seen heat this heavy since 9/11 and the ass whooping we took for not connecting the dots between that terrorist we detained and the eventual attacks. Now, National wants to bring some interrogators in here and line all my men up and start flaying them to the bone until someone rips open a vein for them."

The Special Agent In Charge leaned in again, with a *don't bullshit me or I'll eat you alive* look on his face. "So tell me, what do you know?"

Knowing he had no other choice, Kyle spilled it all. He told his boss everything he knew including everything Anna had told him. When he had finally finished Brian looked at him with a sober, unflinching expression.

"So what are you going to do?" Kyle asked a bit fearfully.

Brian rubbed his face hard, as if trying to decide right then and there. But finally he said, "I don't know. Give me 24 hours . . . in the meantime go home. You're off all cases until further notice."

"And then what?" Kyle pressed. He didn't really care anymore—his career was probably over anyway.

"You'll know when it happens," his boss replied pensively.

As Kyle walked out the door, not sure if he should expect the Calvary or the Gestapo to come knocking on his door, his boss picked up the phone and placed a call.

When the call went through his first words were. "I need to cash in that favor."

CHAPTER 104

INN KAHOOTS

"74 Hamel Road," Anna told the Taxi driver. She had slept little the previous night, and when she did it was fitful. After talking with Kyle and Tom—as good-hearted and willing to help as they were—she realized she couldn't just sit around and wait. After her dreams last night, she was certain everything was not as it seemed. There might be other avenues to explore, and today she knew of one.

She left before either Kyle or Tom woke up. Only Molly greeted her on her way out the door, but thankfully the dog was good-natured and didn't bark. It had taken a while to walk through Kyle's winding residential neighborhood and locate a coffee shop that opened its doors at 6 a.m.

When she arrived, Anna had some time to kill so she ordered a coffee and counted her remaining money. With what Sophia had given her, Anna realized she had more than enough for the coffee, a little breakfast and the eventual cab ride—plus drinks at the bar she intended to visit: Inn Kahoots.

The place held unique significance, as did this day itself. For today was the day she and the rest of the Naturals were supposed to reconnect at the small-town bar, to raise a toast to their freedom. The bar also happened to be the place Anna had visited many weeks ago in an attempt to track down Mary Jane. Before she'd left Grafton, she'd been instructed to seek out a bartender there named Olivia, who'd been tasked with protecting the secret to Mary Jane's whereabouts.

Now the idea of a reunion was gone. All that was left was to go and raise a drink to fallen friends, to put to bed once and for all some impossible hopes and confront a few lingering doubts. Those doubts raised by visions she'd had in Paris—visions suggesting another reason to come—perhaps for a confrontation, or perhaps to face down the evil that had been dogging them since their escape. Although she wondered if those visions were simply lingering phantom images of a universe that had not yet fully peeled away from her own.

Anna finally left the coffee shop at a little past noon, after four painful hours alone, with little to distract her from her thoughts. In that time she'd wondered if Tom or Kyle might stumble upon her there, looking for her. By now one of them would have noticed that she was gone. But she thought they were probably better off without her. She could only bring them trouble. It was better for her to deal with this on her own.

The ride took about thirty minutes and as Anna stepped out of the cab, she easily recognized Inn Kahoots from her earlier visit. The bar was truly unforgettable: a run-down two-story building with straight lines, a flat roof and a long wooden porch, with rickety steps on the right that lead up to the main entrance. The whole place appeared as if it would fall down in a good stiff wind.

Out front at least twenty motorcycles, most of them classic Harleys, leaned in a long row. Anna remembered Mary Jane affectionately called it her biker bar—saying that while the outside gave the feeling that a barroom brawl could break out at any moment, the regulars who frequented the place had big hearts, welcoming anyone who didn't care to judge them.

At one-o'clock, precisely two hours early, Anna walked into the bar, sat down and said hello once again to Olivia. The young bartender poured Anna a beer and made small talk with her between serving other customers. Quickly the two women fell into an easy kind of friendship.

After a while, Anna decided to ask a quick favor, to which Olivia agreed, and the bartender slid down the length of the bar to mention something to one of the biker regulars while pouring him another beer. The man nodded, looking back over at Anna with a smile.

Time passed slowly, and after her second round, Anna decided to take a walk outside, thinking it would be good to get up and stretch her legs for a few minutes. Besides, she didn't want to be here when *he* came. The walk was short but therapeutic, and promptly at three, Anna returned.

Approaching the bar, her feet didn't seem to want to move as fast, and her heart began to race. She was anticipating what was now there, behind those doors. *Had she allowed him enough time to come?* Slowly she mounted the porch steps, shuffling her feet over the dusty floorboards, which creaked out in protest with every step. Reaching for the doorknob her mouth went dry and her hand began to shake. It took every ounce of strength inside of her to pull open the door and step inside.

And as her eyes slowly began to adjust to the darkness, Anna saw and knew instantly. Even from behind, even before he turned to face her—the form, the figure, the way he held his body—the person sitting at the bar was Curt.

CHAPTER 105

LYING IN WAIT

Inside Inn Kahoots, The Kid receded deep into the shadows, watching Curt sip mindlessly at his beer. He couldn't let him know he was here, and was working hard to block him. Curt must have sensed something because he looked around nervously, like he was being watched. Perhaps he was just anxiously awaiting Anna's arrival. Still, to ensure he wasn't found out, The Kid slid deeper into the shadows and waited.

Curt had survived The Kid's attempt to drive him to his death, with the deep plunge off the Golden Gate. But what The Kid had come to realize was that his attempts to kill Curt had been a mistake. He knew now that Anna would never come here without the lure of Curt. Their inevitable meeting never would happen if Curt weren't alive and available to be served up as bait. The Kid had used that to his advantage when he was in Paris, serving up stray visions for Anna to pick up on, letting her know Curt was still alive.

In the end, the fact that Curt was alive wouldn't matter. Soon enough he and Anna would be reunited and not even Curt could get in the way of that. The Kid would make certain of it. So both young men waited anxiously for the love of their lives, for the woman that had made them both feel whole, and yet had rejected them. And while one hoped only to be loved by her, the other longed only for the day he could keep and control her.

When the door finally opened, both men turned to watch her glide into the room. She wore a simple pair of close-fitting jeans that held every inviting contour, a simple white blouse that hugged the swell of her breasts, and a chunky turquoise necklace that road in and out of her cleavage. Her hair bounced with a softness and sway that made both men weak.

As Curt rose to greet Anna, The Kid felt exposed and vulnerable and wanted to move farther away. He felt too close, but he couldn't go any farther away and still see everything that was happening. Curt embraced Anna and The Kid could see from his vantage point that she was crying—and once more The Kid felt a jealous rage well up within him.

Anna let Curt embrace her, but she felt numb and her arms barely made it around his back before she let go. Curt held on for a moment too long, like a desperate lover trying to hang on to something that was never meant to be. When he released her, and looked her in her eyes, he saw something cold and uncaring.

"Anna. What? Have I done something?"

"Don't play this game with me, Curt. Just don't," she said firmly through gritted teeth. "Not after everything you've done."

Curt looked visibly hurt as they took a pair of stools; he tried to take her hand but Anna refused the gesture. "I don't understand. What are you upset with me about? I thought you'd be happy to see me."

"Not after Mary Jane . . . not after Trent . . . not after Grady, and God only knows about Joe. And for what?" Anna said almost yelling now, as couple of locals looked ready to rise up out of their seats. "Don't you dare tell me you did it all for me," Anna seethed. "Because I can't live with that."

"But I don't understand," Curt said pleading now. "I don't understand," and tears began to trickle down his face.

"Cut the crap, Curt. I know you're The Fifth Seed. I know you've been helping Northwoods, that you staged your death so that you could help them without any of us picking up on it. If you were presumed dead, we'd never suspect you."

"Please Anna, please," Curt continued to plead. "I can't take this . . . not from you . . . I need you now more than ever. I swear I don't know what you're talking about. I woke up three days ago in a San Francisco hospital. I could barely remember how I got there and then someone told me I jumped off the Golden Gate Bridge. It all came flooding back. The Fifth Seed, he was there, he was chasing me. I couldn't do it alone. I was so scared. I was so tired. And so I just . . . I just . . ."

But Curt's voice trailed off, unable to complete the thought. "And I think he's still nearby, Anna. I can't seem to shake the feeling of him, and it scares the hell out of me."

Anna wasn't sure what made her doubt. Maybe it was his tears. Maybe it was the open and bare look in his eyes, the sheer fear of losing her, or the primal fear of The Fifth Seed. But it was emotion that was so raw she didn't think it could be faked. And now, Anna became more confused that ever.

"I don't understand, Curt. You say you weren't in Paris, but I felt you behind the door outside the Hotel le Clos Medicis. I touched a doorknob and images of you began to flit through my head. I felt you out on the streets of Paris the morning Grady and I went to Chinon. Then finally I had this overwhelming sense that I'd see you here today.

And the others. All their memories and experiences that we shared in the Chateau du Chinon point to you, Curt. Joe felt you at Montmartre, chasing them. Sophia saw you on the subway. She had no idea who you were but when she shared her memory with me it was you. Then there was the candle in Notre Dame—that was the hardest one. But I finally figured it out. In Trent's split universe you died on that bridge, but in Joe's you survived. And finally, I saw definitively last night that you were alive and yet I still couldn't bring myself to fully believe it. To believe you were capable of it all. But Curt, it all points to you."

Curt tried to grab Anna's hand again and this time she didn't resist. "Anna, I swear I was never in Paris. I was in a hospital bed. I had dreams of you, and Trent and Joe, but I don't know this Sophia, although maybe I saw her in a vision," Curt said, shaking his head as if trying to get a memory to fall back into place. "But that's all I know. I don't even know about Trent and Joe. Has something happened to them? What? You've got to tell me."

Finally Anna broke, and she wrapped her arms around Curt and hugged him. "I'm so sorry. I thought it was you. It had to be you. Nothing else makes any sense anymore."

Curt hugged her back, wanting to know more, wanting to know about the others, but not wanting to press her. God, he didn't even know who Grady was, or what happened to Mary Jane. Had Anna found her?

From a distance, The Kid watched. He hated that Curt was hugging her, and he imagined that it was him—to the point he could almost feel the warmth of her body on his and the sweet taste of her tears on his lips. He wanted it so badly for himself. Just a little longer he'd let it go on, and then he would make his move.

Anna and Curt broke their embrace, and Curt stared down deep into her eyes as she search his for anything that might make sense of it all. In that face-to-face Curt misread the moment they shared, and he moved in close to kiss her. For a second, Anna almost let him—before placing her hand gently on his chest to stop him.

"I can't," she said with a regret aimed only at sparing Curt's feelings. "Not with Grady out there. I tried to reach out to him last night, to see if he was alive, but I got you."

Curt sat back hurt, and picked up his beer to take a long drink. When he was done he simply asked, "Who's Grady?"

Anna smiled happily, not for the hurt Curt felt, but because that simple, honest question left no doubt in her mind that she had been wrong about him being The Fifth Seed. "It's a long story, Curt, one I'll have to tell you. But he's the man I love."

"I see," Curt commented, obviously trying to mask the pain as he quickly downed the rest of his beer and called the bartender over for another.

This time it was Anna's turn to reach out to try to hold his hand, and bring him back to her. "Curt, let's go. You don't need another. I

449

have friends in town that can help us. One is with the FBI. His name is Kyle Brady and maybe if we work together we can finally bring down Northwoods."

"But Anna," Curt pleaded, picking up on something she had said and trying to use it against her. "You said you reached out to this guy Grady last night, and you got me. Don't you see that means something? We were meant to be. Can't you see that?"

Anna dropped Curt's hand. It was useless and while she didn't want to hurt Curt anymore, the pain would be even greater if she led him along. "No, Curt. I don't see that. I have to find Grady. And if you can't help me, I'd understand. But if that's the case I think it's time we said goodbye for good."

As Anna stood up to leave, somewhere inside Inn Kahoots, tucked back in the deep shadowy recesses, The Kid screamed, "NO!"

In that instant Curt stood up, grabbed Anna's arm roughly and spun her around. As he glared into her frightened eyes, his fingernails biting into the flesh of her arm, The Kid came forward. Not from the back room, not from across the bar on the other side of the pool table, and not from a dark, dim corner booth. Instead he came forward from the deep, deep recesses of Curt's horribly fractured mind. In that instant, when The Kid took over, and Curt fell away, Anna could swear the eyes of the man she never really knew changed ever so slightly from blue to green.

Instantly Anna realized her mistake. Curt housed a split personality and for the first time in her life, she felt as if she was staring into a black hole of a soul with more vile power than she could fathom . . . The Fifth Seed.

CHAPTER 106

MOMENT OF TRUTH

"You bitch," The Kid breathed through his teeth. "You ruined everything. We were meant to be together."

Anna stared at the monster before her, willing herself to hold her ground. She wanted to get information out of him. Even as every fiber of her being urged her to scream and run. She had noticed a couple of the locals pause from their drinks and pool playing, as if they were about to intervene, but they held back.

"What have you done with Curt?" she demanded.

"He's been tucked away. You see, I know about him, but he doesn't know about me. It makes it easier that way."

"You're a freak," she spat. "What were you going to do? Use Curt to get close to me and then gradually take over and get rid of him?"

"It's interesting you say that," The Kid said in an almost admiring way. "At first I didn't think I needed him, and he was always too strong when he was around you in particular. In fact, when you escaped he had been in control for weeks. But then you left him and I haunted him. It was easy. He ran, but could never run far enough. He thought finding his parents would make him feel safe. But he couldn't get a lead, and I wouldn't give him a moment's rest. He finally broke and threw himself off the bridge.

"And you allowed it?" Anna asked surprised.

"Oh Anna, you of all people should know there was no danger to me. My own visions showed me a future after the fact. Imagine how much easier it is to throw yourself to danger when you know you will survive. But I did figure the jump would drive Curt away once and for all."

"But he came back again when you'd get close to me . . . in Paris by the doorway," Anna guessed. "That was only shortly after Trent and Joe were trying to light a candle in Notre Dame." Anna added thoughtfully to herself.

The Kid smiled a creepy grin. "Yes, he'd been gone since the jump, but he tried to come forward as you drew near. That was when I first knew he was still alive. It's funny, because it was in that moment that I realized he was my ticket to drawing you in. I'd thought for a while, just the physical being of Curt would be enough. And why not, in terms of a mind, mine was so much more advanced. Yet your reaction at the doorway to his presence sealed it. I had to change my approach. It's why I decided to follow Sophia instead of you."

"So you played us both."

"Yes. You had such a weakness for his weaknesses. But Grady seems to be changing that in you," he added with disgust.

Anna tried to wriggle her arm free, but The Kid just dug his nails in deeper. Again the entire bar seemed to pause at the sight of the struggle, but nobody stepped forward to offer a hand.

"How could Curt have woke up in San Francisco when you were still in Paris?" Anna asked.

"Again, if you cared at all about what Northwoods was trying to accomplish you'd see the answer easily. There were drug cocktails designed to replicate and enhance special skills. If you recall Trent was the strongest at implanting false memories or false futures in others' minds. I used his drugs from Northwoods pharmacy to enhance my own natural abilities and simply placed those memories where I needed them. It was part of how I controlled him."

Anna spat into The Kid's face, and he instinctively let go of her arm to wipe the saliva out of his eyes. In that fraction of a second she made her break for the door. Anticipating her move, the Kid dove for her, tackling her to the floor as she began screaming for help.

In an instant three large bikers surrounded The Kid and pulled him off Anna. That had been the favor she asked of Olivia on her first visit to the bar today—to organize a posse to help her if she asked for it.

As the men yanked The Kid away Anna got up and hit the door in full stride. At the front porch, she turned left and flew across the wood planks and down the steps before accidentally plowing into and tripping over someone standing at the base. As she picked herself up she realized she was staring at someone she knew all too well.

"Hi, Anna." Drake said with a smile, pointing what appeared to be a concealed gun in her general direction.

"What the hell are you doing here?" she asked incredulously.

"My dad didn't trust The Kid. Figured he had something up his sleeve, so he had me follow him. Stupid Kid came back from Paris to pick up some drugs when he could have just walked away. He always comes back for the drugs."

"Your dad?" Anna said, confused.

"Oh, didn't you know? Dr. Hauser's my father. I just found out myself a few days ago. Apparently he had an affair with my mom a while back."

"This is insane," Anna groaned.

"Get up!" Drake demanded, looking around cautiously. "We're heading back to Northwoods."

Anna rose to her knees and brushed driveway gravel off her hands and pants. "I'll go, but just tell me one thing. Is Grady alive? Because if he isn't you can just shoot me now."

"Bang!" said Drake with a laugh. "You'll find out soon enough."

As he escorted her to a shiny black H3 Hummer, Drake sent one of Northwood's men to retrieve The Kid off the floor. Before the man got out of earshot, Drake called after him. "Let the bikers finish up before you interrupt them. The Kid needs a little correction. Just make sure they don't kill him. I think my dad would prefer he get to enjoy that opportunity."

CHAPTER 107

THE HAMMER FALLS

Tom and Kyle hadn't heard from Anna all day. Several hours earlier Molly had slipped downstairs, nosing her way into the guest room. Tom had gone after her, trying to chase her quietly back upstairs—that was when he discovered Anna missing.

Thinking back, it didn't surprise him Anna chose to run, but he was angry with himself that he hadn't seen it coming. He knew Anna was edgy and anxious and wasn't about to wait around to hang Grady's survival hopes on a wing and a prayer handed to the U.S. government.

Then, when Kyle came back from work at 11 a.m., Tom knew that wasn't a good sign. Kyle filled Tom in on what his boss had to say, and Tom filled Kyle in on Anna's disappearance. Given what they knew, both started to wonder if Anna hadn't had the right idea, to get out while she still could.

They still had that option. Neither knew what would come of the conversation with Kyle's superior. It wasn't hard to figure out that at some point they'd either be called to testify, or called on the carpet for their crimes. It depended on who received the message up the chain, and if that person was friend or foe.

Kyle offered to let Tom walk away. He told him he'd cover for him as long as he could. But Tom only had one question for Kyle: "How far do you trust your Special Agent in Charge?"

Kyle's response was simple. "With my life."

That sealed it for Tom. If he was going to be of any help to Grady or Anna, they needed to find help fast. This was their last, best hope. If Anna was off working her own angle, then Tom knew he needed to do his part even if that meant buying time in jail. There was no time for plan B, even if they had one. So the two men waited for whatever was to come, hoping that Kyle was right about the intentions of his superior.

Night came and both men knew with a sense of finality, Anna was not coming back. Too much time had passed. This actually complicated their case with Kyle's superiors; without Anna they no longer had an eyewitness to corroborate their story.

At about 11 p.m. both men decided to get some sleep, retiring to their separate rooms, with Molly following Tom to sleep on the edge of his bed. A couple of brandy Manhattans between the two men had left them warm and comfortably numb to the possibilities, good or bad, of the coming day. Neither realized they wouldn't have to wait until sun-up to discover which side of the law they had ended up on.

Four hours later, in the dead of night, four men dressed in combat black began their advance on Kyle's home. Two swept in through the front door, the lock defeated in mere seconds. In the rear of the house, the other two made quick work with the sliding glass door. They swept through the dark home, weapons drawn, prepared to shoot on sight.

They secured the entire home in seconds, only the two upstairs bedrooms remained. The four met in the hall, outside the doors, using hand signals to coordinate their approach—both rooms were to be taken at the exact same time.

The count was given and the doors exploded inward with a couple of expertly placed kicks as splinters of wood exploded from the doorjambs. It was the first sound any of the men had made since coming within fifty feet of the home.

Inside the rooms, laser dots danced across comforters, locking on their targets, before three shots were placed into the prone figures lying under the covers. The silenced high-caliber rounds shredded the bedding, throwing tuffs of stuffing, feathers and other debris all over the room and high into the air.

CHAPTER 108

LOSING CONTROL

The two men found themselves back out by the lake at Northwoods. The mallards were gone, but somewhere off in the morning mist a loon voiced a wavering call. Mitch looked out at wisps of fog rolling off the lake and tried to locate the source.

"Hate those damn things," Mitch said, referring to the loon. "Their call is just so . . . I don't know . . . it's like fingernails on a chalkboard."

Allan gave Mitch a look that was less than respectful. "Have any updates on the two possible leaks?"

Mitch ran his hand through his thinning hair. He would rather have started with the good news, but at least this wasn't his mess. "You know I'm on the outside looking in on this one, so at this point I've heard nothing new."

"What do you think that means?" Allan asked, concerned.

Mitch didn't like the question, but the answer was even more troublesome. "Well, we knew they were going in to try to take out a friend of Grady's—Tom Hanson—and a rogue FBI agent by the name of Kyle Brady. And from what I know that went down last night. I don't have final confirmation, which probably means our high-level sponsors decided we are no longer on their need-to-know list."

Allan swore under his breath. Their government sponsors were becoming more and more willing to throw resources at the problem, which would have been fine, but they were doing it autonomously, which was not good. Now someone high up had made the decision to go after Tom and Kyle. This worried Allan, because that probably meant someone at the top was concerned. And if they were concerned, that meant they didn't trust Allan to manage the situation.

"How's Grady doing?" Allan asked, changing the subject abruptly.

"Sir, I know what you are thinking and I would have to advise against it," Mitch said. "It's time to get rid of all the loose ends. That includes Anna and Mary Jane."

"I disagree," Allan replied. "The leaks to Tom and Kyle were directly through Anna and Grady. We don't know yet if Tom and Kyle have been taken care of. And even if they have that doesn't mean that Grady and Anna couldn't have sprung a couple more leaks. We need to find out everyone they talked to, determine risk and, if necessary, run them down. If need be, Mary Jane can be used as leverage against Anna. Anna can no longer ignore what we can and will do to her. And if I am correct, Anna can be used against Grady."

"But sir," Mitch continued. "The risks are . . ."

"That's the end of the conversation, Mitch," the doctor said, shutting him down. "I'm directly responsible for the risks I've already brought on my superiors. If I eliminated information that could help mitigate that risk, then I'm done—I might as well be at the bottom of that lake. And if I'm done, then you know what that means for everyone here. So just give me what I asked for."

Mitch gave up. He knew his boss was in full-fledged damage control, which meant all decisions from here on out would be thoroughly over-thought. "Grady is recovering. The wound was not life threatening. The bullet mostly hit muscle tissue in the upper left shoulder and nicked some bone, but otherwise passed clean through. The biggest concern was loss of blood, but he seems to be out of the woods now."

"And Anna?"

"Surprisingly calm."

"Really?" Allan asked with curiosity.

"She seems resigned to be here. Not happy about it for sure. But almost as if it were inevitable."

"Could have been . . . in her mind, anyway," Allan added thoughtfully. "That's a good sign."

"The Kid is locked up for now, just as you requested. He's licking a few wounds from the bar fight, and even more severe trauma to his ego. He insists that Curt had come forward strong and took over so that he could meet up with Anna. Says none of it was him, that he never would have gone to meet Anna without telling us." Mitch added with obvious skepticism. "Says he now has Curt completely under control."

"Unlikely," Allan said, agreeing with Mitch for once. "You sure you are okay with me sending Drake on that errand?"

Mitch was angry about it, but wasn't going to fall into the trap. "That was your call to make. I was still en route back from France when The Kid took off, so you had to get a tail on him." Mitch didn't add that it would have been easy for him to divert to the Twin Cities and take over surveillance from Drake. But there was nepotism at play here.

"Any word from the French?" Mitch asked, turning the tables on his boss.

"Not much. We wound them up pretty good. They never expected the kind of resistance they got at the chateau from four escaped Naturals. Obviously they wasted no time in throwing you out of the country. We were lucky enough to negotiate Grady's release with you. A French faction wanted to hold him and try him on their soil, but the CIA stepped in and insisted the espionage charges they were preparing to bring against him warranted extradition. Needless to say, it's all been a little heated."

"What we do know is that Joe and his accomplices are still at large—and that's about all they will tell us. That could be a lie. Really no way to know until tensions get smoothed over, or we get a man on the ground there."

"So now what?" Mitch asked, uncertain of his next move.

"We need to interrogate Anna and Grady, but we need to wait until later today. I have another delegation coming through for a tour . . . a suggestion from the top, The Head of National Security, to share more of our success with a greater audience . . . and it appears critical I get their continued buy-in," Allan replied.

"Does that mean what I think it means?" Mitch asked cautiously, knowing the answer could be a sore spot for Allan.

Allan eyed Mitch, wondering if he should tell him, and in the end he decided there was no harm. "Yes. It's time the twins were shared with our sponsors. With everything that has gone on over the last month, Northwoods needs to make some amends. Our government and the power elite have been drawn in too close for their own comfort—having to deal with renewed French tensions and Tom and Kyle's situation. We need a win to get back on their good side. The best way to do that is to demonstrate exponential progress with a new strain of seeds."

Mitch didn't need to remind Allan how much that would upset his daughter Melody. So he didn't. He knew the first rule of survival was to never purposely piss off your boss. He'd done enough of that over the last few weeks.

As they stood silently by the lake, weighing their next moves, from somewhere deep in the mists came the lone loon's wavering call, and both men reflexively cringed.

CHAPTER 109

AIR FORCE ONE

The President of the United States sat in a spacious debriefing room near the mid-section of Air Force One. The room was designed to accommodate a table of twenty or more—although at the moment it only held four. Of the three men who sat across from the president, two appeared anxious and on edge, while the other smiled warmly.

The president leaned in, folding her hands as she eyed each of the men before her, until her gaze fell on the only man in the room who looked comfortable.

"It's good to see you again, Brian," the President offered, her eyes belying a certain twinkling fondness that the other two men were too distracted to notice.

"Good to see you again . . . Elizabeth," the man replied, before realizing his impropriety and quickly adding, ". . . Madam President."

It was this slip that Tom and Kyle picked up on, and each shot an awkward glance at Kyle's boss. Both men had been surprised when they had been roused from their sleep shortly after midnight, mere hours before the armed assault on Kyle's home. The President's secret service detail had whisked them away in stealth to the Minneapolis-St. Paul International Airport where they were held in the bowels of the facility for several hours.

At about 5:30 a.m. they were reunited with Kyle's superior, Brian, before being led down a series of winding corridors, out onto the tarmac, and into a black limo. Through the early morning darkness, the car sped the trio to what felt like the farthest reaches of the airfield and a large military hangar, where a generic white Boeing 787, with no distinguishing markings sat waiting for their arrival.

Once there, the three men were immediately ushered onto the plane, shown to their seats and the plane quickly taxied away, taking off just before the break of dawn. It wasn't until they were a good half hour into their flight, and shown to the room they were in now, that they even realized they were on a top-secret version of Air Force One for a private tête-à-tête with the President. It was the plane used when she didn't want to make a big show to the press or public over her travels or activities.

"By the look on your companions' faces you haven't told them how we know each other?" The President said with mild surprise.

"No Madame President," Brian said briskly.

"Cut it, Brian," the President scolded. "You know you've always earned the privilege to address me by my given name."

"Yes, Elizabeth," Brian replied out of respect.

"Let's get a few things out of the way, before we get down to the real business at hand," The President said, turning toward Kyle and Tom. "Brian and I go way back, about fifteen years now, to when I was governor of Wisconsin. He was part of my security detail back then, and helped me through some difficult times. I'm not certain if you know the history, but when I was running for governor, it became known that my husband of ten years was an abusive man, whom I left shortly before I entered the race. That was one of the most difficult times in my life, but it built me into the woman who eventually would be ready for this office—of course, this is all public knowledge."

Brian shifted uncomfortably in his seat, wondering how much detail the President would go into, but he let her continue.

"Anyway, the fact that the story went public was not of my doing. It was so-called dirt that the incumbent had dug up on me. It turned out the information only served to solidify my base, and drew a significant contingent of the female vote from my opponent. The bastard thought, just like my ex, that I was weak and wouldn't fight. Well, I learned to fight."

Anyway, what I'm going to tell you next only a handful of my closest confidants know, and if it ever comes out, I will know exactly who to come down on. And I can come down hard. Am I clear?"

Kyle and Tom nodded respectfully, uncertain where this was going, but whatever was going on was obviously out of their control.

"As the polls began to swing my way, the incumbent governor, instead of backing off the story, dug deeper, floating an uncorroborated story that I was having an affair with one of my security staff, and the real reason I left my husband. He also tried to reverse-engineer the story so it looked like I had leaked the story of my husband's abuse as a politically viable cover to leaving my husband."

The President paused and looked to Brian to gauge his comfort level before continuing. Seeing no objection she went on. "This second angle of the story never took, as the press was already down on the current governor for the previous rounds of mud-slinging, and no concrete facts ever surfaced to support his claims. Again, my base dug in deeper and the governor lost even more of his fringe and some of his base to me. In the last two months of the race, I overcame a ten-percent margin in the polls and unseated the governor in narrow vote. I held that office until I took this one."

Finally Brian felt like he should step in, "You don't have to say anymore, Elizabeth. I think they both get the picture."

Elizabeth raised her hand to Brian, and offered a reassuring smile. "The reason I'm telling you both this is that enough of the story is already public record. And if I had not been straight with each of you . . . well you might have put two and two together and made your own connections and assumptions about Brian and me. Some of those assumptions might have been wrong or misinterpreted. But what you must know is that during that time in my life, after I had left my husband, I found a friend and confidant that I needed to help get me through that difficult period."

Again, Brian wanted to interrupt, to protect Elizabeth, but he bit his tongue—she had gotten this far on her honesty and integrity and she obviously felt she needed to be straight about their relationship.

Elizabeth smiled at Brian, sensing what we wanted to do for her, and admired him for letting her have her say. "That man was the utmost gentleman and I care for him dearly. My only regret was that when the story broke, we agreed it was in both of our career interests and aspirations to part ways."

Both Kyle and Tom realized that what the President was saying was more for Brian's sake then theirs, and each took a moment to look down at the magnificent mahogany table to allow whatever fleeting moment the President and her ex-lover wished to share.

"So where are we headed?" Brian asked, hoping to change the subject and get down to the business at hand.

"That all depends on what you all have to tell me," the President added, turning to face Tom and Kyle. "Brian has filled me in a little on the story you both have to share, and the only thing that I will tell you before you begin is that today was the first I had heard of Northwoods and some of the events surrounding it."

Kyle's eyes shot upward at that instant, looking directly at the President as she held his gaze. He couldn't tell for certain, but he thought she was telling the truth, yet curiosity made him prod. "You mean to say that you have no knowledge at all?"

The President sighed, and sat back into her leather wing chair, gauging the appropriate response. "Let's just say, I have knowledge of certain programs that the United States has interest in, and that some of those programs included studies of brain function, capacity and telepathy, including some research into predictable futures. So that is not news to me. Northwoods and their alleged methodology was most certainly off my radar until now."

Tom, starting to regain his comfort level, found his voice. "How can that be?"

Kyle flinched at the directness of the question, but the President smiled and leaned back in again, spreading her hands in a wide gesture.

463

"This is a big country, Tom. There are innumerable problems to solve, civil needs to address, foreign affairs to tend to, threats to investigate, and yes, top-secret initiatives. There is absolutely no way I can have line of sight to it all, unless I am briefed on it."

Tom sunk in his chair. Normally he allowed little to faze him—it was an essential quality he needed in his line of work. But somehow this woman in her neatly pressed navy blazer, dyed blonde hair and piercing blue eyes had him a little off balance.

"Unfortunately, my predecessor was a little loose and free with civil liberties, and during his tenure the CIA ran unchecked, the FBI was emboldened, and from what I understand, innumerable black-ops initiatives were implemented with no overtly visible or tangible threads back into our government. These operations were designed to be self-sustaining, with minimal oversight and government involvement. All that was given to them was a directive, a set of objectives, and various milestones that had to be met. Each operation is different, but most are given a single secretive thread, or contact back into a power center such as the CIA, State Department, or other covert agencies you'll never hear of but that do exist. These connections offered access to numerous slush funds that are prevalent throughout our wonderful government, introduced in virtually every non-descript bill that gets passed these days."

Tom thought he saw a solution in the logic and tried to point it out. "If there is a thread back, and you've discovered a few already, isn't it possible to follow those threads back to the source—perhaps a holdover from the prior administration—and shut off the flow at the source?

The President laughed, and through this gesture she seemed to be just another person on the other side of the table, instead of the most powerful woman in the world. "I love your optimism, Tom. But as an ex-thief," she added, with pointed emphasis displaying her knowledge, "you should know better about how deep and prevalent corruption can be. There is no one source that links all black or covert operations. In fact there are some that still continue to operate autonomously all the way back from the Kennedy administration. And before you start thinking I'm an innocent in all of this, I have, in fact, initiated several of my own."

Kyle smiled at this. He knew enough about the way government worked to know that no matter how noble and righteous a candidate for any position in the federal government might be, eventually you fall in line with the way the system operates and use it to advance your public or private agenda. Otherwise you get trampled on and stabbed in the back without ever accomplishing anything you ever set out to do. It was the way of the world, and the general public could not even begin to fathom the complexities at play or the grand façade that the three branches of their government provided for the true inner workings beyond.

"So where does that leave us, and more importantly what about my friend Grady who may be locked up in this government fed human test laboratory?" Tom asked with a spite and cynicism he didn't regret one bit.

"Wait right there," Brian interjected, not exactly appreciating the tone with which he was addressing the Commander In Chief. But the President shot him a glance that said it was okay, she was ready for it.

"I didn't say I couldn't or wouldn't help. But I need to hear it from you and Kyle, what you know and what you've heard. Brian has obviously filled me in as best he could, but every detail is important in terms of what our options and avenues might be . . . or even whether I feel it is in the nation's best interest to intervene."

Tom wished Anna were here now. She would have been so much better prepared to debrief the President, to impassion her to action. "Have you at least had a chance to look over Grady's file?"

The President nodded, adding a final thought to the discussion. "Before you begin I want to impress something upon both of you," indicating Tom and Kyle. "Shortly after my secret service detail removed you in the middle of the night, I was made aware of another group that came to call on Mr. Brady's home. Apparently they shot up the beds where you'd both been sleeping."

A look of fear shot through Tom's eyes, but the President reassured him. "Molly is fine. My men removed her shortly after they ushered you out."

"Anyway," the President continued, "you've uncovered something that people believe is worth killing you over. From what I understand, if Northwoods is a black-ops program, they are drawing upon more government resources and support to cover their tracks. That leads me to believe there is significant harm that could be done to the reputation of the United States, or our security as a nation. Possibly both."

"So yes, in answer to your question, I have skimmed the file and understand the stakes better than you might think. I encourage you to leave out no pertinent detail that might have bearing on my decision."

"Then let's start at the beginning," Tom said with resignation.

CHAPTER 110

SAVING FACE

"Notice the two boys," Allan directed his entourage of four individuals. The group consisted of a powerful businessman with no official government ties, though he was wealthy enough to buy and wield power amidst the highest political circles. He was part of the power elite, the mechanism behind the government that drove policy and agenda. Also in attendance was a high-ranking member of the State Department—technically a diplomatic agency—but more accurately a front for espionage and the trafficking of secrets. There was also the Science and Technology Undersecretary from the Department of Homeland Security, and finally the Deputy Director of National Intelligence.

Their roles and reasons for being here were diverse. The businessman had been at Northwoods often. This was his baby: he had initially bankrolled Allan's early research with his vast wealth and resources. Once he and Allan had established enough influence and support in sympathetic government circles, Northwoods was able to tap into slush funds and lean on shadow organizations erected to prop up their ongoing operations.

On the other hand, the State Department representative in attendance technically did not exist—at least her job didn't appear in any public record. Her role was to organize the United State's diplomatic assets in an effort to gather secrets from foreign countries and advance

467

Northwood's cause. This involved everything from the buying of secrets from disenchanted nationals to outright infiltration and espionage across the globe. These acts were perpetrated, not only against unfriendly governments, but also the governments and businesses of the United State's own allies. This was her third trip to Northwoods.

The Undersecretary was relatively new to the group. He had been brought on in the last five years as an advisor to Northwoods on some of the advancements in understanding brain chemistry and the outright manipulation of it, as well as helping in matters of bio-engineering. He brought in experts in the field as needed and had worked closely with the late Dr. Benjamin Olson.

Finally, the Deputy Director was here for one reason: to leverage the vast intelligence assets and networks available to his office, as needed. He was here to keep Northwoods secure and off all political and public maps, while keeping the heads of such agencies as the CIA, the FBI and the NSA out of their business. He had been instated to his role by the director himself, though even the director was kept intentionally in the dark on the full operations of Northwoods.

This isolationist method was designed to limit collateral damage in the event of the unthinkable, and it was understood and embraced by every member of this Black Ops leadership team. While the government was involved, and a beneficiary of the work Northwoods did, it was essential that it be kept at arms length for two important reasons. One, so no one who might misunderstand Northwoods' work could build a power base against it to topple it. And two, to provide plausible deniability for the agencies that employed each representative should Northwoods' secrets ever be exposed. If Northwoods folded, there were layers of people set up to take the fall, acting like built-in firewalls to ensure the core United States powerbase never be shaken.

"This is a game that both like to play." Allan continued, referring to the boys. "They don't know what they are doing, or how they are doing it, only that to them it is as natural as breathing is to you or me."

The group stared through the observation glass. The twins had been brought down to the sub-level for this show, to avoid any unnecessary interruptions. Ethan sat cross-legged, holding a ball out in front of him. This time it almost looked like he was going to throw it to his brother. But suddenly it vanished, and his brother Owen now sat holding the ball. He held it over his head, laughing before the ball flashed back to Ethan again.

Allan watched as the entourage began to murmur among themselves. It wasn't often one got an audience like this, with representatives from deep within the secret underbelly of the government. He guessed it was even more rare that anything truly shocked any of these individuals—as they clearly were now.

He let it play out a little longer before explaining. "You are watching the next generation of Naturals. We can't be one-hundred percent certain, but we believe that these boys are not only peering into alternate parallel universes, but are exhibiting some level of control over the momentary overlap of those universes."

"I'm not certain I follow," the businessman said, impressed by the trick, but wanting to get to the meat of it . . . to know how he could use it for future gain. "What does that have to do with a ball that seems to appear and disappear?"

Dr. Hauser chose his words carefully. Even though the two had a civil history together he did not, in any way, want to talk down to or offend a man of such power. This was a man who could make him disappear in an instant, or raise him up to a position of such power and significance he alone could alter the course of the country for the next hundred years.

"Like the other Naturals you all have seen before," Allan said, addressing the entire group, "these children possess what we believe is the ability to look into convergent, divergent and parallel universes. The more like the universe we are experiencing now, the more likely the twins could pick up on it. What is interesting here is that both twins may be peering into different universes. In one universe Ethan has the ball, and in the other Owen has it. For the first time ever, we are experiencing Naturals who seem to be able to exert some level of control and influence over these alternate universes in the brief moments they overlap."

"Are you saying that these children are altering reality?" the woman from the State Department asked incredulously.

Dr. Hauser again tried to keep his explanation simple, and not in the least bit condescending. "Perhaps. What is hard to tell is whether they are really changing anything or simply acting as windows for us, allowing you and me to see what already exists—two distinct, but very similar universes."

"We could surmise that they are actually changing the physical practicalities of the current universe and altering the outcome. In this case, which child actually possesses the ball? On the other hand we could simply be observing the convergence, coming together of, or divergence, splitting apart of, of two universes. If we believe this, then the universes are still separate, and nothing has actually changed in either. We're just seeing them laid over one another like transparent pieces of film."

"Impressive," said the Undersecretary, understanding and perhaps imagining the immense possibilities of either scenario to his own world.

Allan was just about to build on the individual's awe, when one of his assistants slipped through an unseen door in the black wall of the observation deck.

"Excuse me, please," Allan said, leaving their side momentarily to brush off the intrusion. He'd left very strict instructions that he was absolutely not to be disturbed for any reason.

Before he could lay into his attractive assistant, she whispered three words that made him rethink his position. "It's your daughter."

"Oh, Christ. Don't tell me," Allan said. "She knows."

Allan's assistant simply nodded her head. "I wouldn't have interrupted you sir, but she is, for lack of a better description, freaking out. I actually had to have her restrained in your office to prevent her from interrupting you here."

Allan nodded grimly. "Let me move things along here, and I'll be right up."

His assistant excused herself, leaving the room the same way she had entered. Allan turned to his guests, the stress on his face now replaced with a broad, but fake smile. "That about concludes today's briefing. I hope you have found the work we are doing here to be of immense value to the future of our great country. I have several matters to deal with."

The entourage nodded, looking back at the two boys playing ball. Each of them now thinking of more and more frightening ways to harness and exploit what they were seeing. Ways in which each might entrench or even alter the complex geopolitical landscape surrounding the balance of global power. What sat before them was the next nuclear arms race.

CHAPTER 111

FATHER AND DAUGHTER

"**G**o to hell!" Melody yelled at her father as he entered his office.

"How in the hell did you find out?" Allan roared, facing his daughter.

"Oh Dad, cut the crap right now. You know damn well that you can't keep something like this from me. What did you think I'd do when I found out? Run to you and say go right ahead and use my own kids—your own fucking grandkids—as guinea pigs?

"This is different, Melody . . . honey. It's not going to be like the other Naturals. I promise."

Melody picked up a glass vase from the table beside her, tossed out the flowers onto her dad's prized tapestry rug and flung it at him. "Don't you lie to me! Don't even . . ." she shouted as the vase burst into shards at her father's feet.

Allan jumped as some of the glass fragments cut into his pant legs. "I'll admit it. I made mistakes. You of all people know that. But honey, I can't change those mistakes. And you don't understand the kind of people we are dealing with here. They won't tolerate mistakes—especially ones that result in loose ends. The stakes are too damn high."

"So is that your plan. Now that you've got Mary Jane, Anna, Curt and Grady all under one roof, you can just wipe the slate clean? Erase them all?"

"Melody," her father said, pleading now, trying to get her to understand. "This is not to protect me. This is to protect the future of our country. This is the next big global power struggle. Information is power. And whoever controls that information controls the future. If we don't do it someone like the French or the Chinese will. And whoever perfects this next new weapon of future knowledge will control the global markets and vault to the lead in the race to be the next superpower."

"Save your patriotic speeches for your visiting dignitaries and government bureaucrats. I've always had a blind spot for you, Dad. Always wanted to believe that you were an innocent, pulled along in a stream that you realized too late was a raging canyon river. But I now have little doubt that you'd sell me and my kids out to the highest bidder."

Allan flinched at his daughter's words, and for a moment a seed of doubt broke the surface of his resolve, but he quickly buried it. He buried it deep under his rising anger, telling himself that she was completely wrong. That he was caught up in the raging waters of a flash flood with no way out but to try to ride it out to the end. So he said the one thing, through firmly clenched teeth, that he regretted immediately. "I'm certain the boy's father would be okay with it, why can't you be?"

Melody exploded on her father. "Curt would never have agreed to this, even in the midst of his drug issues. He's the man I loved . . . not that monster you helped foster inside of him."

"But he never loved you, did he?" Melody's father spat back, each of them no longer trying to convince either of their case, but only to hurt the other more severely with their words.

"Oh, and in your twisted world that makes perfect sense. Because Curt loves Anna, that means I should hate him and Anna. In your mind, I should wish for the woman Curt loves to be dead, so that I could have him to myself. Really? It doesn't work that way. You of all people should know that."

"What the hell does that mean?" her dad spat back, already knowing where Melody was headed.

"Mom, Dad! Mom! You know, Laura . . . your wife . . . the one you drove to her death because you couldn't keep your hands off of Becky Slater."

Allan looked at his daughter aghast. "Don't you even go there!"

"Oh, I will, Dad. Because you loved Becky, and you couldn't stop loving her even after you fathered that horrible excuse for a human being, Drake. Or even after mom found out so many years later. You remember! The night she left you in an emotional rage and wrapped her car around that telephone pole."

"I didn't know you knew," Allan said, sinking down into his leather couch, placing his head into his hands.

Melody stood watching him, her arms crossed in defiance across her chest. "You always underestimate me, or overestimate yourself. Try as you may you can't shut me out. But I guess I really didn't know everything for certain until you confirmed it now."

She hoped she was breaking him. Even though he was a monster, he was her dad, and she held out hope she could change him. It was what she had tried to do with Curt as well. It was what she looked for in men . . . someone she could fix.

"Why do you stay with me, Melody? Why did you agree to leave the twins here?" Allan asked. The voice was not one of sorrow, but utter frustration.

It was then that Melody knew if she hadn't broken him by now, she never would. And for the first time in her life she allowed herself to believe someone, even her father, to be a lost cause.

"Because I was eighteen and pregnant Dad—pregnant with twins of one of your Naturals. I had no place to go! Mom had just died. And I still thought I loved you. And of all things I needed you. I don't know if you remember but the years before mom died you were different. You treated the Naturals well. So I stayed, and agreed to your stupid plan—to raise the children and find out if they were Naturals. Then things became even more complicated when we found out some of the things they could do. Where was I to take two boys who even their own grandfather could not resist exploiting? At least I thought I had some control over it here."

"You treat me like a monster," Allan said ruefully. "But you should look into the mirror. You are not without sin. I know exactly what you did to Mary Jane. We are not so different, you and I."

Melody sighed, and turned to find her way out. When she got to the door she turned to her father, who simply watched her through a fierce, steady gaze. It was his fighting look. She had seen it many times when she was younger and he'd argue with her mother. This was the first time she could recall him using it on her. "You really don't know, me do you Dad? Because if you did, you would never, ever compare what, or why, I did what I did to Mary Jane with any of the things you have done. There was a higher reason." Melody insisted.

"And Melody, what you don't realize is that we are more alike than you think. If you knew your dad better, you'd understand I had a higher reason for everything I have done here."

And with that, Melody left the room. It was over. She'd lost the battle for her dad. It was time she tried to wake up Mary Jane and pay a visit to Anna. The final sequence of events needed to be set in motion.

CHAPTER 112

ANNA'S VISITOR

A light shuffle near the heavy metal door grabbed Anna's attention, and she looked up from her cot to see a shadow fall across the door. She sat up and curled her knees up to her chest. Her clothes had been taken, and she had been given a medical gown to wear and she pulled the hem in around her ankles, waiting for whomever it was to enter. *Was this it? Were they coming for her now?*

In her brief time in her cell, she had been left in relative isolation. Food had been brought for her on two occasions, but she did not eat fearing it might be drugged. A couple times someone had come and taken her vitals, which only reaffirmed her belief that the food might be drugged, but nobody complained when they returned to carry away the untouched tray.

While she waited for whatever was to come, she hoped her earlier visions might be true—those horrible visions that included her and Grady together again in The Room. She found it ironic that what she had dreaded over the course of the last few days was now what she desperately wished for. For it would mean Grady was alive.

A few times she tried to close her eyes and shut out the harsh light from the metal-caged light bulb directly above her bed. She'd tried to reach out to him . . . to feel him . . . and a few times she got a vague sense of his smell, a brief flicker of his grim hard face, or a silky sense of his hand brushing across the hairs on her arm, but these she attributed to more wish than evidence of his survival. She did the same trying to think of Mary Jane, and she received the same strange peaceful and restful feeling she'd gotten before, but little else.

The door to her room began to open slowly. It seemed almost as if someone were trying to enter quietly without notice. A moment later, Melody stuck her head around the door as she entered the room.

For some reason tears began to well in both women's eyes, and Melody quickly ushered the heavy door shut behind her and raced to Anna's side. The two women embraced, old childhood friends who still shared a common bond no matter how distant they had become, or been forced to become, over the last five years.

"I'm so sorry," Anna said to Melody as they separated.

Melody's heart broke. "Why the hell are you sorry?" she asked with bittersweet disbelief.

"Because you risked everything with your dad to help us escape, and I've squandered that freedom, and your sacrifice, by getting myself caught."

Melody patted Anna's arm reassuringly. "You haven't squandered anything. And if you are worried about my relationship with my father, you shouldn't. He's been nothing but brutal to you and your friends, and for the first time in my life I now realize he has been just as vile to me."

Anna reached out and held Melody's hand and for a moment she felt an odd happy feeling come over her.

Melody simply looked back at her, understanding what she was experiencing. It was time for her to stop hiding. It was time for her to face reality and truly face down her father. She knew deep down she would need Anna's help and trust to do it. It was why she was here, a place she knew she would be all along.

CHAPTER 113

STOKING THE FIRE

Allan stormed down the Natural's residential corridor on sub-level one to The Kid's room, fresh off of his argument with Melody. It was time to put an end to it all. Mitch would certainly be happy about that. It was what he had been begging him to do this morning out by the lake. The usefulness of Grady, Anna, Mary Jane and even The Kid were coming to an end. One last task and he'd be done once and for all with that phase in Northwood's history. It was time to enter a new era. It was time to move past his daughter, and the memory of her mother that she brought back to him every time he saw her.

For too long he had hidden his feelings for Becky Slater. And for what—for a daughter who didn't understand him and never would? He'd also ignored his other flesh and blood, Drake, simply for the sake of his half sister's feelings and the memory of her mother. He'd just begun to rectify that.

"They're part of my family too, goddamn it," he swore under his breath as he walked along.

He was fueling his anger, throwing log after log of bile, bitterness and self-righteousness on top of the flames. He'd need it for what was to come next. When he got to The Kid's door he unlocked it, and kicked the door open for good measure.

The Kid sat looking at him from a chair, near a small one-person table in the corner—almost as if he was waiting for him. His curly red hair hung down into his eyes, the blue ballcap he wore so often, crushed and twisted between his hands in a vise-like grip.

Allan recognized the body language, realizing the turmoil going on deep inside him. This is the way The Kid looked when he needed a fix. He guessed somewhere in the deep recesses of The Kid's mind, Curt was waging a massive battle to come forward. Without the drugs, The Kid wasn't nearly as strong as he'd like others to think he was. The drugs helped keep Curt down.

Allan reached inside his white lab coat, his hand brushing the gun holster beneath, and he saw the The Kid's eyes widen. Immediately following his argument with Melody, Allan had indeed paused in front of his open desk drawer, considering the gun that lay there . . . weighing the deaths he could orchestrate if he so chose. "Pick it up," he'd told himself, it would be easy. Instead, the doctor's hand found a small bottle in one of his inside pockets. This is what The Kid was dying for, and Allan pulled it out and tossed it to him. For now, the gun had been left in his office, Allan deciding to leave the firepower to Drake and Mitch.

The Kid grabbed the white bottle out of the air, fumbling awkwardly with the cap. He'd already started to develop the shakes, and the tremors in his hands made even the simplest tasks difficult. Finally The Kid got the top off, extracted two pills and tossed them back, dry-swallowing them. For a moment his eyes rolled back into his head and he sagged back into the chair.

Allan watched dispassionately, letting this scenario he'd seen so many times over the years play out. When he finally sensed that The Kid's involuntary twitches and muscle contractions were subsiding, his mind unthawing from the deep-freeze of withdrawal, he spoke.

"I'm going to need you in the observation room in a half hour. This time don't screw with me. You're going to help us read Anna and Grady—and then if you're good, I'll let you kill one of them. Whichever one you want."

The Kid's head just lolled back, reveling in the moment as the drugs began coursing through his blood stream. Right now he'd do anything for the drugs.

CHAPTER 114

THE FIFTH SEED

In a private room, off one of the main corridors on the third level of Northwoods, the true Fifth Seed took a private moment. A hand reached out to a small plastic bottle on the marbled bathroom vanity and removed the top and gently tapped out three little red pills. They danced wildly upon the washbasin's surface before coming to rest.

Two eyes viewed the pills with distaste. There was a moment's pause, an instant of uncertainty before the hand set down the bottle and scooped up the tablets. Palming them, they were quickly tossed back, chased with water from a crystal tumbler that rested nearby.

These little red pills were a necessary evil, rarely used . . . but essential to what was to be accomplished in the next hour or so. The Fifth Seed's skills were indeed stronger than any of the other four Seeds. It was the reality behind the myth, kept secret by an ability to hide in plain sight. No one ever realized that when they looked into those eyes there was a freak of nature behind them. Not even the Naturals themselves could sense the raw power raging just beneath the surface. The Fifth Seed relished the anonymity. Over the years, only one knew the identity of The Fifth Seed, and that individual would never tell.

Of all the seeds, the Fifth had rarest visions, but when they did come they were almost never wrong. Then there was the ability to transfer emotions, memories or visions with a simple touch. But perhaps most frightening of all was The Fifth Seed's ability to rip open another's mind, lay it completely bare, and expose the deepest buried secrets within. It created an uncanny ability to know others and use it against them.

But the process could have horrifying effects on the individual whose mind was laid bare. The human mind had a natural ability to erect walls against itself, rationalize actions and choices, and bury the most painful moments and memories of an individual, and that individual's life, into small compartments . . . never be opened again. The Fifth Seed could open those compartments and read it all. That same process allowed the other person to see all of their life's wretched moments in an excruciating blur. That compounded effect, of releasing what was never supposed to be released in one massive flood, could drive someone whose mind was laid bare to the brink. This was the most horrifying of any of the Natural's talents.

The Fifth Seed also had one more talent. Underdeveloped though it may be, the drugs would help counteract that. Today The Fifth Seed would have to call upon every one of these talents—and once and for all, let everyone know the true identity of fear itself.

CHAPTER 115

NEMESIS

G rady lay handcuffed on the floor of a small eight-foot square holding cell. The floor was cold concrete, and the walls were more of the same. Like many of the other rooms in Northwoods, this room had a heavy, metal door to seal people in—but no window. Only a tiny peephole set into the door allowed outsiders to look in, preventing insiders from seeing out.

Once Grady's so-called doctors had decided that his gunshot wound was not life threatening, the IVs had been torn from his arms, patches monitoring vitals had been ripped off his skin and his bed had been taken away. He was handcuffed to a gurney and wheeled blindfolded to this room. Several times he had been injected roughly in the arm. He guessed it was not medical related, as the drugs often made him extremely drowsy and his limbs like putty—probably so that he couldn't resist.

In his lucid time in this cold, gray cell, Grady was visited by disturbing visions of the Naturals, particularly Anna, being thrown here for solitary confinement whenever they chose not to cooperate. They weren't visions like a Natural might have, rather they were horrific figments of his imagination—and whether accurate or not, they only served to fuel is anger.

No food had been provided to him, but occasionally a guard would come and drop a metal cup of water in the corner and leave. He drank it, assuming if Northwoods wanted to pump any more drugs into him, they'd just prick another vein. But the task of getting the water into his mouth was a challenge with his arms secured behind his back. After some scuffling across the floor he'd been able to grab the cup in his teeth and tilt his head back enough to splash the contents across and into his mouth. It wasn't much, and more water hit the floor than his stomach, but he wanted to keep his strength up for whatever was to come next.

To that end, he needed to start forming some sort of a plan. He had few hopes of getting out of this modern-day dungeon, much less beyond the fortress he assumed was Northwoods, but he had to try. Since he had been taken from Chinon, he had been given no word of Anna or the others' fate. This surprised him a little, as he thought that Northwoods would use that against him in a psychological battle for his spirit, by telling him that Anna was dead—whether it was true or not.

In fact, it seemed no one of significance had handled him since he had been here. Not the man that had become his nemesis, Mitch—and not man he knew to run the place, Dr. Allan Hauser. He was confident that hour would come; otherwise they would have found a quiet way to dispose of him already. The only reason he was alive right now was because they needed him for something: information. Grady was going to make it hard to get.

His plan for escape was simple. There were no magic tricks up his sleeve. His goal: try to take down the next person who walked through the door, and hope they had a gun. If he could get a gun, anything beyond that door was possible, though not necessarily probable.

The peephole was the problem. No one would enter if they saw him up on his feet waiting to ambush them as they came through. So he had to be down on the floor. He also had to get his hands out in front of him. It took some work, stretching his cuffs until they bit deep into the sides of his wrists, drawing blood, but he was able to lower his hands far enough to get them below his butt. He nearly had to dislocate his shoulders to do so and in the process, severely aggravated his gunshot wound. He could feel the flesh re-tearing where it had only recently begun to mend, new blood flowing once again beneath the medical dressing.

With his hands low, resting at the bend in his knees, he was able to slip them down below his feet and out in front of his body. He lay back down on the cold concrete, positioning his body in a way he thought only the lower part of his body could be seen through the eye in the door. He needed whoever might be checking on him to see and believe he was still incapacitated on the floor. Now he waited.

It seemed to take forever before he heard someone working the lock in the door. Assuming whoever was entering had already checked the peephole, Grady didn't waste a second. Rolling to his stomach, he pressed his hands into the floor, as if doing a push up, bringing his knees underneath him. Springing to his feet he positioned his body near the hinges of the door, as it swung inward.

From the other side, a body moved into the dimly lit space. Without hesitating, Grady threw his entire weight at him, keeping his cuffed hands high, using them like a metal-enhanced club and swinging them down across the person's head with a violent blow. The hit staggered the man, and Grady pressed him forward, using his body weight like a plough, forcing the man up against the wall, where his head collided hard with the concrete wall. Grady watched him crumple to the ground.

He'd barely had time to appreciate his small victory, when Grady sensed movement behind him. Whipping around, he prepared for an attack, but the man just stood there pointing a gun at his head. He didn't recognize the face, but the person Grady had attacked . . . the one who was now picking himself up off the ground was certainly familiar.

"Good to see you, too," Mitch said with heavily laced sarcasm.

Grady turned away from the gunman to face Mitch again, which would have been his fatal mistake, had Mitch not saved him.

"Hold on," he said to the guard holding the gun. "Don't shoot him just yet. The doctor would like to see him." But as the words evaporated from Mitch's mouth he snapped a lightning-quick roundhouse, throwing his foot into Grady's jaw.

Staggered by the blow, Grady regained his balance, refusing to drop. He didn't want to give Mitch the satisfaction. Though his jaw screamed out in agony and his shoulder seared in pain, Grady returned glare for glare with Mitch, a kind of mutual respect and shared hatred.

"Lets go see the doctor," Grady said.

But Mitch wasn't quite done with taking out his frustrations.

CHAPTER 116

FORETOLD

Anna found herself crouched on hands and knees as a foot violently kicked up from out of nowhere, grazing her cheek. She fell back, laying face up, staring at an unblemished white ceiling raised over white padded walls.

Gently she touched her face where the foot had landed, tracing her fingers over what she guessed was a split lip. Producing her hand in front of her face, her fingers returned sticky with new blood. Anna winced as the salty-tasting liquid seeped slowly into her mouth as the cut bled out.

It was happening. Her vision had come true. Had nothing she had done over the last several days done anything to alter it?

She looked up at her attacker: Drake, the one who had brought her here on the Doctor's orders. His eyes were full of hatred, and his body was tensed as though he wanted to deliver another kick into her ribs, but he held back, knowing he wouldn't be in his father's good graces if he beat up on Anna too much.

"That's for dumping me, bitch," he spat before turning and leaving her alone in the room.

Hearing the door close, Anna gathered herself and sat up, gazing at the walls of pure white. Yes, she was in the room, and facing that awful door, the one padded in tufted quilts of fabric-covered foam. The same little window, crisscrossed with wire. And there was the long expanse of mirrored glass along one side—the one where people observed the agonies the Naturals had been put through.

She lay there, hoping it was all a bad dream, but anxious to see Grady. She knew he'd come. She knew, no matter what, she'd have at least one last chance in this lifetime to look into his eyes, and maybe even feel his touch. Those thoughts carried her through the solitary moments of the next few minutes until the door opened again and two orderlies entered. They grabbed her off the floor by each arm and roughly forced her into a white dentist-style chair that blended into the center of the room. Its angle could be rotated, but it was currently fixed so that she faced the mirrored wall. They strapped her in, but she chose not to struggle—not out of defeat, but because she believed she might need every ounce of strength she had to weather the ordeal to come. The orderlies went about their task of setting up an IV and Anna's eyes gazed up angrily at the clear bag that dripped drugs in a steady trickle into her veins.

She didn't try to fight off the narcotics; instead she let them gradually consume her, envelope her completely, ever so slowly relaxing her muscles as her senses began to heighten. The scent of something like almonds and horrible body odor stung her nose, her fingertips felt as if they were on fire, and the light within the room scorched her eyes. Oddly, her anticipation began to heighten for she knew exactly what was next.

The door opened and her heart leapt before she even saw Grady. Mitch wheeled him into the room on a gurney, securely strapped down to its metal frame. Behind him came Drake and two other armed guards including one Anna knew all too well . . . Gabe. A deep sorrow filled her heart, her mind flashing back to days when the same man had been a part of something that was never so sinister. He was trapped in the quicksand, where something that once looked so solid gradually sucked you in against your will until you could no longer hold your head high, above the murk.

Anna turned her attention back to Grady, seeing his mouth had been gagged and his body severely beaten, but his eyes were still strong. It was this that she did love about him; those strong eyes caught hers as they wheeled him by, telling her to be strong and to trust him.

Mitch seemed to be enjoying the reunion, making a mockery of it. "I see the lovebirds are back together. Do you want to get a good last look at each other?" he jeered as he tilted Grady and Anna's seats up and set them face-to-face. "What, no emotional embrace, no goodbye kiss? I'm disappointed," he laughed.

Neither Grady nor Anna took notice. They just looked at each other, Grady's eyes sending a clear message to Anna: *No fear. Stay strong. Don't let them take your dignity away.*

Anna's head swam, the drugs in her system playing with her mind and her senses, realizing how easy it was to read Grady now. She knew that was why they were together and the reason for the drugs. Northwoods was going to try to extract every last bit of information from them, and then dispose of them. Of that, there was no doubt.

"We're just waiting for the doctor," Mitch told the assembled group, as if leading a tour. On cue, the door opened and Dr. Allan Hauser strode through, dressed from head to toe in medical whites.

Seeing his captives held securely in place made him smile. "Welcome back, Anna," he said in fluent French.

Anna just turned her head away.

"No!" he shouted, still in French. "Do not look away from me. Do not look away from your lover. You and Grady will tell me everything you know, everything you've told others and whom you have told. And we won't leave this room until I know it all."

Anna ignored his commands, and she shut her eyes tightly, to Grady's eyes, to his soul, and the soulless devil she knew with near certainty was lurking behind the mirrored glass . . . The Kid. The one who had almost literally consumed Curt.

The instant her eyes closed her mind wrapped around the blow she knew was coming, and the hand that would deliver it. This time, unlike in her previous visions, it landed hard across her face, her head thrown violently to the side against the vinyl cushioning of the chair. She could hear Grady's muffled protests, and his writhing against his restraints, trying in vain to free himself, to help ward off the attack. Anna couldn't help but open her eyes just in time to see Mitch taking the gag off Grady.

"Have anything to say to us, Mr. Hamilton?" he asked evenly.

"Yeah. Go to hell," Grady spat as the gag fell away.

Without warning, Mitch raised his fist and drove it hard down into Grady's shoulder wound. Grady writhed, shouting out in mix of agony and anger. Then, just as Grady was beginning to regain his breath from the blow, Mitch did it again.

"Stop!" Anna screamed.

Allan, who was standing closest to Anna, turned at her protest. "Does that mean you'll tell us what we need to know?"

Grady shot Anna a warning with his eyes, beseeching her not to give in. He wanted her to know he could take more, but at the same time he wondered how much she could take. He spoke up before she could spill it all. "Tell us what you want to know."

Allan turned to face Grady, eyeing him as though he were nothing, realizing his first request had been delivered to Anna in French. "Fair enough. I want know what you've been telling others about Northwoods. But more importantly, I want to know who you've been telling it to."

Grady's mind instantly and uncontrollably thought of Tom, his close friend and confidant, and the files he had shared with him and the phone conversations they'd had. Little by little he'd given Tom more information.

But Anna yelled at him, "Close your mind Grady! Shut them out! If I can read you so can they."

But Allan was already smiling. "Mr. Hamilton, you'll be happy to know we already know about Tom, and his recent acquaintance, Kyle Brady."

For a moment Anna wondered how Allan had gotten the information so fast. She knew Allan wasn't a Natural. Then she saw the tiny receiver pressed into his ear canal. Its presence almost certainly meant The Kid was behind the mirrored glass, feeding on the information.

"I'll kill you," Grady yelled, his anger getting the better of him.

Mitch found a new spot to apply pain and drove the flat of his palm down hard into Grady's sternum. If the restraints weren't holding him down Grady would have doubled over. Still, he retched in pain, gasping desperately.

"I'm guessing Mitch just broke a rib or two," Allan suggested. "He could have done much worse damage if I had allowed him. But anyway, where was I? I think it was Tom and Kyle. Why don't you tell me what you've told them?"

"That's great news," Grady said, finally regaining his breath, as each rise and fall of his chest brought new stabs of pain to the mix. "You wouldn't give a damn what I might have to tell you if they were dead," Grady guessed.

"Not. For. Long." Allan said tersely, and perhaps a little too defensively, only confirming Grady's presumptions.

Now Grady knew the stakes. He was trying not only to save himself and Anna, but sharing information would now also bring harm to his best friend and ex-partner. Both were exposed.

"So Kyle was your FBI partner," Allan asked, moments after Grady thought it.

Again Anna pleaded with Grady, "Keep your mind shut. He's playing you Grady, baiting you. He's got another Natural behind the mirror trying to read us both."

For most of the time Drake had just been standing nearby, observing the interchange and enjoying the violence immensely, but he'd been feeling left out. So when Anna raised her voice again, he moved over to her side and slapped her hard across the face. "Stop interfering, bitch."

Anna took the blow, turned back to face her attacker, and spit in his face. "Look in his ear," she said to Grady.

Another blow from Drake silenced her for the moment, but Grady was already beginning to understand, that it wasn't talk the doctor was interested in. He wanted to raise the emotional stakes, chum the waters, and let the thoughts flow, and the shark in the cage would be let loose to feast on the tasty morsels of information. All of it was being fed into the doctor's ear. But Grady had no practice in shutting off his mind, so his best bet was not to get sucked into the game, to avoid thinking about anything that could betray them or their friends.

He focused on information he wanted, placed all of his mental emotion behind wanting answers. "So who the hell is behind the window?" Grady asked no one in particular.

Anna was the first to speak, understanding by intuition what Grady was trying to do. "Curt."

"What the hell?" Grady asked, completely caught off guard.

"My name is not Curt," came a disembodied voice, cutting in across a room-to-room intercom. The voice sounded angry.

Mitch shot a look at Allan that implied he was less than thrilled, but Allan tried to back him down with a calming hand gesture. They were losing control of this situation.

"It's a long story," Anna said to Grady, in a tone that was softer, and sorrowful. "He's not who or what I ever thought him to be."

"And what the hell is that supposed to mean?" The voice came across the intercom again.

Allan finally interrupted. "Kid . . . back off . . . you are not helping here."

"I'm not The Kid, either," the voice snapped back again in anger.

"Then who the hell are you?" Allan asked, he too being baited into this side conversation.

"You know damn well who I am," The Kid shouted, the speakers in the room ringing with amplified feedback. "I am The Fifth Seed. I am the one everyone talks about here at Northwoods. I am the legend . . . the one they all fear."

"You are NOT The Fifth Seed!" Allan shouted up at the ceiling. "We've been through this before."

"I was born from another, I have powers beyond all other Naturals. I am a mystery and an enigma. Who else could it be?" The Kid said, sounding both high and deranged.

Allan was near the breaking point and realized now too late that The Kid had begun to completely unravel. He was losing his mind . . .

fragmented and fractured as it was. For a moment Allan lost track of where he was and who he was with . . . and more importantly what he had set out to do here. "Shut up! I know who the Fifth Seed is and the true Fifth Seed puts every freak-of-nature talent you and the other Naturals have to shame!"

Everyone in the room stared at the doctor as spittle flew from his mouth and his body shook in furry, waiting for the voice on the intercom to return.

When the voice did return, it seemed more distant, more distracted and genuinely surprised. At the moment he didn't even appear to be talking to those in The Room, rather to himself or someone else inside the confines of the observation room.

"What the fuck are you doing here?" Then silence.

CHAPTER 117

TRUTH BE TOLD

M elody entered the observation room as The Kid was arguing with Allan. She watched silently and observed. He was breaking down and she knew what she came here to do would only encourage that road to insanity. There was no other choice.

"You are NOT the Fifth Seed!" came Allan's voice over the intercom. "I've told you that before."

Hearing this, The Kid picked up a clipboard with papers on it and flung it against the side wall. He grabbed the microphone in front of him with a fierce grip as he seethed. "I was born from another, I have powers beyond all other Naturals. And I am a mystery and an enigma. Who else could it be?"

Melody almost started forward but stopped herself, something told her to wait another moment or two. She wanted to hear the response and it came almost instantaneously.

"I know who the Fifth Seed is and the true Fifth Seed puts every freak of nature talent you and all the other Naturals have to shame!"

There it was, it was time—and she, the one who had hidden all her life, the one who had been protected and preserved for reasons of such deep-seated complexity, made the slightest of movements back in the shadows of the observation room.

Melody knew it had caught The Kid's attention even before he rounded to face her down. But he must have been expecting someone else—because the surprise and shock in his eyes was apparent.

"What the fuck are you doing here?" he said, before lifting his finger from a button on the control console, ending his transmission into the room behind the glass.

"He's right, you know," Melody said, referring to Allan's last comment. "I've come to show you the truth."

"What . . . you?" he asked with a sarcastic laugh. "What truth can you show me? I am the truth. Yeah . . . you heard me tell them," he said waving his arms to represent everyone beyond the glass, inside The Room. I'm the Fifth Seed of Northwoods. I am the face of fear."

"You're mistaken, Curt."

"Don't call me by that name!" he yelled. But his voice carried no further than the highly soundproofed walls.

"Why not, Curt?" Melody needled. "What's wrong with Curt?"

The Kid's hands reached up and grabbed the sweaty tendrils of his curly red hair and pulled on them with his fists as if trying to ward off something deep inside him. "He's weak! He's too damn weak. He could never have brought this about."

"So it's you who has accomplished this alone?"

"Yes." The Kid said without doubt. "I wrote this future."

"Anna never would have come to you in Inn Kahoots without Curt?"

"How did you know about that?"

Melody ignored the question and went on. "You would have found Trent and Joe without hitchhiking off Anna's dreams?"

"How do you know that?" The Kid asked again, fear creeping in.

"You would have produced the next line of Seeds without the ability of Curt to love?"

"What the hell are you talking about? What next Seeds?" he asked, completely confused.

"Hmmm. Interesting," she said playing him, waltzing seductively toward him. "You yourself fathered the next generation of Naturals and yet you don't even know your two five-year-old twin boys exist? And that they exist here, under the roof of this hellish torture chamber called Northwoods. Really! How all-powerful can you be?"

"You're lying! You always lied! I have no children."

"Yes you do, Curt and you have seen them. They are here at Northwoods, but if you were as powerful as you say, you would have known that. You don't even know they are Naturals more powerful than you could ever dream to be."

"But that would mean . . ." The Kid began.

Melody interrupted. "Yes, that would mean my father has been misleading you all along. Playing you and your need for his drugs and your need and desire for Anna."

"Are they hers . . . Anna's?" The Kid asked about the twins, with a hopeful joy in his eyes . . . longing for any reason to feel closer to her . . . more connected to her.

Melody looked through the glass. It looked as if they were once again resuming the interrogation of Grady and Anna. She knew she had to hurry and take her place at the glass window. There was more work to be done, and she needed to get rid of Curt.

"No," she said with a slight, awkward smile. "They are yours and mine."

"But how?" The Kid asked, not fully comprehending.

"You don't remember? You were mostly Curt then. Mostly. And you loved Anna. But I loved and admired you. At least as much as any eighteen-year-old thinks they can love someone. You and Anna had a fight . . . like I knew you would . . . like I had dreamed you would."

"What do you mean by that?" The Kid asked with skepticism.

Melody ignored the questions and continued on. "I was going off to college in a month or so, and realized it might be my last chance to let you know how I felt. So I came to you that night, wanting to comfort you, to be there for you and to tell you how I'd felt for so long. And in your grief, and my blindness, you made me believe for a few secretive weeks that it could be true. But like it always happened back then, you and Anna couldn't stay apart for long. The day I found out I was pregnant was the day you told me you and Anna had gotten back together. So I postponed college and my Dad sent me away to bear our children."

"You lie!" The Kid yelled. "You deceitful . . ."

But Melody wouldn't let him continue, couldn't bear to let the shell of the man she loved be hurtful to her. In that moment she locked eyes with The Kid—lashing out through her mind—using all of her long-hidden abilities to dive deep into the shadowy recesses of Curt and The Kid's fractured psyche, ripping both personalities up for the first time—at the same time—laying them exposed for the other to see. It was a horrifying experience, never intended to be—where two minds that were created to protect one from the other, fused into one—and it drove the newly born and fully unified mind of Curt and The Kid completely insane.

He ran shrieking from the room trying to escape something he could never escape: himself. Nor would he ever forget those hooded and haunting eyes. Eyes that had revealed to him the deepest, darkest depths of an incomprehensibly frightening soul; one with a mind so powerful it could only belong to the true Fifth Seed of Northwoods: Melody.

CHAPTER 118

CONVERGENCE

An uneasy silence hung over The Room as each person waited for the next word to come from the intercom. As each moment passed it became apparent that was the last they would hear from The Kid.

"Go check it out," Allan commanded, turning to Mitch.

"Yes, sir," Mitch replied, leaving Grady's side, striding quickly out of the room. It would take a few minutes for him to get into the observation room. For security purposes, these rooms were not directly connected, so Mitch would need to retreat to the secure wing and access the warren of administrative tunnels from there.

Allan watched the door close before turning his attention back to Grady and Anna, who had been using the distraction to try to send silent signals between each other. "It looks like we will be doing this the old fashioned way."

Allan moved closer to Grady and spun his gurney around so that Grady faced him. "What I'm going to do now is start taking fingers off your pretty friend over there. One for every answer I don't like from you. Is that understood?"

Grady nodded. He could no longer see Anna's face without craning his head around in an unnatural way, so he wasn't certain how she was handling it. But he knew the game of cat and mouse was over. Either he needed to make some kind of move with Mitch out of the room or allow Anna to be tortured to death while he looked on.

"To make this a little easier, and to be more certain you are telling me the truth, I've got something prepared." Allan said. Immediately, as if on silent command, Gabe and one of the orderlies stepped forward to assist. The orderly held out a prepped syringe full of a red viscous liquid, which Allan took in his gloved hand, eyeing it for a moment. "Do you know what this is?"

"By the looks of it and given the circumstances, I'd say a highly experimental version of a narcoanalytic," Grady guessed, his unblinking eyes set firmly on the doctor, not the drugs.

Allan smiled back at Grady. "Good answer, Mr. Hamilton. Yes, it's what one might call a truth serum. This one has been designed for use in the field against terrorists and other unwilling informants. It makes a good testing ground, particularly since it appears to have some particularly nasty side effects, including a high possibility of brain damage. If it works as advertised, it should give us twenty to thirty minutes of lucid conversation, before we have to start wondering whether you'll be one of the unlucky one in four that never recover—left to live out their lives in a highly vegetative state."

"Nice," Grady said with obvious sarcasm. "Do I get a last meal?"

Allan ignored the comment and nodded to Gabe, summoning him closer. "Unstrap his arm . . . his bad arm," he added. "I'll need access to a vein and his restraints are in the way. But whatever you do, don't let go of his arm."

Gabe nodded, and quickly began undoing the thick Velcro straps that had been fastened about Grady's wrist, elbow and bicep.

"Oh, and if you struggle at all, Drake here gets his way with Anna," the doctor suggested.

Drake, still standing near Anna's head laughed, but the doctor gave him a steady glare that quickly shut him up. With the restraints removed Grady held out his arm, displaying full cooperation. If his odds were three in four that he'd come through without serious damage, he'd take those chances. He needed to buy time. Grady had some limited experience with serums like this in his training, and he knew nothing was foolproof. Depending on the mental rigidity and emotional stamina of the individual, anything could be beat—even a polygraph—and he steadied himself to weather the worst, telling himself it was all for Anna and Tom.

As the doctor leaned over Grady, searching for the ideal spot to start the injection, his white lab coat draped open to reveal a shoulder holster for a gun. Grady's eyes locked on hopefully, looking for any opportunity to turn the tables, but to his disappointment the holster was empty. The sight though, caused Grady to hesitate momentarily and he pulled his arm away from Gabe.

"Christ." Allan muttered as he jumped back from the table, wary of Grady's free hand. "What did I tell you? Hold his damn arm!

"And you," he said, indicating Grady. "What did I tell you about resistance?"

Grady said nothing, and instead quickly reoffered his arm to Gabe. Having been rebuked, Gabe obediently grabbed Grady's wrist in his big meaty palm and clamped down on it with much greater force than before.

Watching both men carefully, gauging the security of the situation, Allan seemed satisfied and stepped closer to the gurney. Again he leaned over Grady's arm looking for a vein. Once again his coat fell open and Grady saw the holster. Only this time, for a moment, the briefest moment, Grady was struck with the oddest impression—as if there now was a gun hanging heavily inside the shoulder holster.

The doctor set the needle down for a moment on a nearby medical supply tray. He had located a vein, picked up an alcohol swab, and began rubbing it in the crook of Grady's elbow. It was a completely unessential step, as the doctor didn't really care if Grady developed an infection in the injection site, but old habits were hard to break. As he performed this step, working over Grady's gurney, his lab jacket again flashed open and the gun was gone. As he discarded the cotton swab, and returned to Grady's arm with syringe in hand, to Grady's surprise the gun once again seemed to resolve back into reality. What Grady did not realize—like the twins playing ball or the candle that would and would not light—two Naturals were now temporarily drawing two convergent universes into one physical reality.

"What the hell," Grady said, almost too loudly.

In that same moment, Grady thought he heard voices in his head telling him—or more accurately willing him—to reach inside the doctor's lab coat and take the gun, "believe it is there."

He recognized one of the voices: Anna. He tried craning his neck around to bring her into view to the point he could just make out her reclined form, restrained in the white seat. Her eyes were closed, as if in deep concentration. He also took note of Anna's personal guard, Drake, at least a pace behind her head; oblivious to what was going on.

"Not me!" came Anna's voice again inside Grady's own head. "Focus on the gun with us. Believe it is there."

"Looking for something?" the doctor asked Grady—his ability to eavesdrop on his thoughts now apparently gone after the last cryptic sentence uttered over the intercom. "She can't help you now," he said, noticing Grady's interest in Anna.

Grady gave no reply, his mind too distracted—instead he simply turned back to watch Allan work on his arm. The doctor had already isolated one of Grady's veins with a rubber armband and was preparing to plunge the serum into the bloodstream. As the doctor broke the skin and began to depress the syringe, Grady did the only thing he could think of: he yelled out in mock pain.

Grady's obvious over-reaction startled Allan, and the doctor paused, pulling back on the needle slightly. In the same moment Gabe reacted by momentarily loosening his tight grip on Grady's wrist.

It was now or never. Grady knew if he acted and the voices were wrong—well he didn't want to think about those implications. Instead he went all in on a bad hand, hoping the bluff would carry him. So with all his might, Grady yanked his arm free tearing it from Gabe's big clutches. To Grady's utter surprise Gabe's grip actually slackened with his effort.

"Grab him!" the doctor yelled frantically, seeing Grady's arm pull free. Yet, rather than step away again, Allan rushed to finish the injection, fumbling as he attempted to hang onto the syringe and plunge its contents into Grady's moving arm. The effort was wasted though, because the needle tore easily from the superficial skin puncture and popped out of the doctor's hand, where it flew through the air before landing squarely in Grady's lap.

Seeing an opportunity, Grady's instincts and training kicked in. In a fraction of a second, his free hand had gathered up the syringe, palming it. Then, with lightning-fast reflexes, he raised it up, over and around the side of the gurney driving the needle deep into his nearest access point—the thigh of the doctor.

Screaming in pain the doctor leaned forward, grabbing at his leg, desperately trying to remove the foreign object and prevent Grady from depressing the syringe. But that was all Grady wanted from the needle: a distraction. And as the doctor tried extracting the needle from his thigh muscle, Grady waited for the opportunity he was now certain would come. Sure enough, a second or so later, the doctor's lab coat fell open, again revealing the gun holster.

Not even bothering to check whether a gun was there or not, Grady's only free hand shot out, reaching up and inside the doctor's coat, grabbing for something that in reality shouldn't have been there—at least not in this reality. To his amazement, Grady's fingers wrapped around cold steel, and he pulled out a gun like a magician pulling a rabbit out of a hat.

Not wasting a moment, Grady expertly spun the weapon in his palm until the hilt of the gun slipped comfortably into his hand. Raising the barrel, he aimed it directly between the eyes of the doctor.

In that fraction of a second when decisions are made, Grady felt an overwhelming and uncontrollable urging from an anguished voice. It was something fierce and ugly, and it rose up out of the darkness of his mind, something not entirely him, that bit into him, fueling the anger and hatred that was already there . . . anger that had been boiling inside him over the last few days.

As Grady struggled mightily to be in control of his own mind, his eyes caught anger, disbelief and abject fear reflected in the eyes of the doctor. Almost without thought, he pulled the trigger.

CHAPTER 119

MINOT

The wait had been agonizing for Tom and Kyle. It had been well over an hour since they had finished retelling Anna and Grady's story to the President, including their own roles in the ongoing saga. When they were done, the Commander-in-Chief had said little. Instead she sat there, with hands folded in front of her, eyes cast down, thinking it all through.

When she finally did look up, if she had made any decisions, she wasn't revealing them. Instead she thanked Tom and Kyle for their information and excused herself from the room. Minutes later they had been escorted back to their seats, and shortly thereafter they could feel the plane begin a fairly significant bank as though it were changing course.

Now as plane began its descent, Tom and Kyle contemplated what was in store for them. For security reasons, the window shades had been drawn automatically—not allowing them to even glimpse the landscape and hazard a guess as to their final destination.

As Kyle waited for the plane to touch down, he couldn't help but feel that the lack of information from the President was a bad thing, and he wondered if the strength of Brian's past relationship with her was enough to save their skin—especially if she felt she needed to silence them.

While she appeared to have no involvement in the current doings at Northwoods, he knew how these things worked. If Northwoods were ever exposed to the public, and the link made back to the government in any way, whether the President had knowledge or not, the public would hold her accountable. She'd be damned either for endorsing such a project, or for not knowing about it. Either way Northwoods represented a political nightmare for her unless the public never found out. It didn't take a genius to realize that was bad for them.

The plane touched down, and they taxied for a short while until Air Force One came to a stop. They were ordered to sit tight, as arrangements were made for their arrival. Twenty minutes later they were allowed to get out of their seats, depart the plane, and walk down the gangway that had been pulled up to an exit just forward of the wings. Kyle assumed the wait meant the President had disembarked before them, and did not want to come back into contact with them. Another bad sign.

Kyle wasn't surprised to see that as they exited, they were not outside, but inside what appeared to be a large airplane hangar.

"What gives?" Tom said, nudging Kyle as they walked down to the concrete apron, just ten paces behind Brian.

"Wait and see, I guess. But I'm starting to wonder if we made our point too well with the President," Kyle replied under his breath.

Tom's curiosity was piqued. "What do you mean by that?"

"They seem to be going out of their way to keep us under wraps and out of the know. That can't be good from our point of view."

Tom smiled ironically at the thought, noticing the wealth of Air Force military personnel milling about the plane and the hangar. The tempo about the facility seemed to be crisp and serious. As they reach the bottom of the steps, two Air Force MPs waited for them.

"Come with us, gentlemen," one commanded. "We have a place prepared for you where you can wait."

Brian nodded to the men, and they led the way across the vast expanse to a small room that looked like a shed with a window on the far side. Once there Tom and Kyle were ushered inside the small cramped room by a single guard who excused himself to take up station outside the door. Kyle's boss was asked to continue on with the remaining guard to a destination yet unknown.

"They just removed the one person who I thought might be able save our asses," Kyle said with disgust.

"You think this is heading in the wrong direction?" Tom asked. There was no fear or anxiety in his voice, simply curiosity.

"Tom, do you really want me to answer that?"

"Only if you are a damn good liar."

CHAPTER 120

THE BOWELS OF HELL

I nside Grady's head the voices had suddenly gone silent as the bullet began its journey out of the barrel of the gun—accelerated off a flash of gunpowder, smoke and thunder. Grady watched—as if in slow motion—the doctor's eyes widening in fear at the realization he'd lived his last microsecond.

As the doctor fell, only Grady knew the eventual outcome. At the last possible moment, Anna's voice came to him, drowning out the angry goading from a woman he'd never met: Melody. She'd begged him for quick, unmerciful revenge, even as Anna's voice pleaded with him to be humane to a monster who'd never given her such dignity. So he shifted the barrel a hair to the right. In the end the bullet hit its mark, but barely—its tip tearing through the top quarter-inch of the doctor's right ear, sending him spinning to the tiled floor.

As the blood flowed and the doctor screamed out in pain, Drake, still standing behind Anna, tried to regain control. Pulling his own gun he pressed the barrel hard into Anna's skull with a viciousness fed by the sight of what he believed was his father's agonizing death.

"Drop the gun!" he roared at Grady, who still lay belted to the gurney, facing away from Drake.

Helplessly restrained and without a clear view of Drake, Grady realized he'd miscalculated his position. He was out of options. And just when Grady was about to give up, Gabe did something noble and completely unexpected. Standing near Grady's gurney he spun the bed on its wheels a full 180 degrees, stopping on a dime so that Grady faced Drake head-on. The move was so sudden and unexpected it caused Drake to hesitate, before he made the fatal mistake of removing his gun from Anna's head and pointing it at Grady.

This time for Grady there was no compassion, no hesitation and no voices inside his head twisting his thoughts. All he could rely on were his own instincts, his FBI training, and his marksmanship skills. It was a tough shot, from a reclined position, but it was his only shot. Grady had already lifted his arm to aim before the bed stopped its spin. The barrel of the gun was already tracing a perfect bead on Drake's forehead, only a foot above Anna's, as Drake tried to steady his own weapon. When the bed came to a stop, all Grady had to do was center himself with a breath and pull the trigger. This time the bullet whistled through the air and took the son of the doctor down in a heartbeat, the slug landing just off target—a few stray centimeters left of center of Drake's forehead.

Drake's momentary threat had turned everyone's attention away from the doctor, who remained low and out of sight, dripping blood, as he scrambled along on hands and knees until he was to the door and out of The Room, the remaining security guard and orderlies close behind.

Gabe, realizing there was little time before the general alarm was raised, fought feverishly to release Grady from his remaining restraints. As the final one was ripped off, Grady tore his ravaged and beaten body off the bloodstained mattress and rushed to Anna's side.

"Thanks," Grady said to Gabe, as they both struggled with Anna's bonds. The simple exertion was already taking its toll on Grady. He tried to bury away in his mind the sharp, stabbing pains that racked his body with each movement—all so he could gather an occasional breath of air. In addition to his injured ribs, Grady's shoulder wound was a bloody mess . . . and to make matters worse, his head was beginning to swim from the small amount of truth serum Allan had been able to administer.

Gabe removed the final restraint and Anna flung herself from the chair into Grady's arms, nearly knocking him off his feet. She kissed him hard and told him again how much she loved him.

The feeling of being close to Anna—to feel her body against his, to smell her soft fragrance and to run his fingers through her hair—gave Grady new strength and served as temporary painkiller. He would have loved to hold her longer, but he knew they weren't safe standing still. Trying to get his bearings, Grady was about to usher them all to the door when a voice from intercom cut through the air.

"They're trying to come through the observation room! I've locked the door from the inside, but it won't be long before they override the system," Melody shouted, fear creeping into her voice.

"Who the hell is that?" Grady asked, turning to Anna.

Anna flashed Grady a weak smile, "It's the doctor's daughter. She's okay," she said, knowing there was little time to elaborate.

In that instant the institute's alarm system began to sound and the lights throughout the sublevel flashed off. The lights replaced by an ominous emergency lighting system that hugged the base of the walls, leaving the floors in light, while everything above receded quickly into shadows.

Adrenaline was beginning to surge into Grady's veins and the effect helped to further numb his pain and clear his head as he began shouting orders. "Close that damn door and see if you can't cover the window with something," he yelled over the alarms to Gabe, pointing at The Room's only entrance and exit.

For a moment, Gabe looked at him with a question in his eyes, believing he'd be shutting off their only means of viable escape. But in the end, he followed the voice of authority and did what he was told. Though the security effect of closing the door was temporary—Grady knew a closed door with a blocked window kept what little element of surprise there was on their side.

With Gabe securing the door and stuffing a pillow off the gurney into the recessed window, Grady turned, gun still in hand and yelled at the mirrored wall. "Get down and out of the way!"

Though he'd been speaking to the intercom and Melody in the other room, Anna moved away from Grady's side to give him room, but stayed comfortably near. She wasn't going to let him out of reach if she could help it. She watched anxiously as he raised the gun, centered it on the mirrored panel and fired a single round into its center.

The one-way window fragmented into a spider web pattern with a small hole in the center, but it didn't shatter, and Anna felt her heart sink at the bullet's failed impact. But Grady was only emboldened, since it told him the pane wasn't bulletproof—just thick tempered glass—designed to prevent an out-of-control patient from pounding on the mirror and breaking through it.

Looking around the room for a battering ram, he saw what he thought might work and rushed back to the gurney he'd been brought in on and began wheeling it over to the fractured panel.

Gabe, guessing what he was going to do, came over and took the other side of the gurney. They retracted the legs into the bottom of the bed, making it easier to lift and manhandle. On the count of three both men raised it up and started running one end into the bullet hole and the center of the spider web pattern.

"Hurry, they're almost in," Melody shouted again over the intercom.

Grady and Gabe were moving as fast as they could, taking three steps back and racing three steps forward to jam the end of the bed into the fracture. With each blow the mirrored surface began to fragment and fall away . . . the hole in the center growing wider and wider. Each new jarring hit took its toll on Grady and he winced in agony. Seeing him hurting, Anna jumped in to help out on his side of the gurney.

"Why not just shoot it again?" Anna said, trying to spare Grady the trauma and get things moving faster.

"Because I've already used three bullets and don't know how many we will need to get us out of here."

The thought seemed to drive each of them a little harder, and on the last push the front of the gurney crashed through, exploding a five-foot-round gaping hole in the center of the glass. Melody could now be seen, through the opening between the rooms, hanging back by the door, looking agitated and afraid.

"One more hard drive!" Grady said through gritted teeth, hoping they could clear away some of the final shards near the bottom of the broken panel. Just as the three were moving forward to slam the gurney back through the mirror, the door to the observation room swung wide and Mitch came barreling through with his gun drawn.

The shock in his eyes showed clearly, as he'd been expecting to enter a private room with only The Kid inside. Instead he was staring past the observation room through one massive shattered hole, into The Room itself. The room he'd left only minutes ago. He certainly hadn't expected to see Grady and Anna, who had been firmly bound when he left them in the doctor's care, now having smashed through the window to get to the doctor's daughter. The one person he thought would be there, The Kid, was nowhere in sight. It was a completely different situation than he'd been anticipating and it took him a moment to process. That hesitation and confusion played into Grady's hand and cost Mitch.

Grady finished the charge with the gurney and the moment it crashed into the window he dropped his side and let the weight fall to Anna. Deftly he stepped away from and around Anna as he drew his gun, his feet crunching on shards of glass as he leveled the weapon and fired a single shot at Mitch.

But as Anna recoiled from the charge into the window, staggering with the unexpected weight of the gurney, she'd brushed Grady's arm, throwing off his aim, sending the bullet low, where it lanced into the muscle of Mitch's thigh. Shouting in pain, Mitch crouched down, reaching for his injured leg as he spun off his good leg, back out of the observation room through the door. But Grady wasn't about to allow Mitch to retreat to security if he could help it. He had wounded prey on his hands, and a good hunter never allowed an injured animal to escape into the wild.

Grady threw himself through the hole, grabbing the mattress off the gurney as he went, using it as a protective bridge over the broken glass and across the control console before falling to the floor on the other side. He was on his feet in a second, gun forward, resting on his free palm, as he rushed the door in pursuit of the hobbled Mitch.

Anna, not wanting to let Grady out of her sight, hopped through the window and raced after Grady, only a few paces behind. She caught up with him at a bend in the corridor as he paused, trying to peer around the right angle, hoping Mitch hadn't already set up an ambush farther down.

"Stay with the others!" Grady said, his voice full of concern rather than anger.

"No. I can't bear the thought of being separated again," Anna said, her hand finding his, letting him know they were in it together.

Grady nodded, understanding exactly how she felt. He was just about to turn the corner to check the hall when Melody came up from behind with the much heavier Gabe laboring along several paces behind.

"You're going to need someone who knows the layout. I've been wandering these back hallways since I was seven to get places my dad never wanted me to be," Melody said, dismissing Grady's objection before he could even voice it.

Grady didn't have time to argue with them. He was already wasting time, so he rolled out into the hallway in a crouch and popped up on one knee, this gun pointing down the length of the corridor. But it was empty.

He didn't bother to give anyone the safe sign, but leapt to his feet, sucking air deeply into his damaged chest and sprinted down the hall, the others following a safe distance behind. They ran along the hall for about one hundred feet, passing several locked doorways with bold lettering indicating they were more observation rooms. The group turned left at a fork based on Melody's direction and traveled another two hundred feet past more one-way windows that peered into strange rooms. Melody caught Anna's questioning expression, and explained that these were "environments"; places Northwoods conducted studies and experiments on normal individuals, in a quest to artificially recreate what the Naturals did naturally.

Anna glanced into each room as they passed. Each appeared temporarily deserted as the environments glowed ominously with the pulsing emergency lighting. She'd been in rooms similar to these during her time here, but had never known the experiments extended to others beyond the four naturals. She shivered at the thought. It wasn't just the creepy feel of the place that was getting to her. There was a real sense of foreboding starting to build inside her and she thought it had something to do with these rooms.

It wasn't until the next series of windows that she actually paused and let the group get ahead of her for a moment. To her right was a row of windows opening to a very long, dim room. It was sunken, a story below her feet, and it too flashed with the lights from the general alarm raised throughout the sublevel of Northwoods. In this dark, ugly room, the emergency lights strobed on shadowy outlines of human forms—recessed into a mock-urban landscape—some torn to shreds by bullet holes. Not certain why, Anna walked up to the window and pressed her hand to the glass. She was observing the gauntlet—and while it was empty right now, the flashing emergency lighting gave the illusory effect of intermittent gunfire. From her hand touching the glass and the visual cues below, Anna's mind flashed with images of what the room was for, and the monsters it was designed for.

Seeing the group getting too far ahead of her, Anna released her hand from the surface of the window and followed. She would have liked to try to understand more about the room, as she had a sense it played into their future, but she had run out of time. Back with the group, Melody continued to talk Grady through the maze, as he tried to pick up the blood trail from Mitch. They'd been lucky so far in that whenever they'd come to a fork, it took only a few paces in either direction to find a crimson drop or two on the concrete floor, clearly indicating which route they should take.

Grady knew that they were running out of time. They'd only been in the access corridors for a few minutes now, but he was certain that people were coming for them, following up from the rear. If he stopped to listen, he could catch an occasional voice or footstep echoing from the far reaches of the darkness behind them. He knew that if they didn't get out of these hallways it was only a matter of time before they turned a corner and came face to face with Mitch, or more likely, back-up security that Mitch called in to assist.

Grady thought their luck might be changing when they reached the next fork in the hallway and found a drop of blood to their left. He turned to Melody, as he had done at previous forks, waiting for her to tell him where the corridor led.

"That's odd," she said, thinking something through.

"Why? What?" Anna asked.

Gabe had been silent for most of their journey, simply content to follow, and hoped these people had a way out, not only from this current mess, but also the mess of his lifetime. "That hall leads to a secure staff entry to the Northwoods grounds."

"What's strange about that?" Anna asked, clearly not following.

Grady gave the answer, as he worked it through in his mind. "I think all along we thought Mitch was going to try to lead us into an ambush, one he's been buying time to set up. Logically that would be back into the heart of the Northwoods complex. What's odd is it seems he is actually leading us out."

"Is that bad?" Anna asked, still trying to follow the thought.

"It is because I can't think of any reason for him to do it, unless he's setting the trap outside, which is just that much closer to freedom for us. It's always harder to control an environment outdoors."

"Okay. Then think about it—what does your gut tell you?" Anna directed, helping Grady along his own path with her thoughts—her eyes strong and determined. "Trust your own instincts Grady—it's not just the Naturals who can read these signs."

Melody looked between Anna and Grady, wondering what was going on between them, both verbally and non-verbally. Even in her few minutes with them, she could tell how connected they were, and already knew how deeply their love went. For a moment she wondered how heavily that must have played into Curt's slide toward insanity, which she had simply pushed over the edge with her mind.

This stray thought sparked something deep inside, and Melody knew this was the end of the line for her. She needed do something. And she needed to act now or lose the opportunity. The corridor to the left only took her farther away from that opportunity.

"Sorry to break up this party but I can't go out there. I think I have some unfinished business back inside," Melody said, inclining her head back down the hallway in the other direction.

The group nodded, understanding what must be eating away at her—nobody willing to stand in her way or convince her otherwise.

Melody smiled and grasped Anna's hand, giving it a reassuring squeeze. "Just do me one favor, please. A little farther down, if I remember correctly, you will reach another fork in the corridor. Whatever you do, don't follow the blood trail . . . trust me on this."

Anna squeezed her hand back in a silent promise, and then let go. Without pausing for further discussion or objections, Melody set off in the opposite direction to find her father.

A worried look spread across Anna's face and on impulse she turned to Gabe. "Go with her," Anna said. "She's going to need a big guardian angel like you."

Gabe grinned, glad to do something that might set his own part in this horror right, and with an appreciative nod he set off to follow Melody. Once they were gone, Anna turned back to Grady. "Do you have an answer? Do you think you know why Mitch is heading out instead of in?"

Grady nodded thoughtfully. "Yes. If I were to hazard a guess, I'd say he wants to make a game of this. He doesn't want help. Or at least his bruised ego won't allow him to ask for help. Instead he wants to turn the tables."

"How so?"

"He wants to hunt us."

CHAPTER 121

WEIGHT OF THE WORLD

Brian sat in front of the President again, in a secure area of the hangar. The room was bare, except for a small desk, a table with four chairs, and several filing cabinets that hugged the square walls.

"You understand my situation?" the President asked, concern in her eyes.

"Yes, clearly," Brian answered. "You are faced with a rogue black operation that you knew almost nothing about, but the fact is, your knowledge or lack thereof is a liability to you if this ever goes public. What I can't understand is, you've been in office for five years now, a year into your second term. This can't be the first issue like this that you've had to deal with. Our government is full of individuals and secret groups hoping to further their own agenda under the guise of national interests. What do you need from me?"

"I trust you, Brian. I need to understand how deep you think I need to scrub." This was said with no emotion or concern, simply an honest open question inviting Brian to make his case.

"So you want to know about the two men and their tendencies—whether they can be trusted?"

"Yes."

Brian leaned back in his chair and put his hands behind his head in thought. "Kyle isn't a problem. He understands the world has secrets . . .

secrets that the public should never know . . . for their own sakes. Tom is more complicated, but he is a high-priced thief . . . or ex-thief, depending on who you believe. What I know of him, and men like him, is that they hate publicity and high-profile situations. He lives in secrecy and gains his status and power from anonymity."

"I would have guessed that," the President interjected. "What I need to understand though, is whether they will sit in my corner when I decide a course of action."

"You mean when you invade Northwoods?"

The President leaned forward. "How did you know that was my next move?"

Brian pulled his hands from behind his head and gave the President a serious look. "Elizabeth, do you underestimate me as well? It's clear we are at Minot Air Force Base in North Dakota. It's the perfect choice for an air infiltration or even an outright air strike on Northwoods—although that would be hard to cover up—but not impossible. Anyway, it's nearby, and it involves the military, versus the FBI or any other security agency at your disposal. A military force allows you to control the situation yourself as Commander-in-Chief. That way you don't have to tip your hand to any of the various security agencies that might be unfriendly to your decisions."

"You're quite astute. I always admired that about you." The President smiled.

"The way I see it, those two men sitting back there in the holding room are the least of your worries. It's the man that drew them into all of this that you should be wondering about, or perhaps even a bit fearful of."

"Grady Hamilton?"

"Yes, he was one of mine," Brian offered, knowing he probably wasn't sharing anything new with the President. "Their loyalties are to him. For each of them, he is why they are neck-deep in this situation. It goes directly to his innate leadership abilities and the irrational loyalty he engenders, almost as if by accident. They will follow his cue."

"And what if Mr. Hamilton doesn't make it out of this alive?" the President asked, not making a threat, but exploring her options to their fullest.

"Then those two men would also be your problem," Brian said seriously.

"So it hinges on Grady," the President stated, more to herself.

"And one of the Naturals . . . Anna. In the case of Grady, he was drummed out of my field office on bogus murder charges that were never brought against him. It was a bad break for him, and truly nothing against him as an agent or as a vigilant arm of the United States Government. He was a damn good and loyal servant. But because of that history he may carry a grudge. And because of Anna, and his apparent feelings for her, he may now have the perfect excuse to try to bring people down around him. On the other hand, if Grady has fallen for one of these Naturals then he will do everything he can to protect her and her friends. Public exposure of Northwoods might close some festering wounds, but it will rip open new ones as the public clamors to better understand and come to grips with their unique talents."

"I see," the President said thoughtfully.

"Elizabeth, you know me. I'm not going to judge you one way or the other. I've been around too long. I'm not naïve . . . sometimes there is no right that can be done, just less wrong. I know you've dealt with that before. This isn't the first or the last time, but here's the way I see it if you're interested."

"Go on," the President prodded. "You know I trust you."

"Take Northwoods down before it takes you down. You are too good a President to be dragged down by, or into, something someone else started that just happened to blow up on your watch."

"And whoever gets in my way be damned?"

"I didn't say that. But it appears you are trying to decide between a fast, efficient scorch-and-burn policy or political brain surgery that requires careful, painstaking extraction and prevention. Both solve the problem and both carry various levels of risk. While one ensures the problem has been expunged, it's like taking off an arm to ensure an infected finger doesn't spread to the rest of the body. The other is less certain of success, but does the least damage to the whole. The question is which, if it ever did get out into the public eye, could you justify to the American public?"

"Thank you for your time, Brian," the President said dismissively. She wasn't rude in doing so, but he had given her enough to think about. "A transport will be waiting to take you home."

Brian realized he wouldn't be going home with Kyle and Tom. As he walked to the door, he paused for a moment. He was trying to push the President to a course of logical, prudent action that was most justifiable—because like all secrets, someday this would come out. It was just a matter of when. Perhaps he had danced too delicately around that with her.

"How far away is the strike force?" Brian asked, his back to the President and his hand on the door.

"The F-15s are en route if necessary, ready to enforce a temporary no-fly zone within fifty miles. The helicopters are still here at the base—loaded and ready to fly—they're just waiting for my command. They're our new V-22 Ospreys, so they can be there in a little over an hour if need be, from tarmac to turf."

"Godspeed Elizabeth," And with that Brian walked out the door.

CHAPTER 122

THE HUNT

Grady shook his head as though trying to free the cobwebs in his brain. "Excuse me. Did I actually hear you right? You think Mitch is going to use one of these bio-engineered soldiers to hunt us down?"

Anna looked at Grady helplessly. "I'm not certain, but it's the sense I have."

"And like those are ever wrong," Grady said with frustration.

Anna looked hurt, and Grady instantly regretted his choice of words. He hadn't meant it that way. "I'm sorry Anna, but how . . . where . . . ?"

"You know, Grady, I can't always explain what or why I feel what I do. But when we passed one of those darkened rooms I felt this overwhelming dread. When I looked into the room, and saw the flashing emergency strobes it gave me this odd impression of gunfire and war games. Then there was Melody's mention of human experiments on non-Naturals. But it wasn't until you talked about your own sense that Mitch was baiting us outside, to hunt us down on his own, that it clicked. It all fueled and fed this sense."

The conversation had to end there. The occasional sounds coming from behind them in the hall were much closer now, though their pursuers still remained out of sight.

"Let's get moving," Grady said, looking behind him as they set off.

It wasn't long before they reached another branch in the corridor . . . the very one Melody had warned them about. Grady, feeling the pressure building behind them searched quickly for a trace of blood from Mitch. But by now Mitch had most likely staunched the wound with a torn piece of clothing. He finally found a small drop about fifteen feet down the hall to the left, near where the floor folded into the wall.

"This way," he ushered to Anna.

"No! Melody told us not to follow the blood trail."

"Anna, it's time to end this. We can't run forever," Grady rationalized.

"Grady, I'm not saying we aren't going to do everything we can. But what if this is the ambush we've been expecting? Melody was adamant."

Grady nodded with resignation. It probably wasn't a good idea to start ignoring the advice of a couple Naturals simply because he was so close to his prey that he could taste revenge. He gave one last desperate look up the corridor before turning to following Anna.

This hall ran perfectly straight for several hundred yards, and both began to wonder if it would ever end, and if so where? But it finally dead-ended in a concrete stairwell that rose up three stories from the depths. There was no other choice but to go up. When they reached the top, it appeared their only option was to go through a door set into one wall of a ten-foot-square chamber, with the stairwell rising out of the middle.

"What do you think?" Grady asked Anna while they both eyed the door. "Any sense of what we might be up against when we open that door?"

"What, you think I'm a superhero now who can see through doors?" Anna joked awkwardly, only trying to lighten the tension. Opening a door to the unknown wasn't easy, particularly when there could be a new generation of soldier waiting to cut them down the moment they opened it.

"Seriously, what do you think we could face in this ultimate soldier? We're going to need a plan of attack and it's best to know your opponent."

Anna sighed. "This is more a guess than anything, but at worst—a predictive fighting machine who will always be one step ahead of his prey. He will know our next move before we make it. At best, if I'm wrong, we'll find an injured and very angry Mitch, all alone."

"I'm going to need you," Grady said, a weary smile creasing his face. "You'll have to lead us . . . lead me. It's the only way I can see us overcoming something like that—to be one step ahead ourselves."

Anna nodded. "I'm guessing that's why Melody gave me these when she visited me. They helped when we were back in The Room with the gun, but she expressly told me to save a couple and not take them all at once. I think she knew something like this might happen. They seem to enhance my receptive abilities and concentration."

"You'll have to tell me about her and everything else that has happened between you two another time. I still can't believe the doctor did all of this with a Natural as his own daughter. But we need to keep moving."

Nodding, Anna popped the pills back into her throat and swallowed. Steeling her courage, she hit the door hard with her hands and thrust out into the wooded grounds of Northwoods with Grady hot on her heels.

Outside, morning had arrived and the mists hung heavy, rolling up from the distant lake to the west. It floated like wispy ghosts riding over the tall grasses and dodging between the thick tree trunks. Both Grady and Anna realized that they had completely lost track of time inside Northwoods. With no clocks and no windows where they were held, they had little concept of the time of day or even the day of week.

They found themselves in a small clearing about twenty yards wide, impinged on three sides by a lush and wooded landscape, thick with hardy pine trees, broad maples, burly oaks and mammoth hickory nut trees. The one side of the clearing that was open fell gradually away, down a lazy hill toward the lake.

Anna quickly realized how exposed they were, and began running toward the security of the trees. Both made it to the edge of the clearing and into the woods without incident. It was then that Grady noticed the twenty-foot tall chain link fence.

"That runs the length of the rear grounds," Anna explained matter-of-factly. There are cameras mounted on a motorized swivel about every forty feet or so, mostly to monitor exterior threats, but we should be careful not to get caught in their sweep. I've also heard that they can electrify the fence during emergencies, so we should avoid direct contact."

Grady was still trying to get his bearings. He took a moment to look back at where they had came from and found it odd to see that the door they had passed through to get to the grounds looked so unassuming. "If we hadn't come up through that," Grady said, indicating the door, "I would have guessed it was just a service shed for the fence."

"Rumors were that Dr. Hauser had a tunnel installed as a means of escape if anything ever went seriously wrong." Anna suggested. "He was always a paranoid bastard. That might also explain why that tunnel leads to nowhere. Probably means there is a gate around here somewhere as well, but it won't do us any good unless we have a code."

"So where do you think Mitch came out?"

"Most likely back by the main Northwoods complex," Anna pointed out, "which from here is back toward the lake."

Grady looked back down the hill, over the rolling white fog and imagined the sinister complex resting somewhere out there, obscured by trees. "You know, maybe you're rubbing off on me, but I have this weird feeling that if we had followed the blood trail we wouldn't be breathing right now. I think Melody knew that's where the ambush was being set. Anyway, it appears to have bought us some time. Let's get moving, and stay close to the cover of the tree line."

Grady was about to move off when Anna's hand shot out, slamming him in the chest, stopping him in his tracks. In that same split second a soccer-sized crater erupted from the trunk of a hickory tree, precisely in line with his next step.

Anna and Grady crashed to the ground, landing on a bed of wet, rotting leaves. If she hadn't realized it before, Anna now understood, with incredible clarity, the game that was about to be played out. A vague sense of danger had only come to her a moment before the gunshot, and if she had hesitated a second, Grady would be dead. The shot was definitely fired in anticipation of his misstep, which made Anna realize the enhanced soldier was out there and very real.

"You're a good shot, Grady. But I think you'll meet your match today," Mitch yelled from somewhere off in a pine thicket, across the clearing between them and the lake.

Grady put a finger to his mouth, telling Anna not to be baited by Mitch into a response and pointed behind them to the security of a large hickory tree. "Crawl," he whispered, as they both began to back themselves to a more secure position.

"You surprised me, Anna," Mitch yelled again, still trying to bait his prey. "We never expected you to take the other corridor. That tells me you know a little about what you're up against." Mitch laughed.

Anna remained silent, as both she and Grady made it to the tree and slid up the backside, keeping it between them and the first gunshot.

"I'll tell you that you're no match for him," Mitch continued, obviously not satisfied with their silence. "He's a gifted hunter, a killing machine, and he'll know your next move before you take it."

No sooner had Mitch said his last word and a bullet pulverized the side of a pine tree just a half step away from where Anna had planned to step.

"What did I tell you, Anna?" Mitch yelled again laughing.

But Anna was emboldened by the shot. While much too close for comfort, she was trying to understand how to play this game of wits. She had certainly been contemplating that next step, but again her mind had stopped her. That was now two shots she had been successfully able to anticipate.

Thinking through the options, she suggested to Grady that they continue to backpedal from their spot even deeper into the security of the woods. She felt an overwhelming sense that this game of cat-and-mouse would come to an end, one way or another, somewhere nearer the lake. She began leading Grady in that direction.

For Anna, it was an odd feeling—making a decision, avoiding that decision and deciding an alternate course of action. She tried to keep her decisions fluid and unexpected, often contrary to what she originally thought was right, hoping it would keep the hunter thinking while she tried to get inside his mind and figure out his next move. This game would not be won until they were able to turn the tables.

Mitch remained silent now, probably frustrated that he couldn't toy with his prey, as Anna kept picking her way through the dense pine forest, leading Grady by the hand, while trying to keep as many thick tree trunks between themselves and the direction the last gunshots had come.

Two more times bullets landed in places near a path she had been planning to take but thought better of. It seemed to be working, because the shots had now stopped, and she and Grady were buried in a sea of pines and underbrush that made any shot, even one from a visionary soldier, virtually impossible.

For the next twenty minutes they continued on, with Grady following faithfully behind, trusting Anna's instincts. Occasionally he'd encourage her, letting her know that she was doing well. But he actually worried about influencing her in any way that might make her deviate from her extremely cautious approach.

When Anna paused, concentrating, unmoving almost a full minute, Grady needed to know what was bothering her.

"I'm not sure I'm doing this right." Anna said with self-doubt. I'm suddenly getting this terrible sense that we are about to stumble into a *checkmate* in this game."

Grady looked worried. "Why would you say that?" he whispered, crouching down by her side to peer through the tapestry of branches, pine needles and leaves. He felt blind in every direction except for a ten- to fifteen-foot circumference around them, and even that was fragmented and obscured by brush.

"I thought we were doing well, particularly since we haven't heard a gunshot for the last fifteen or twenty minutes. But it's too comfortable, too easy."

"They're flanking us!" Grady said in a revelation.

"What do you mean by that?" Anna asked apprehensively.

"Mitch was goading us back there, letting us know where he was with his voice. He was probably doing it intentionally to drive us in a certain direction. Once the hunter knew we could anticipate his attacks, I'm guessing Mitch told him to circle around to a spot, to focus his energy not on tracking, but on where we might emerge from the tree line."

Anna looked at Grady with fiery eyes. She knew he was right, and she was angry with herself for not picking up on it. She'd been too concerned with trying to avoid an individual misstep, instead of worrying about where they were ultimately headed.

"Must mean the lake is nearby," Anna said thoughtfully, her mind working the angles again. She knew the broad, vast lake well—having wandered around its banks many times over the past few years. Trying to concentrate on where they might be and where they might come out, Anna's mind centered on a hilly wildflower meadow that ran from the edge of the pines, down to the edges of the eastern shores.

"I think I know where we might be," Anna said with concern. "And if I'm right we were about to accidentally wander right out into the open. We can't be more than twenty yards or so from a wildflower meadow near the lake."

"Makes sense. I think the fog is getting thicker. It's happened so gradually I didn't even notice at first."

"So what do we do now?" Anna asked, hoping Grady had a better answer than she did. Her goal in all this had been to keep them way from Mitch and his enhanced killing machine, but she realized Grady's goal was eventually to get much closer to them. It was really their only way out, to get rid of their threat.

"Tell me as much as you can about the layout of the lake and the meadow. I'll need to know the lay of the land if I'm going to turn this to our advantage."

Anna told Grady everything she knew, and watched him as he processed the information. She could see his mind working hard, and he came back with a single question.

"Who do you think this guy out there is trying to track? You or me?"

Anna eyed Grady, trying to figure out where he was going with this. "Me, if he knows I'm the Natural and leading the way, which I'm guessing he does. Occasionally I can feel him trying to reach out, almost like a sonar ping—though I don't think he can get in my head—not being a full-fledged Natural and all."

Grady nodded, listening intently for any opportunity he could exploit.

"Anyway, he's bound to know he's got to get ahead of me to beat us. Right now we are both working off sheer instinct, intuition, and an occasional flash vision of a near-term future event. At least that's where my focus has been—on the very short term and individual actions and reactions. We're not talking about trying to foretell the future, just predict and anticipate near-term outcomes."

"I see," Grady said thoughtfully. "It probably won't work."

"Grady!" Anna scolded under her breath. "Just because you're worried about me doesn't give you the right to hold out on me. If you think you have a plan to get us out of this, you damn well better tell me."

Grady just shook his head. "I'm sorry, but I'm just starting to work through it in my mind. You're not going to like it. It's going to mean we're going to have to go our separate ways."

Anna began to protest, but Grady explained in detail why it was the only choice that made any sense. In the end, Anna realized if their final goal was to expose Northwoods, once again they would have to separate to survive.

So Anna watched as Grady began heading back in the direction they had come before changing course to his ultimate destination. He had the longer route to travel and he needed a good head start before Anna would set off in the opposite direction. When she finally thought it was safe to go on, she remembered the promise she had made to herself and already broken—never to leave Grady's side again. But Grady was right . . . it was the only way. It hurt like hell not to have him here. She wanted him to give her courage for what she was about to do—to keep the attention off of his flight.

Her path took her through the last of the pines, and she could already tell that they were beginning to thin. She was thankful for the underbrush that still provided her some measure of cover, though it made the going very slow and difficult.

As she cautiously approached the tree line, she worked through some thoughts. She allowed herself to find some ounce of joy knowing that Grady could be heading off to get help, and incredible sadness at their split. She loved him, so she hoped he could make it while she tried to occupy the gunman's attention. Even the trained killer out there couldn't possibly track them both down. Anna was the best equipped to prolong this game of cat-and-mouse, to buy Grady more time. Of course there was still the issue of Mitch out there somewhere as well, but his injury was likely limiting his mobility.

At the edge of the woods the mist hung heavy, and Anna tried to peer out toward the lake, but it was virtually impossible to see. In fact, she could barely see twenty yards in front of her, as the blanket of white boiled over the tall wildflower meadow. She hung back behind a tree, trying to decide if it was safe to proceed, to cross the meadow, to round the lake and hopefully find the hole in the fence that friends on the outside had agreed to cut into the fence if she was ever recaptured. These were the specific thoughts she was concentrating on.

At last she decided the path seemed safe enough to venture out. It was in that split second, that moment of decision that a ghostly figment rose up through the mist, from the cover of the wildflowers and fired a single shot into the tree line.

Anna screamed, staggered, and fell face first into a sea of wild daisies.

CHAPTER 123

PREY

G rady loathed putting Anna in danger like he had. It was tearing at his heart and with every step away from her, he wanted to rush back to her and come up with a new plan. But it seemed to be their only hope.

It was all based on hunches: a hunch that the artificially-enhanced gunman would take the bait and keep tracking Anna; a hunch that Mitch was the coward Grady thought he was, hiding behind others' brute force; and a hunch that while the gunman tracked Anna, he'd be too distracted to sense the real danger.

He'd told Anna to stay behind the trees and trust her senses while she tried to feed false information into the environment—information that perhaps the gunman might pick up on. They weren't even sure the man's mind worked in that way. But if it did, Anna's thoughts were designed to create confusion, doubt and uncertainty.

Grady had backtracked for a bit, and then circled around, working his way toward the clearing that led down to the lake. It took a while, as he had to ensure his movements created no noise, and finding places to land his feet without snapping a twig, or whipping a bent branch took great concentration and effort. He'd been trained in the art form, from his days as an agent, on how to approach one's prey.

When he finally made it to the edge of the clearing he was probably about one hundred yards behind Anna's position, which was nearer the lake, and even here the swirling mists turned solid ground into a cloud. He had to close some of that distance to reach the tall, grassy wildflower meadow where the slope of the hill began to slide more steeply down to the lake. He could see it now, as the fog ebbed and flowed creating momentary windows of sight—even then everything appeared to have a layer of vellum draped across it.

He hit his belly as he reached the meadow, and checked his flank for the last time—making certain Mitch wasn't hanging back in a position where he might spot Grady. He began his crawl, not certain how far he should go, or how close he should get. As he moved, his ribs began to ache again—the adrenaline in his system long since depleted, and he sucked in shallow breaths, trying to hold himself on his elbows to minimize the pressure on his rib cage.

He wasn't sure why he decided to stop when he did. He only had a sense that where he was felt close enough. Another hunch . . . another guess . . . and he was beginning to experience genuine second thoughts about the plan, but it was much too late to turn back now. The wheels were in motion.

It took only five minutes of lying in wait before he heard her approach. Anna was certainly not trained in the art of stealth, and even though she tried to be quiet, or thought she was being quiet, there were occasional sounds from the dense tree line, far forward and to the right of his current position, signaling her slow arrival.

Grady anticipated this, and he was going to try to use the distraction of Anna's approach to make up more ground and get himself in a better position. He hoped now was the time that the gunman would be preoccupied with Anna. He hoped right at this moment the gunman was reading her thoughts—caught off-guard by the splitting up of Grady and Anna. Was he trying to figure out how to get word to Mitch that Grady was making a race for the fences? This is what Grady hoped: the distraction he wanted.

On knees and elbows Grady reached his next zone of comfort, and took up new position under the cover of wildflowers and fog. It was a position he thought would give him the best angles based on Anna's own angle of approach into the clearing. Then he thought he saw it—the flash of Anna's white medical gown against the earthy hues of the autumn leaves. Yet the haze was so dense he wondered if it was truly her, or some ghostly figment of the mist.

Grady's mind told him it had to be Anna and if so she had picked the perfect approach, reaching the security of a broad tree trunk. Grady guessed she was using it to set up her next move, to survey the open expanse between her position and the lakeshore. He felt like he had to wait forever, and for a moment, thought they both had been ridiculously wrong in their assumption that the gunman had been trying to outflank them. Just as his nerves felt like they were going to break, and his ribs felt like they were going pierce through his skin and suck the very breath from his lungs, *he* rose. The movement came barely inside Grady's field of fog-impaired vision, a lone figure firing three compact bursts into the tree line.

Grady had steeled himself for this moment. He knew for the next few agonizing seconds he wouldn't be able to tell if Anna was acting the part they had planned or had actually been hit. He couldn't let that lingering question distract him from his task. Even before Anna started to crumple, before her limp body crushed a bed of wildflowers, Grady had exploded up from his cover, raging forward in a silent fury, using his worst fears to fuel his vitriol.

To his dismay, Grady realized the gunman was already turning to face down his attack, with uncanny reflexes that where so quick after having just fired at Anna. And Grady knew without a doubt the gunman was anticipating his move rather than reacting to it. But Grady still had the split second jump—having started his attack the instant the gunman's first shot was fired. While artificial headgear and narcotics could replicate some of the Natural's unique talents, nothing could speed up muscle twitch and motor skills, and Grady's were as fast any. A hair before the gunman could line up his shot, Grady sent his own rapid-fire burst of bullets at the gunman.

The first was low, but hit home, shattering the man's kneecap. As the gunman's leg began to collapse on him, it forced his own return fire high over Grady's head. Steadying himself, Grady got off a second shot that slammed harmlessly into the man's protective armor. Instinctively, he micro-adjusted his aim so that that final bullet drilled a hole through the gunman's left eye socket and dropped him to the ground.

Grady hit the deck himself, anticipating possible return fire if Mitch was anywhere nearby, but to his horror he saw Anna rising up and come running toward him.

"DOWN!" Grady yelled as loudly as he could, but the sound of a gunshot had already exploded across the field, the sound echoing from the hazy soup near the lake. Grady couldn't see where the shot had come from, but he witnessed its effect. One moment Anna was running along and the next she was swallowed up by the grass.

He scrambled on hands and knees, dying for breath, wrenching in pain, but fear consumed him as he hurried over to Anna's last position. He found her there—lying on the ground with her eyes staring, unblinking, up at the heavens. For a moment, he died inside until she turned her head to him and smiled.

"That wasn't acting," she said, breathing heavily, with a bit of a dry laugh. Grady's eyes instantly searched her for the wound.

"I think he just grazed me." Anna said removing her hand from her right side and producing a bit of blood. Grady crawled closer and ran his fingers over the torn, bloodstained cloth, but based on the small amount of blood, Grady saw she was right—the bullet had only cut across the surface of her skin.

Impulsively Grady kissed her, wishing he could remain by her side. But there was one last thing he had to do. "Stay here. Mitch is still out there."

Anna nodded, a convenient lie. But it was a directive she would ignore the moment he ran off. She'd already promised herself she wouldn't let him out of her sight, and she'd broken that promise already. She didn't intend to do that again.

Grady kissed her again, got up, crouched low and started down the hill—knifing through the mist to face down Mitch once and for all.

CHAPTER 124

DEVIL'S DAUGHTER

"How long have you been sitting there?" Allan asked, looking out his windows at the Northwoods grounds. He'd been standing there for the last fifteen minutes, trying to peer out over the grounds and figure out what was happening beyond the thick veil of fog. Mitch had checked in briefly, telling Allan his plan to lure Grady and Anna out into the open and utilize one of the enhanced soldiers to hunt them down. Allan had instantly approved, it all needed to end now.

"Only a few minutes," Melody explained. "I had to make a stop."

"The twins okay?" Allan guessed her first destination.

"Yes. I left Gabe with them. They're playing with their nanny in the art room."

Allan nodded, his eyes not leaving the grounds. He wanted to know what was going on. He'd seen several flashes of gunfire and his eyes tried to pierce the white veil.

"I thought maybe you'd be out there, with the others," Allan offered without emotion. "You've established your allegiance."

"What does that mean, Dad? You can't take it away from me: I'm a Natural. And no matter how you try to rationalize it, everything you've done to them, to the other four, you might as well have done to me, your own flesh and blood."

"You don't understand, and I guess you never will," Allan said with a sigh. "As a child you were fascinating to me, not only to the brain surgeon I was back then, but also as your father. I couldn't imagine what was going on in that pretty little head of yours—but I knew it was fantastic, unprecedented, and that there had to be others like you."

"So you went in search of others you could use as your guinea pigs, because you couldn't bring yourself to experiment on your daughter?" Melody asked incredulously.

"No!" Allan shouted in anger, then immediately calmed himself. "You were here, you knew what it was like. Northwoods was a comfortable place, an easy life, and a refuge for children whose parents didn't understand and couldn't deal with the challenges of raising a child who could read their minds and glimpse the future. You're just now beginning to understand that as a parent yourself. We rescued those kids."

"Then what happened, Dad? What made it all change? Was it Mom's death? Was it your greed for power? What was it?" Melody shouted angrily.

Allan rounded on her. "I had no choice! This whole thing, all my research, all my advances and the understanding we built about how Natural's minds work was funded with the government's money. I built this research facility on their grants to further what became my life's work—to help understand you better. This is revolutionary, Melody. What you can do is revolutionary. It has to be understood or . . ."

"Or what?"

"We've been through this before. The world is not as innocent as you'd like it to be. Part of my agreement in advancing my own research was to achieve certain milestones for our government sponsors. We made tremendous progress in understanding the Naturals, but suffered setbacks in our studies on enhancing non-Naturals. It's just not that easy to find Naturals with all the physical skills or psychological makeup to be predictive battlefield solders, a new breed of world-class spy, or even a top military advisor. We needed to find ways to merge the two. Other countries were moving ahead of us in developing these human weapons. Then, five years ago the pressure was put on to accelerate those results . . . we were falling behind the Chinese, and even our French allies."

"Don't play the innocent card with me, Dad. Don't talk to me about a new global Armageddon based on countries that control the future. It won't work anymore," Melody seethed.

Allan turned back to the window to see another gunshot flash. "I wouldn't think of it, Melody. One, because I now know you'll never understand. Because I did what I believed needed to be done. It was important to the country and our future as the sole superpower in the world. This is bigger than you or me. I've said that before. Nothing has changed."

Melody walked closer to her father, preparing for what was to come. She could see out the window and saw another gunshot flash. For a moment she forgot about her father as she too tried to peer through the mist, hoping that Grady and Anna were okay.

"It's over, Dad," Melody said. "You're going to lose this one."

"Is that a prediction or a threat?" Allan asked with interest, once again turning to look at his daughter with a distant contempt.

Melody wasn't going to answer that with words. Instead her hand flashed out and grabbed his, and she looked deep into his eyes.

In that instant Allan knew what she was trying to do, and he desperately tried to look away. On some level he knew every secret he'd buried inside him and every painful, gut-wrenching decision he'd made was locked away in a place to keep him sane. But somehow he couldn't manage to remove his eyes from his daughter's piercing, fierce gaze.

For the second time today, Melody dove deep down into another's soul, and ripped it bare. She flayed open her father's rationalizations and thrust them inside out, laying every bleeding flaw before his eyes. She tore off the locks to the deep-seated anguish he held at some subconscious level for his sins. She caved in the heavily reinforced walls of the room he'd built in his mind, the one in which he hid his deepest darkest secrets to spare even himself. Melody ripped them up, root and all, to the surface of her father's mind, laid his wretched life exposed before his eyes, to feast on in horrible agony.

For the first time he truly experienced the complicity he had in the death of Melody's mother, viewed second-hand his own arrogance that led to the recent death of his illegitimate son, and exposed to him the horrors of a grandfather who would sell out his own grandchildren for personal gain. Melody even unearthed the love he once held for the Naturals so long ago—when he treated them as if they were his own children—but now cast them aside as sacrificial lambs sent to slaughter for some higher good.

The hardest blow came through Melody's touch, where she transferred all her pain, all of the anguish that her father had caused her in life. For the first time Dr. Allan Hauser saw it all for what it was. He saw himself for who he was. Not able to bear another moment of this anguish, he tore his hand from his daughter's and fought for his own sanity in the only way he could. He raised his hand and slapped her violently across the face.

Melody went down hard, crashing across the floor. But she was not defeated, because she knew what he saw, and she knew that no mind could manage to keep a burden like he was suffering now. She could see it in his eyes. Just as Curt had gone completely mad, her father was now on his own journey there. As she picked herself up off the carpet, she glanced out the window and saw something that surprised even her.

"I told you it was over," Melody said wiping a bit of blood from her lip and nodding out the window.

Her father's wide eyes gazed upon her for a second—furious at what she had done to him. But eventually he turned and saw it, too. As her father accepted the inevitable, Melody turned to make her way out to the grounds to try to find Grady and Anna.

Allan watched the scene unfolding outside through his immaculately polished windows with dead, uncaring eyes—until he finally heard the door close behind Melody. He moved silently over to his desk. For a moment he just stared at the drawer, wondering if he had the courage to go through with it. He'd been a coward all his life. Melody had ripped it open for him to see plainly. He took one last glance out the window and steeled his mind to the task. There really was no other choice. No other option.

His trembling hands slid open the drawer where his eyes expected to behold the polished handle of his gun. But it wasn't there. In that excruciating moment he realized exactly where Grady had got the gun, and he finally understood the depths of Melody's hatred and treachery. Perhaps she was more like her father than he'd given her credit for.

CHAPTER 125

ROLLING MIST

G rady navigated his way down the hill in a direction he assumed the lake to be, though he could not see it. If the fog was dense up on the hill, the white churning swirl was pea soup down here.

As he moved, he remained in a low crouch, the thick carpet of wild grasses and wildflowers brushing across his arms, thistles tearing at his pants. He paused, listening for any sound that might give him a clue as to where Mitch might be holed up. Yet all he could hear was the soft lap of water against the shore. He felt blind and vulnerable, but he knew he had to press on.

He tried to replay in his mind the audio of the single gunshot Mitch had fired down near the lake, layering that over his sense of his current position, trying to make an educated guess as to how to proceed. He decided he'd been coming in at too flat an angle—too direct, which could create a head-on confrontation. Grady started moving to his right, farther up the shore of the lake, and farther away from where he guessed the Northwoods complex to be.

The uncertainty and confusion of the situation was unnerving, and oftentimes he thought he would glimpse a figure moving laterally against his position, stalking him at the periphery of his impaired vision. Several times he wanted to raise his gun and fire, but if he was wrong and the shape was a figment or a tree, anything other than Mitch, a gunshot would expose his position and the disadvantage would instantly transfer to him.

Grady had moved a good fifty feet off to his right, and he began pressing forward again, the sound of the lapping water growing closer. He guessed he was only about twenty feet or so from the lake's edge now, as the wildflowers transitioned to tall reeds and lakeshore grasses. A small breeze rustled the stillness, and the white world around him began to swirl even more. But the effect created momentary rippling windows in the fog. As he searched desperately for Mitch, a gunshot from behind him spun him on his heels.

The round didn't come anywhere near him, and Grady knew Mitch was getting as jumpy as he was. This was the break Grady had been hoping for, and he rounded to face the source of the blast. For a moment, as the wisps ebbed, he thought he had a bead on Mitch, but another blanket of white rolled through and the figure was lost. He knew he couldn't wait for a better opportunity—he might never get another one—so he took careful aim and fired.

Assuming he'd missed, Grady dove to the cover of the grasses and began moving back along the shoreline toward Northwoods. As he picked his way along he listened for any sign that he'd gotten a lucky break and hit Mitch, but he heard nothing and there had been no return fire.

He continued to move along, realizing either he was getting closer to the water or it was getting closer to him. His shoes began to sink into a cool, wet muck and water seeped into and filled up his footprints as he lifted his feet. Grady adjusted his course a bit more inland to avoid the water. To his right, over the reeds, he could just make out the surface of the water, and he realized the grasses actually flowed out into the lake. There was no rocky beach to tread on here.

Somewhere off in the distance he thought he heard something familiar: a low, distant thump and he wondered what it meant. He took a moment to listen close, wondering if his enemy had heard it as well, and what that might mean to him. Would it encourage him into more hasty action, or cause him to beat a retreat? Grady wasn't even certain what it meant for himself and Anna. Either way, he didn't really have a good feeling about it.

In his distraction Grady made the second of his mistakes. His first had been to assume that Mitch was up and on the move, but after Grady's shot had come within a hair's breadth of taking him out, Mitch took a new approach. He'd hunkered down, under cover of the grass and knew sooner or later Grady would move near his position, as he tried to follow the source of Mitch's last shot. The second mistake Grady made was looking up to a sky he couldn't see in an instinctive reaction to what he now was guessing were at least three helicopters moving in from the west.

As Grady's eyes left the ground, Mitch erupted from his makeshift grass blind, just a mere ten yards away—and gathering himself into a shooting crouch he pulled the trigger.

Anna was blind. Trying to follow Grady through the fog had been almost impossible. If not for the three gunshots, she would have been lost as well, but she'd used her ears to draw herself closer to the action. Her long white medical gown proved to be an asset, helping her blend into her surroundings. A few times the mist parted enough that she thought she could see Mitch in the distance, his eyes searching; occasionally in her general direction, but he'd never seen her. But now as she crept ever closer, trying to maintain the utmost quiet, he'd seemingly disappeared.

Then, at that moment she'd convinced herself she'd been following ghosts, Mitch exploded up from the grass, facing in the opposite direction, less than 10 yards in front of her. Gun drawn, he prepared to fire at a dim silhouette that just stepped into view.

Anna knew it had to be Grady, and her heart raced, as twelve years of buried hatred took over, fueling her. She rushed Mitch from behind, covering the ground between them in a matter of seconds. In full stride she bowled into him, lowering her shoulder into the small of his back, just as Mitch got off his first shot. The collision was jarring, and both Mitch and Anna rolled hard to the ground. But Anna wasn't done. She rolled onto Mitch, one hand clawing at his face, the other reaching desperately to tie up his gun hand so he couldn't turn the weapon on her.

As they wrestled across the soft, marshy ground, Mitch landed a hard elbow to Anna's gut, and she doubled over, coughing violently.

"You bitch!" he yelled, tossing her from his body like a rag doll and thrusting himself up on his hobbled leg, screaming through the pain that tore through it. Anna crashed to the ground in a heap, and it took all of her energy to roll to face her attacker. She expected to see the barrel of Mitch's gun aimed at her. Only Mitch knew where the real threat was, and rather than deal with Anna's, he'd rounded to face down Grady. But the man had quickly disappeared; having hit the deck after Mitch's shot went astray.

"Grady!" Mitch yelled, in full, furious disgust. "I'm going to kill you and then your lover here," he said, glancing back at Anna, but she was gone, having rolled out of view. Angry at himself for losing sight of both, Mitch knew he needed to end this dance, once and for all. Abandoning all caution, he rushed Grady's last position, keeping his gun trained low, letting off round after round into the reeds, trying to flush out his prey.

The shots whistled into the muck, much too close for comfort, but Grady had taken the time during Anna's attack to retreat ten yards back and right of his last position. Sensing his own opportunity, Grady popped up from his cover to return fire, only to be caught off guard by Mitch wildly crashing toward him, less than five feet away.

Mitch was more prepared for the next shot . . . his gun already up and in position to fire. Realizing his disadvantage, Grady knew he had no chance to get his gun up and into position before Mitch could get off his shot. So instead, Grady did the only thing he could. He dropped his gun and launched himself at Mitch, tackling him to the ground.

"You're dead!" Mitch yelled as he rolled with Grady's tackle, keeping his knees up between himself and Grady's chest, launching his attacker over his head as Mitch himself somersaulted across the ground.

Flying through the air, Grady hit the ground hard, but sprang to his feet quickly, as Mitch followed suit, favoring his left leg. Advancing aggressively, Grady tried desperately to keep the fight in close quarters, since Mitch still had his gun and Grady's was currently lost to the grasses. But when Grady moved in, Mitch caught him off guard with reverse sidekick that connected just under his chin. Again Grady flew backwards, this time crashing into shallows of the lake.

Sensing an opening, Mitch launched himself on top of Grady, quickly wrapping his free arm around his neck and dragging his adversary under the water. But Grady went with it, letting his body go loose, allowing himself to be dragged down beneath the surface—as the frigid water knifed into his body like tiny spears.

While Mitch worked to tighten his hold, Grady, searched for and found the target he wanted. Striking out violently with the palm of his hand, Grady connected directly with the bullet wound in Mitch's leg. Instantly Mitch's grip around Grady's throat loosened, and he crumpled to a knee into the water, as Grady resurfaced gasping for air.

Not wasting a second, Grady was back on top of Mitch, grasping whatever he could get a hold of—hair, clothing, bare skin. But Mitch also knew Grady's biggest weakness, and drove a vicious blow into his midsection. Grady collapsed on hands and knees, retching into the water, trying to fight through the fierce pain caused by the new trauma to his already broken ribs.

Disgusted, Mitch threw Grady off of him and drew his gun, ready to put a bullet in the back of Grady's head just as the first Boeing V-22 Osprey aircraft broke over the tree line. It swooped down over the lake and hovered—its massive twin tilt-rotors, rotated into vertical hover position. As the blades beat the air, they created a violent rotor wash that dispersed the ground fog in an instant, driving the white wisps off to a thirty-yard radius where they waited to return. Suddenly the world around Mitch was clear and he gazed up at the immense U.S. Air Force aircraft, wondering if it was friend or foe.

The answer came without warning, as a tethered body swung out of the rear cargo hold, traced a bead on Mitch's forehead and pulled the trigger. It was a tough, precision shot even for a trained marksman such as Kyle Brady, invited along on the trip by the President herself. But the bullet—with the angle, distance and the slight but constant shift of the helicopter as it floated on air—flew just off Kyle's intended trajectory.

Still, the shot decimated a significant portion of Mitch's left arm and he screamed in agony and rage as blood sprayed from the fresh wound. But instead of returning fire on the military craft, Mitch executed his last act of vengeance on the man who'd succeeded in bringing down Northwoods. The man Mitch had personally invited into this game only a few short weeks ago.

Gutting through the pain, he trained his gun once more on the back of Grady's head and without hesitation, pulled the trigger. There, in the span of a single second, two shots echoed out across the water. In the aftermath Anna stood alone on the shore, holding one smoking gun, the one Grady had lost to the grasses. And as the gunshots' echoes faded, a lone loon answered their chorus with its quavering call.

CHAPTER 126

FACE OF THE FUTURE

In the distance Anna heard a bird's sweet song mingled with the soft rustle of wind through the trees, and the distant lapping of water on a sandy beach. Her eyes had been closed for the last few minutes, her mind traveling over the details of the last several days. She was trying to reach out—trying to understand the loss of someone close to her—and to find answers. She didn't want to open her eyes, didn't want to see this place anymore, and she was dying to leave it behind. But open her eyes she did, bringing into focus a beautiful landscape of manicured grasses, towering trees and a serene lake.

It had been 24 hours since she had traded her white chair deep in the bowels of Northwoods for her less restrictive perch here in an Adirondack crafted of natural teak. While most would find the view calming, it obviously held too many hurtful memories—all compounded by the trauma of yesterday. She had sat here in this very spot many times before, crying softly, as she was now, longing for her freedom. Even though the future held promise she still wasn't free—at least not quite yet.

Things had happened so quickly after she had shot Mitch down by the lake. Men dressed in combat black had swarmed out of the V-22 Ospreys on rappelling ropes to secure the lakeshore and Northwoods' grounds. Three other Ospreys had taken the grounds by storm in a coordinated military strike.

One had landed in the courtyard to the facility and unloaded its strike force on the front entrance of Northwoods, while two others dropped more military elite onto the rooftops where they blew open the emergency stairwell doors and began an orchestrated effort to secure the facility. Each soldier had been debriefed on key Northwoods personnel and peripheral human targets. They had been given file photos, memorized faces, and been given strict orders to detain certain individuals.

Each man and woman on the their "take" list, including Anna, had been detained, isolated and debriefed by top-level security advisors that were understood to report to the President herself. Stories of the detainees were compared with follow-up interrogations that occurred throughout the day. Little information was offered or shared with the captives. One thing was obviously clear to Anna—Northwoods was, at last, going through a complete and final shutdown. How deeply the government chose to scrub was what needed to be determined and would ultimately decide her fate as well as the others.

For Anna it had been an excruciating process, requiring her to relive and retell her life story and the story of the last month in painful detail. At the same time, she was trying to mourn the horrific loss of someone so close to her. She longed desperately to have Grady by her side to comfort her. The only bright spot in the last 24 hours was that she'd been allowed to visit Mary Jane. The night Melody had visited her at Northwoods, she had told her of Mary Jane's condition, and offered a confession, that she herself had carefully induced the medical coma that she was just starting to come out of. Before Anna could ask the questions that such a possibility raised, Melody had revealed to Anna on that night she was a Natural too, the so-called Fifth Seed of Northwoods. What she had done had only been to protect Mary Jane—otherwise her death would have been a certainty at the hands of The Kid.

Mary Jane had seen Curt alive—and understood he was complicit with Northwoods. In the end, The Kid simply couldn't risk Anna reaching out to Mary Jane and discovering this truth. As a med student and Natural, Melody knew with near certainty that the extended sleep she had induced in Mary Jane would help to keep The Kid away from her, and could eventually be overcome.

As the world seemed to spin around her now, Anna tried to wipe away her flood of tears on her sleeve. Trying to be strong, to finally forget but never forgive. It was what she realized she would need to do to move on. From behind, a hand touched her on the shoulder and she looked back to see who it was. Through a stream of tears, the person's face was washed into a soft blur—but she knew the touch, and she leapt from her chair and fell into an embrace with Grady as he dropped his crutches to hold her.

It was their first contact since she'd killed Mitch. Her bullet had caught the Northwoods security advisor a mere fraction of a second before Mitch could take out his revenge on Grady. Still, with his last breath in him, Mitch had found a way to pull the trigger as he himself went down. Grady now had a fresh cast on his leg where Mitch's parting volley had torn into the muscle and shattered his femur.

Their embrace lingered and Anna let her body meld like liquid into Grady's own. She sobbed even harder at the mix of happiness and sadness that overwhelmed her. When her tears finally began to subside, she released him and placed her hands on his scruffy face, gazing deeply into his eyes.

"You heard about Melody?" Anna asked through the last vestiges of her tears.

"Yes, I'm just catching up. But they shared a little with me. I didn't even know she and Curt had fathered twin Naturals."

"Nobody knew. It was a secret she shared only with her father. And now her twins are gone. Nobody knows for sure, but when the military stormed the grounds they found Gabe and the children's nanny dead in the nursery, and the boys were nowhere to be found. They've searched every bit of this god-forsaken place. They reviewed some of the security camera footage to figure out what happened, and they are saying Curt, or The Kid, or whoever he is now, took them. So far they've had no luck finding them."

"How's Melody doing?" Grady asked with concern.

"Not well. They let me visit with her for a few minutes before I asked them if I could come out here. You know they found her dad, in his office with a rope around his neck, hanging from the ceiling."

"What's she going to do?" Grady replied, as he gently wiped a tear from under Anna's eye.

Anna's sad eyes looked up into Grady's. "Who knows? I guess if they let her go, she'll try to find them. But nobody knows yet what they are going to do with all of us."

"They'll let us go," Grady suggested in a way that implied there was a catch. "We just need to make some agreements."

"Whatever they want," Anna said, wanting to make it all disappear, to go and live her life with the man she loved, to finally be free.

"They want us to sign top-secret clearances. They are going to bury what happened here. The public will never know. But with that the government, including the President herself, will give us assurances that those responsible will be brought to swift justice."

"What does that mean?" Anna asked skeptically.

"It means we have to trust them. But if you watch the headlines over the next few months, my guess is some very high-level people will either meet unfortunate ends, or be implicated in things that the government deems more palatable a topic for public consumption. It also means that if we step out of line, then we will be subject to the same ends."

"How far do you think it goes?" Anna asked.

"Honestly, not sure . . . and they're not going to tell. It certainly went high enough to bring the FBI into the periphery, and I've always had my suspicions about the NSA and CIA, but I have no proof. The involvement of those agencies would indicate someone with power had knowledge. But they're not going to admit that if they don't have to. And frankly, we wouldn't be allowed to walk away if we had anything concrete to back up our suspicions. The people who questioned me wanted to make it very clear that the FBI involvement was the product of their own investigation into improprieties at Northwoods."

"And?" Anna asked in a low whisper, realizing they were discussing things that might alter someone's decision to let them leave.

"It's a lie. You and I know that," Grady answered, his raised voice carrying a bit before he brought his emotions back under control. "That said, based on the highly secret military response here, the efforts they seem to be going through in order to shut Northwoods down, and the fact they they're willing to let us walk with conditions, means Tom and Kyle got this in front of someone high up who didn't like certain things going on behind her back. My impression is that today is just the tip of the iceberg in what will be a long, drawn out power realignment."

"So is this really the end? Or will we always be looking over our shoulders?" Anna asked with a shiver. The Indian summer of the last week had faded, and the autumn cool-down was in full force this morning, but the chill she felt came from inside.

Grady looked around first before he answered, and realized he might be giving an answer to his question with his actions. "I really can't say. A lot depends on us, and more importantly, you."

"You don't know or you don't want to speculate on what you presume to be true?" Anna asked.

"Both, I guess," Grady said. "I do know Melody, Tom, and Kyle have all been given the same deal as you and I have. They're taking a risk with all of us—although a very calculated one."

"So, what do you think? You've been around these people and their back room dealings. Is their offer to us a good one?" Anna asked. "It's you I trust."

Grady sighed with resignation, for he had only one answer, and not a very good one. "We really have no other choice, Anna. The illusion of a choice is only to make us feel better about our final decision—and perhaps make us more likely to play nice and cooperate. But even if they allowed you to walk out of here today and talk to the press or to lay Northwoods bare to the world—exposing everything that happened here—would you really bring that attention and scrutiny down around you? Or around what you are capable of?"

Anna looked up into the sky as if searching for the answer amidst the clouds. "No."

"Then we can leave today," Grady said with a smile, hugging her close, letting Anna know he'd stand by her no matter what she chose.

As she drew into Grady, Anna tilted her head up to look into the eyes of the man she loved and she knew—not from any visions of a future together—rather she knew this from the center of her heart and soul, exactly what he represented to her. He was her future—and she kissed him deeply and embraced that future with all her being.

The End

PART 1

The President of the United States sat in a comfortable suite on Air Force One. She had spent the entire day at Minot Air Force base overseeing the infiltration of Northwoods from afar. No action was undertaken without her authority. No movement was made without her consent. No lives were taken unless she expressly approved it. She insisted that as much knowledge and intelligence be obtained before final preparations were made.

If she was going to clean up the mess, she was going to make sure it was done right, with little chance of it all coming back to bite her in the ass. But to do that she also had to solidify her allegiances, cut some back room deals with some of her enemies and set in motion the pre-established plans to wipe away the threads that implicated entire organizations—instead isolating damage to individuals who'd been set up to take the fall.

There was a knock at the door and the President, expecting the visitor, invited her top advisor in. The aging Air Force general, the President's Chief of Staff, entered and took a seat opposite her.

"I'd like an update, Kevin."

The general didn't have to ask which updates she wanted. There was already a list that had been established over 48 hours ago, of over fifty different to-dos, action items and loose threads that needed to be resolved. The list had been whittled down to a handful now and it seemed that the cover-up was going to be a success.

"I'll start with Northwoods leadership. As you know, Dr. Allan Hauser has been taken care of. The official word will be that the good doctor was found in his office having hung himself. This story has been spread to all individuals being held at Northwoods. In another 24 hours, a story will be released to the press, by a puppet Northwoods representative, loyal to you, who will indicate that the doctor has committed suicide. No links will be established to our government, and all records linking any government involvement, either directly or indirectly, have been expunged.

"Good," the President interjected.

"The doctor's passing will also provide the opportunity for Northwoods to reconsider its charter, having lost its heart and soul with the death of its leader. Northwoods puppet leadership will play on the emotion of the suicide and will mention that the facility's reason for being will be evaluated over the next several months. After a two-month waiting period, a quiet decision to fold Northwoods will be made. By that time the facility will only be a shell of itself and the news will only be of local interest. No one will care."

"And the people who had been working there and the patients?"

"I'll start with the staff. We have interviewed and interrogated each of them. We had psychological experts as part of those interview panels, adept at understanding human character and behavioral patterns and have assigned each a risk number of 1-5, with 5 being greatest risk. Of the lot we only had seven individuals that fell into the high-risk categories of 4 and 5. Over the next six months each will meet with some form of unfortunate accident—heart attack, stroke, car accident . . . the usual. We will monitor their activities between now and then, and take emergency corrective action as needed. Highly loyal individuals in the 1-2 range will be offered generous relocation packages and they will assume immediate positions at Northwoods' sister site. They have already been told they will be instrumental in helping the sister site merge and marry findings from both locations to further research. Any individuals who have graded as a 3 will be put on our watch lists—but the likelihood is that they neither pose threat of harm—nor would they make loyal participants in the new site."

The President nodded her head, indicating that what she had heard so far was to plan, and encouraged her Chief of Staff to go on.

"As for the patients, Dr. Hauser had taken your advice five years ago when you first toured Northwoods. Over the last five years they have been migrating their patient lists to focus only on Naturals, and the enhancement of non-Naturals. He also leveraged the new streams of slush funds funneled to Northwoods to accelerate those experiments—with varying degrees of success I might add. It appears the doctor had been sharing only what he thought we'd find interesting and hiding the rest. In any event, it has been over four years since Northwoods has had a traditional civilian patient population. So all existing patients will be moved to the sister location."

"You should also know our four friends have already met with some unfortunate accidents. They left the facility the morning of our infiltration. We were hoping to reach them before they left, but their timetables were out of our control. Their small charter plane landed at the Minneapolis International Airport at about 8:52 a.m. CST. At which point their departures were delayed by several hours due to some mechanical issues with their charter plane back to Washington."

The President's Chief of Staff paused for effect before he moved on. "Madam President, I am here to inform you that it is now being confirmed by press agencies across the country that the charter jet carrying a member of The State Department, our Science and Technology Undersecretary from The Department of Homeland Security and the Deputy Director of National Intelligence and their pilot are believed to have perished when their plane went down over Lake Michigan, near Wisconsin's Door County peninsula."

"In addition to that, the nation has suffered another significant loss, when one of our significant philanthropic supporters, the technology mogul Edward Starks, died en route to his southern California beach house in a nasty head-on collision with a semi on one of the cliff-shore roads.

"Tragic," the President offered. "I appreciate the update, Kevin. I will need to address a mourning nation on the loss of our friends and colleagues. Anything else?"

Her Chief of Staff shifted uncomfortably in his chair. He'd always known the President to be open to hard questions, or even advice from her closest advisors. She believed it was ridiculous to surround oneself with highly intelligent individuals only to do her bidding. She not only counted on their candor, she demanded it and often came down on aides who held out on her. "Tell me again why we are letting Anna and Grady go free?"

The President eyed the military commander before her. "Because it would be overkill. If I understand correctly they are about as averse to exposing Anna's talents to the scrutiny of the real world as Anna is to living a future in Northwoods. And they believe my administration is doing everything we possibly can to bring those behind Northwoods to justice. I believe we now have an allegiance with them through our handling of the situation. This is something that Dr. Hauser could never accomplish with the Naturals—building a trust, and then getting them to do his bidding. Because he couldn't handle them, he wanted to get rid of them—which put us in this mess in the first place. He squandered opportunities by mismanaging that simple relationship—one that I aim to exploit. I may wish to call in the favors we are extending to them some time in the future."

Kevin had never heard the opportunity expressed in that way, and could find no argument against it as long as the individuals involved saw the President to be on their side. "That reminds me. We still have no update on Joe, the Natural who was wounded in France. He has disappeared like a ghost, along with a gypsy, purported to be friendly to his cause. As far as we can tell the French have raided the home of this gypsy's aunt, who owns a vineyard near Chinon, but their efforts have turned up no trace of either. The French continue to hold us at arm's length on this one, and they have made it clear to us that they are rededicating their resources to matters of greater importance and will take no further questions on the matter. For the time being we cannot mitigate that risk to any level of satisfaction."

"Keep an eye on that for me," The President said with mild concern. "I'm comfortable as long as that risk remains overseas, and enamored with French street trash. Also be sure his face appears on all airport security facial recognition systems. I want to know the moment he returns to this country."

Kevin nodded, making note of her request.

"That reminds me, your report failed to mention the final loose thread on our list . . . Curt . . . or the one some people at Northwoods called The Kid."

"He's been the hardest to nail down," Kevin offered. "Nobody has seen him since the events that unfolded between him and the doctor's daughter at Northwoods. The word is that he was a clinical split personality and that various recent events may have caused him to go even farther off the deep end. He's a wild card—although the risk to you seems minimal—but the risk that he might take the existence of the Naturals public, not in a pre-meditated way, but of his own recklessness is a concern. We will continue the search."

"How has everyone taken the news of the twin's abduction?" the President asked vaguely.

"That's an interesting one. Whether people are loyal to Northwoods, or at least the idea of it, or whether they'd prefer to see it destroyed, all seem to gravitate to one side. They all believe The Kid took the twins to spite Melody and all would love to see him strung up for it. That is something you should take particular note of."

"That is good to know," the President replied with interest. "For the truth is the one thing we can hang over Melody's head if she ever steps out of line—and it would be of grave concern if anyone were to ever discover that we took the children."

TWO MONTHS LATER

The attractive couple sat across from each other, the older man gazing at the magnificent young creature he had met only recently. As they waited for their food, over a candlelit table for two, tucked in a secluded back room of W.A. Frost, he imagined her laying next to him—her lithe, lean body intertwined with his as he roughly took her under the sheets. Yes, she would be his next conquest, and he had ordered a second bottle of expensive Chardonnay just to help get her in the mood.

Playing the sensitive, caring role he developed so well over the years, he feigned interest. "Tell me more about yourself; I want to know all about you. What makes you tick?"

The young lady sat back and smiled coyly. "That's an interesting question and it comes with a long answer. But I guess there's plenty of time before we get our food."

The man smiled politely, but in his head he was dreading the entire pre-coital conversation.

The woman who couldn't be any older than 23 or 24 leaned in seductively, as though she wanted only his ears to hear what she had to say—but the microphone she wore ensured many more people would hear before the night was through.

"I'm going to tell you something that only a handful of people know, and I'm pretty sure it's going to blow your mind. You see, as a child I was found to be gifted—blessed, some might say, with a mind that could learn at a pace twice as fast as others, and see things others could only dream of. In layman's terms, I can read other people's minds."

The man just stared back at her blankly, unsure of what to say next.

He didn't need to say a word. The young woman, upon seeing his unbelieving expression, took it as a challenge and continued on. "Let me prove it to you. Think of something I would never know and I'll tell you what it is you are thinking."

Not wanting to play the game, the man began to look around. "Where the fuck's our food?" he thought. "I don't need this shit." As attractive as she was, the man didn't think he had the stomach to entertain a nutcase for an entire evening.

"Ah, I see you don't want to play." The young lady frowned playfully, her full red lips forming a mock pout. "But your mind's always working, so I'll tell you what you were thinking anyway. You wanted to know where the fuck our food was so you could ditch the nutcase. Is that about it?"

Not wanting to admit she was right, the man scoffed, figuring that would be easy enough to guess given the circumstances.

"Okay, you want something harder I can see," she said, sitting back and staring thoughtfully out into space as if trying to come up with a fabulous idea. "I know, let's try this. Think of the worst thing you've ever done in your life and I'll tell you what it was."

The man shifted uneasily in his comfortable high-back chair. Though he tried not to let the image flash through his mind, he couldn't help but envision that fateful night. The two had been standing together on a lonely dark street in the midst of winter as he struck the woman—her body taking a blow to the gut before a backhand caught her across the face. It was this crunching blow that had caused her to lose her balance.

He could see her so clearly, as though it happened yesterday. The woman grasping at air, hoping to regain her traction, as her feet skidded on a patch of ice. She never recovered, and her body crashed heavily to the sidewalk with a thick, ugly thud. In a fraction of a second, Nancy's skull fractured as it met violently with solid ice-sheathed concrete. The man recalled the hard kick he had given her, telling her through tightly clenched teeth to get up. When she didn't stir, he knelt down beside her, begging her to stand, but she never moved again.

The woman at the table watched the man closely, seeing it all in his eyes—the anger, the horror and the sudden sadness coupled with vivid visions that made her sick. Suddenly she felt frightened to be at the same table with this monster, but she still had another question to ask, and she knew she had to get it out while he was at his most vulnerable. "You killed her, didn't you?"

The man looked up across the table at her, aghast at her knowledge and fearful of her penetrating eyes . . . eyes that seemed to bore deep into the darkest reaches of his soul. Almost breathlessly he whispered, "No."

Ignoring his answer, she persisted, driven to expose the truth. "I can see it in your eyes . . . I can see you hitting her . . . striking her violently like you had done so many times in the past." A revelation coming to mind, her eyes intensified. "This time it was worse, wasn't it? This time she had cheated on you, but you let it happen. You were there all along, following her that night, letting your anger build the whole time they were together, but you never tried to stop them. You wanted her to cheat. You wanted to beat her. This time you wanted to have a reason for your abuse . . . to justify the violence and pain you had inflicted on her over the years. The pain she just took from you and kept coming back for. But this time it was different, this time you wanted her dead."

"No!" the man screamed as the entire restaurant turned to see who was causing the disturbance. "No," he said this time more softly, as patrons turned slowly back to their dinners, tears welling in his eyes. "I didn't mean to kill her, it was just an accident," he sobbed. "It was all just a horrible accident."

Immediately, three plainclothes cops seated nearby rose from their tables and approached the scene. A fourth man, who had been seated with them rose as well, crossing the four paces to the young woman's table as rapidly as his legs would carry him. Anna rose and threw herself into Grady's arms. There, the two stood for the longest time, hugging each other as the police cuffed the man, escorting Nancy's husband away.

"Lets go home," Grady said, with his own tears forming in his eyes, as he led Anna out the door into a swirl of white fluffy snow—where a pair of not quite blue and not quite green eyes watched from a distance.

ACKNOWLEDGEMENTS

A lifelong dream, my first novel would never have made it into print without the support of so many individuals along the way. Thank you to my friend and neighbor, Mike Finstad, who convinced me to dust off a half-finished manuscript. Your constant encouragement and thirst for more chapters helped me discover an elusive ending, and in turn a new beginning. To Jason Sawyer—fellow writer, friend and confidant. Your sage advice and passion around the concept—particularly the theoretical science and mechanics of multiple universe theory—kept me believing I had a story worth sharing. To Brett and Wendy Rouleau—as some of my earliest readers you became my earliest advocates, and gave me one of the most important gifts of all: belief in myself. And to my editor, Scott Rohr, thank you for your straightforward honesty and tireless attention to detail—beyond cleaning up my numerous errors your careful suggestions and objective eye brought strength and emotion in the text. I could not have asked for a better editor. Any errors that remain are mine and mine alone.

Also special thanks all of my early readers and reviewers who offered critical feedback and encouragement along the way, including Adrian Clift, John Bernier, Tom Lord, Connie Ashba, Mark Brust, Mark Pafko and my cousin Josh Linderman. Your willingness to dive into a raw manuscript by a new, unproven writer humbled me. An author is nothing without his readers, and each of you touched and inspired me along this journey. To Liz Pedersen, Andrea Vollmer and Ziba Sarabia Lennox—you each inspired me in your own way and made me believe anything was possible as long as you have passion.

To my family, including my sister Kristen (Jacobsen), brother Mark, aunt Pat, and my mother and father, Deanna and Mike. You not only read and critiqued this endeavor, but you supported me throughout a lifetime of writing. There would be no book without you.

And finally, thank you to my wife Shelly. You watched me start and stop many stories along the way, spending innumerable late nights at the computer in pursuit of an elusive ideal. Your belief in me, through all our years together, inspired me every day to keep searching for that next idea . . . that elusive *seed*.

AUTHOR'S NOTES

*T*he *Fifth Seed* is inspired by the work of physicist Dr. Julian Barbour. His theories about the universe and his quest to prove time doesn't exist formed the seed around which this novel was written. If the subject interests you, I suggest reading *From Here To Eternity* and *Is Einstein's Greatest Work All Wrong—Because He Didn't Go Far Enough?* Both can be found in the back issues of *DiscoverMagazine.com*.

Many of the settings in *The Fifth Seed* are borrowed from my travels. While each locale is described faithfully to my memory, many of these destinations have changed over the years. The Chateau Chinon is one such example. I've been told the entrance, in recent years, has switched from the old stone bridge described in these pages, to an entirely more modern entrance. In addition, during my prior visits much of the Dauphine Apartments were in ruins. Today the Chateau has been dramatically reconstructed. Yet, for the purposes of this novel, I chose to live within my memory and remain faithful to my mind's eye.

On the subject of the Chateau, and the existence of the Agnés Sorel tunnel, I stumbled across a rare reference to it in my book research several years ago. It came at a moment where I was struggling for a means of escape for Anna and her friends from the Chateau. In an ironic twist of fate, my wife Shelly and I originally stayed at the beautiful Agnés Sorel Hotel in Chinon on an earlier visit to the region. With that said, the description of the tunnel is purely a product of my imagination, but the small hotel does exist and is faithfully described to my recollection—including the room with the two French doors that open to the river. I highly recommend a stay if you have the opportunity.

Apparently the FBI headquarters in Minneapolis moved while I was drafting the novel. I preferred the idea of the original downtown location instead of the suburb they are now located in, so I left it there.

Unfortunately Bailey's Bed and Breakfast does not exist, nor do the beautiful A-frame condos in Lanesboro. Someday perhaps I will have one commissioned in its image.

And finally, Northwoods is purely a figment of my own imagination. No such place exists . . . at least to my knowledge.

Edwards Brothers Malloy
Oxnard, CA USA
September 23, 2013